SCARPIA

SCARPIA

Piers Paul Read

B L O O M S B U R Y
LONDON · OXFORD · NEW YORK · NEW DELHI · SYDNEY

Bloomsbury Publishing
An imprint of Bloomsbury Publishing Plc

50 Bedford Square   1385 Broadway
London   New York
WC1B 3DP   NY 10018
UK   USA

www.bloomsbury.com

First published in Great Britain 2015

British Library Cataloguing-in-Publication Data
A catalogue record for this book is available from the British Library.

ISBN: HB: 978-1-4088-6749-5
TPB: 978-1-4088-6750-1
ePub: 978-1-4088-6752-5

2 4 6 8 10 9 7 5 3 1

Typeset by Integra Software Services Pvt. Ltd.
Printed and bound in Great Britain by CPI Group (UK) Ltd, Croydon CR0 4YY

MIX
Paper from
responsible sources
FSC
www.fsc.org
FSC® C020471

To find out more about our authors and books visit www.bloomsbury.com.
Here you will find extracts, author interviews, details of forthcoming events and the
option to sign up for our newsletters.

SCARPIA

PART ONE

One

I

In 1777, after the fall of his patron, the Marchese Tanucci, the *cavaliere* Luigi Scarpia returned to Sicily with his wife and youngest son Vitellio to live as best he could off the income from his estate. He did not reside on his estate but, like other Sicilian landowners, in a baroque villa in Bagheria, a suburb of Palermo. He rarely descended into Palermo but remained alone in the library of his villa, brooding on the reversal of his fortunes which he ascribed, correctly, to the Austrian influence at court. During meals he muttered abuse about anyone or anything that came from north of the Alps – the French *philosophes*, German painters, the English minister General Acton, and most particularly the Austrian Queen of Naples, Maria Carolina, who had engineered the fall of Tanucci.

Italy in the eighteenth century was not a single nation as we know it now but a geographical area divided into a number of different sovereign states. Most were ruled by hereditary monarchs with absolute powers, the exceptions being Venice, a republic, and Rome, governed by its bishop, the supreme pontiff of the Roman Catholic Church. Besides the city, the Pope also ruled the Papal States – a swathe of territory that straddled the Italian peninsula from the city of Bologna in the north to Gaeta in the south.

The largest and richest of the Italian principalities was the Kingdom of the Two Sicilies – the first of these two Sicilies being the Kingdom of Naples which included the southern half of the Italian peninsula, and the second the island of Sicily itself. This double realm was ruled by a Spanish Bourbon, Ferdinand, who had been made king at the age of nine by his father, King Charles III of Spain. The governance of the kingdom was left in the hands of the Marchese Tanucci who deliberately neglected Ferdinand's education. As a result, Ferdinand thought only of hunting, preferred the company of his grooms and whippers-in to that of his courtiers and ministers of state, spoke the coarse dialect of the Neapolitan underclass, the *lazzaroni*, and like them ate macaroni with his fingers.

In 1768, a marriage was arranged between King Ferdinand and the Archduchess Maria Carolina, daughter of the formidable Empress of Austria, Maria Theresa. By the terms of the treaty, Maria Carolina was entitled to a seat on the royal council once she had given birth to a male child; and when this came about in 1774, though she was still only twenty-two years old, the force of her personality led the government of Naples to forsake Spain in favour of Austria. Tanucci was dismissed together with his allies, among them the *cavaliere* Luigi Scarpia.

Like King Ferdinand, Luigi Scarpia had a strong-minded wife, Marcella di Torre della Barca, who on most matters took a contrary view to that of her husband. In common with other women at the time, she had received only a cursory education but her ignorance did not lead her to doubt her own judgements. She might not be able to prove to her husband that Voltaire was a great writer, or that those German artists living in Naples, Tischbein and Kniep, were great painters, but they were considered so in the best circles throughout Europe and Marcella had more faith in fashion than in her husband's opinions. She yearned for Naples, where their house had had a magnificent view over the bay towards the volcano

Vesuvius: in Bagheria her bedroom looked out over a scrubby, neglected garden. She loathed life in Palermo, blamed their exile on the *cavaliere*'s irascible nature and was impatient with his gloom. The man she had married had thought the world an oyster that would slip down nicely with a glass of chilled white wine. Now it was something toxic and indigestible. Isolated and bored in the villa in Bagheria, she watched him succumb to a paralysing depression that left him unable to address either his wife's ennui or his son's education.

*

Vitellio was aged fourteen when he returned to Sicily with his parents. In Naples he had attended a school run by the Jesuits until the order had been suppressed by Tanucci in 1767. There he had studied Latin, mathematics and ancient history. Like most young men of his kind, he could speak French and Spanish as well as Italian. Again, like other young noblemen of the period, he learned to ride a horse, load and fire a pistol, fence with a rapier and handle a heavier sword. He was aware that the many quarterings on the family's coat of arms signified descent from Norman knights. In Sicily he had a tutor, the *abate* Eusebio, a priest who fed his love of history but had more difficulty when it came to Latin and mathematics.

During the summer the family left the villa in Bagheria for their estate at Castelfranco. The castle of their Norman ancestors had been demolished after an uprising of Sicilian nobles against the Hohenstaufen Emperor Frederick II; only the chapel with the family sepulchre remained intact. A villa had been built a mile from the ruins with a garden that had run wild and here Vitellio's parents would sit semi-comatose in the terrible heat, the *cavaliere* with a book on his knee, his wife with a fan on her lap. They showed no interest in their land or the tenants who farmed it. The running of the estate was left to their agent, Ottavio Spoletta – a devious and brutal man, as agents of absentee landlords often were at the time. He extracted rents and taxes from the impoverished peasants and exercised the judicial powers delegated by Luigi Scarpia, their feudal lord.

Ottavio Spoletta had a son, Guido, who was Vitellio Scarpia's seasonal friend, and together they would ride out among the olive groves early in the morning, and up into the hills above Castelfranco, filling their lungs with the cool pine-scented air. The physical appearance of the two young men reflected their different stations in society as if nature was conversant with rank. Vitellio was handsome – not tall but slender with blue eyes, a small sharp nose, good teeth and dark hair tied in a pigtail. His habitual expression was one of amusement as if he could see the comic in every aspect of life. In adolescence he was perhaps a little vain, glancing sideways at a looking glass every now and then, and giving what he took to be an aristocratic tilt to his head. He was mercurial – mostly cheerful but occasionally, particularly when thwarted, falling into a black mood. He could be earnest when planning a day's hunting, as if the chase were a military exercise – a frown coming onto his delicate brow if his troops – the beaters and stable boys – disobeyed his orders; but his expression would change to a look of delight when, with a shot from his musket, he brought down a partridge or, with a thrust from his pike, he skewered a wild boar.

Guido Spoletta was taller than Vitellio Scarpia and stronger. His skin was a shade darker than Scarpia's, his eyes brown, his hair black – a colouring from Byzantine or Saracen ancestors. Each admired the other for the qualities he did not possess. Scarpia wished that like Spoletta he could climb trees, dive into pools and gut a boar or a deer with a few deft strokes of his jagged knife – drawing out the warm entrails with his bare hands. Spoletta admired Scarpia for his handsome face, his slender form and for his learning. But neither envied the other, ascribing their particular advantages to their birth and upbringing. Scarpia saw Spoletta's practicality – his readiness to do what had to be done – as a quality reserved for those raised close to the soil; while Spoletta knew that Scarpia's intelligence and refinement came not just from his education but a pedigree stretching back to days when Roger de Hauteville and his Norman knights took Sicily from the Saracens.

Like King Ferdinand, the two young men loved hunting, in particular pursuing wild boar where there was real risk of being gored after falling from a rearing horse. For Spoletta, riding alongside the son of his feudal lord was an honour that raised his standing among the peasants. For Scarpia hunting was a simulation of battle, giving substance to the fantasies sown in his mind by the books he had read from his father's library such as Gatien de Courtilz's *Mémoires de M. d'Artagnan, capitaine lieutenant de la première compagnie des Mousquetaires du Roi,* which stood on the shelf next to Cervantes's *El ingenioso hidalgo don Quijote de la Mancha.*

*

As he passed the age of sixteen, Vitellio became aware that his ability to ride a horse bareback, parry with a sword or bring down a partridge with the shot of a musket might not be enough to make a mark on the world. He began to pay more attention to the lessons of the *abate* in Latin, history and rhetoric; to converse with his mother in French; and, sitting in the library, to attempt to draw his father out of his dejection to talk about politics and his past. Vitellio came to enjoy sitting in the corner of this library, confident that, though his father rarely spoke, he was content that his son should be there. On the leather-topped desk lay open ledgers and the half-dozen books that the *cavaliere* was reading at the same time – Montesquieu's *Esprit des Lois* side by side with Augustine of Hippo's *City of God;* Voltaire's *Candide* and

Febronius's Galician manifesto alongside Francis of Sales's *Introduction to the Devout Life* and Thomas à Kempis's *Imitation of Christ*.

Vitellio left to his father the reading of works of philosophy and religion, but progressed from the adventures of d'Artagnan and Don Quixote to Herodotus, Suetonius, Froissart, Joinville and other chroniclers of war. He continued to enact scenes of triumph and glory in his imagination, and decided that he would like to be a soldier even though in the Kingdom of the Two Sicilies it was not a calling that brought wealth or prestige. Should he seek his fortune abroad? Vitellio knew enough about the King of Prussia to imagine himself as one of his grenadiers, but he did not speak a word of German and he had heard that recruits had to be at least six feet tall. And then he thought that Prussia would be cold and misty and he was told by the *abate* Eusebio that it would jeopardise his salvation if he was killed in the service of a Protestant king.

Sometimes Vitellio Scarpia looked at his parents, wondering whether, when he reached their age, he would come to resemble one or the other. It was hard to think of himself as his mother because she was a woman but he noted that, in the few years following their return from Naples, she had seemed to grow taller and more commanding; while his father, so imposing when he was a child, appeared now to shrink and shrivel behind his desk in his book-lined library. Sometimes in the dusk, before the servants brought in a candle, it would seem as if a gnome were sitting on the *cavaliere*'s chair.

Vitellio also noticed that his parents did not say much to one another beyond the discussion of everyday practicalities. Even here, his mother's questions often went unanswered; or they would be answered later in the day with a handwritten note delivered not by a servant but by the *cavaliere* himself. 'It is easier to collect one's thoughts in writing,' he once said in reply to a puzzled look from his son. 'And it is more discreet. The servants can hear, but they cannot read.'

In 1780, when Vitellio was seventeen, his mother finally cajoled her husband into considering the future of their younger son. He would have to make his own way in the world. The income from the estate in Sicily could not sustain two households. Her estates in Basilicata on the mainland, her dowry, had been made over to her first-born son, Domenico, and the rest of their substance had gone on the dowry of their daughter, Adelina, who had made a good marriage before their father's disgrace. In Naples, Marcella had thought of a career in the Church for her younger son – a quite plausible calling to consider, even in an anti-clerical household. Not all priests were Jesuits and a bishop could live as a prince. The Archbishop of Taranto, for example, never visited his see, delegating all his duties to a coadjutor and devoting his vast revenues to his magnificent collection of art and antiquities.

As Vitellio had grown older, it had become clear that he was not made for the life of a priest. By aptitude and inclination he was better suited to a military career. Influence at court could obtain a commission but, after Tanucci's fall, the Scarpias had lost any that they had once possessed. More could perhaps be done in Madrid. At his wife's dictation, the *cavaliere* therefore wrote four letters of introduction to Spaniards he had known when working with Tanucci, and a fifth all-important letter to the Spanish king, Charles III. One morning, he summoned Vitellio to the library. From the drawer in his desk he took out a leather bag containing one hundred Sicilian piastres and twelve Spanish dollars. He handed it to Vitellio together with the five letters and his German sword. 'You may need this. I will not.' It seemed to Vitellio that there were tears in his father's eyes.

Beyond the money, the letters and a sword, Vitellio would need a valet, and so Guido Spoletta was summoned from Castelfranco and from there went daily to Palermo to learn from a tailor how to take care of a gentleman's clothes, and from a barber how to shave off stubble and dress a wig. Before Vitellio left, his mother gave her son the new tunics, breeches and linen that had been prepared over a number of months and put fifty Venetian sequins into his purse. On 17 April 1782, Vitellio Scarpia, with Guido Spoletta as his servant, set sail from Palermo for Barcelona.

2

The Spanish brig set a course north to distance itself from the coast of North Africa and passed through the strait of Bonifacio between Corsica and Sardinia. Spain was at war with Great Britain, but all the British warships were at the western end of the Mediterranean defending Gibraltar. A greater danger for any ship from a Christian country came from North African corsairs. In the war between Christendom and Islam that had lasted a thousand years, the Saracens had been driven out of Italy, Sicily and Spain, but the Ottoman sultan still ruled lands in an arc running from Belgrade to Tangier. In reality, his viceroys in Egypt, Algiers and Morocco were left to rule as they pleased, and what pleased them, because it was profitable, was to allow pirates to use their ports. Scarpia half hoped for an encounter with these Barbary pirates in which he could show his skill with his pistols and wield his father's German sword – until he became seasick and for the rest of the voyage lay groaning on his bunk.

When the boat reached Barcelona, he disembarked with Spoletta and, after three nights in the Catalan capital, took the diligence to Madrid. There, from modest lodgings, Scarpia went daily to the Escorial. After two months of waiting, he was admitted to an audience with the king who, remembering the father's services to Spain under Tanucci and needing any good men he could find for the army then besieging Gibraltar, granted Vitellio a commission in the Royal Guards. A portion of Scarpia's funds was spent on a uniform, a horse and other equipment an officer was expected to provide for himself. On 10 September 1782, with Spoletta as his servant, he reported for duty to the commander, Martin Álvarez de Sotomayor, in Algeciras.

Three days later, the Spanish launched their long-planned assault on Gibraltar, watched by a crowd of fashionable spectators. It was thought that the assembled gunboats and floating batteries would soon demolish the British defences, but three of the batteries were set on fire and exploded, while the remaining seven were disabled and scuttled. The 35,000 Spanish and French troops waited in vain for an opening in the British lines. However, Scarpia – untrained, undisciplined and frustrated by the inaction – broke away from the main body of the Royal Guards and led a small contingent newly placed under his command in a sortie against an outlying battery of the defenders. It was a futile excursion; two Hanoverian gunners were wounded, one by a pistol shot from Spoletta, another by a thrust of Scarpia's sword; but no other officer had followed his lead, and the gun could not be turned. Scarpia and his troop galloped back to the Spanish lines.

Few of the Spanish spectators saw this act of bravado, and those who did could not identify the young officer. The colonel of the Royal Guards was enraged by Scarpia's act of insubordination; so too the commander-in-chief, General Álvarez de Sotomayor, who had waited passively for the Spanish navy to clear a path into Gibraltar. When Admiral Barceló came to hear of the Sicilian's madcap escapade, he made much of it to his staff. It exposed the pusillanimity of the 35,000 soldiers and diverted attention from the naval fiasco.

There was talk of a court martial, but in the end it was decided to punish Scarpia's excess of zeal with a transfer from the Royal Guards to a more mundane regiment then on garrison duty in Almeria. There were no opportunities here for acts of valour. The Moorish Alcazar, with its fine view of the Mediterranean from the ramparts, was like a mausoleum, with ageing, embittered officers the cadavers. Scarpia saw no alternative but to sit it out and wait for a return to favour.

Spoletta distracted himself with forays into the cantinas and bordellos in the town below; but Scarpia was too fastidious and too romantic to follow his example, and he was aware that the moral climate was less clement in Spain than in Italy. Even in Almeria there were agents of the Inquisition, making sure that anyone in a position of authority attended Mass on a Sunday and, at Easter, confessed their sins and took Communion. And there was a reason beyond fear of God or the Inquisition that made Scarpia behave correctly at this time. He fell in love with the daughter of the commander of the garrison and, to judge from appearances, she with him.

Colonel Rodrigez Serrano was a kindly man married to a younger woman. They had a single child, a daughter, Celestina, who at the time of Scarpia's posting to Almeria was aged seventeen. Scarpia himself was still only twenty and so it was quite natural that, when he was invited to dine by his commander, the daughter should enjoy his company and he hers. The mother, too, Doña Inez Serrano de Romero, was pleased to receive this young officer who, despite the disgrace that had brought him there, was 'a breath of fresh air'. Doña Inez was also quite conscious that it was time to start thinking about a husband for Celestina and, had she the means, would have taken her to Valencia or Seville. She and her husband had relatives in both cities, but she knew a girl with no dowry to speak of was never welcome and so it might be better to find a husband for their daughter closer to home.

Would the young Lieutenant Scarpia make such a husband? Doña Inez knew next to nothing about him and her husband, when questioned, turned out to know little more. He was from the Kingdom of the Two Sicilies and had many obscure quarterings on his coat of arms. Scarpia clearly was not rich, but nor, perhaps, given his lack of connections in Spain, would he expect to arrange a marriage that would make his fortune. She calculated that Scarpia was probably the best they could hope for and that, if the two young people were brought together, nature would take its course.

Vitellio Scarpia, as we have seen, was handsome – slim with thick black hair, pale skin and an intelligent look in his blue eyes – sometimes angry, sometimes kindly, always acute. All this would seem to complement the apparent docility of Celestina. She was not a great beauty according to Castilian taste; she was shorter than the ideal, with wide, low-slung hips and a large bosom. Her black hair, however, was thick and shining; her teeth even and white; her lips pink and plump; her nose delicate and small; her brown eyes unusually large and with an expression that, normally docile, showed occasional mockery, irony, even impertinence – glances which her parents failed to notice but which were intercepted across the table by Scarpia and, covertly, returned.

Twice a week, Scarpia was invited to dine with his commander and his wife and daughter. Sometimes other officers or visiting dignitaries were present. Sometimes they were not. When it became warm enough – and it quickly became warm enough in southern Spain – Scarpia with one or two other young officers would accompany Doña Inez and her daughter on picnics in the bare hills behind the city. He was attentive towards Celestina and it was clear to all that the two took pleasure in one another's company. At the regular fiestas, they would dance but then retire to their respective corrals – Scarpia to stand among his fellow officers and young men from the town, Celestina to sit with the other young women under the eyes of the duennas, their enticing eyes half hidden behind their fluttering fans.

The enticing eyes of Celestina more often than not settled on Scarpia. If they settled on anyone else, it was simply a feint to avoid the humiliation of seeming too obvious. The looks, and also the touch of her hand when they were dancing – a hand that, again, did not give itself away with a squeeze but made quite clear by the way it lingered in his that it would have been quite happy to have been held for longer – had the intended effect on Scarpia: each night, as he lay in the narrow bed in his quarters – a modest, low-roofed set of rooms built into the battlements – he would imagine himself holding Celestina, kissing her soft lips, caressing her silken shoulders, running his fingers through her thick hair. Yet the obstacles to making a reality out of these imaginings were considerable. Scarpia felt that he was too young to marry and, if he were to marry, it should not be to someone unknown to his parents and without their consent. Scarpia was impetuous and romantic, but he was not incapable of calculation, and it had been made clear to him by his mother – one might say drummed into him – that those sequins and ducats and dollars given to him as he set out for Spain were not a down payment but the entirety of what he could expect from his family.

Spoletta, who felt that Scarpia's future was also his, saw the danger posed by Celestina. He saw that his master was being pulled one way by prudence and another by desire. Spoletta would have seduced the girl and left it at that; but he understood that Scarpia, as a *cavaliere*, had to take other factors into account. Spoletta also saw, as Scarpia did not, that what was to be done or not done lay in the hands of women – Celestina, her mother and Celestina's maid Tula, who canoodled with Spoletta when both were off duty. It was

Tula who told Spoletta that her mistress, pining for Scarpia, had decided that the time had come to move things along. A note was passed by Tula to Spoletta and, reluctantly, by Spoletta to Scarpia. *'Think! To see the stars at midnight from the ramparts by the winch.'*

There were a number of winches on the ramparts of the Alcazar used to raise cannon balls, gunpowder or provisions from below; but there was one in particular close to the steps from the chapel which Celestina and Scarpia had agreed in earlier conversations was the spot from which there was the best view of the sky and the sea. It also had the advantage that there was an alcove in the ramparts behind it with a stone bench where one could sit without being seen. And there was dead ground between the *jefatura* where Celestina lived with her parents and the winch, which made it unlikely that she would be seen by the sentries whose duty, after all, was to look out to sea for British warships or Barbary pirates.

Scarpia kept the assignation: for the first time, the two young lovers kissed and embraced; and, as Scarpia felt Celestina's body press against his, he made protestations of eternal affection. Celestina, too, murmured words of love, and the name Vitellio over and over, as his arms encircled her waist, his hands rose and became entangled in her hair, and his lips left her lips to stray onto her bare shoulders.

They stepped into the alcove and sat on the stone bench hand in hand to exchange further whispered words and intimate gestures. How delightful for Scarpia to feel the smooth warm flesh that he had imagined; and for Celestina to discover that she could inspire such devotion and desire. It was almost four when there was to be a change of the guard before Scarpia and Celestina decided that it would be wise to return to their respective quarters. They discussed another tryst – not the next night, when Scarpia would be on duty and so under the eye of his men – and not the night after that, because Celestina was to go away for a week to visit her aunt in Valencia – but in eight days in the same place and at the same time.

3

Celestina was unable to keep this rendezvous because, two days later, the diligence in which she was travelling with her maid Tula to her aunt in Valencia was seized by Barbary corsairs. The Arabs' longboats had emerged suddenly out of the early-morning mist and they surrounded the coach as it left the village of Vera. Celestina, Tula and the other passengers were the first to be rowed out to their galley. Most of the able-bodied inhabitants of Vera followed before the nightfall.

Celestina and Tula were now to be counted among the million Europeans who had, over the previous two centuries, been seized from the shores of the Mediterranean to be ransomed or sold in the slave markets of Tunis and Algiers. Scarpia and Celestina's parents were tormented by visions of Celestina at the mercy of a lascivious Moor, but they also knew it was possible that, coming from a good family, she would be held *intacta* in the hope of a ransom greater than the price she might make on the market. Such ransoms were arranged by religious orders, the Lazarists and Redemptorists, whose humble friars acted as intermediaries between distraught families and the Algerian Dey. Their negotiations were sometimes successful; the fetters and manacles of freed slaves are still to be seen on the wall of the cathedral in Minorca; but more often they failed. Though charitable funds were available to pay the ransoms, they were insufficient to redeem every captive – particularly the young, the strong and the beautiful whose price, inevitably, was high.

A month after Celestina's abduction, a Redemptorist friar returned from Algiers with the news that her captors were indeed open to a pre-emptive offer for Celestina and mentioned a sum. It was immense, and wholly beyond the means of her parents or the religious orders. Even the king who, though he was mindful that Celestina was the daughter of one of his officers, was loath to set a precedent that would involve a future outlay that the royal treasury could not afford. Rather than encourage such abductions by paying ransoms, better to spend the money on equipping warships with gunpowder and shot. King Charles ordered Admiral Barceló to take his fleet and bombard Algiers.

Celestina's parents, having come to see Scarpia as their daughter's future husband, now treated him as a son: he dined at the *jefatura* almost every day. The atmosphere at table was hard to bear as the evasive replies to their appeals to relatives, religious orders and government ministers were read out aloud at table. It became clear to Scarpia that the ransom would not be raised and his mind turned to other solutions. When the Redemptorist friar returned to Almeria on his way back to Algiers, Scarpia asked if it might be possible to mount a counter-kidnapping as audacious as that of the Barbary pirates. Was there someone in Algiers who might know where Celestina was being held? Could he be bribed to lead a small party of disguised men to rescue her?

The friar was evasive. He had to be careful not to compromise his neutral standing with the Dey, but the project was not altogether impossible: there *were* people in Algiers – covert Christians or venal slaves – who could discover where prisoners were held and guide visitors through the narrow alleyways of the Casbah. On his return to Algiers, he would make enquiries and prepare the ground.

*

Scarpia now petitioned Admiral Barceló to be allowed to join the force that was to mount a punitive expedition against Algiers. The admiral, remembering Scarpia from the siege of Gibraltar, and how grateful he had been for his escapade, petitioned the king to have him seconded temporarily from the garrison at Almeria to the contingent of marines. The order for the transfer came to Celestina's father who, understanding the reason for Scarpia's request, counter-signed the order and gave Scarpia his blessing. In Cadiz, a Lazarist friar recently returned from North Africa told Scarpia that a covert Christian had been found who would lead him to Celestina. He gave Scarpia Arab clothes and made a map from memory of the city of Algiers on which was marked the small jetty where a small party might land unobserved and the house where they would find their guide.

The fleet set sail. Scarpia, in command of a contingent of marines, was not on the admiral's flagship but on an auxiliary galleon, the *Santa Fe*. He left it to Spoletta to befriend the sailors and, on the fourth day, as they approached Algiers, Spoletta reported that he had found five men who for ten Spanish dollars – two apiece – would in the dark or during the action lower a boat and row to the shore.

All went according to plan. Soon after the bombardment started, Spoletta shouted 'man overboard'. Permission was given to lower a boat to retrieve him and, preoccupied by the bombardment, the ship's captain did not notice that it did not immediately return. As the sailors rowed towards the jetty Scarpia and Spoletta covered their uniforms with Arab kaftans. They could hear the boom of the cannons and see the fires started by Admiral Barceló's cannonade.

The sailors lay low behind the jetty while Scarpia and Spoletta disembarked. At the house marked on the map, a man was waiting who at Scarpia's whispered '*Benedicamus Domino*' replied with a '*Deo gratias*' and then silently beckoned for them to follow him through the narrow alleyways on the edge of the city. Distracted by the bombardment, no one showed any interest in the three men. They stopped by some gates to a courtyard. 'She is there,' said their guide. 'It is the house of a janissary … a Turk.'

While the guide waited outside, Scarpia and Spoletta climbed over the wall into the courtyard. A dark figure stood by the door into the house watching the fires in the centre of the city. He turned as they approached: Spoletta ran him through with his sword. Were there other guards? Where were the slaves held? With Spoletta, Scarpia passed through the door and glided silently up a shallow stone staircase. The corridor at the top was dark and silent. Light came from an open door. Scarpia, with Spoletta behind him, crept up and looked in. On the far side of the room by an arched opening looking out over a garden stood two figures – one a man, the other a woman. The man was tall and swarthy – his figure loosely clothed. The woman, naked, stood sheltering behind him, her left arm raised, the fingers fondling the tight curls at the base of his neck. The man was watching the fires visible through the palm trees over the tiled roofs; the woman could see nothing but his shoulder which occasionally she bumped with her lips, giving gentle kisses.

Scarpia's eyes were at first caught by the pink orbs of the woman's low-slung buttocks. He looked sharply away, as if ashamed of his intrusion, and found his eyes resting on a deep divan with rich-coloured cushions and drapes in disarray. It required no imagination to realise that the couple, alarmed by the sounds of the bombardment, had risen from a bed of love and, apparently in no danger, were watching the spectacle as if it were a firework display. And now Scarpia, overcoming that first brief embarrassment, realised that the plump buttocks and broad hips of the woman were familiar – that he had seen them often covered in cotton and silk in the Alcazar of Almeria.

Scarpia stepped forward, Spoletta behind him, both men with swords drawn. 'Celestina!'

She turned. So did the man. She gave a cry as one hand fell to hide her pudenda and the other rose to cover her breasts. The man had moved even before she did, dashing towards a sideboard on which lay his scimitar.

'Vitellio, no!' cried Celestina; then, 'No, Spoletta,' because it was Spoletta who had intercepted the Turk and held him, his back against the wall, at the point of his sword.

Scarpia, still confused by the nudity of his beloved, and yet to make sense of what he had seen, turned and took from the divan a garment. 'Put this on,' he said. As he stepped forward to hand it to her, he opened his arms to embrace her; but as soon as she had snatched it, she stepped back.

'Vitellio, you must go.'

'No, you must come. We have a boat…'

'Oh, Vitellio, if only you had come sooner. Now it is too late.'

Scarpia looked at her, now dressed in the silken kaftan, in anguish and confusion. How could he have come sooner? How could it be too late? 'Celestina, my dearest,' he said, 'I have come to take you home.'

'This is now my home.'

'With him?' Scarpia turned to the Turk, his body still motionless but his eyes darting to and fro in search of some advantage, or for a sign that Spoletta had dropped his guard.

'He bought me,' said Celestina. 'I am his.'

'But you are mine,' said Scarpia. 'I am here to reclaim you.'

'It is too late,' said Celestina again. 'I have been with him and … Vitellio, I love him.'

Now the anguish sank and the rage returned. 'You love that? A Turk?'

'He is a man, Vitellio. He has been kind to me and … I love him.'

'Then love his corpse,' said Scarpia, turning in a fury and lunging at the man's chest.

'Bravo,' said Spoletta, pressing forward the point of his own sword and severing the artery in the Turk's neck so that, even as the man fell and writhed from Scarpia's thrust, blood gushed in intermittent spurts onto the patterned tiles of the floor.

Celestina shrieked, 'No, no, Vitellio,' and ran to her groaning, gurgling lover.

'And you, you whore…' said Scarpia, raising his sword to strike Celestina.

'No, no,' said Spoletta, taking hold of his arm. 'Not her. Not a woman. But this one – we will send his soul to Hell.' He turned and drove his sword through the breastbone of the bloodied man, who then stopped twitching and lay still.

There were the sounds of voices. 'Come,' said Spoletta, 'we must go.' He drew Scarpia towards the door. Scarpia staggered backwards, his eyes still on Celestina, sobbing over her lover's body. She turned, her face streaked with blood and wet with tears. 'Take me, then,' she sobbed. 'I have nothing to stay for.'

Scarpia hesitated.

'No,' said Spoletta. '*E rotto.* Leave her. You'll find another.'

'But her father, her mother.'

Abruptly, Celestina stopped weeping, went to the divan to take up some more clothes and put on slippers, and followed Scarpia and Spoletta as they went back down the shallow stone steps, across the courtyard and through the gate. As they ran down the narrow alleyways behind their guide, they heard cries behind but reached the jetty unimpeded. Ducats were thrust into the hands of their turbaned friend, and gold dollars into those of the sailors. Celestina sat alone, a bundle in the back of the longboat, and as a bundle she was carried on the back of a sailor up the webbing onto the ship's deck.

The next morning, the punitive bombardment completed, the fleet returned to Cadiz. When it turned out that the man overboard was in fact a girl swathed in silk and smeared with blood; and that five sailors, an officer in the marines and his servant had been absent from the action, the sailors and Spoletta were flogged. Scarpia, saved from the indignity because he was an officer, was confined to his cabin until the boat reached Cadiz. There, Celestina was sent back to her parents in Almeria while Scarpia was detained for two months in comfortable quarters in the Castillo de Santa Catallina.

In the event, there was no will among the authorities to proceed with a prosecution for desertion. A number of the junior officers could not but admire Scarpia's act of daring. The ship's commander feared ridicule if it was revealed in open court that the five sailors and two marines had gone missing without being noticed. Admiral Barceló retained a soft spot for the wild young Sicilian, and King Charles, who was appraised of the case, again remembered the loyalty of the older Scarpia to Tanucci. It was therefore decided that there would be no charges but that Vitellio Scarpia would forfeit his commission, be dismissed from the service and expelled from Spain.

There was one concession. Scarpia was given a permit to travel to Almeria to visit the girl he had rescued and her family. But, as soon as he was released from the Castillo de Santa Catallina, Scarpia, with his servant Spoletta, took passage on the first ship they could find – a French sloop sailing for the Italian port of Civitavecchia. It would be more than a year before a letter reached him from his former commanding officer in Almeria, Colonel Rodriguez Serrano – dignified words of thanks written on a stiff card on which was pasted a fragment of a bone of St Idaletius, giving the news that Celestina was now married to one of his officers, a Lieutenant Alfonso Valdivia, whom Scarpia remembered as decent but dull.

Two

Floria Tosca came from the Veneto, that territory on the mainland of northern Italy ruled by the Republic of Venice. There were in the Veneto important cities like Padua, Verona and Vicenza, but also unimportant cities such as Golla. Golla was significant only as the seat of a bishop. That bishop had an assistant or coadjutor, Monsignor Tochetti, among whose duties was the bestowing of the sacrament of Confirmation on the children in outlying parishes.

It was in performance of this duty that Monsignor Tochetti was to be found on a day in the spring of 1789, travelling in a shabby barouche from Golla to the small town of San Lorenzo. Beside him in the barouche sat Father Carnevali, his secretary, and, on the box holding the reins, the coachman Bruno. It was a fine day; the hood was down; and neither the horses nor the humans showed signs that they were pressed for time. It was a journey of two hours or so from Golla to the village of San Tomasso where they were to stop for lunch, and two hours more from there to San Lorenzo. The sky was clear, the air warm and scented by the budding acacias that lined the road.

Monsignor Tochetti was now fifty-three years old and aware that, with no patents of nobility, influential relatives, outstanding sanctity or exceptional administrative skill, he was unlikely to be appointed to a diocese of his own – unless it was some impoverished and out-of-the-way see where life would be less agreeable than it was in Golla. Tochetti liked his subordinate role. If he once had ambitions they had been, like his carnal passions, feeble and easily suppressed. He had one enthusiasm and that was music – not an unusual enthusiasm for an Italian and one wholly appropriate for a priest in the late eighteenth century when there was no clear distinction between compositions that were sacred and those that were profane. Paisiello, Cimarosa and Pergolesi wrote operas as well as sacred music. True, the popes in Rome would not permit women to sing onstage, but that was not the case in Venice or Milan; and in Rome there were sufficient celebrated castrati to play female roles. Indeed, there were some who considered the contralto or soprano voices of these eunuchs finer than those of women.

Tochetti knew that some outside Italy were disconcerted, even horrified, by the employment of castrati. An Englishman visiting Golla had berated Tochetti in the salon where they had met for what he described, in his poor French, as *'abominable et inhumain'*. Tochetti had explained that it was surely good that the misfortune of boys who had suffered disfiguring accidents in their youth – perhaps mutilated by pigs after falling into a sty (the parents of such choristers did not usually go into details) – should profit from their misfortune? Would a Girolamo Crescentini or a Luigi Marchesi have achieved such fame and fortune as tenors or baritones? And had not Jesus himself spoken favourably of eunuchs, praising those who had chosen the condition for the sake of the Kingdom of God – monks and priests and bishops like Tochetti?

As a celibate priest, Monsignor Tochetti felt in no position to judge whether the knowledge that the heroine of a drama such as Cimarosa's *Il matrimonio segreto* was in fact an emasculated male affected one's appreciation of the sounds that filled the theatre. He had heard both women and castrati sing in churches and by and large felt that the tones of the castrati were somehow more sublime than the richer warbles of women: but was that because he knew these richer warbles were the voices of women, and so imagined a measure of carnality in the sound? Tochetti had a number of friends among the ladies of Golla, and had presided over the weddings of many of their daughters; but he also heard their confessions and knew how fragile was the flower of chastity – how quickly and easily it wilted when transplanted from a convent into the world.

One reason why Monsignor Tochetti was content not to be transferred to a see of his own was the thought that this would mean relinquishing his responsibility for the cathedral choir in Golla. Golla itself was not a diocese of great importance; its bishop was hardly a prince of the Church; and its cathedral, Gothic with later baroque embellishments, was architecturally undistinguished; but the cathedral choir, Monsignor Tochetti liked to think, was the equal of any in Italy – as fine as that of St Mark's in Venice or St Peter's in Rome. The monsignor's confessor – a holy and irascible Franciscan – had warned him against tainting his soul with the sin of pride when it came to the choir which, though he did not personally direct it, was his creation: he had even gone so far as to augment the salary of the choirmaster from his own resources to entice a man of ability to move to Golla. And, suggested the severe confessor, did the monsignor perhaps go easy on the matrons of Golla when it came to the propriety of their relations with their *cavaliere servente* in the hope that this would make them more likely to contribute towards the commissioning of cantatas, *Te Deums* or Requiem Masses by fashionable and so expensive composers?

Tochetti would listen and ponder and make his act of contrition with a firm purpose of amendment; but then, like the matrons themselves who returned week after week to confess the same peccadillos, he would tell himself that beauty too, like truth, was an aspect of the divine; and that, while the end does not justify the means, a donation of ten scudi for the commission of a cantata would surely, to some small extent, help atone for a sin; and that the creation of a choir that drew many eminent people to forsake their private chapels to attend Mass at the cathedral, and add lavishly to the collection made during the Mass, surely contributed not just to the diocesan coffers but the greater glory of God.

*

Monsignor Tochetti and his entourage stopped at midday at the village of San Tommaso where the parish priest gave them lunch and provided the bishop with a bed for a short siesta. They then continued on the second leg of their journey and reached San Lorenzo at six in the evening. Father Giacomo, the parish priest, came out to greet them. He was around the same age as Monsignor Tochetti but, while the coadjutor bishop was tall and heavy, he was a slim, restless figure, bald under his dusty, horsehair wig. The two men greeted one another with a genuine warmth. Temperamentally they might have nothing in common – the one cautious and phlegmatic, the other talkative and sharp – but they shared a lack of ambition and both steered a steady course between the extremes of worldliness and religious enthusiasm.

An agreeable smell of roasting meat wafted into the parlour, and a pitcher of wine with three glasses was waiting on the sideboard but, after greeting Father Giacomo, and introducing his secretary, both the bishop and the priest went to wash the dust off their faces, and then passed from the house into the church to pray before the altar and thank God for their safe arrival. Monsignor Tochetti, while meditating upon the painful martyrdom of St Laurence who was roasted on a grill, could not prevent his thoughts from turning to that other roasting that he had sniffed a few moments earlier, wondering whether he could look forward to lamb cutlets or a beefsteak.

It was lamb cutlets, preceded by an antipasto and pasta, and followed by stewed pears with a rich custard. Father Carnevali, the bishop's secretary, ate in respectful silence while the two older men chatted and exchanged learned quips. Father Giacomo shared the bishop's love of music but was more interested in the written word. The *Gazzetta Veneta* was delivered a couple of days late to the presbytery at San Lorenzo and kept the *abate* Giacomo up to date on gossip and worldly affairs. Father Giacomo admired the Gozzi brothers, Carlo and Gasparo, who wrote regularly for the *Gazzetta*, *Modo Morale* and the *Osservatore* of their love of tradition and loathing of Voltaire, Rousseau and d'Alembert.

The food was eaten. The wine was drunk. At nine, pleading fatigue after his journey, Monsignor Tochetti rose from the table. His friend, Father Giacomo, escorted him to his room and then, after wishing him goodnight, leaned towards him and whispered: *'We have an agreeable surprise for you tomorrow…'*

2

Veni, creator Spiritus, mentes tuorum visita, imple superna gratia, quae tu creasti pectora. The ever-familiar words of the ancient hymn, and the sounds of the Gregorian chant, mingled with the smell of incense and candlewax as Monsignor Tochetti processed in a line of priests, deacons and altar boys – his own position, as befits the humility of a man *in persona Christi*, at the very end of the procession – followed only by an eight-year-old boy holding his train. His thoughts: 'This church of San Lorenzo has some of the best acoustics in the diocese,' and, 'Father Giacomo has done good work with his choir; it is really quite excellent. *Is this the surprise?'*

The ceremony proceeded. An acolyte removed his mitre and handed it to the little cherub while another took hold of his crozier. Tochetti rose to deliver his homily – a set text that he had used many times before, though he tried to vary it so that it would not seem stale to the congregation, which he did with a few ad hoc embellishments such as a warning about the perilousness of reading impious books, a remote danger because few in the congregation could read, and none would have heard of Voltaire or Rousseau.

The homily over, the coadjutor bishop, flanked by acolytes, moved to the steps of the altar. The fourteen young men and women – the girls in white dresses, the youths in their best clothes – now came forward with their sponsors and knelt before Monsignor Tochetti. He laid the palms of his hands on their head – as the hands of Cardinal Buranzo many years before had been laid on *his* head to transmit invisibly the powers he was now exercising as a bishop in a direct and unbroken line from the twelve Apostles of Christ. And Tochetti believed as he touched the bare hair of the young men, and the lace veils of the young women, that a benevolent force was indeed descending from Heaven that would help these poor souls to resist the blandishments of Satan and deal with the vicissitudes of life; yet even as the supernatural powers flowed through his long, elegant fingers, Tochetti was thinking: '*But where is the surprise?*'

The last of the confirmed together with the sponsors returned to their seats. The ceremony was running towards its conclusion. Now that the Holy Spirit had received his due, it was the turn of the Virgin Mary, whose statue was festooned with flowers. Sitting on his throne adjacent to the altar, Tochetti heard from the organ the familiar first bars of Pergolesi's *Stabat Mater*. And then came the voice.

Stabat mater dolorosa
juxta Crucem lacrimosa,
dum pendebat Filius.

Tochetti turned, stupefied, and looked up for the first time at the organ loft over the entrance to the church. Never before had he heard, from a woman or a castrato, a voice so rich and strong yet ineffably pure. Sunlight shone through the stained glass – the coloured shafts of light given substance by the candle smoke and incense. In the shadow beneath these bright beams, the choristers, facing their choirmaster, were imprecise figures with featureless faces. Tochetti could not make out which mouth was open or shut; which figure was the soloist; which form was the source of such an exquisite voice.

Yet even though intoxicated by the ethereal sound coming from the organ loft, the coadjutor bishop Tochetti understood that it was unseemly for him to remain with his head crooked and his eyes fixed on the back of the church. He turned back to face the acolytes across the chancel, and resumed an expression of placid piety. Then, as the cantata ended, and he rose to give the congregation a final blessing, he met the eye of Father Giacomo. To his discreet look of amused interrogation, the bishop responded with a gentle nod: *yes, the surprise had indeed been a surprise.*

*

The sharp sounds of laughter and chatter in the dialect of the Veneto echoed in the red-tiled floor of the parish hall. There was a brief hush as the coadjutor bishop, divested and now in his black soutane with red piping and broad purple sash, entered the room with Fathers Giacomo and Carnevali at his side. He waved his raised hand, a gesture that all recognised as a sign that they should carry on laughing and chatting and eating their ices and maca-roons. The bishop mingled with the newly confirmed children, their parents, grandparents, cousins and aunts and uncles. He held out his elegant hand to enable genuflecting peasants to kiss his episco-pal ring. He pretended to remember the mothers whose elder children he had confirmed in earlier years. But all the while his eyes flitted between the wide shoulders of the thickset men and the coiffured heads of their bedecked wives looking for the source of the angelic voice. Finally, frustrated, he turned to Father Giacomo, who remained by his side, and said: 'And is she here?'

Already, in the sacristy, as they had disrobed, he had asked Father Giacomo about the voice. 'Most beautiful singing,' he had said.

'I am glad Your Grace was pleased,' Father Giacomo had replied.

'You must have a fine choirmaster.'

'He does what he can.'

'And the voice? The *Stabat Mater*? That was the surprise?'

'Indeed. I had hoped that Your Grace, as a connoisseur, would remark on it.'

'A woman.'

'A young woman. Even … a girl.'

'From the village?'

'From the village, yes, but she has been raised by the sisters.'

The sisters, Tochetti knew, were the Carmelite sisters whose house was outside the walls of San Lorenzo.

'Is she a nun?'

'Not as yet. Her parents are poor. The father works as a gardener at the convent. That is why the nuns took her in.'

'Not for her voice?'

'I think then, aged ten or so, it was not yet clear that God had endowed her with such a precious gift.'

Tochetti had said no more. He knew the convent: he had made a number of visitations. The sisters were discalced Carmelite – the stricter branch of the order – and had an unusually large proportion of genuine vocations – women who had not been sent there for want of a husband, as was so often the case, but who wished to devote themselves to God. The prioress, Sister Monica, was a formidable woman, the daughter of the Venetian patrician, a Chigi: she treated her chaplains as lackeys and, during Tochetti's visitations, behaved as if she outranked him in both the spiritual and temporal domains.

Now, standing among the noisy parishioners of San Lorenzo, the bishop received the reply from Father Giacomo he had not wanted. No, the singer was not there. She had returned to the convent.

'Without even a macaroon?'

'Sister Monica keeps her cloistered. It took some persuading to let her sing today.'

'But she has taken no vows – the young woman?'

'No. But I suspect that Sister Monica would like her to do so. She has been prepared, as it were, for a religious life.'

'But that would be absurd.' This was an involuntary expostulation – not addressed to Father Giacomo but heard by Father Giacomo all the same.

'The sisters are very fond of her,' said the priest.

'But what do the parents say?'

'They are very poor. Faced with Sister Monica…'

The bishop understood, but he also felt rise within him a certainty that the voice he had heard should not be confined to the chapel of a convent or the parish church of a village in the Veneto. Like a rare bird with exotic plumage, that voice must be free to fly in the wide open spaces of … a cathedral!

His duty done, Monsignor Tochetti returned to the parlour of the presbytery, asked for pen and paper, and wrote a note addressed to Sister Monica.

Reverend Mother, I find to my delight, by the providence of the Lord, that I am to spend another day in San Lorenzo and would be glad to say the first Mass of the day for your community. With God's blessing, Alfredo, Coadjutor Bishop of Golla.

He folded the sheet of paper, called for wax, and sealed the letter with his episcopal ring. It was sent off at once and, two hours later, a reply was received from the prioress, Sister Monica, expressing her pleasure at what the bishop proposed.

3

Sister Monica was courteous and correct when Monsignor Tochetti, accompanied by Father Carnevali, arrived at the convent at six in the morning. All was ready in the sacristy and, after listening to the nuns hidden behind the grille sing matins, Monsignor Tochetti said Mass, and was then served breakfast in Sister Monica's private parlour with the prioress sitting at the same table but eating nothing. As he ate his brioche and drank his coffee, the coadjutor bishop and the prioress talked about this and that, with Father Carnevali speaking only when spoken to; and eventually the conversation turned to the subject of music, the cathedral choir and from there to the beautiful voice of the young woman he had heard in the church of San Lorenzo the day before. 'It really is exceptional,' he said. 'I have never heard anything quite as lovely before.'

'God has given her a particular talent,' said the nun – a sallow face and wary eyes visible under her cowl.

'Who is this young woman?' asked the bishop.

'The daughter of our gardener. We took her in to live with the novices and get some kind of an education, though sadly she still struggles to read and write.'

'Have you thought … has her father thought … of having her voice trained by a professional, and developing her talent?'

'They are content to leave her as she is.'

'But she is … what? Sixteen years old?'

'Fifteen.'

'Do you sense that she has a vocation to the religious life?'

'Not as yet.'

The bishop sat in silence for a moment; his brioche was eaten, his cup empty. Then, in a tone unusually imperative for a man who seemed so bland, he said: 'I should like to see her. And her parents.'

'That would be difficult,' said Sister Monica.

'Why difficult?'

'It might take time.'

'I am in no hurry.'

The nun bowed her head in reluctant acquiescence. 'Very well.' Her tone had an edge of irritation – irritation perhaps at the bishop's request or at her own inability to think of a reason to refuse him. Strictly speaking, he had no jurisdiction over Sister Monica and her community of nuns; but the gardener, his wife and his daughter were not part of that community; they were parishioners of San Lorenzo and so came under the rule of the Bishop of Golla and now the bishop's coadjutor acting in his place. Moreover, to refuse his request would be a discourtesy that would reflect badly on the community: what difficulties could there be in calling the gardener from the garden, his wife from her house and their daughter from within the convent?

*

Sister Monica left the parlour. Monsignor Tochetti and Father Carnevali rose from the table and sat on the two straight-backed upholstered chairs placed on either side of the fireplace. Father Carnevali handed the bishop his breviary, took out his own, and both clerics started to read silently the Office of the day. Monsignor Tochetti considered that he would probably have to wait for a while, if only to justify the prioress's talk of difficulties, but twenty minutes later she returned, followed by two peasants, a man and a woman, and behind them a girl.

The bishop stood. The two peasants went down on their knees. Both seemed older than the bishop had anticipated – almost fifty, perhaps, which suggested that they had married late in life. The gardener was still dressed in his work clothes, but his wife was wearing her Sunday best – a clean, embroidered dress with square-cut bodice and a bonnet, slightly askew as if put on in haste. The bishop held out his hand to proffer his episcopal ring, first to the husband, then to the wife, which both kissed with lowered heads.

The girl, who stood behind her parents, did not, at once, go down on her knees. Only when her parents were raised by a gentle gesture by the bishop, did she first curtsy and then, with a bounce, kneel, kiss the ring and stand again: and as she did so, she looked briefly and quizzically into the eyes of the august successor to the Apostles, before lowering her glance demurely to the floor.

Monsignor Tochetti may have successfully made himself a eunuch for the sake of the kingdom, but he was quite aware that God bestowed physical beauty unevenly on his creatures, male and female alike, so that some, like Father Carnevali, despite the advantage of youth, were unpleasing to the eye, while others, like this young woman, were a delight. The questioning glance had come from large brown eyes decorated with long lashes and crowned with elegant black brows. The hair beneath her bonnet was black with a sheen, and her pale brown complexion was free from pockmarks or any other blemish. She was recognisable as the daughter of her mother, but just as the older woman was now heavy and bent, the younger one was erect and slender. As in the mother, her features were strong, but none were out of proportion: and her pink lips, when they parted, showed an even row of bright white teeth.

The prioress, Sister Monica, who had been standing by the door, now came forward and directed the gardener and his family to sit on a bench that was placed against the wall. The bishop and Father Carnevali resumed their seats on the straight-backed chairs, and the three whom he had summoned sat facing them on the bench – the girl between her two parents. Sister Monica, and an accompanying nun, remained standing.

'My very dear children,' Monsignor Tochetti began, 'I have asked to see you because yesterday in your parish church I heard this most beautiful voice, and after the ceremony I asked Father Giacomo to whom it belonged. He told me it was yours…' The bishop moved his eyes from the parents to their daughter. 'He told me of your presence, here at the convent, and Sister Monica kindly acceded to my request to meet you. And this meeting, I should say, is not simply to satisfy my curiosity. You may not know it, but in the cathedral of Golla we have a choir that is famous throughout the Veneto, and it would, it seems to me, add to the greater glory of God if you, signorina, would come to Golla under my protection and sing in that choir.'

There was silence. Neither the parents nor the daughter raised their eyes and remained not just silent but entirely still as if they were not present, or wished they were not present, or thought the bishop's short speech had somehow nothing to do with them. Then, suddenly, the mother directed a furtive look at her daughter, before going back to the contemplation of her embroidered skirt.

Monsignor Tochetti had addressed them in Italian, and it now occurred to him that perhaps they had not fully understood what he had said. He therefore repeated his proposition in Venetian, adding to his proposal an assurance that the girl could reside with one of the many religious communities in Golla and would be treated with every respect and consideration.

Now both parents spoke at once. 'It is a great honour,' said the gardener.

'She is still young,' said the wife.

'How old are you, my child?' the bishop asked the girl.

'I am fifteen, Your Grace.' She looked up to say this, and her expression encouraged the bishop: it seemed to suggest that she felt that at fifteen she was quite grown up.

'But in Golla, in a great city…' said the mother.

Monsignor Tochetti smiled. Golla, a great city!

'I understand Tuscan,' said the girl. 'I can read and write ... almost.'

'There is much wickedness in the city...' said the mother.

'Would she perhaps find a means to ... to earn her living?' asked the father.

'Her voice, which has such natural beauty,' said the bishop, 'would be trained to perfection by one of the finest choirmasters in all Italy.'

'So that...' The gardener hesitated to put it bluntly.

'She would earn her living,' said the bishop. 'And more.'

'It would be a wonderful opportunity,' said Father Carnevali with an ingratiating glance at the bishop.

'Yes, for sin!' said Sister Monica. She did not move; her hands remained folded under her habit; but her words were as strong as a fist thumping upon a table.

'Yes, for sin,' repeated the old peasant woman, the mother, raising her eyes and turning with gratitude to the nun standing behind her.

'There is sin everywhere,' said Father Carnevali.

'But the walls of a convent keep the Devil at bay,' said Sister Monica.

During this exchange, Bishop Tochetti watched the girl closely and he noticed how, at the mention of sin, her eyes slightly widened and, when she turned to look at Father Carnevali, she wrinkled her nose. Could she smell his malodorous breath from where she was sitting, or was it just his appearance that had produced this reaction? And why had the word sin led to a widening of the eyes?

'Both these things are true,' said the bishop, speaking in Venetian. 'High walls can protect from worldly temptations but, as Our Lord tells us, good and evil are a matter of our inner disposition. And he also told us that we must not hide our light under a bushel; and we must remember the parable of the talents in which the man who keeps his one talent buried is consigned to everlasting torment in Hell.'

'With all due respect to Your Grace,' said Sister Monica, 'the talent may be spiritual and a calling, even for one with a fine voice, may be to be a saint.'

'There are saints outside the cloister,' said the bishop.

'The path is harder for a young girl.'

The bishop turned to the girl. 'Do you feel, my child, that Almighty God and the Blessed Virgin would like you to take the vows of the nun?'

'I prefer singing to praying!' The girl blurted this out. The bishop and Father Carnevali laughed. The two nuns did not. Nor did the mother.

'But to sing *is* to pray,' said the bishop. '*Laborare est orare* – and it is not just to pray but to preach, to evangelise, to clothe truth in beauty, to make it shine and delight!'

When a bishop, even a mere coadjutor bishop, points at a path towards sanctity and salvation, it leaves little more to be said.

'Let me suggest this,' the bishop went on. 'If the signorina is willing, let her come to Golla with her mother and father, and they will be shown where she might reside, and by whom she would be taught – all this, of course, at my expense. Indeed –' the bishop now stood up and turned to Father Carnevali – 'let us give you now ten scudi to cover the expenses.' Father Carnevali bowed. 'If, that is –' the bishop turned to Sister Monica – 'the services of your gardener can be spared for two or three days?'

Sister Monica, too, bowed to signify her acquiescence.

'And if all does not seem satisfactory –' the bishop turned back to the parents – 'then of course the three of you can return to San Lorenzo.'

Monsignor Tochetti and Father Carnevali moved towards the door. Father Carnevali gave the ten scudi to the incredulous gardener. Then, at the door to the parlour, the bishop stopped, held out his hand to be kissed and, after the three had kissed it, added an episcopal blessing.

'But I do not even know your name,' he said to the girl.

'Our name is Tosca,' said the father.

'And she is Floria,' said the mother.

'So,' said the bishop. 'Floria Tosca. I look forward to seeing you in Golla, my child.' And, after giving her a final blessing, he left the room.

Three

Vitellio Scarpia and Luigi Spoletta disembarked with their few belongings at Civitavecchia – the port, fifty miles from Rome, used by priests, pilgrims and cultivated sightseers on their way to the Eternal City, and the base for the warships of the Papal States. The two Sicilians were there fortuitously: Civitavecchia had happened to be the destination of the first boat leaving Cadiz after Scarpia's release from the Castillo de Santa Catallina. They took rooms at an inn near the port and as they ate dinner Spoletta dropped oblique remarks to make clear that in his view they should find another boat to take them on to Palermo. Nothing that he said required an answer from Scarpia who, throughout the voyage from Cadiz, had been silent and, even now that he was back in Italy, remained in a sombre mood. Spoletta also made the point, as if thinking aloud, that their funds were running low; but he did not press it. He realised that Scarpia might not want to return to his parents penniless and in disgrace.

The next morning they travelled on the public diligence to Rome. Arriving at the Piazza del Popolo, the driver directed them towards an inn which he promised would be suitable for a *cavaliere*. It was above an eating house and so filled with the smell of burning fat. On the second day they found better lodgings close to the

Piazza di Spagna – an apartment on the *piano nobile* and a garret for Spoletta under the roof. The wallpaper was faded and carpets threadbare, but the place was clean, the owner was agreeable and his daughter, who offered to wash their clothes, was good-natured if plain. The plainness, like the shabbiness of the rooms, suited Scarpia's mood: he looked away from pretty girls.

Rome was a good place for a disheartened man to hide away from the world. The city that had once been the capital of a great empire was now an anomalous backwater, ruled as it had been for the past thousand years by its bishop, the Pope. In antiquity, two million inhabitants had lived within the Aurelian walls: now there was a tenth of that number and much of what had once been a city had returned to nature as vineyards and fields. There were magnificent basilicas, grand palaces, innumerable churches and fine fountains and piazzas; but cattle and sheep grazed among the ruins of the Baths of Caracalla, and chickens scratched the earth of the Forum. On the bend in the Tiber, where the Romans now lived, pigs fed off the rubbish, which lay in heaps on the mostly unnamed, unpaved and unlit streets.

The Pope at the time of Scarpia's arrival in Rome was Giovanni Angelo Braschi, Pius VI. Handsome, amiable, vain, he had risen through the ranks of the papal civil service and had now reigned for twenty-three years. He was not especially devout, but liked to preside at the elaborate liturgies on the innumerable feast days of the Church. He had ennobled and enriched his nephew, Duke Braschi Onesti, but far from being offended by this nepotism, his subjects admired their *papa bello*: popes who did not share their good fortune with their relatives were considered stingy. He was extravagant, spending large sums of money on grandiose projects such as a magnificent new sacristy for St Peter's Basilica, Egyptian obelisks in many of Rome's piazzas, the Pio-Clementino museum, and fruitless attempts to drain the Pontine marshes.

There was, at the time, a large gap between the rich and the poor, but so imbued were all the citizens of the Eternal City with the values of the Gospels that the poor were respected, even revered. Monasteries, convents and lay fraternities vied for the privilege of caring for the needy – feeding them, clothing them, educating them, giving them shelter and tending them when they were sick. There was free primary education, funds for dowries for impoverished girls, and the newly built prison, the *carcere nuovo*, was the most advanced in Europe. Foreigners who lent themselves airs or showed contempt for the poor were despised: in Rome a prince or a cardinal would happily share a pinch of snuff with his coachman or a beggar on the street.

As a result of the free provision of life's necessities, few Romans did any work. Those not attached to one of the many ecclesiastical establishments worked as servants or artisans or were wholly idle. Even those who worked took a siesta that lasted from midday until six in the evening. Sundays were days of rest, and no one worked on the many feast days that punctuated the year. Such holy days saw magnificent singing by choirs in the basilicas and churches and jubilant celebrations later in the day. On the feast of St Peter and St Paul, the facade of St Peter's Basilica was illuminated by six thousand lamps, and there was a fireworks display from the Castel Sant'Angelo judged to be finer than that put on for King Louis XVI at Versailles. The Roman nobility shared their pontiff's sense of *noblesse oblige*. The magnificent collections of art in their palaces were open for all to see, and given some pretext such as the state visit of a foreign monarch, they laid on sumptuous entertainments with a free distribution of cakes and ices and paid for orchestral concerts in public squares.

*

Each morning, after Spoletta had helped him dress, Scarpia set out to explore the city. He mingled with the foreign visitors among the ruins of the Forum and the Baths of Caracalla, read the gazettes in the Caffè Greco or the Caffè degli Specchi, and at midday ate lunch in one of the many *alberghetti*. In the afternoon like everyone else he returned to his lodgings for a siesta. In the evening he watched the *passeggiata* on the Corso and at night explored the dark streets lit only by candle lamps beneath some image of the Madonna or a saint.

On Sundays, Scarpia went to Mass in a nearby church or in one of the great basilicas – St John Lateran, Santa Maria Maggiore or St Peter's itself. He was awed by the grandeur of the buildings. The rich decor of painted putti and marble saints led his eye upwards towards images of the Saviour whose suffering had won Paradise for the repentant sinner, and to his gentle mother surrounded by angels reigning as Queen of Heaven. Never hitherto devout, Scarpia had been obliged by experience to discover a new side to his mercurial character, one that was reflective and susceptible to remorse.

Scarpia could not remove from his mind the memories of what had happened in Algiers. Images recurred over and over again in his mind's eye of Celestina's buttocks like sides of ham; of her body pressed gently against the dark hirsute body of the Turk; of her finger twirling the lock of his tight-curled black hair – then of the man, his back against the wall, held paralysed at the point of Spoletta's sword; his eyes flitting to and fro; and then Scarpia's sudden fury, and lunge at the man's breast.

Scarpia had attacked the Hanoverian grenadier during his sortie at the siege of Gibraltar, but that was war. The janissary, Celestina's lover, was also an enemy who, had he had the chance, would have killed Scarpia. But he did not have the chance. It was not a fair fight. When Scarpia had killed him he was unarmed, ungirded – half-naked, bristly like a pig. And like a stuck pig he had died – blood pumping from his carcass; and there was Celestina crouched beside the body, her face wet with tears and blood; and, had he not been restrained by Spoletta, he might have killed her too – possessed for that moment by a jealous rage, the terrible hatred of someone he had so recently loved and had thought was his.

And then there was the shame he felt at disappointing those who had helped him on his way to preferment and good fortune – Celestina's father, Admiral Barceló and the King of Spain himself; and his father and mother who had sent him off to Spain with their prayers and blessings. What shame, embarrassment and disappointment they would have to endure when they learned that he had been dishonourably discharged from the Spanish army. What kind of welcome would he get after dissipating the favours they had called in as well as the ducats, dollars and sequins they had put in his purse?

Scarpia feared the disappointment of his father less than the disdain of his mother: his father, after all, had lost so many illusions that he might even be pleased to lose another. There was also the parable of the Prodigal Son which was familiar to any Christian; but that story told by Christ of a father's forgiveness of a wayward son made no mention of the mother, who, if she was like Marcella di Torre della Barca, would have been less likely to forgive the shame that her son had brought on the family.

These were the thoughts that led Scarpia to linger in Rome. He could live there cheaply – even for nothing thanks to the many soup kitchens. If he could no longer afford the clothes of a gentleman, then he could wear a soutane and pass himself off as a cleric: a third of the city's male inhabitants wore soutanes or the habits of one of the many religious orders, and, as he mused on his own failure as both a soldier and a lover, it struck Scarpia that perhaps he had mistaken his vocation and was called, like Ignatius Loyola, to be a soldier of God – not as a Jesuit, because the Society had been suppressed, but as a member of one of the many other religious orders each of which had a church in Rome – the Augustinians, the

Benedictines, the Carmelites, the Franciscans, the Redemptorists, the Theatines, the Barnabites – the choice was vast.

By chance, as these thoughts were passing through his head, Scarpia found himself outside the Oratorian church of Santa Maria in Vallicella. He went in. A Mass was in progress: incense thickened the air, rising past the gilded columns to the sumptuously decorated dome. In a side chapel there was a confessional with a line of penitents waiting to be shriven. Scarpia knelt behind them. His heart thumped because, although he had been to confession many times before, his sins had hitherto been insignificant peccadillos.

When his turn came, Scarpia knelt before the grille. Behind it he could discern the gaunt face of an older man. To him, he told his whole story. The priest listened, interrupting only to clarify one or two points. Did he appreciate that indiscipline was itself a sin? Was his escapade at the siege of Gibraltar perhaps less a case of courage than of pride? What had been his intentions towards Celestina? Had they been honourable? Had he meant to marry her? Had he not anticipated that her chastity might have been compromised during the many months she had been held in Algiers?

Scarpia explained that the Redemptorist had said she was being held untouched in the hope of a ransom.

'But by the time you had reached Algiers, the friar had already returned?'

'Yes. He had arranged for the guide to lead us to her.'

'And if you had found her unwillingly seduced?'

'I would not have blamed her.'

'It was that gesture of affection that enraged you?'

'Yes.'

'And yet, poor girl…'

Scarpia was silent.

'But you returned her to her parents?'

'Yes.'

'And told no one of her disgrace?'

'No.'

'So you behaved honourably.'

'But I killed a man.'

'Yes, a Turk, but you are right to be sorry because you did not kill him in defence of Christendom, or even to free the girl, but in a moment of passion. But, of course, passion is often involuntary, and the acts it inspires are not premeditated.'

Scarpia, moved by the Oratorian's understanding, now told him that he felt called to take holy orders. He had had enough of the world. Enough of the flesh. He abjured the Devil. Did the priest smile? Scarpia thought he saw through the grille some movement of his thin lips but, if it was a smile, it was not one of mockery and ridicule.

'How old are you, my son?'

'I am twenty-four.'

'You are still young and there can be no doubt but that Almighty God has something in mind for you. He would not want a spirit as fervent as yours to go to waste. But does He want you to take holy orders? There is nothing in your life until now that would suggest this. Moreover, when we feel impelled to do something, even something apparently good, we must be sure that we are heeding God and not unwittingly using Him for purposes of our own. You have made mistakes. You feel you have disappointed your parents. You fear returning to them with their hopes dashed, their ambitions for you unfulfilled. But God never asks one to avoid difficulties; He never sounds the retreat.'

The priest told Scarpia that for his penance he should pray the Five Glorious Mysteries of the Holy Rosary, pronounced the solemn words of absolution – *Ego te absolvo a peccatis tuis* – and, raising his right hand, gave him his blessing – *in nomine Patris et*

Filii et Spiritus Sanctus. Amen. Then, as Scarpia rose to his feet, the priest said: 'If you will wait in the church, I have some thoughts about how I might be of use to you while you are in Rome.'

Scarpia knelt before the high altar saying the prayers that were his penance, counting the Ave Marias on his fingers since he was without a rosary. After half an hour or so, he felt a hand on his shoulder. The priest introduced himself as Father Simone Alberti, and invited Scarpia to follow him out of the church into the presbytery. They went into a parlour, one wall lined with books, the other with a portrait of the founder of the Oratory, St Phillip Neri. Father Simone sat down at a table, and Scarpia, at his host's invitation, on a chair that faced him. The priest drew paper out of a drawer and dipped a pen into an inkstand. He wrote – the scratch of the pen the only sound other than the chirruping of birds in the Oratory garden – and when he had finished and dusted the paper to dry the ink, he closed the parchment and sealed it, saying: 'This is a letter for the Treasurer of the Pontifical Household, Fabrizio Ruffo. He may be able to help you. I can promise nothing, but it is worth a try. Do not hide anything from him. It is always best to tell the truth.'

2

Fabrizio Ruffo, the Treasurer of the Papal States, was a tall, portly man with an air of natural authority. He wore a black soutane with purple piping, a purple cummerbund and a purple cotta – the short cape worn over his soutane – but he was not a priest. The second son of the Calabrian Duke of Bagnaro, he had been raised to pursue a career in the Church – dispatched to Rome at the age of five to be educated by his great-uncle, Cardinal Tommaso Ruffo, Dean of the College of Cardinals. There was a second cardinal in the family, Antonio Maria Ruffo, and Fabrizio had influential relatives in Rome: his mother Giustiniana, was a Colonna – Princess of Spinosa and Marchioness of Guardia Pertcara. He had studied at the Collegio Clementina and La Sapienza University, and, after graduating at the age of twenty-three with a doctorate in civil and canon law, he had served as secretary to Giovanni Braschi, who himself, early in his career, had served as secretary to Cardinal Tommaso Ruffo. When elected Pope as Pius VI, Braschi had appointed Ruffo to the papal civil service – the *chierici di camera*. Now, at the age of forty-one, he had reached its apex as Treasurer – a post that made him responsible not just for the administration and finances of the Papal States, but also for its defence. He was prefect of the Castel Sant'Angelo, commissary of the coastal fortifications and administrator of the pontifical armed forces – in effect, the Pope's Minister of War.

Ruffo had been a fellow student of the Oratorian priest, Simone Alberti, at La Sapienza, and after graduation the two men had remained friends. They met regularly to discuss the myriad perils that faced the Church, in particular the virus of scepticism that had spread from France to Rome itself, where fashionable *abati*, despite papal prohibitions, joined Masonic lodges, took part in theistic rituals, and expressed the opinion, sotto voce, that the Gospel was a fairy story and Jesus of Nazareth a gentle rabbi who never claimed to be the Son of God. Ruffo was dedicated to both the Church and to the papacy, and foresaw catastrophe should either be undermined, but he had taken no vows of poverty and had amassed benefices that sustained a princely way of life.

The note Father Simone Alberti had written to his friend Ruffo said simply that he might find a use for a young Sicilian *cavaliere* in his capacity as Minister of War. 'He has shown great courage in the field of battle, which, here in Rome, as we know, is in short supply.' The reference was to a recent conversation between the two churchmen about a play currently at the Argentina theatre in which a character said: 'I don't like to bathe in the Tiber because I might drown. I don't like to ride a horse because I might fall off. And I don't like to go to war because I might get killed.' They had both agreed that this was a true depiction of the Roman mentality. Banditry was rife throughout the Papal States, but soldiers escorting travellers fled at the first sign of a fight.

'Perhaps,' Father Simone had said, 'they have taken too literarily Our Lord's admonition to love their enemies?'

'Not at all,' Ruffo had replied. 'Every man carries a knife and thinks nothing of killing a man over a woman or some imagined insult or a game of cards. And the women have *stiletti* disguised as hairpins to use on their rivals. But no one wants to risk his life going after bandits. They admire the bandits. They consider theirs a reasonable way to earn a living.'

As a Calabrian, Ruffo knew that his fellow countrymen were better at pursuing vendettas than fighting in a disciplined military force, and that Sicilians were much the same; but he was less unworldly than his friend Simone; he delighted in gossip, and remembered being told the story by the Spanish ambassador Azara of a young Sicilian who had gone ashore during the bombardment of Algiers by Admiral Barceló. Had not his name been Scarpia? Might this not be the same man? He therefore gave instructions to his secretary that, when Scarpia presented himself at the Quirinale Palace, his name should be put at the top of the list of petitioners waiting in the antechamber.

When, in the middle of the next morning, the young man was shown into his presence, Ruffo was agreeably surprised by his pleasant demeanour. Ruffo had long since subdued any carnal desires that might have impeded his career in the Church, but he was not insensible to beauty in either men or women and this young *cavaliere* was unquestionably handsome – his even features enhanced by black hair, blue eyes and a manner at once shy and defiant. The

Sicilian knelt to kiss the churchman's ring, but Ruffo raised him by the elbow, saying: 'I am not a bishop, signor, nor even a priest. The Lord has not deemed me worthy of holy orders.'

Scarpia blushed. 'I am sorry, Monsignor. I didn't know.'

Ruffo pointed to an upholstered chair, inviting Scarpia to sit down. 'You are recommended by Father Simone,' he said, 'but he does not say why. No doubt the seal of the confessional prevents him from telling me more.'

'I served until recently in the army of His Royal Highness, King Charles of Spain, but I was dismissed.'

'For what reason?'

'Indiscipline.'

'Indiscipline?'

'There were two instances, Monsignor. At the siege of Gibraltar I broke ranks and made a foray on my own initiative, and during an assault on Algiers I commandeered a longboat and went ashore without permission.'

'You landed in Algiers? During the bombardment? May I ask why?'

Scarpia blushed, which, to Ruffo, added to his charm. 'For personal reasons.'

'Personal reasons. I see.'

'For the first offence, I lost my commission in the Royal Guards; for the second, I was discharged.'

Ruffo paused. The letter was still in his hand. 'Yes, Scarpia. I remember now. I was told something. Your father served with Tanucci. I remember hearing about your escapade in Algiers.'

'It was not worthy of being brought to your attention,' said Scarpia, his eyes looking modestly at the floor.

Ruffo smiled. 'Stories like that amuse the ladies,' he said.

'It will have brought shame to my parents.'

'And you would like an opportunity to make amends?'

'Yes, Monsignor.'

'Would you say you have learned a lesson?' Ruffo asked. 'Would you now be more inclined to obey orders?'

'Most certainly, Monsignor.'

'Would you be willing to take service in the pontifical army?'

'It would be an honour, Monsignor.'

'To us,' said Ruffo, 'the reasons for your dismissal from the army of the King of Spain are not a mark against you, but rather the opposite. The Romans make poor soldiers. They are unwilling to risk their lives.'

'I am not afraid of death,' said Scarpia.

'So I imagined. And are you prepared to serve outside Rome?'

'I will serve wherever I am sent,' said Scarpia.

'Excellent. Then, if you are willing, I shall arrange for a commission as lieutenant in the pontifical army. Your pay will be fifteen scudi a month.' Ruffo rang a bell on his desk. A clerk entered the room. 'You will write out an order to the Banco di Santo Spirito,' Ruffo said to him, 'for this young man to draw his salary: and the decree for a commission to go to the Governor of Rome.' He turned back to Scarpia. 'You will be told where to report for service. Now, may God be with you.'

Ruffo smiled benignly as Scarpia thanked the Treasurer, bowed deeply and departed; then, though he knew that there were other petitioners waiting to see him, he did not ring his bell to indicate to his secretary that he should show the next one in, but sat back in his chair and considered how best he could make use of his new recruit. Banditry was ubiquitous in the Papal States, but most shaming for the authorities was the way in which the coaches of diplomats and dignitaries on their way from Rome to Ancona, the chief port of the Papal States on the Adriatic Sea, en route to Venice and Vienna, were frequently stopped by brigands as they crossed the mountains from Perugia, and the passengers robbed. This happened so regularly that rich travellers disguised themselves as paupers and important officials went incognito – the ambassador wearing the worn tunic of his clerk, the nuncio the shabby soutane of an impoverished *abate*.

Ruffo decided that he would send Scarpia to Fazetta, a town in the Apennines between Perugia and Ancona. He did not want the wild Sicilian to be infected by the pusillanimity of the regular officers and would tell the garrison commander that the young lieutenant should have his own quarters and choose his own men. It was unlikely that the commander or anyone else in the military hierarchy would raise any objection when all had failed thus far. No doubt they would like to see Scarpia fail too, and certainly, with his impetuosity, there went risk. It would seem that he had been extraordinarily fortunate at Gibraltar and in Algiers. Would he be so lucky in the Apennines?

Four

Monsignor Tochetti, the coadjutor bishop of Golla, kept the promise he had made to the parents of Floria Tosca. The fifteen-year-old prodigy was placed with the Ursuline sisters in Golla, lived there under the same regime as a postulant, and left the convent only to sing in the cathedral choir. Even here, she was kept apart from the male choristers and, though she spent much time with the choirmaster, Antonio Faglia, she was always chaperoned by one of the older nuns, who sat silently telling the beads of her rosary while her charge went through a rigorous training.

When Faglia decided, a month or so after Tosca's arrival in Golla, that she was ready to make her debut at High Mass on the feast of the Ascension, she was still kept from the view of the cathedral's congregation; but nothing could hide the exquisite sound of her voice, and all at once the bishop, the priests, the deacons, the acolytes, the dignitaries of the city, and those matrons with whom the coadjutor bishop was on such good terms, turned and looked up, in search of the source of the angelic sound that filled the cool vastness of the cathedral.

They looked in vain. Floria Tosca, on Tochetti's instructions, was to be heard but not seen. This absence of an identifiable source only compounded the curiosity of the congregation. She was the talk of the town and, since the cathedral choir already had a wider reputation, news of its new singer quickly spread throughout the Veneto. The celebrated composer Antonio Granacci came from Ferrara to attend High Mass at Golla. He was quite as overwhelmed as everyone else by the power, range and sweetness of Tosca's voice and asked the bishop if he could meet this prodigy. The bishop referred him to his coadjutor, Tochetti. Tochetti, though pleased that Granacci should have recognised the quality of Tosca's voice, regarded him as primarily a profane composer and refused.

Just as Bruno, the deputy coachman of the diocese of Golla, put blinkers on the horses that pulled his barouche, so too Monsignor Tochetti's obsession with his choir concealed problems that lay ahead. The bishop ignored, for example, the reports of his choirmaster Faglia that the situation of Tosca would become untenable over time. Faglia was a man of around fifty – thin, nervy, a musician to his fingertips, but also a man who, unlike Tochetti, had experience outside the Church. He had recognised at once the value of Tochetti's 'find', and felt privileged to be called upon to train such an exceptional voice, but he was the one who had to listen to Tosca's grumbling about her incarceration; and he repeatedly told Tochetti that 'la signorina Tosca' did not have a religious vocation and so could not be expected to remain cloistered in a convent.

Faglia was married; he had daughters of his own, and he asked permission from Tochetti to introduce Tosca to his family, and even let her lodge with them rather than with the nuns. Tochetti refused. He had made a promise to Tosca's parents that she would reside in a convent. Faglia suggested that he might ask the parents if they would release him from his promise for the sake of their daughter's happiness, but again Tochetti refused: it would be improper for a bishop to ask a peasant to dispense him from a vow. Faglia said nothing more. He told Tosca to be patient.

Monsignor Tochetti's refusal to present Tosca to Antonio Granacci was much discussed in Golla. It was said that the great composer had asked Bishop Sarlo to overrule his coadjutor, but that the bishop had replied to his request, as he had done to a number of others, with a smile and a shrug. Tosca was young; Tochetti had promised her parents; the wider world was full of perils for a talented young woman: how many divas led chaste lives? But Bishop Sarlo saw what his coadjutor did not – that it was one thing to disappoint Granacci, but what if a request to meet Tosca came from someone he would be powerless to refuse?

*

Prince Alberigo XII di Belgioioso d'Este came to Golla from Milan. It was said that he was on his way to Venice and had chosen to break his journey at Golla because he had matters to attend to nearby. No one specified what these matters might be, and it would have been impertinent to ask why a man of his eminence had chosen to attend to them in person. It was enough that the prince was honouring Golla with his presence: house-proud residents on the route into the city tidied up their window boxes and the municipality made sure the streets were swept.

Prince Alberigo was a widower of sixty-four. He was descended from the celebrated *condottiere*, Alberigo de Barbiano, who in the fourteenth century had founded the first of Italy's mercenary militias, the Compagnia San Giorgio, defeating a predatory band of Bretons which had threatened Rome and receiving from the grateful Pope, Urban VI, a banner with the slogan *Liberata Italia ab externis*, which became the family motto. Later generations of this family of warriors served the Sforzas, the Viscontis and the Holy Roman Emperor, Charles V. After the French King Francis I was defeated by Charles V at the Battle of Pavia in 1525, he was held in the castle of Belgioioso.

Alberigo XII had added to his already extensive estates by marrying Anna Ricciarda d'Este, the daughter of Carlo Filberto d'Este, and added d'Este to his name. Milan was then a possession of the Austrian Habsburgs who, because of their hereditary entitlement, were not regarded by the prince as foreigners. Indeed, his father Antonio had been made a prince of the Holy Roman Empire by the Emperor Joseph II with the right to mint coins with his effigy imprinted upon them. Alberigo's younger brother, Luigi, had been the Imperial ambassador to Sweden and Britain; and was later the lieutenant governor of the Netherlands, also a Habsburg possession. Alberigo had served as the Imperial viceroy in Milan, and had been made a Knight of the Order of the Golden Fleece by the Austrian emperor, the highest honour he could bestow.

Such power, such wealth and such honour should have a concrete manifestation and in 1772 Prince Alberigo had commissioned Giuseppe Piermarini, the architect of the palace of Caserta in the Kingdom of Naples, to design a dwelling suitable to his status – the Palazzo Belgioioso – which, now completed, was the largest and finest in Milan. Here he entertained not just diplomats and statesmen but writers and artists from the middle class. He was proud of his appointment as the first Prefect of the Academy of Fine Arts in Brescia, and was himself a collector of rare books and works of art. And of course he loved music. He rarely missed an operatic performance at La Scala. The prince was a connoisseur of beauty in all its forms.

Cardinal Albioni, a patron of Bishop Sarlo, had let it be known that his friend Prince Alberigo would be passing through Golla and would be glad if he could stay for a night or two with his entourage in the bishop's palace. The suggestion was accepted with professions of gratitude: it was considered a privilege to receive a man of Prince Alberigo's standing. The bishop had reached a stage in his life when he had no expectations of further preferment, but an innate respect for power, whether secular or ecclesiastical, led him to fuss about the rooms the prince would occupy and personally order a new coat of distemper on the walls of the quarters for his grooms.

The bishop fretted because, beginning at the back of his mind but increasingly coming to the front, was the puzzling question as to why Prince Alberigo should have chosen to make a deviation to spend two nights in Golla on his way to Venice. He must surely have known that there was a straighter route, and he must also have had the pick of a number of castles and villas where he might have stayed along the way. Could it be that he had heard about Floria Tosca? Could it be that the devious Granacci had tipped him off? Did Tochetti realise that, if the prince should ask to meet her, it would be impossible to refuse?

Perhaps the prince could be thwarted. Bishop Sarlo suggested obliquely to his coadjutor Tochetti that the sung Mass during the prince's visit should be one without a role for a soprano, or that 'the voice of your young protégée' should be given a rest. But the blinkered Tochetti ignored the warnings. He could not understand why his bishop should want to hide from his distinguished visitor the glory of the cathedral choir – particularly when the prince would be there on 15 August, the feast of the Assumption of the Blessed Virgin Mary into Heaven. Could it be that he was envious of his coadjutor? Was he afraid that Tochetti's achievements would somehow detract from his own?

*

Prince Alberigo Belogioiosa d'Este arrived in Golla in a cavalcade of coaches and outriders with his secretary, chaplain, major-domo, valet, a cook, two footmen, two chambermaids, four coachmen and two grooms. Also with him was his twenty-year-old daughter, Carlotta. It was hot. The prince and his daughter were tired and dusty. After being met by Bishop Sarlo and served iced drinks, they were shown to their quarters. While they rested, their servants unpacked trunks and then themselves settled into the newly distempered rooms. The prince's secretary discussed with the bishop's secretary the programme for the prince's visit; the major-domo conveyed to the bishop's servants the prince's habits and expectations; and the prince's cook went down to the kitchens to run through the menus for the meals that would be served to the prince and his daughter during their stay.

Twenty-four sat down to dinner at the bishop's palace that night – eight of the higher clergy of the diocese, among them Monsignor Tochetti, and a dozen from the nobility in his diocese. The wives wore the sumptuous dresses that their dressmakers had prepared; the husbands were bedecked with medals and orders. All were taken aback to see that the prince himself was dressed simply – no sign of his Order of the Golden Fleece – and his daughter, too, wore only a modest gown. The contessa on the one side of the prince, and the marchesa on the other, talked about the writers and artists he was said to admire. The prince, still vigorous and handsome, listened politely as these provincials showed off their familiarity with the Horatian odes of Giuseppe Parini.

The next morning, these same dignitaries and many lesser citizens crammed into the cathedral of Golla to hear Mass on the feast of the Assumption. A special plush prie-dieu had been placed before an elegant upholstered chair for the prince, and a similar if smaller piece of ecclesiastical furniture for Princess Carlotta. Recovered after a good night's sleep, the heat not yet sufficient to exhaust and enervate, and well-rehearsed in the role that grandees were expected to play, the prince and princess entered the cathedral through the doorway that led from the bishop's palace, knelt humbly before the statue of the Virgin Mary in the Lady Chapel, musing on the miraculous nature of her bodily assumption into

Heaven, then proceeded with their retinue to their small thrones at the front of the congregation. Organ music mixed with the sounds of whispering and shuffling in the packed church. The prince and his daughter first spent some minutes on their knees on the prie-dieux, then took their seats. Behind them, necks, mostly those of women, craned to see what the prince and more particularly the princess were wearing. The objects of their curiosity did not move, their profiles as motionless as the effigy on the coins minted by the prince's father.

A blast from the organ, and triumphal music from the full orchestra, announced the advent of the column of servers, acolytes, deacons, priests, canons, the coadjutor bishop Tochetti and finally the Bishop of Golla, Giuseppe Sarlo, all wearing richly embroidered vestments – the gold braid glinting in the light of the candles, or flashing more brightly when caught in a shaft of multi-coloured sunlight from the stained-glass windows to the church. All took their places around the altar and the Mass started. *Introibo ad altare Dei*, chanted the priest. *Ad Deum qui laetificat juventutem meam*, the acolytes responded. Then came the *Confiteor*, the confessions of sins, and, at the words *mea culpa, mea culpa, mea maxima culpa*, the prince and princess, together with the rest of the congregation, struck their breasts with clenched fists, for no one is without sin.

Then came the Kyrie – an unfamiliar Kyrie that the citizens of Golla had never heard before. It exploded with the full choir and full orchestra, and then the voice of a solo soprano soared above all the rest. The bishop glanced at Tochetti; Tochetti did not meet his eye, but could not hide an expression of agonised excitement. It had been at his insistence that Faglia had brought forward a work he had been rehearsing for some months – the Great Mass in C minor by the Austrian composer, Wolfgang Amadeus Mozart. Both men knew that the music was sublime. Fortuitously, six years before,

Faglia had been in Salzburg when the work had been first performed with the composer's wife, Constanze, singing the soprano part. He had later been able to obtain copies of the sheet music. The Mass was incomplete. The Credo ended with the exquisite soprano rendering of *Et incarnatus est* and there were gaps in the Sanctus that Faglia had to fill with his own extemporisation.

The part of the first soprano was, however, the perfect vehicle for the voice of Floria Tosca, first in the Kyrie, then in the Gloria singing *Quoniam tu solus Sanctus* in tandem with the second soprano and finally the solo singing of *Et incarnatus est* – a passage so beautiful, so transcendent, so sublime that, when sung by Tosca in rehearsal, Faglia had had to turn away to hide his tears. And the effect now on the congregation was equally power-ful: curiosity, impatience, distracting thoughts were all doused by the beauty of the sound, and it was not even noticed that, during the singing of *Et incarnatus est*, Princess Carlotta glanced sideways at her father and saw that, as with Faglia, tears had come into his eyes.

Mozart had written no Agnus Dei and so Faglia had composed one in the same style of his own. The contrast was marked, but added to the appreciation of what had gone before. It enabled the prince to leave the church with dry eyes, and afterwards it happened as Bishop Sarlo had feared. The prince asked to meet the young soprano who had so enchanted the whole congrega-tion; he asked in a tone that was at once nonchalant and imperious. The prince had never known a request of his to be refused. Tochetti overheard it: he opened his mouth, but a gesture from Bishop Sarlo closed it before a word had emerged. 'Of course, Your Excellency.'

'And perhaps she could sing for us?' asked the prince – still nonchalant, still imperious. 'Something by Galuppi, perhaps, or Paisiello. Or does she only know church music?'

'I shall ask the choirmaster,' said Bishop Sarlo. 'I am sure that some small recital could be arranged. This evening, perhaps, after the girl has rested, and when it is a little cooler.'

*

Evening came. The bells tolled for the angelus at six, and shortly afterwards the bishop and his curia assembled once again with the city's notables, and the bishop's guests, the Prince and Princess Belgioioso d'Este. The conversation was desultory. All waited for the promised entertainment and, when there appeared at the door to the long gallery a girl accompanied by the choirmaster, Faglia, and followed by a nun, they fell silent and stepped aside. The girl, Floria Tosca, walked forward with no sign of shyness. She wore the embroidered dress of a peasant – the same that she had worn at San Lorenzo – clean, colourful, but ill-fitting – a little too short and a little too tight. She walked up to the bishop, curtsied and, leaning forward, kissed his ring. She then turned to Monsignor Tochetti, smiled at her patron and protector, but, as she was about to kiss his ring, saw from his look and the nod of his head that her next obeisance should not be to him but to the resplendently dressed older man standing next to the bishop. She looked up at the prince, then lowered her eyes and curtsied. The prince looked at her kindly – his glance lingering on her constrained bust.

'Your Excellency, may I present Signorina…' The bishop hesitated, struggling to remember the girl's family name. 'Signorina Tosca,' he said.

The prince leaned forward and with the gesture of a friendly uncle took hold of her hand. 'Your singing enchanted us, signorina.'

Tosca gave another curtsy to acknowledge the compliment.

'And I have asked His Grace,' the prince went on, 'if you might possibly sing something for us here.'

'As Your Excellency pleases,' said Tosca – her strong Veneto accent leading the Princess Carlotta to smile.

'The signorina's repertoire is limited,' said Faglia, 'but purely for the purposes of training her voice –' he glanced anxiously at Tochetti – 'we have learned one or two arias from the operas of Scarlatti and Paisiello.' Faglia snapped his fingers. From nowhere, there appeared a lank young man with a lute. 'With your permission, Your Grace...' The bishop nodded his assent. Faglia gestured to the lute player to sit down on a chair. Tosca moved to stand beside him. All had clearly been rehearsed. The lute player strummed a few opening bars, then, taking his cue from Tosca's intake of breath, began his accompaniment of her song.

First she sang an aria from Scarlatti's *Il Pompeo*, then 'Quella Fiamma che m'accende' by Benedetto Marcello; and finally 'Vittoria, mio core' by Giacomo Carissimi. Her voice was both rich and pure; the sounds flew like canaries released from a cage; and, to the dismay of Tochetti, she acted the roles she was playing, the anguish and triumph of the lover alight in her eyes, her body bending and then rising as if the words and sounds were the gusts of a breeze. Her eyes, when they were not raised in supplication to Heaven, or not mistily dreaming of an absent lover, were directed at those who had asked for this command performance, Prince Alberigo Belgioioso d'Este and his daughter, the Princess Carlotta; and if they wandered on to others among the select audience, they avoided those of the coadjutor bishop who watched her acting with a frigid dismay.

The prince raised his hand. Enough. The performance was over, but Tosca was not dismissed. Quite to the contrary. After a gesture from her father, the Princess Carlotta came forward and took her by the hand as if she were a long-lost sister and, with the familiarity that only a true aristocrat can muster, told Tosca that everything about her was delightful and asked what plans she had to develop her talent and share her God-given gift with the world.

Tosca pursed her lips and blushed. She was not confused, but she could not give the answer she would have liked. The Princess Carlotta, as if reading the girl's mind, turned to Faglia. 'But surely, signor, you are not going to confine the signorina to a church?'

Faglia leaned forward, a modest bow. 'It is not for me to decide on the future of Signorina Tosca.'

Carlotta turned to the bishop. 'Then you must tell us, Your Grace, what you have in mind for this most exquisite voice.'

Bishop Sarlo frowned. 'What I have in mind? Well, no more than it should continue to sing in our choir for the greater glory of God.'

'But surely, Your Grace, such a light cannot be hidden under a bushel.'

'We do not think of our cathedral as a bushel,' said the bishop drily.

'That is not what I wish to suggest,' said the princess, with a blush and a glance at her father.

'What my daughter wishes to suggest, I think,' said the prince, 'is that clearly Almighty God has endowed the signorina with gifts that might flourish in a theatre rather than a church.'

Now the coadjutor bishop, Tochetti, stepped forward and, after a nod from his superior indicating permission to speak, turned to the prince. 'Your Excellency should understand,' he said, 'that promises were made to the signorina's parents that she should reside in a convent and sing only in a church. These are promises that we are not at liberty to break.'

'But perhaps,' said the prince, in an easy-going manner, 'the mother and father are not aware of what their daughter might achieve?' He turned now to Tosca, who had been listening intently to what had been said. 'And you, signorina? Would you not like to sing those beautiful arias on a stage?'

Tosca appeared to hesitate before making a reply, but it was not really a hesitation. It was rather that she could not find the words to express what she felt. Never before had this fifteen-year-old daughter of peasants from the Veneto been in such glittering and august company. The seed pearls that lined the bodice of Princess Carlotta's dress would in themselves have been enough to astonish her; serving merely as a border for one part of a dress of rich silk, and framing an amethyst necklace with matching silver-and-amethyst ear-rings, it seemed as if this girl, only a year or two older than she was, had been dipped in a tub of treasure. Moreover the princess was beautiful and gracious and treated her with a soft kindness that she had not known either from her rough parents or the austere nuns. Added to this, there was the intoxicating effect of praise and applause. Tosca knew she had a fine voice; she had been complimented from an early age. But never before had she seen the effect of her movements and expressions upon an audience. True, Faglia who had taught her the arias had, on occasions, acted out of character – dropping for a moment his tutorial manner, letting slip his usual expression that was dry, even severe. But here, in the prince and princess, there had been no reluctance to surrender to the beauty of what they heard and saw. She had not hitherto been confident that the plaintive sighs and ardent looks that were demanded by the arias about love would be convincing – she who had never known love; but from the expression on the faces of her audience, she saw that they were; and she saw too how the prince's glance flitted intermittently between her face and her bust.

Tosca was devout. She prayed every night and every morning to the Virgin Mary whom she found more approachable than God. She knew that Mary was ever-virgin, and that the nuns who had taken her in hand had vowed to emulate her chastity. But Tosca also knew that she was not called to the religious life. She took a delight in her effect on men, even on a man who was old enough to be her grandfather, like Prince Alberigo Belgioioso d'Este. While a

Sister Monica might shroud her pale body in the robes of a nun, Tosca was happy that her pretty face and fresh body should be seen and admired. Concurrent with her piety was a peasant shrewdness that told her that everything had a value and so everything had a price. A pretty girl could hope for a better husband than a girl who was plain, unless the gifts of nature were unbalanced by the size of a dowry. It was not just the eyes of the prince that had lingered on Tosca's bosom; others too had seemed more attracted to the swelling flesh of the peasant than to the paltry bust of Princess Carlotta, despite its frame of gold thread and seed pearls.

Thus the question put by the prince: 'And you, signorina? Would you not like to sing those beautiful arias on a stage?' had an obvious answer. Yes, Tosca would like to sing on a stage. However, she sensed that she should act with caution. The prince was a Milanese. She did not know the extent of his powers. She was not concerned that her parents would raise objections; everything had a value, everything had a price. But was she not now the ward of Monsignor Tochetti, whom, she knew, would want to keep Tosca for his choir? She, therefore, after the long pause that was not a hesitation, said to the prince: 'Most certainly, if it was thought right by my lord bishop.'

'And what of his vow to your parents?'

'My parents?' She looked up at the prince and with a smile conveyed what he, who also understood the mentality of peasants, already knew: that everything had a value, everything had a price.

'Precisely,' said the prince. 'They would want what was best for their daughter.'

'She is to be protected from the world,' said Monsignor Tochetti. 'That was our assurance.'

'The world?' said Prince Alberigo. 'Is it really so dangerous? Well, perhaps it is, but not all who live outside the cloister are necessarily doomed.'

'La signorina Tosca could live with us,' said the princess. 'I would treat her as a sister.'

Monsignor Tochetti's already pallid face went a shade paler. He opened his mouth to say something, but closed it again. To suggest that Tosca might be at risk in the Palazzo Belgioioso would be to impugn the honour of the princess and her father.

Bishop Sarlo, who missed nothing, now intervened. 'Your Excellencies must temper your generosity or our poor chorister will be overwhelmed. We shall talk about this further, but now it is time for dinner.' He turned to Tosca. 'Dear child, you have delighted us this evening. We thank God for your great gifts, and we pray to Him for guidance as to how they can best be used for His greater glory. Retire now. We will consult others – Monsignor Tochetti, Signor Faglia and, of course, your parents. You are precious to us all here in Golla. God will guide us for the best.'

2

The struggle for Tosca lasted many months. Prince Alberigo, who had filled his newly built palace with rare manuscripts and beautiful works of art, wished the music in his household to be as magnificent as all else. He could not listen to a cantata or an aria without remembering the girl who had sung for him in Golla. He lapsed into reveries in which this flower from the Veneto sang in the grand salon of the Palazzo Belgioioso – among the audience all the notables of Lombardy with the viceroy, a cardinal and an Austrian archduke or two. *Che meraviglia! Che prodigio!* The joy would be theirs, the praise hers, but the glory his.

The prince became obsessed. An emissary was sent, incognito, to her parents in San Lorenzo, causing a sensation despite his discreet manner and modest dress. He repeated the offer made by the prince that their daughter should be taken into their household and trained as a singer by the best teachers in Milan. She would be treated not as a servant but as a member of the family. The prince's children themselves were accomplished musicians; one daughter played the viol, another the pianoforte, and Princess Carlotta was a talented composer. Music was their passion, and Signorina Floria Tosca would therefore be treated with the greatest respect. And, of course, something would be done to make up for the help in the house and the kitchen that parents can reasonably expect from a daughter. The prince proposed an annual stipend of twenty sequins.

The parents absolved Monsignor Tochetti of his vow, but the prelate was as stubborn as the prince, and refused to release Tosca, whose voice now brought so many to High Mass at the cathedral. Bishop Sarlo supported his coadjutor, not for the sake of his cathedral's choir, but because, missing nothing, he had seen the prince's eye rest on Tosca's bosom. He did not trust the prince. He did not trust the prince's daughter. He saw that Tosca had an exceptional talent, but also knew that all operatic divas were subject to temptation and invariably succumbed. He felt responsible for Tosca: it was his coadjutor who had plucked her from her innocent bucolic surroundings and in so doing created an occasion of sin. How could the poor girl not be flattered by the praise of a prince? How could she not enjoy the admiration of musical connoisseurs? How could she not wish to accept an invitation to live with the family of such prominent Milanese? He felt angry with Tochetti whose vanity had brought Tosca to Golla, and with Faglia who for his own amusement had taught her to sing operatic arias and mimic the looks and gestures of women enslaved to their passions.

Bishop Sarlo therefore ruled that Tosca must remain in Golla. She could leave the convent; she could lodge with the family of the choirmaster, Faglia; but he could not in good conscience permit her, whatever her parents might say, to go to Milan. To defend his position, he lapsed into consequentialism – the formula used by Jesuits, that the end justifies the means – and told the prince, falsely, that

Tosca had made a legally binding commitment to sing in the cathedral choir at Golla until the age of twenty-one. The prince sent an emissary to Tosca to see if this was true, but the emissary was not permitted to see her. A letter to Tosca was sent under cover of a letter to Father Acquaviva, Monsignor Tochetti's secretary, from a friend of his in Milan, but Father Acquaviva, in obedience to his conscience, and in the hope that Bishop Sarlo might give him some preferment, exposed the ruse. The letter never reached Tosca.

Then, a little over a year after Tosca had first come to Golla, Bishop Giuseppe Sarlo received by special courier from Rome a thick parchment letter bearing the seal of the Secretary of State, Cardinal Zelada. Bishop Sarlo looked at it with apprehension. He had little doubt as to what it was about. Five years before, to his bitter regret, he had been persuaded by his friend Bishop Scipione de' Ricci to attend a synod in his diocese of Pistoia. It had been summoned by Leopold, the Grand Duke of Tuscany, to reform the Church in his principality. Radical ideas had been put forward to restrict the powers of the Pope, to abolish indulgences, to burn fake relics, to permit the saying of Mass in the vernacular, consider the ordination of married men, abolish most monastic orders and forbid women taking vows before the age of forty. Bishop Sarlo had been dismayed and had hastily returned to Golla.

The synod of Pistoia had alarmed Pope Pius VI; more dramatically, it had enraged the populace of Pistoia, who, when their bishop ordered the demolition of a shrine and the destruction of bogus relics, had rioted in their defence. The Grand Duke Leopold deserted his protégé. Ricci was under pressure to resign his see. It was known to Bishop Sarlo that a papal bull was being prepared in Rome condemning the decrees of the synod. It was also known to Bishop Sarlo that Rome was aware of his presence at the synod, and that printed copies of the synod's first decree, *Decretum de fide et ecclesia*, had been found in his diocese.

Bishop Sarlo's immediate superior in the hierarchy of the Church was Monsignor Giovanelli, the Patriarch of Venice. Giovanelli knew that Sarlo was no Jansenist and had accepted Sarlo's assurances that he would never have gone to Pistoia had he known what his former friend Ricci would propose, and had had nothing to do with the distribution of *Decretum de fide et ecclesia*. Monsignor Giovanelli had assured Sarlo that neither he nor the Venetian Inquisition had any doubts at all about the orthodoxy of his beliefs. Sarlo had been only partially reassured. He might be in the clear with the Venetian Inquisition and confident that it would not pursue the matter further, but what of the Inquisition in Rome? Its proceedings were slow but inexorable, and the five years that had passed since Pistoia were, *sub specie aeternitatis*, a mere blink of the eye.

Bishop Sarlo waited until he was alone in his study before breaking the seal on his letter. It was a good portent that the coat of arms impressed on the wax was that of the Cardinal Secretary of State, not the Holy Inquisition or the Congregation of Bishops. He took a deep sigh, raised his eyes to the crucifix on the wall of his study, said a brief prayer – *Libera me, Domine* – and read the letter.

Beloved brother in Christ,

I am commanded by His Holiness Pope Pius VI, Pontifex Maximus, etc. etc., to summon you to submit to his adjudication on the question raised by His Grace Simone Maria Visconti, Archbishop of Milan, on behalf of His Excellency Prince Alberigo di Belgioioso concerning the young woman Floria Tosca who, it is charged, you are directing towards the religious life against her will. You are hereby commanded to bring the said Floria Tosca to Rome to be heard by the Supreme Pontiff so that he may give his ruling.

Yours in Christ,

+ Francisco, Cardinal Zelada +

The game was up. Even before he had finished the letter, which was written in Latin, and the bishop's eye had seen the name 'Floria Tosca', he knew that he had been out-manoeuvred and outgunned. His eyes avoided the crucifix; he dared not face the image of his Saviour with a look of disappointment in his eyes. A jumble of doubts passed through his mind. Had his motives been pure? Had he wished to keep Tosca in Golla to protect her chastity? Or had that been a pretext – the real reason being to keep her for the cathedral choir? Had he been infected by Tochetti's vanity? Was it the common failing of churchmen that, renouncing glory for themselves, they pursued it for institutions – building ever grander churches, monasteries, palaces, shrines? Or were these doubts put into his mind by the Jansenist Tempter? The bishop did not know. He would consult his confessor. For good or evil, Tosca was off his hands. Resignation replaced resentment. He now dared look up at the cross.

3

Three new dresses were made for Tosca, the costs met by diocesan funds. The choice was left to the two matrons closest to Tochetti who, resigned like Sarlo to losing Tosca, nevertheless felt some satisfaction that the girl he had plucked from an obscure village in the Veneto was now to sing before the Pope. Tochetti absented himself as Tosca stood in her shift, surrounded by the seamstress who fitted and unfitted, pinned and stitched and sewed, and the three matrons arguing about what was appropriate – whether the dresses should be loose and flowing to conceal the contours of her body, or tight at the bodice as was then in fashion. Every now and then, when Floria was fully clothed, Tochetti was summoned to give his view. He dithered. Would too close a fitting give rise to lascivious thoughts, as one of the matrons suggested?

Tochetti was immune to carnal thoughts yet he loved Tosca and, when he saw her looks of impatience, excitement and the little laughing smiles at the carry-on of the matrons, tears came into his eyes and he quickly withdrew.

For the visit to Rome, a lady's maid was seconded from the household of one of the matrons of Golla. Monsignor Tochetti did not join the party: Bishop Sarlo had been summoned in person and Tochetti as his coadjutor remained to undertake his duties while he was absent. Bishop Sarlo, then, was accompanied only by his valet, his secretary and Faglia, the choirmaster. They stopped for one night in Ferrara, another in Orvieto, guests of the bishops in both places. In Rome, Bishop Sarlo and his small entourage stayed, as he always did, in the convent of Santa Marcella; and while they waited for the papal audience, Faglia was charged with taking Tosca and her maid on a tour of the city.

What were Tosca's thoughts as, her face shaded under a parasol, she strolled among the elegantly dressed tourists – the English milords with their ladies, the earnest German professors with their tall blond pupils, and the puzzling though handsome young Frenchmen who wore neither hats nor wigs? At Santa Maria Maggiore, she knelt devoutly before the statue of the Virgin, and at the basilica of St John Lateran she genuflected with a grave expression before the Blessed Sacrament and lit candles before the statues of different saints; but once out of the church she became like a dedicated entomologist, catching in the net of her large eyes the fluttering looks of admiration from the young men she passed in the street. Tosca was happy and excited. She had prayed to the Virgin to ask God to free her from the confines of the convent and it now seemed as if the Virgin had heard her prayer. Tosca loved to sing; she had always loved to sing; but it was only in Golla that she had come to understand the value of her voice. Prelates and princes were fighting to own it. And now she was to sing before the Pope!

*

Tosca's recital before Giovanni Angelo Braschi, Pope Pius VI, *il papa bello*, was held in the Sala dei Corazzieri in the Quirinale Palace – a large, light room with a superb gilded ceiling. A small chamber orchestra had been assembled by the Pope's master of music, who had been told by Faglia what accompaniments to prepare. The Pope had let it be known that he did not wish to sit enthroned as if presiding over a court of law but be merely *primus inter pares* in an audience of musical cognoscenti. Around fifty chairs had therefore been placed as in a concert hall with some larger and plusher in the front row for the curial cardinals and the largest and plushest for Pope Pius. A harpsichord and the chairs and music stands for the small string orchestra were on a raised dais with space at the centre for the singer, Floria Tosca.

Among those invited were the Pope's intimate advisers – Cardinal Zelada, the Secretary of State; Treasurer Ruffo with an equerry; Fra' Emanuel de Rohan-Polduc, the Grand Master of the Knights of St John; Bishop Franchetti, representing Archbishop Visconti of Milan; the composer Granacci with unnamed companions and friends; and of course the plaintiff-in-chief (though the proceedings had by now dropped all appearance of a legal hearing) Prince Alberigo Belgioioso d'Este and his daughter, Princess Carlotta. Next to the prince was Cardinal de Bernis, the French ambassador, with two exquisitely but modestly dressed women, one on either side, their heads covered with mantillas as decorum demanded; the Spanish ambassador, Don José de Azara, was there with an equerry, and next to him the ambassador of the Kingdom of the Two Sicilies, the Marchese d'Ambrogio, and in the third row Bishop Sarlo. The fifty seats were quickly filled; the word had got

71

around about this extraordinary hearing and what was at stake. Rome had divided into rival parties – one supporting Bishop Sarlo, the other Prince Belgioioso and his proxy, the Archbishop of Milan; and despite the restricted number of invitations, a crowd pressed in and stood at the back of the room.

Promptly at a quarter to six in the evening, the coach carrying Floria Tosca and the choirmaster Faglia drew up in the courtyard of the Quirinale Palace. Faglia was dressed in a new tunic and new breeches, Tosca in the most modest of the three dresses made under the guidance of the matrons of Golla – the dark blue silk cut close to her figure, but the bodice raised to expose no more than the base of her throat. They were awaited at the entrance by a papal equerry who led them up the shallow steps, along the marble-floored landing and through the high wide door into the Sala dei Corazzieri. Tosca raised the skirts of her pretty dress as she went up the steps onto the platform. Faced with the rows of prelates and courtiers, she hesitated for a moment; then, seeing the handsome old man wearing the grandest robes and sitting on the largest and plushest chair, she stepped forward and gave a deep curtsy while Faglia, coming up behind her, gave an equally deep bow. Faglia then went to the conductor's podium, tapped it with his baton to alert the orchestra and the audience. The room was silent. The recital began.

Tosca sang, first the soprano solo from the Credo of Mozart's Mass in C minor; then the arias that she had sung before Prince Belgioioso at Golla. Finally, as an obeisance to the great composer who was in the audience, she sang an aria from Granacci's *La morte di Dido*. Bishop Sarlo, who had placed his last hope for the salvation of his protégée in the acoustics of the Sala dei Corazzieri – praying that the notes would echo or be muffled or be lost in the vast chamber – now discovered that his hope was vain. There was no distortion: the sound of Tosca's voice, as it filled the room, was exquisite. All fidgeting ceased as if the audience was suddenly

72

paralysed or mesmerised by the stare of a snake. Faces took on a look that approached veneration and the bishop noticed tears come into the eyes of both men and women, courtiers and priests.

The recital ended. At first the applause was muted; with so many in the audience whose prospects depended upon the approval of the Pope, too great an enthusiasm might be considered unseemly; but then the Pope himself, to everyone's astonishment, got to his feet, clapped his venerable hands, shouted *Brava, signorina*, and beckoned to Tosca to come down from the stage. This was enough to release the constrained enthusiasm of the audience. There was frenzied clapping and cries of *brava* and *bravissima*. The Prince Alberigo Belgioioso d'Este and his daughter not only applauded, but exchanged looks of triumph. Cardinal de Bernis, his applause restrained by a French sense of *mesure*, caught the eye of Prince Alberigo and gave a slight bow to acknowledge the good taste of a fellow connoisseur.

Tosca came down from the stage on the arm of Faglia and, suddenly nervous, looked out for Bishop Sarlo who, in his last moment *in loco parentis*, took her arm from Faglia and presented her to the Pope. 'Your Holiness, Signorina Floria Tosca.'

With perfect poise, and with a fervour that was by no means feigned, Tosca stepped forward and knelt to kiss the Fisherman's ring. While her pretty lips were on this symbol of his holy office, the Pope extended his left arm to raise her up. 'My child,' he said, 'the Lord has given you an exceptional gift. You have touched my heart and surely the hearts of many others.'

Tosca gave a deep curtsy; again the pontiff raised her up. By now he was attended by the interested parties – Prince Belgioioso d'Este, Bishop Franchetti and the composer Granacci. 'Is it your wish,' the Pope asked Tosca, 'to accept the invitation of Prince Belgioioso to join his household?'

'It is, Your Holiness.'

'And is it the wish of your parents?'

'It is, Your Holiness.'

'We have a certified attestation of the parents,' said Bishop Franchetti, the auxiliary from Milan.

'Then their wish shall be met.' The Pope looked down on Tosca. 'If you have taken any vows in regard to the religious life, which in any case you are too young to have made –' this with a side glance at Bishop Sarlo, the only acknowledgement by the pontiff of the lowly prelate's existence – 'then they are hereby dispensed. You are free, my child, to use the gifts God has given you for His greater glory. *Laborare est orare, sed etiam cantare est orare.*' He turned to the Prince Belgioioso d'Este and the Princess Carlotta. 'Take good care of your precious charge. May God bless you all.' He raised his hand and made the sign of the cross. 'Now go in peace.'

*

Tosca travelled from Rome to Milan seated in the same coach as Prince Alberigo and Princess Carlotta. There had been some sadness when she took her leave of Faglia and Bishop Sarlo, but it had gone by the time they reached Orvieto. With her limited experience of life, Tosca had imagined that noblemen and their daughters would treat a little peasant as a servant, and their servants with an imperious disdain. What she learned on the journey was that even the servants of such elevated grandees were an aristocracy of a kind – performing their duties with solemnity and precision. The secretaries, the major-domos, the valets, the coachmen were treated by the prince with a respectful nonchalance. There was no need to cajole or chastise.

Tosca also discovered that the prince and princess had been sincere when they had said that she would be treated as a member of the family. Not just with the Belgioiosos but throughout Italy, even throughout Europe, the talent of an artist was equal to any pedigree. And so just as Voltaire became the honoured guest of King Frederick the Great or the Tsarina Catherine, so Tosca, with her giggling peasant charm and harsh Veneto accent, was treated by the prince and princess and their servants with the respect they would have accorded the daughter of a duke or the niece of a pope. When they stopped for the night on their journey north, she shared a bed with Princess Carlotta; and when they finally reached the Palazzo Belgioioso in Milan, she was given a room like that of the prince's older children. She was also assigned a maid and, guided by Princess Carlotta, a wardrobe of fine dresses matched with equally fine shoes. Instructions had been given, presumably by the prince, that she was not to be *denaturée* – which the dressmakers and hairdressers perfectly understood to mean that the freshness of the *campagna* should not be lost. Tosca was Tosca and must remain Tosca, though perhaps not entirely Tosca: with a little laughter, and a little teasing, and a friendly solicitude, Tosca was taught the meaning in Florentine Italian of some of her Venetian idioms.

With the utmost tact, some of Tosca's rough peasant manner was smoothed: she learned how to eat with silver cutlery and *sip* from a glass of wine. She was given romantic novels by Carlotta, and taught by the tutors of the prince's musical children how to play the harpsichord and read music. The best teachers in Milan were employed to further train her voice and she practised singing for several hours each day. She joined with the prince's children in an amateur performance of an opera written by the prince himself; and then, in October, Tosca made her first professional appearance at La Scala in Cimarosa's *La ballerina amante*. It was a small role, but she enchanted the audience. The prince was delighted. His children fussed happily over Tosca after this, her first appearance on a public stage.

And later, when the children had retired, the prince – the illustrious Prince Alberigo Belgioioso d'Este – went to Tosca's room to praise her in person. She awaited him in a loose silk gown. She was now sixteen years old. He was more than sixty, but healthy and handsome and so immense in his grandeur that a peasant girl from the Veneto could no more refuse him than she could refuse Zeus. And ever since she had seen his eye linger on her bosom that day in Gallo, Tosca had known that in due course she should expect to repay the man who had given her so much in the only currency she possessed. And in the mind of the illustrious prince? An assumption of a *droit de seigneur*, perhaps, or a feeling that, having been taught music and manners, it was time for Tosca to learn about love.

Five

I

The equerry who had accompanied Treasurer Ruffo to the recital by Floria Tosca at the Quirinale Palace was Vitellio Scarpia. After fifteen months serving in obscure garrisons on the routes across the Apennines, and on the borders of the Papal States, Scarpia had been recalled to Rome. He had amply justified all Ruffo's expectations; wherever he had served, banditry had declined. The brigands captured by Scarpia, among them the infamous Ponzio Adena, had been tried, convicted and given the prescribed sentence of ten years in the galleys. Since there were no galleys, they were held in the comfortable Carceri Nuove and, after three years, benefited from one of the amnesties that the popes periodically extended to all convicted criminals to demonstrate the merciful nature of Christ's vicar on earth. Scarpia had been rewarded with promotion to the rank of captain, an increase of his pay to eighteen scudi a month, and a posting to the garrison of the Castel Sant'Angelo. On Ruffo's recommendation, his protégé had received from Pope Pius VI the Order of the Golden Spur.

Scarpia had returned to Rome with few acquaintances and no friends, and having spent so long in the company of men, he now hankered for the company of women. The painful memory of what had transpired in Algiers had faded and Scarpia found himself glancing at pretty girls at Mass on a Sunday or walking up and down the Corso. Many met his glances with a smile: the months of active service had given depth and maturity to his handsome face. However, these young women were all strictly chaperoned and Scarpia had no introductions to the homes where they lived.

Spoletta, noticing his master's renewed interest, offered to introduce him to willing women – not just whores but young wives in Trastevere whose husbands turned a blind eye to their earning some pin money through discreet liaisons with richer men. Scarpia declined Spoletta's offer. He retained a high-minded vision of love, which Spoletta considered an aristocratic affectation, like a powdered wig.

Spoletta did not suffer from solitude: in all their postings he had quickly found the tavernas where he could satisfy his simple needs for food, drink, talk and a woman. Spoletta saw himself as a straightforward, uncomplicated son of the soil, but he was not as simple as he seemed. His father had been a brute and his mother a bully, who punished her son for the sins of his father – a violent, irascible man who exacted sexual favours from the wives and daughters of the peasants of Castelfranco in lieu of unpaid rent. There had been no joy in the home, and, such was the isolated position of the factor between those who owned the land and those who worked it, little chance of finding joy elsewhere. Spoletta had only been happy in those summer months when the Spolettas' feudal lord, the *cavaliere* Luigi Scarpia, took up residence in the villa and he rode out into the olive groves with his son.

Spoletta had been taught to read and write, but there had been no books other than rent books in his home; and though Vitellio Scarpia had lent him the odd history or romance, Spoletta found reading laborious and did not see the point. With long hours of brooding during the winters in the Apennines, he had developed his own philosophy which lay between that of the Church, which taught that human nature was fallen but might be redeemed, and that of the French *philosophes* to whom man was perfectible if only he could break the shackles of oppression and superstition. To Spoletta, man was an animal, and it was vanity to think he was something better. Like the friends he made in the tavernas, he wanted to be neither perfected by the *philosophes* nor redeemed by the Church. He was careful not to mock the Church; he did not want to be called before the Inquisition; but at times, to a suitable audience, he would suggest that the clerical calling was a clever way for cowards to avoid fighting, get a good income, yet still retain the moral high ground.

*

Around six months after his return to Rome, Scarpia received an embossed invitation to a ball at the Palazzo Colonna. He had walked past this magnificent building at the foot of the Quirinale Hill on a number of occasions; he had even wandered in to look at the collection of paintings and sculpture that rivalled that of the Vatican, but never had he imagined that he would ever enter the palazzo as a guest. Who was behind the invitation? Was it Father Simone to whom he had returned to make his Easter confession, and had confided his isolation and lack of friends? Or was it Treasurer Ruffo? Both were cousins of the princess.

The invitation produced in Scarpia elation, excitement, confusion and finally panic: it demanded more strategy, planning and courage than any encounter with brigands. He would have to buy a new suit of clothes, a new powdered wig, new shoes with new buckles – all in tune with what was worn at the court in Versailles. Had Scarpia been a Knight of Malta he might have worn his uniform, but better, he thought, the coat of a civilian than that of a mere captain in the despised pontifical army. A tailor was found and money was borrowed from a Jew in the ghetto to buy an elegant tunic, a white silk shirt with exquisite ruffles, soft grey breeches with silk stockings to mould his fine calves, and large oval silver buckles on his brightly polished leather shoes.

*

The night came. Scarpia was delivered to the palazzo in a sedan chair, a tricorn hat loosely placed on his head, and a silk cloak covering his tunic on which was pinned the Order of the Golden Spur. A hundred torches lit the entrance, where Scarpia's hat and cloak were taken from him; and two lines of footmen in sumptuous attire held silver candelabra to illuminate the wide stairs. Scarpia followed his fellow guests to the top, gave his name to the major-domo and then heard it bellowed over the chatter to a decrepit old man and a shrivelled old woman who were receiving the guests – presumably the Prince and Princess Colonna. His name meant nothing to them: both shook his hand briefly with the dead smile and empty expression of those who wish to show a minimum of politeness, but no more. Then Scarpia was carried by the flow of guests into a huge and magnificent galleria, offered a goblet of punch from a gilded tray, and finally, as the flow ceased, he found himself alone and ignored in a crowd of people he did not know.

But then, in the distance, he caught sight of a familiar face – that of the Treasurer, Fabrizio Ruffo, dressed resplendently in a black soutane and purple cotta, with gold-braided cuffs appearing below his purple mozzetta and three bejewelled orders pinned to his chest. He was standing at the centre of a group of four others – one a cleric, one a layman and two of them women. Should Scarpia approach him or would such an august figure consider it an impertinence? He moved closer, and stood pretending to admire a painting. He turned. The treasurer caught his eye and beckoned for him to approach. Scarpia stepped forward and gave an elegant bow.

'This is the young man I was telling you about,' said Ruffo to the older of the two women.

'Ah, yes, the fearless soldier who has made it safe for us to travel to Ancona. I am told you do not know many people in Rome.'

'No, signora,' said Scarpia. 'I have spent more than a year in the mountains.'

The woman shuddered. 'You poor boy. I am surprised you survived the cold.'

Ruffo introduced Scarpia to his friends and his friends to Scarpia – the layman, the *abate* and the two women – Principessa di Marcisano and Contessa di Comastri. At each introduction, Scarpia bowed.

'You must call on us,' said the younger of the two women, the Contessa di Comastri. She was aged around thirty, her features even, her skin flawless, her hair piled high, her dress cut low – the bodice richly embroidered and studded with sequins framing the soft rise of her breasts.

The Principessa di Marcisano was a good ten years older and dressed with the same elaboration, but in a way that suggested this was only for form's sake. She flickered a look of suspicion at the contessa, then turned to Ruffo. 'Shouldn't I take him to meet some other young people, Monsignor?'

The treasurer bowed. 'By all means.'

'Come with me,' said the principessa to Scarpia, then set off at a fast pace, her hooped dress parting the flotsam of guests like the blunt prow of a ship – acknowledging the bows and smiles of those she passed with an almost irritated nod of her head, but stopping for none as she pursued her mission.

Scarpia followed in her wake into a smaller side room where there stood a group of young people around Scarpia's age – languid, saying little, glasses in their hands, two of the girls with thick powder covering their pockmarked faces. From upholstered banquettes set against the wall older women kept watch on the young.

At the approach of the principessa, the young men bowed and the girls curtsied.

'Ludovico, Paola,' said the principessa, 'this is Vitellio Scarpia. I want you to look after him. He knows no one in Rome.'

'And we know *everyone*,' said a girl with a clear complexion, and a shadow of an impertinent smile on her lips.

'He does not need to meet everyone,' said the principessa, with a sharp look at her daughter.

'Don't worry, Mother,' said the young man. 'We shall look after him.'

The principessa turned to Scarpia. 'You know how to dance, I take it?'

Scarpia bowed. 'If the steps are the same in Rome as they are in Palermo.'

'A Sicilian!' said one of the young women. 'Well!'

What the 'well' was meant to signify was not clear to Scarpia. He felt welling up inside of him a rage at being treated like some strange beast from a zoo.

'Your card,' said the principessa to her daughter.

The girl handed her mother the thick parchment programme listing the dances against which were written a number of names.

'You have some free, I see,' said the principessa. Then, turning to Scarpia: 'Would you like to dance the next quadrille with my daughter, Paola?'

Scarpia bowed towards the young woman, and in a tone tinged with sarcasm said: 'If the signorina would be so kind.'

'With pleasure,' said Paola di Marcisano, investing the word 'pleasure' with an equal irony, and a sharp look of annoyance directed not at Scarpia but her mother.

*

Paola became kinder when the two were alone. 'What brought you to Rome?' she asked, as they came face-to-face during the quadrille. Before Scarpia could answer, they were swept apart; then, as they came together again, before giving him a chance to answer, she said: 'Not as a pilgrim, surely?' The same impertinent smile. Back, forward, their hands touched for a turn.

'I was in Spain,' said Scarpia, 'and the boat brought me to Civitavecchia.'

'Like Aeneas.'

'More or less.'

'And clearly, if you found yourself in Civitavecchia, it made sense to come to Rome.' She was swept away again. Then, when they were momentarily reunited: 'What did you do in Spain?'

'I was a soldier.'

She seemed unable to think of a smart rejoinder; then, when the dance ended, she said: 'I dare say there's more to being a soldier in Spain than there is in Rome.'

'I am a soldier here too.'

'A Knight of St John?'

'No. Just a soldier.'

'Well, that's original. I don't think I've ever met an ordinary soldier before.' They walked towards the buffet: she seemed in no hurry to return to her friends. 'But then, though we know *everyone*, as I said, it is only in a *social* sense. I was locked away in a convent until last year, and so have in fact met few people outside our circle.'

Scarpia followed her to the table.

'Do you like ice cream?' she asked, taking a small porcelain plate on which sat three coloured boules. 'We love it here in Rome.'

Scarpia took a plate from a flunkey. 'Also in Palermo.'

'Shall we sit down?' Holding the plate of ice cream, she sauntered towards the side room from which they had come. 'We had better remain in view of Aunt Adolina. We don't want to cause scandal. It's a sin. Did you know that? Causing scandal is a sin, even if what causes the scandal is entirely innocent.'

'I would not want to compromise your honour,' said Scarpia.

'Oh, you couldn't do that. No one could think –' She stopped, turned towards Scarpia, looked him up and down, and said: 'You really shouldn't wear that order, the Golden Spur. His Holiness hands it out to everyone. Most people pass it on to their valet.'

Scarpia blushed. 'Alas, I don't have a drawerful of orders to choose from.'

'Better none than the Golden Spur, I can assure you. It marks you out as a provincial.'

'I *am* a provincial,' said Scarpia, looking for some way in which he could avoid sitting down next to Paola on a banquette. 'But I am most grateful to be taught the ways of the world by someone who has spent her life in a convent.'

Paola patted the place on the seat next to her. 'Come and sit down. I didn't mean to upset you. And you're quite right, I really have no idea as to what is or is not *comme il faut*. It is only that I overheard someone saying that about the Order of the Golden Spur. But, as you say, an Order is an Order and it looks quite pretty. And me, do you think I look pretty?'

Scarpia glanced at her – the small, sharp nose, thin lips, white teeth and large eyes. 'Yes.'

'You didn't take long to come to that conclusion. A first impression. Why not? You don't think my features are too severe? My ancestors, over the centuries, married into families from Tuscany, Lombardy, the Veneto – even the Thurn and Taxis who are German – which perhaps accounts for the colour of my hair.'

Scarpia looked at her elaborately dressed hair. 'What colour is it *au naturel*?'

'*Au naturel*, as you put it, my hair is brown. You would probably prefer it to be black like that of the girls in Sicily or in Spain.' She glanced at him mischievously – the same look of impudence that she had directed at her mother.

'I would not judge a woman's beauty simply by the colour of her hair,' said Scarpia.

'And yet,' said Paola, 'St Paul himself – he's my patron saint – said that *a woman's glory is her hair*, so it must play some role in one's overall judgement of a woman's beauty. Perhaps you judge beauty simply by the quality of the soul?' – another impudent smile. 'We were taught in the convent that that is what matters, but then as soon as we were released we are bedecked and adorned as if the soul is the last thing a man has in mind when he is looking for a wife.'

'Perhaps the way a woman looks says something about her soul?'

'Less in Rome than in Paris where Frenchwomen put rouge on their faces. We don't do that here.' She pointed to her cheek. 'That's its natural colour. *Au naturel*. Perhaps we'll start painting our faces sooner or later. We always follow the fashions of Versailles, though we're usually ten or twenty years out of date. That dress my mother is wearing. Did you notice? It's ancient. It might have been worn by Madame de Pompadour. It's not that she couldn't afford a new one. She simply can't be bothered. She'd much rather fuss about what I'm wearing.' Paola finished her ice cream. 'That was most enjoyable, but now I must get back to my friends. I can see a worried look on Aunt Adolina's face.' She stood. 'You must forgive me for prattling on so much. You can't imagine how dull life was in the convent with no one to talk to but the other girls, the nuns and the occasional *abate*.'

*

Was she pretty? Lying in his bed that night, and over the next several days, Scarpia tried to raise images from his memory of Paola di Marcisano. She had been pretty, but how? She was tall, and thin – quite the opposite of the buxom Celestina. The skin of her cheeks to which she had pointed, untainted either by smallpox or rouge, was

85

part of a pale complexion but, perhaps because of her adolescent chatter, her prettiness seemed like that of a child. Her dress had been a pale blue, with little scarlet bows beneath the bodice, but, when he thought of her bodice, there came into his mind the gentle swelling of the breasts of the Contessa di Comastri. The more Scarpia mused on the two women – and one or two others he had met at the ball – the more his mind returned to the contessa.

*

Scarpia was now made welcome at the regular receptions in both the Palazzo Marcisano and the Palazzo Comastri which he attended whenever his duties at the Castel Sant'Angelo allowed. These *conversazioni* were held on particular days – the Marcisanos received on a Thursday, the Comastris on a Monday. At first Scarpia appeared at the earlier part of the evening, soon after the bells of the churches had rung the Ave Maria, but was later given to understand that he could remain for the later and more exclusive *conversazioni della seconda sera*, which continued late into the night. Biscuits, ices and cool drinks were served by liveried footmen, and guests could choose to listen to a string quartet or the singing of a fashionable castrato in one room, demonstrate his wit and learning to a group in another, catch up on the latest gossip in a third or play faro in a fourth.

At the Palazzo Comastri he watched, but as yet did not join in, the games of cards on which the Romans laid wagers with no coins placed on the table or even ivory counters, but all the bets noted by the players themselves on a card, together with gains and losses – the reckoning to be made at a later date. Letizia di Comastri always spent the last hour or so of her soirées at the tables and, having taken Scarpia 'under her wing', liked him to stand behind her, saying he brought her luck.

Scarpia himself did not gamble; he had already been obliged to borrow more money to pay for new sets of clothes and have a purse full of *baiocchi* ready for the *mancia* – the tip he had to slip into the hands of the footmen as he came and went. His new life was expensive, far beyond the salary of a captain in the army, but he thought of the costs as an investment: advancement in Rome largely depended on influence, and at both the Comastris and the Marcisanos Scarpia met powerful men – the Papal Secretary of State Cardinal Zelada; the Pope's nephew Duke Luigi Braschi Onesti; the French ambassador Cardinal de Bernis; and the Spanish ambassador José Nicholas de Azara.

Few of them noticed the young Sicilian: both by nature and experience, Scarpia was a poor courtier. When some grandee made a clever remark, Scarpia could only come up with a witty repartee several hours later as he lay sleepless in his bed. He ground his teeth in frustration at his lack of what the French called *esprit*. At times he felt that his inarticulacy was an embarrassment to the Contessa di Comastri, who had introduced him to her distinguished guests. He began to doubt his ability to compete for preferment with the suave *abati* in their elegant black habits, silk stockings and silver-buckled shoes.

Only the Spanish ambassador, Don José de Azara, paid him some attention, and this because he had known Vitellio's father, Luigi Scarpia, when he served with Tanucci. At one of the *conversazioni* in the Palazzo Comastri, he took Scarpia aside and asked after his father. Scarpia replied that as far as he knew he was well, but that he had not seen him since leaving to serve the King of Spain.

'Ah yes, of course,' said Azara. 'Now I remember. It was you ... yes. But you have found service in Rome? That is excellent, though you will not find glory as an officer in the pontifical army. You have to be a cleric to rise in Rome – not a priest, necessarily, Ruffo is not a priest. But then clerics have one disadvantage. They are limited in what they can do for our contessas and principessas, and these ladies often have the ear – and on occasions, more than the ear – of influential gentlemen. And quite clearly you are appreciated by our Contessa di Comastri. Make the most of that. She is one of the most beautiful women in Rome, and there is a vacancy, as it were, in her entourage. You are aware, I am sure, that here in Italy every married woman has her *cicisbeo*, her *cavaliere servente*? It is a custom that came, as it happens, from Spain. The husbands don't mind or, if they do, they are too proud to show it. And someone of the quality of our Contessa di Comastri has three – *il buono, il brutto* and *il bello* – *il buono*, the man who pays her bills, *il brutto*, the one who runs her errands, and *il bello*, the one who ... how can one put it? The one for the exchange of tender emotions. She has *il buono*, the amiable Prince Paducci, who is too old to ask for more than the privilege of paying for her losses at cards; and she has *il brutto*, the idiotic Chevalier Spinelli, whose tastes are not really for the opposite sex, but he likes to be seen with the contessa for that very reason; but there is a vacancy for the post of *il bello*, and, indisputably, my dear Scarpia, you are a handsome young man – also with a reputation for courage and daring which may not be fashionable among the faint-hearted Romans, but always appeals, though they may not admit it, to women. *Bello. Coraggioso. Intrepido.*' The ambassador patted Scarpia on the shoulder. 'Yes, you are made for the role.'

2

Scarpia, after his conversation with Azara, realised that what the ambassador had recommended had already come to pass. He now went everywhere with the contessa, often in the company of the doddery Paducci and the prancing Spinelli, and no one seemed to mind – least of all Letizia's husband, the count, who treated Scarpia as a favoured *amico della casa*. A tall, thin man with an aloof manner, and twelve years older than his wife, he spent less time in her company than in that of Adelina di Prato. He laughed when shown a *pasquinade*, one of the anonymous pamphlets left by the mutilated classical torso situated near the Palazzo Braschi named Pasquino, informing the Romans of the contessa's newly acquired taste for Marsala.

It was now clear to Scarpia that in the eyes of the Romans there was nothing shameful in paying court to someone else's wife. It even seemed proper that he should fall in love with a married woman, because to the Romans love had nothing to do with marriage. Marriage was a contract made in the interests of the two families involved. It was the duty of a wife to provide her husband with children, but no one thought that the vow to forsake all others should be taken seriously, or bothered whether or not children born of the marriage looked like their fathers.

Scarpia, then, decided that he was in love with Letizia di Comastri and, from all outward appearances, Letizia di Comastri was especially fond of him. She was five or so years older than he was, and had two children whom she saw at most for half an hour a day. Having borne these children when young and supple, her figure remained taut and graceful. She was aware of its effect on men of all ages and walked with gently undulating hips. Much of the time spared from attending to her children was spent on the meticulous preparation of her hair, her face and her clothes: Scarpia, who was admitted to her boudoir if his duties permitted him to call on her in the morning, would sit on a stool behind her, catching glimpses through the weaving bodies of the hairdresser, seamstress or chambermaid of Letizia's face reflected in the mirror on her dressing table, catching her eye and in it the expression: 'All this is for you.' And in company those same lovely eyes, flitting around the many handsome and distinguished men who always surrounded her, would seek him out and settle for a moment – widening, brightening and triggering on her lips a sweet, complicit smile.

What was not clear to Scarpia – what remained ambiguous in the *moeurs* of the Romans – was whether or when or how the love would or should come to fruition. Sometimes in an alcove, or behind a pillar, Letizia would draw him towards her, whisper some term of endearment, hold and press his hand, even permit a kiss on her cheek, but then break away and return to the party. They were never alone. In her boudoir, there were not just the maid, the seamstress and the hairdresser, but also the hosier showing his selection of silk stockings and the chemist with a tray of powders, creams and unctions which, Letizia assured her lover with a look of mock misery, were most important 'for a woman of my advanced age'. Once the contessa was free of their ministrations, the two had the run of the Palazzo Comastri with its forty-five rooms, but here again they were never out of the sight of footmen and maidservants; and there was no place where they might not be disturbed by the major-domo, resident *abate*, the house guests – cousins, nephews, scroungers, and the petitioners who wished to enlist the count's influence to secure a preferment, or plaintiffs from some dispute on one of the Comastris' country estates.

And both in the palazzo and out and about, the contessa was invariably accompanied by her other *cavalieri serventi* – *il buono*, Prince Paducci, and *il brutto*, the Chevalier Spinelli. At their first encounter of the day with Scarpia, both men acknowledged his presence with a cursory nod of the head and then ignored him. Scarpia felt insulted; his hand went to the handle of his sword, but then he noticed that they also ignored one another and indeed anyone else when in the presence of the contessa: clearly, fashionable devotion required that while in attendance it should be as if she were the only other person in the world. All this Letizia acknowledged almost with cruelty. When the prince presented her with some expensive bibelot, she took it with the same cursory word of thanks she addressed to the chemist who gave her a pot of face cream; and while she was a little more effusive with the unctuous chevalier, she sent him on the most preposterous errands both to test his devotion and, she whispered to Scarpia, 'to get him out of the way'.

To get him out of the way for what? Scarpia was hot-blooded. He thrashed around on his bed at night, imagining the soft body of the voluptuous contessa in his arms, but then was obliged to recognise, as the months passed, that perhaps the smiles, conspiratorial glances, squeezed hands and occasional kisses, were all that a *cicisbeo* – even *il bello* – should expect. She seemed to treat him as a child – giving him little gifts – a silver snuffbox, a flacon of expensive pomade, a fashionable shirt, and once taking him to Prince Paducci's tailor and ordering a beautifully embroidered frock coat with matching waistcoat and breeches. Perhaps the contessa's love was no more than a silken leash for a pretty lapdog.

When it came to July, the Comastris moved with their whole household to their estate in the Sabine hills to escape the heat of Rome. The Torre San Domenico had been built by a Cardinal Comastri in the seventeenth century on the ruins of a castle, destroyed during the wars between the Guelfs and the Ghibellines. A long avenue of cypress trees led up to the stuccoed villa with its slatted shutters. The count and contessa took up residence with their two children, the children's governess and a complement of servants from the palazzo in Rome. To the usual crowd surrounding the contessa there was now added gardeners, grooms, tenants, more *abati* and guests from neighbouring villas. Prince Paducci, *il buono*, was elsewhere but the Chevalier Spinelli was staying, pattering after the contessa, or cocking his head to assess the social weight of some new visitor and, if a lady of sufficient distinction, sliding across the room to whisper gossip into her ear.

Scarpia was greeted with the usual sweet smile and squeeze of the hand by the contessa, and presented to those he did not know as 'the courageous captain'. No doubt anyone who noticed the hard look in his eye thought it was an expression you should expect from a soldier who was ready either to take or lose a life. In a sense they were right, because the source of that hard look was Scarpia's resolve to risk all on a frontal assault on the virtue of Letizia di Comastri. He realised that she might not want to be seduced, and that the count was complaisant only in so far as his wife's dalliance was limited to those smiles, squeezed hands and whispered endearments. He was aware, too, that if he went too far, he might lose his position as *il bello* and with it all the influence that the Comastris could exercise on his behalf: he was aware of all this, and that as a Sicilian he was ignorant of the nuances of local custom, but nevertheless determined that the contessa would be his mistress by the time he returned to Rome.

*

The Torre San Domenico had large gardens laid out in terraces with gravel pathways. Umbrella pines gave shade, hedges of laurel and ilex formed a wall with mossy stone and weathered brick, and peacocks scratched the gravel paths between hedges of box and yew. One of the carefully contrived vistas led to a gazebo, the others to statues on plinths and fountains fed by springs from the hills – water spouting from the mouths of the acolytes of a Neptune holding his trident, and from those of Laocoön and his sons struggling with serpents – the features of these pagan gods and heroes roughened by exposure over the centuries, and the patches of burned lichen a reminder that in winter it could be both wet and cold.

Between ten in the morning and five in the afternoon the garden was empty and silent: it was too hot to leave the shade of the house and even the crickets lay low; but early in the day when the air was damp with dew and in the evening when it became cooler without than within, the Comastris and their guests would stroll in these gardens, either in groups or alone.

On the fourth evening, at around six, Scarpia joined a small group sitting on the edge of a fountain at the back of the garden – the contessa, her two children and the children's governess, a Swiss, Fräulein Bisenschmidt. The children – a boy of ten, a girl of twelve – were trailing their fingers in the water and, as Scarpia approached, the son was being rebuked by Fräulein Bisenschmidt for flicking water in the face of his sister. Letizia had on her face the serene expression that Scarpia had noted before during those brief moments that she spent with her children – a serene and benign approval of something that had little to do with her, rather as if she were being shown hounds by the huntsman or horses by the groom; and she now seemed as indifferent to the bickering of her children as she would have been to the hounds yelping or the horses nodding their heads. The picture she presented, sitting with her children, was unquestionably charming, bringing to mind a painting by Watteau or Fragonard; and the contessa was undoubtedly aware of how charming it was, having the ability to step out of the frame and see herself as others might see her and, like those others, admire what she saw.

The only flaw in the tableau presented at that moment, and indeed at any moment when she received Scarpia in the company of her children, was that her daughter, Giulia, now aged twelve, was already developing from a scraggy child into a woman. Clearly, it was not unusual for women who married young to have mature daughters while they themselves were still in their prime; but it was aggravating all the same when a man's eye, upon entering her drawing room, was drawn to the daughter rather than the mother.

As yet, there was no question of Scarpia noticing the two children except as details in the pretty tableau. He was, in any case, not looking upon the scene with the eye of an art connoisseur but rather as the huntsman alert for his prey; and the prey, Letizia, to get rid of the evidence of her age, took the bickering and flicking of

93

water as an excuse to suggest to Fräulein Bisenschmidt that it was time for the children to go in. The Swiss woman and her two charges did as they were told. Giulia and Antonio kissed their mother, Fräulein Bisenschmidt curtsied, and all at once Scarpia and the contessa were alone.

Letizia perhaps had not meant this; she looked around, almost flustered, as if there were someone she could call upon to prevent what she sensed might happen; but there was no one, and her sense was correct. Scarpia went up to her, took her hand, raised her from the edge of the basin and drew her into a shaded alcove where the yew hedge hid them from view. He said nothing. He knew what he was up to. So did she. He kissed her, gripped her and fumbled beneath her skirts. Feebly, she tried to stop him. 'No, no, Scarpia…' but even as she spoke the arms that had feebly pushed him away now drew him towards her. He kissed her lips, then her neck, then her shoulders which, despite the cooler air, were moist with salty sweat. Her words became murmurs as his hands prowled under her skirts and found her flesh. Scarpia was triumphant. He had crossed the Rubicon. There could be no going back.

They straightened their clothes, came out of the alcove and sauntered side by side along the gravel paths. The garden was on a terrace cut into the side of a hill: the elegant basin where the contessa had been sitting with her children was beneath the bank to the north, while to the south, which they now reached, over a low parapet, was a fine view towards Rome and the Tyrrhenian Sea. The parapet had been built on the foundations of the ramparts of the *castello*, and in the corner, marking the boundary of the garden, was a former turret that now served as a gazebo. They stood together looking at the beautiful view – the distant tower of a church, a line of cypresses on the horizon. Then they strolled to the extremity of the garden – in other words, to the gazebo. Here they stopped and it became clear to Scarpia that the contessa had gently led him there for a purpose. She opened one half of the double doors and, though she did not go in, pointed to an old sofa that had been placed at the back of the gazebo against the wall. 'My father-in-law used to come here for his siesta.' Then she added, not in a whisper but in a low, quiet voice, 'Be here at midnight. I shall come if I can.'

*

Letizia, when she appeared in the moonlight, was a different woman. Her hair was undressed, and fell over her shoulders: her complicated, corseted dress had been replaced by a loose silk wrap which, though it revealed less of her bosom than the décolleté gowns she wore during the day, clung to the body that was naked beneath. She was there like a fawn, as much a part of nature as the scent of the eucalyptus or the chirp of the crickets. The sofa they lay on had lost some of its stuffing, perhaps as a result of gallant encounters over many years, but was nevertheless soft enough for the two to make love and, after a short spell in one another's arms, make love again. 'Dear Scarpia,' she said, stroking his flat stomach or, when he was over her, running her hands from his shoulders down his back. 'Dear Scarpia...' And her Sicilian lover, so imperious in the chase, felt humbled to find himself the lover of such an exquisite woman and was exultant that her rapture appeared to equal his own.

Before they parted, at three in the morning, they agreed they would return to the gazebo at the same time – 'But not tomorrow,' Letizia whispered sweetly. 'If we do it every night, we will look exhausted, it will show on our faces.' And so, for the rest of his stay, it was one night on and one night off – their trysts unnoticed and their behaviour, in the company of the count and Letizia's other admirers, no different from what it had been before.

Six

I

The Castel Sant'Angelo, the huge cylindrical fortress on the west bank of the Tiber, had been built in the early second century as a mausoleum for the Emperor Hadrian and members of his family. Three hundred years later, it was converted into a fortress – surrounded by ramparts and crowned by castellated walls within which were barracks, the papal treasury, prison cells and elegant quarters with frescoed walls in which popes and cardinals, when necessity demanded, could take refuge from their foes. In 1753 a magnificent bronze statue of St Michael the Archangel wielding his sword had been erected on the pinnacle of the castle reminding anyone who might choose to besiege it that supernatural as well as natural forces could be enlisted in its defence.

The principal duty of the soldiers who formed the garrison of the Castel Sant'Angelo was to guard the papal treasury and protect the pontiff should the city of Rome fall into the hands of his enemies: this had happened in 1527 when the unpaid German soldiers of the Emperor Charles V ran amok – murdering, raping and pillaging the inhabitants of the Holy City while the then Pope, Clement VII, looked on helplessly from its ramparts. But there was a secondary duty, which was to act as gaolers of the prisoners consigned to the Castel Sant'Angelo. These were not ordinary criminals but those convicted by the Holy Inquisition of moral sedition, or committed by a *lettre de cachet* of the Pope – an order that could not be disputed in the courts and that was used sparingly, often as a favour to some illustrious family to prevent a spendthrift son running up more debts, or a lovelorn heir marrying an unsuitable bride.

In Spain or in Venice, the Inquisition was feared for its arbitrary and despotic powers. In Rome at the time it was a relatively benign institution whose main concern was to preserve the integrity of the Catholic faith. One or two prisoners such as the occultist Cagliostro had been imprisoned for dabbling in black magic, much in fashion at the time. Freemasonry, also in fashion, was considered a serious crime and those who attempted to found lodges would be sent to the Castel Sant'Angelo: so too those, whether or not they were Freemasons, who disseminated the dangerous ideas put forward by the French *philosophes* that priests were parasites and there was no God.

The half-dozen or so prisoners whom Scarpia had charge of during his tours of duty were housed in rooms with views towards St Peter's Basilica and the Vatican Palace. They were allowed to read and to write and to receive visitors, though, since the visitors would themselves become suspect, there were few of them. The chief source of suffering, then, beyond the deprivation of liberty, was boredom, and, given the approval from the Pope for a compassionate regime, Scarpia sometimes alleviated that boredom – and, indeed, his own – by entering into conversation with some of his prisoners.

One in particular, Count Vicenzo Palmieri, was agreeable company, and Scarpia liked to spend time talking to him in his cell. He was around the same age as Scarpia – thin, good-looking, but with, on occasions, a crazed look in his eyes. He came from an ancient Roman family, and had been sent on a tour of Europe north of the Alps from which he had returned with a mind filled with new ideas – democracy, which he had witnessed in England, industriousness, which he had seen in the Netherlands, and, finally, the free thought of Voltaire and the *philosophes* he had found in France. In Paris he had joined a Masonic Lodge that included pupils of the painter Jacques-Louis David. David was then at the French Academy in Rome, and on his return Palmieri had looked him up and was shown David's work in progress, *Oath of the Horatii*. Intoxicated with the idea that the Romans should throw off their tyrannical ruler and re-establish a republic like that defended by the Horatii, Palmieri had set out to recruit some of his friends into the Masons and conspire with them to depose the Pope.

Palmieri's project never got off the ground. The writings of 'Monsù Voltaire', as he was known by the Romans, were regarded as ridiculous and malign – the work of the Devil from which one was protected by a quick sign of the cross. The only Romans who took an interest in the French Encyclopaedists were the spies of the Inquisition. Free-thinking was tolerated among the French students at their Academy, but in a native Roman it was considered seditious. Palmieri was arrested, summoned before the Inquisition and, after refusing to recant, sentenced to five years' imprisonment in the Castel Sant'Angelo.

Scarpia had read some of the works of 'Monsù Voltaire' in his father's library; and had discussed with his father the ideas of the Encyclopaedists. He was therefore curious to know why the young Palmieri was so sure of his convictions. At first Palmieri would not be drawn; he treated his gaoler with a simmering contempt, calling him the Pope's *sbirro*, the Romans' derisive term for a policeman. He received the few favours that Scarpia granted him with no word of thanks, as if it were Scarpia who should feel grateful to be of service to a Roman patrician. Then, little by little, he lowered his guard, dropped his stern demeanour and began to give Scarpia looks of appreciation, if not gratitude, that seemed to acknowledge that two men of the same age and speaking the same language might have something in common.

'Are you not ashamed of what you do?' he once asked Scarpia when he was making a routine inspection of his cell.

'It is one of my duties,' said Scarpia, as he cursorily sifted through Palmieri's belongings.

'Yes, of course, you must obey orders, and the gaoler must search his prisoner's cell. But you might be ashamed of serving a relic from the Middle Ages, the supreme hypocrite, who even as he claims to be the successor to a Galilean fisherman, lives the life of a pagan despot.'

Scarpia, unused to hearing the Pope referred to in this way, controlled his indignation. 'He lives according to tradition. He is not simply the successor to St Peter and Bishop of Rome. He is also sovereign of the Papal States.'

'An absurdity based upon a fraud,' said Palmieri. 'The famous Donation of Constantine has been shown to be a forgery; and anyway, a state belongs to its people, not to any emperor, and so was not Constantine's to give away.'

'So you are a democrat?' asked Scarpia, using the term that most Romans would find insulting.

'Of course I am a democrat,' said Palmieri. 'It is not the will of a priest that should govern a nation, but the will of the people.'

'And how is that will to be expressed?'

'By elections to a parliament, as in England.'

'Don't the English have a king?'

'Yes, they have a king.'

'And not everyone has a vote, I understand.'

'No, not everyone has a vote. But here *no one* has a vote.'

'Except the cardinals. It is they who chose our oriental despot.'

'Cardinals who have been appointed by a previous pope.'

'Some of them good men, and so some popes are good men.'

'Some may be better than others, but whoever they are they live extravagantly off the widows' mites and share the spoils with members of their family – Duke Braschi, for example, who has built a palace to rival that of the Farnese.'

'It is the custom,' said Scarpia.

'A corrupt custom. The endowments made by the devout over the centuries were to provide for those who would pray for their salvation, not for the idle and grandiose living of prelates or the relatives of the Pope.'

'No one starves in Rome. There is much charity.'

'Charity indeed! They divert a trickle to the people from the flood of revenues from the universal Church. What cardinal lives in evangelical poverty? What parasitic priest would, if he truly believed in Christ, be able to look Christ in the face at the Last Judgement? I tell you, they don't worry about judgement because they don't believe in the whole farrago any more than I do! But why question a system when it provides for them so well?'

Scarpia frowned. 'You fail to distinguish between weakness and treachery. St Peter was weak; he disowned the Lord and the cock crew; but Judas was treacherous: he sold his Saviour to the Chief Priests. His Holiness may be weak like Peter, but today's Judas is a French philosopher. He denies and he betrays.'

'For fifty pieces of silver? No. Our reward is persecution and imprisonment, while it is the priests who receive the fifty pieces of silver – and more!'

Palmieri's contemptuous tone – *lèse-majesté* veering on blasphemy – made Scarpia uncomfortable, and he now finished his search of the prisoner's quarters in silence. However, he continued the dialogue in his mind. And when he returned the next day he had prepared a reply.

'There are a hundred reasons why things are as they are. First, the Church must be resplendent and the faithful want it to be so: think of the Transfiguration of Christ. And with riches comes power, and with power authority, and with authority the establishment of truth.'

'What truth?' asked Palmieri contemptuously.

'The truth of the Gospels. The truth that God became man and died to secure our salvation.'

'Salvation from what?'

'Why, from damnation.'

'Damnation! A fairy tale to frighten the people into submission.'

'So, after death? What awaits us?'

'Nothing. It's the end.' Palmieri swatted a fly with the palm of his hand. 'Like that. The end.'

'There is no eternal life?'

'No.'

'No God?'

Palmieri hesitated. 'A Supreme Being, perhaps, who has designed a universe that we can understand through scientific discovery, but not a Trinity of Father, Son and Holy Spirit – that absurd concoction of nitpicking theologians.'

'And how does this Supreme Being tell us what is right and what is wrong?'

'There is no need. It is self-evident, as the Americans say in their Declaration of Independence. "We hold these truths to be self-evident, that all men are created equal, that they are endowed by their Creator with certain unalienable Rights, that among these are Life, Liberty and the pursuit of Happiness."' Palmieri, who spoke some English, recited the famous phrase parrot-wise in that language to impress Scarpia and then, with a look of condescension, gave his own Italian translation.

'All men are created equal?' said Scarpia. 'Yet some of the gentlemen who wrote these fine words own slaves!'

Palmieri blushed. 'It is an institution that will wither with time.'

'Like the papacy, perhaps?'

'We will not wait for that to wither. The tyrant will be overthrown.'

2

Scarpia's arguments with Palmieri invariably ended with the prisoner growing excited, standing (if he was seated), looking away from his gaoler to an imaginary gathering and declaiming as if to a crowd. This was the moment for Scarpia to withdraw and, while he could well understand why a young man who was so eloquent and personable but had such seditious ideas should be prevented from infecting others, he could not see his foolishness as evil and admired his passion for justice – even if his idea of justice would, if implemented, turn the world upside down.

Certainly, his discussions with Palmieri were more interesting than the exchanges with most of those he met at the *conversazioni* in the palazzi where he was now made welcome. There were a few, he realised, who held views similar to those of Palmieri – even the odd suave *abate* who had spent time in Paris and, in the same way as a woman might return wearing a dress in the latest French fashion, would discreetly drop hints that they had adopted some of the *philosophes'* 'enlightened' ideas. They never said anything that would land them in trouble should it come to the ears of the Inquisition, but would whisper and perhaps giggle as they let it be known that they had in their possession some racy novel such as *Thérèse Philosophe*; and, with even greater discretion, persuade some hesitant lady that the *bon ton* in Versailles considered both clerical celibacy and wifely chastity as vices rather than virtues.

Scarpia considered himself immune to contagion by these new ideas – whether whispered in the salons or proclaimed by the would-be Brutus, Count Palmieri. First of all, he did not see his liaison with the Contessa di Comastri as a virtue; nor the asceticism of a priest like Father Simone as a vice. He preferred the gentle 'philosophy', if it can be called that, of Ludovico di Marcisano, whom he encountered at the Marcisanos' receptions. Ludovico was tall, with a gangling figure, even features and the kind of aquiline nose found on the senators in ancient Rome whose busts lined the galleria of the Palazzo Marcisano. Ludovico was aware of this likeness and, after the friendly glance that welcomed Scarpia, he rarely looked into his eyes, or those of anyone else, keeping his head in profile as if posing for the sculptor. He was proud of belonging to one of the thirty leading families of the Roman aristocracy, and would frequently bring up his descent from the Roman consul Lucius Porcius Cato: 'Of course it can't be proved, but it has been a rumour in the family for the past thousand years.'

Unlike Count Palmieri, Ludovico had not made a grand tour of northern Europe; indeed, he had never travelled outside the Papal States. Like Scarpia, he had been taught by a former Jesuit and from him had learned Latin and history – the former important not because he envisaged a career in the Church, but because, combined with history, it enabled him to research his ancestry and establish, if possible, that his descent from Lucius Porcius Cato was not just a rumour but a fact. He hunted, gambled for small sums and played *pelote* with his friends. He felt it his duty to go to receptions in the other palazzi and be seen in his coach on the Corso. He belonged to a number of religious fraternities and regarded doing charitable works necessary to his self-respect. Following the example of his father, he welcomed anyone who wished to look at the works of art that formed his family's collection, though he himself knew little about the masterpieces assembled from the time of the

Renaissance, seeing them simply as part of the decor suitable for the dwelling of a prince.

Ludovico di Marcisano was three years older than Scarpia, who at first felt flattered that the prince should treat him with such familiarity, then noticed that he treated his grooms and footmen in just the same way – as likely to ask his coachman for an opinion on a new opera as one of his noble friends. The touchy Scarpia then felt foolish for having assumed that the young prince's friendliness was specific to him; but later saw that Ludovico in fact sought out his company and was almost in awe of both his heroics in the Apennines and his ability to discuss and dismiss the ideas of the French *philosophes*. He could, of course, speak French, but he considered reading books a pastime for clerics, not princes. He was no simpleton, but felt that his faith was a sufficient source of wisdom, and that it was therefore futile to unpick the certainties of religion with clever arguments and preposterous speculation.

It reassured Ludovico that Scarpia, who had at least read some of the books in question, shared his views. He liked to recruit him, and cite him as an authority, in arguments with his sister Paola who, though by no means a free-thinker, liked to taunt her brother with difficult questions. Would Jesus approve of the successor to St Peter living in numerous sumptuous palaces? How does Jesus's admonition to turn the other cheek fit in with the halberds of the Pope's Swiss Guard, and the raising of a pontifical army – this with a impertinent sidelong glance at Scarpia. Did he not rebuke Peter, who cut off the ear of the Chief Priest's servant with a sword? And what of Jesus's injunction to the rich young man to sell all he had and give the proceeds to the poor? Did her brother mean to do that when he came into his inheritance? 'No,' replied Ludovico, 'only your dowry.' 'Who cares about a dowry?' said Paola. 'If I were to marry – *if* – it would be to a man who loved me for myself, not for my dowry.'

Paola, being unmarried, was kept under strict surveillance, and Scarpia was only tangentially involved in these conversations. Unlike Ludovico, who made no distinction between Scarpia and his other friends – most from the patrician families – she never addressed Scarpia directly. However, it often seemed as if she was in fact addressing Scarpia through Ludovico. She rarely looked him in the eye – but directed darting looks at him every now and then to judge his reaction to something she had said.

Such a look was aimed at Scarpia after what she had said about a dowry. Her head did not turn towards him; her eyes were momentarily half closed as if their direction could be somehow camouflaged by her long eyelashes; but Scarpia caught it all the same and was puzzled. Was he expected to make a rejoinder? What was he expected to say about dowries without which no girl could hope to get married?

'It is something of a luxury to forgo a dowry,' he said. 'Something only a princess could afford.'

Paola frowned. 'How so, a luxury?'

'Because she knows that her parents would never let her starve, whereas a girl from Trastevere, say, who brought no dowry to a marriage, would have no roof over her head.'

'Love should be above such sordid calculations.'

'Love, perhaps, but marriage is about more than love.'

Ludovico moved away, apparently afraid that the topic might turn from the general to the particular – a husband for Paola and a wife for himself. And as soon as he was out of earshot, Paola for once did look Scarpia in the eye, her voice low, her cheeks scarlet, and said: 'Were you thinking of a dowry when you rescued that Spanish girl from a Turk in Algiers?'

Scarpia now blushed as deeply as she did. 'You know about that?'

'Of course. Everyone knows. We were told by Azara.'

'I was in love, or thought I was in love.'

'You weren't thinking of her dowry?'

'No.'

'And why didn't you marry?'

'She didn't love me.'

'Ungrateful wretch.'

'It wasn't her fault.'

'How magnanimous!'

'And also…' He hesitated.

'What?'

'It was for the best.'

'And do you still love her?' Paola put the question intently: again, looking directly into his eyes.

'No. And she is now married to someone else.'

*

Paola had changed since Scarpia had first met her; though she still walked with the bouncy gait of an adolescent, her slightly scrawny form had filled out and her eyes, skin and hair were all flawless. She seemed to disdain fine and fashionable clothes, but nonetheless wore them, and appeared at the grander *conversazioni* bejewelled and with intricately dressed hair. It was the consensus among the Roman matrons who sat in judgement on matters of this kind that she was among the three most beautiful girls available for a young nobleman looking for a wife. Even Letizia di Comastri, who did not think of herself as a matron but certainly contributed towards the consensus, remarked on how Paola di Marcisano's looks had improved. 'Don't you think so?' she asked Scarpia.

'Yes, she has grown from a girl into a woman.'

'You seem to go quite frequently to the Palazzo Marcisano.'

'Only in the hope of seeing you there.'

'Last Thursday, you knew I wouldn't be there, yet you went all the same.'

'I like Ludovico.'

'Of course, Ludovico. I am sure. And Paola has nothing to do with it.'

'Nothing. Though she is sometimes amusing.'

'And I am not?'

'You are far more amusing and experienced.'

'Experienced! You mean old!' As she said this, Letizia pulled up the sheet to cover her breasts because the two were lying naked on a bed in a small apartment provided by the contessa's *cicisbeo buono*, Prince Paducci. The breasts were in fact a perfect shape and size; Letizia had not risked deforming them by feeding her two children herself; but it was true that Scarpia had, once or twice, compared the slightly looser skin and faint lines of her face with the fresh figure and features of a younger woman such as Paola di Marcisano. He had found that, with love, *l'appétit vient en mangeant*, and was attracted to other women; but he considered it would be dishonourable to betray Letizia, and could not envisage a more delightful lover – affectionate, animated and, as he had so ineptly put it, experienced – deftly, discreetly and, without any overt immodesty, guiding his hands and lips to different parts of her body – intimating, with gentle gestures, what pleased her most.

Scarpia did not like to think about the source of this experience, but once asked her, after she had introduced him to a variation on the standard act of love, whether she had learned it from her husband.

'Alfredo? No ... at least, yes, because he had of course had lovers before we were married.'

'And since?'

'I do not ask. And nor does he. It is not done.'

'But you must be curious, surely, where his appetites are satisfied if not at home?'

'His appetites … Oh, you know, he's now quite an old man. He doesn't bother me, I can assure you, if that's what you're worried about. But really, Vitellio, you shouldn't put such questions. It shows you're not a Roman.'

Scarpia reined in the jealousy that posed as curiosity, but could not prevent himself raising questions in his own mind, even if they were not put to Letizia. That quick change from a 'no' to a 'yes' after he asked if her experience had come from her husband: a 'no' would mean, of course, that it had come from someone else, but who? He had heard of no previous *cicisbeo* credible in the role of her lover. Had the Chevalier Spinelli been demoted from *il bello* to *il brutto*? Unlikely, unless his preference for young men was a recent development. And what of *il buono*, Prince Paducci, who paid Letizia's gambling debts, gave her expensive trinkets and, without any exchange of words, had given Scarpia the key to the beautifully furnished apartment with bamboo-patterned wallpaper where he and Letizia now met? Scarpia could not believe that even a Roman would arrange a love nest for a successor. No, Prince Paducci was the same age as Letizia's father. He admired her as he might a painting or a china figurine, and his affection for her was avuncular.

Yet even if Scarpia acknowledged that, as Letizia had reminded him, he was a provincial, unacquainted with the subtle, sometimes paradoxical and even mysterious bonds between sophisticated Romans, he nevertheless remained perplexed by that which existed between his mistress and her elderly admirer. Why, if the Count di Comastri was so rich, did his wife need money from the prince to pay her debts? Why, if he got nothing in return, did he give her an amethyst ring on her name day or a small gold-framed looking glass without even the excuse that the gift was to mark a special occasion? And why, on receiving these expensive trinkets, did Letizia do so with such a bad grace?

'You don't seem to like the prince,' he once said to her.

'Oh, he's all right. I feel sorry for him. He hates his wife and children and they hate him. Life has disappointed him. All that money, and nothing to spend it on ... except me!' She darted a smile at Scarpia. 'But old people ...' She wrinkled her nose.

Scarpia could better understand why Letizia enjoyed the attentions of the Chevalier Spinelli, *il brutto*: he came with all the latest gossip; he amused her; and he would chatter away about fashion. Like a eunuch in a sultan's harem, Spinelli had the kind of privileged access to Letizia's boudoir at times when it was denied to both the count and Scarpia: she did not mind him seeing her with bleary eyes and a crumpled complexion, and he could advise her on what she should wear that morning or how she should dress her hair. On occasions, waiting for Letizia to emerge from her morning toilette, Scarpia would hear cries of 'No, no, *no* ...' as Spinelli castigated the dressmaker or hairdresser, or threw into the outer darkness an evening gown or new pair of shoes; or 'Oh yes, oh yes, oh *yes* ...' as Letizia put on something of which he approved. He also made her laugh – an irritating laugh – but nonetheless an accomplishment since, Scarpia noticed, Letizia had no real sense of humour.

Once the toilette was completed, and Letizia was ready like a refitted galleon to sail out into the world, Spinelli would be at her side – the pilot to guide her out of port. He accepted that Scarpia might also walk with her, though he rarely greeted him, scarcely acknowledged his presence and never looked him in the eyes. He would sometimes glance disparagingly at what Scarpia was wearing, give an involuntary 'humpf' of disapproval and then either look down at his own exquisite tunic or, if a mirror happened to be there, glance with admiration at his own reflection.

Spinelli was always in the Comastris' box at the opera, knew by heart both the music and libretto of most productions and was considered by all to be an expert whose judgement was final. Since this was Rome, female roles were sung by castrati, many of whom Spinelli knew well. Just what his relations were with some of these eunuchs was not clear, though in the intimacy of their love nest Letizia would whisper the names of one or two whom she believed had been Spinelli's lovers. 'And what do they do together?' she wondered. 'Do you think they do *this … or this, or, this?*'

As it would have been bad form for Letizia to ask Spinelli about his relations with his friends among the castrati, so it would have been bad form for Spinelli to ask Letizia for details of her relations with Scarpia; but clearly he, like Prince Paducci, knew that they had progressed from the usual duties of a *cicisbeo*. It was not that either Letizia or Scarpia gave anything away: in public they behaved with the expected decorum. But a young man cannot disguise a certain swagger when he is master of one of the most beautiful and prized women in Rome; nor a woman in her prime the flushed and healthy hue of her skin that comes with regular bouts of making love. Also the chevalier could not but be aware that there were moments of the day when Letizia indicated that she would rather he made himself scarce. If this enhanced his jealousy, he did not show it, treating Scarpia as just one among other minions and tradesmen who saw to the contessa's different needs.

The count, too, seemed to sense that his wife was now sleeping with Scarpia. If he thought it was regrettable and a breach of taste, he did not show it. Quite to the contrary – his pride demanded that he cover for his wife's infidelity by seeming to treat Scarpia almost as an adopted son. Scarpia was always made welcome by the count, but, while the words were warm, their tone was not; and when on rare occasions his eyes met Scarpia's, their look was contemptuous and cold.

Scarpia was so intoxicated with his passion for Letizia that he did not notice the count's coldness or the signs of misgivings in others. Ludovico, who seemed to have heard rumours of Scarpia's promotion from the Contessa di Comastri's *cicisbeo bello* to her lover, blushed if her name came up in conversation, or if he ran into Scarpia in her company at some ball or *conversazione*. Spoletta, whom Scarpia thought would have been proud of his master's triumph, remained oddly reticent, once referring to the matter obliquely in disparaging remarks, as he was shaving Scarpia, about the deviousness of the Romans and their 'over-sophistication', in contrast to the honesty and directness of Sicilians, who would 'put a knife into the heart of a man who put his cock into the cunt of his wife'. To which Scarpia replied, 'When in Rome, do as the Romans do,' the words mumbled through soapy foam.

In his intoxication, it did not occur to Scarpia that while no doubt there were Romans who did as he was doing, there were others who did not. His confessor Dom Simone, when Scarpia first confessed this sin of the flesh, gave a deep sigh. For a moment he remained silent, then counselled Scarpia on the virtue of chastity – the lily of the virtues, even for men – but seemed to regard the sin as somehow inevitable, and therefore venial, and was lenient in the penance he imposed. It was only after he had absolved Scarpia that he added a worldly addendum to the spiritual advice: 'Take care, Scarpia. Letizia is wilful. I have known her since she was a child.'

3

Father Simone's leniency towards Scarpia in the confessional was, he thought, consistent with Christ's treatment of the woman taken in adultery: 'Let him who has not sinned cast the first stone.' True, Jesus had told the woman 'to sin no more', and the priest too had told Scarpia to sin no more, but was aware of how a penitent's firm purpose of amendment can evaporate as soon as he – or she – leaves the musty confessional and comes out into the open air. In such cases, in the view of the Oratorian priest, repentance was what mattered, not simply the avoidance of sin. Father Simone was devout, but he was no Jansenist. He did not think that only the few would be saved. He firmly believed in the visions of St Margaret Mary Alacoque in Burgundy, who had seen Jesus pointing to his sacred heart, aflame with love for all humanity – saints and sinners alike. Did the father cease to love the Prodigal Son when he was cavorting with women in the fleshpots of Egypt? No, he loved him even as he sinned and patiently awaited his return. As with the Prodigal Son, so with Vitellio Scarpia.

This understanding of the frailty of human nature was not confined to a single priest, the Oratorian Simone Alberti; it had taken root in the culture of Catholic countries throughout the world. Over the centuries the Roman pontiffs had sanctioned periods of indulgence as well as penitence – a mix of feasting and fasting that sustained both body and soul. The main period of fasting was Lent – the forty days that preceded the commemoration of the crucifixion of Christ on Good Friday: then, in Rome, the theatres were closed, fiestas were forbidden and all good Catholics fasted and abstained from eating meat. However, it had long been established by the Roman pontiffs that the best way to induce a mood of penitence in the populace was to permit a brief period of orgiastic excess before the start of Lent – the eight-day carnival during which all laws were suspended, and, as the German poet Goethe observed when visiting Rome at around this time, 'Anyone can play the fool as much as he likes, and everything is permitted short of murder and violence.'

The Roman carnival baffled not just Goethe but other visitors from northern Europe. Even for Scarpia, who had been absent on military service and so had yet to experience the carnival, the mounting excitement in the Palazzo Comastri as it approached was beyond anything he had known in Palermo. Though Letizia kept her assignations as before, Scarpia found himself banned from her quarters, 'Because there is something I want to be a surprise.' The Chevalier Spinelli was allowed to attend on her, and unusually – presumably under orders from the contessa – advised Scarpia on the kind of costume he should wear at the forthcoming festivities, and offered to obtain a suitable mask.

The carnival started with the ringing of the bell on the Capitol – something otherwise reserved for the death of a pope. The opening ceremony took place around the statue of Marcus Aurelius, after which civic leaders of the city led a procession from the Piazza Venezia along the via del Corso to the Piazza del Popolo – the palaces bedecked with tapestries and carpets hung from the windows, the pavements packed tight with masked spectators in exotic costumes – Turkish janissaries, English sailors, Barbary pirates, Jewish money-lenders, fairy-tale princes, bloodstained banditti, pagan gods, hairy satyrs, innumerable Punchinelli – the hooked-nosed hunch-backed figure from the *commedia dell'arte* – and Harlequins in their black-and-white garb. Only the costume of a priest or a monk was prohibited, and only Jews, prostitutes and priests were forbidden to wear masks.

Behind the civic leaders of the procession down the Corso came a loud brass band, then fantastical floats decorated by fraternities, academies and some of Rome's princely families. Scarpia watched the parade with the Count di Comastri, Prince Paducci, the Chevalier Spinelli and other friends of the family on the stand erected outside the Palazzo Ruspoli, and he now realised what all the excitement had been about; for, seated in a glade of potted palm trees, fronds of sycamore and trellised ivy on a sumptuously deco-rated float drawn by plumed horses was Letizia di Comastri dressed as the pagan goddess Diana. She wore a short, white, belted tunic which showed a large portion of her elegant legs, and around her sat three cherubs – restless toddlers with their mothers, scantily dressed nymphs. In one hand, the goddess held a bow and arrow, while the other held onto the collar of a whippet. Her alabaster limbs were as still as those of a statue, and her face was fixed in a serene smile, as befitted a deity. Only when the float drew level with the Palazzo Ruspoli, did Diana turn her head and wave to her husband, her lover and her friends.

Behind the floats came the coaches of the Roman nobility, then those of the rich Borghese, and closing behind them like the waters released by an opened sluice gate, the delirious crowd, masked and in fancy dress. All behaved with a cheerful impudence and indiscretion. Women carried switches to fend off unwelcome familiarities, or tickle the men whose attention they desired. False lawyers held disputes which others joined in, charging men with grotesque crimes and listing for women their lovers. All joined in the joke; everyone was ready with repartee. There was no respect for rank, which anyway was impossible to discern beneath the costumes and behind the masks. Marchesas and contessas mingled with shop girls and fishwives; princes and dukes with grooms and coachmen. The carnival, wrote another visitor from northern Europe, Madame de Staël, threw 'all mortal men together, turning the nation upside down as though there were no social order any more'.

Gender, too, was thrown into doubt. Men dressed as women and women as men – slim girls in Harlequin costumes, indistinguishable from adolescent boys; older women covering their more mature figures in the garb of a Punchinello; while men of all classes, with plucked eyebrows and powdered cheeks, thrust through the crowd with straw busts beneath their décolleté dresses. 'They caress the men they meet,' wrote Goethe, 'and allow themselves all the familiarities with the women they encounter, as being persons the same as themselves, and for the rest do whatever humour, wit or wantonness suggest.' His disgust weakened in the face of women dressed as

Harlequins: 'in this hermaphrodite figure, it has to be said, they often strike me as particularly charming'.

*

When the float driven by the Comastris' coachmen reached the Palazzo del Popolo, the goddess Diana descended from her throne and returned with her nymphs and cherubs to the Palazzo Comastri, where she was joined by the party from the stand outside the Palazzo Ruspoli for some refreshment. Friends, cousins and of course the *cavalieri serventi* all bombarded the contessa with compliments, which she received with a beatific smile and pouting lips.

The meal did not last long: the carnival was continuing and the whole party sallied out once again. Now the crowds on the Corso had been pushed back onto the pavements and space cleared for the climax of the day's celebrations – the race of the fierce Barbary horses. Seats on stands were hawked by those who built them: '*Luoghi! Luoghi avanti! Luoghi nobili! Luoghi padroni!*' The Count di Comastri and his party, now accompanied by the contessa with Scarpia at her side, returned to their places on the stand outside the Palazzo Ruspoli. A general of the pontifical army led a troop to clear the course. The horses were taken by their grooms to the starting line by the obelisk on the Piazza del Popolo. The rope was dropped, and the horses tore off down the Corso, cheered on by the excited crowd. Scarpia, who felt he had a good eye for horses, could not judge this Barbary breed. The horses flashed past in a moment. Hurrahs were heard from the Piazza di Venezia, and the winning horse, adorned with its prize, the gold-embroidered *palio*, returned in triumph down the Corso.

In the evening came the masked balls, either in the palazzi or in the Alibert theatre, dazzlingly lit up for the occasion. The Comastris went from one to another and Scarpia noticed that when it came to the cotillion or the minuet, Letizia was quite as happy, perhaps happier, to dance with her *cicisbeo brutto*, the Chevalier Spinelli, because like all Romans he took pride in his balletic talent while Scarpia, though he knew the steps, was a Sicilian who thought it effete and affected to emulate the kind of dancer one might see onstage. He did not mind: there were other partners to be seized from the crowd – some known, some unknown, masked women who laughed and flirted and whispered witty inanities, even daring to comment, as they watched the contessa and Spinelli, that while the *cicisbeo brutto* might serve her better on the dance floor, the *cicisbeo bello* was no doubt to be preferred in the arbour of love.

*

For the full eight days, Scarpia was out in the streets with Letizia di Comastri and her small court of friends and admirers. Sometimes, with Letizia, he broke away from the group and they went alone into the side streets that led into the Corso, stopping to watch the impromptu dramas that were played out by mummers – a pregnant girl suddenly giving birth in the gutter, her baby a bundle of straw; a ferocious quarrel between five men that led to a fight with knives and the shedding of blood – the knives made of papier mâché, the blood, red paint. Then there were the battles that flared up when one group of revellers pelted another with sugared almonds, crystallised fruit or, more perniciously, *puzzalona*, pea-sized pieces of volcanic rock rolled in plaster and painted with whitewash.

The last great game of the carnival came on the eve of Ash Wednesday with the *moccoli* – small tapers lit after dark – when everyone's aim was to extinguish the flames of those next to him and keep his own alight. That night the whole of the Corso became a masked ball with everyone determined to squeeze the last drop of fun from the carnival before the chimes of midnight ushered in

Lent. To be without a taper was a capital crime. '*Sia ammazzato chi no porta moccolo!*' Kill anyone without a candle! Paper lanterns hung from the balconies of the palazzi draped with sumptuous fabrics; lamps were placed on top of carriages to light up the street. To keep their tapers out of the reach of those who would stifle them, some tied them to poles, but others countered with wet sponges, also tied to reeds or sticks. The battle was frenzied but cheerful: the blood-curdling threats good-hearted. *Sia ammazzata la bella signora*, cried a masked young man shouting in the rough accent of the street as he pinched between his fingers the flame of Letizia's candle. *Sia ammazzato lei*, countered the contessa as she in turn squashed the top of his taper with the top of her hand. Flints were struck; tapers relit; candlewax spilt over the finest dresses. The battle went on in the surging, jostling, dancing crowd.

Then, as they reached the Palazzo Colonna, there was a concerted assault on the candles and tapers of the Contessa di Comastri and her entourage, and suddenly the group was in dark-ness. Letizia was parted from her *cicisbeo bello* by a cross-current in the surging crowd – Scarpia was swept away and only saved from falling by a slim young man and a tall woman, both masked, the woman elegantly dressed as a Madame de Pompadour but with a flat chest and manly hands, the youth slim in a black-and-white Harlequin costume, but for all his virile manner unable to hide the swell of a bosom.

Their tapers, too, had been extinguished, and like Scarpia they were carried by the strong current of humanity into the eddy of the small Piazza di San Marcello. Like the survivors of a shipwreck, the three mounted the steps leading to the church – crowded, but above the throng. The door to the church was open; the woman led them in and, after a brief genuflection, went to relight her taper at the stand of votive candles in front of the statue of the Virgin. Scarpia and his young companion followed. They, also, lit their tapers. The masked woman turned to go back to the fray; the young man followed with Scarpia behind him, but, in the darkness between the inner and outer doors of the church, the Harlequin turned, snuffed out first Scarpia's candle, then his own, and enfolded him in his arms. '*Si ammazzato Scarpia*,' he whispered, pressing his soft bosom against Scarpia's chest, and giving him a long but inexperienced kiss. Then he was gone, and when Scarpia came out onto the piazza, both the Harlequin and the Pompadour had disappeared into the crowd.

4

The young count Palmieri, who had somehow learned of Scarpia's position in the Comastri household, warned Scarpia against Letizia di Comastri, whom he knew only by repute, and also against women in general. This came in one of his periodic rebukes of his gaoler for serving tyranny and injustice. 'And all for what? A monthly salary of fifteen scudi? A papal bauble – the Order of the Gold Spur? And the favours of the Contessa di Comastri – a bored, fashionable woman with whom you think you are in love? Have you not read the Scripture? Does it not say in the Book of Proverbs *Give not thy strength to women*? And don't think it is just your physical strength the prophet is talking about – those pleasant exertions – I know all about them – I know they have their charm; but they sap your spirit just as much as your body. They are blinkers to hide the suffering and injustice which surrounds you, a sedative for your conscience, a ruse of those with power to disarm a potential adversary, a man who, if he were not distracted by love, might see through the preposterous claims of divine right and the superstitious buttresses of exploitation and injustice.'

'But you are married,' said Scarpia.

'Yes, I have a wife,' said Palmieri. 'And I have a child. Both are a ball and chain. She visits me. You have seen her. She begs me to recant, to return home; to conform, to wear a powdered wig, like you; to live quietly and comfortably, to go to Mass, to pretend to believe. And it is a temptation, of course it is a temptation. To exchange this cold cell for the warmth of a woman, the embrace of my child. But it would be cowardice – as shameful as deserting one's friends on the field of battle.'

The young Contessa Palmieri was permitted to visit her husband Vicenzo on Sundays and high feast days. They remained under guard. Sometimes she came with her two-year-old son, sometimes she came alone. Out of courtesy to his new friend, Scarpia would meet her at the entrance to the lower ramparts of the Castel Sant'Angelo, excuse her a search of her person, and escort her up the steep tunnel through the bowels of Hadrian's Mausoleum to the fortifications perched on the top. To save his friend embarrassment, he would not himself be present at their encounters and would assign a Swiss guard or German mercenary who would understand little of what they said. Their reports suggested that in fact they were mostly silent: she wept while Palmieri spoke to her gently as a patient teacher might talk to a child.

Simona Palmieri was dark and thin, her face pretty but fixed in an expression of sadness. Following Vicenzo's conviction she had returned to live with her parents and saw no one – disgraced as the wife of a man condemned by the Inquisition. Scarpia took pity on her and, then at the height of his conceit as a lover, imagined that it was a man's embraces that she most missed. After a visit to her husband, Scarpia suggested that they meet to discuss what might be done to help him. She came at night to his lodgings. They talked and when Scarpia drew her towards him, she did not resist him. She succumbed like a corpse and responded to his embraces with reflex movements and joyless cries. She then lay beside him, inanimate, staring at the ceiling – no words, no smile, no expression of hatred or satisfaction or complicity or disgust – saying nothing even as she got off the bed and readjusted her clothes.

*

Now, for the second time in his life, Scarpia felt remorse. He had killed the Turk because he had taken Celestina, whom Scarpia had felt was his. Now he had taken Simona, who rightfully belonged to Count Palmieri. *Post coitus*, the reasoning that had preceded the act – the thought that he was somehow doing his imprisoned friend a good deed by caring for his wife, and that it was a kindness to fulfil her yearning for love – he realised had been the false promises of the Devil. When making love to Letizia a day or two later, he thought of Simona, then of Celestina, and felt a sudden anger against all women for drawing men into the abyss of brute passion and, as if to punish them, made love to Letizia with a brutality he had never shown before.

Letizia was delighted and, a week later, when they met again, she told Scarpia, bashfully, how during those seven days she had only thought of their last encounter, and how he was quite right to have been so brutal because she was shameless and should be punished; and that he must pre-empt her resistance and render her powerless by tying her hands to the bedposts with the cords that held back the curtains – she tripped across the room to unhook them from the wall – and she should lie on her stomach, splayed on the bed, because she did not deserve to look into his eyes.

Scarpia did as he was told, but felt humiliated making love to her in this contorted fashion. Again, he felt angry and treated her with a roughness that only seemed to excite her more. Her cries of pleasure became intolerably irritating, but, because she was faced down into a pillow, they were muffled; and suddenly Scarpia heard other grunts chime in with his and hers – grunts that came from the painting of the Madonna on the wall.

Terrified that this was some terrible trick of the Devil, Scarpia leapt from the bed, and went over to the painting of the Madonna. It was silent, but from a hole in the wall the size of a pea, camouflaged by the bamboo pattern of the paper, came the sound of hoarse breathing. Scarpia seized his sword and thrust it through the hole. There was a cry, then scuffling sounds on the other side.

'Oh no, Scarpia. Don't kill him.'

He turned back to Letizia, still tied to the bedposts and twisting to face him. 'Kill who? Has someone been watching us?'

'Untie me, Scarpia. Let me explain.'

Scarpia threw down his sword on the bed, its blade marked with plaster and a trace of blood. He unknotted the cords, and roughly pulled Letizia by her arms to face him. 'Who was there? What has been going on?'

Letizia raised the sheet to cover her breasts: her eyes, avoiding his, looked with alarm at his sword. 'Have you killed him? Oh, *Santa Maria*. Please God, you have not killed him.'

'Killed who?'

'He is a silly old man. He has few pleasures. What harm did it do to us?'

'He? Who? Prince Paducci?'

'Of course, of course. Who else? And you have killed him!'

'I hope my sword went straight into his eye.'

'Oh no. It is too terrible. Why are you so cruel? He liked to watch, that is all.'

'And you knew this? You let him?'

'Of course – why not? He is so good to me. It cost us nothing, after all. And why, when there is so much pleasure...' – now she gave a timid smile through her tears – 'why not share it? And how much better that a rich old fool should give me his money rather than some whore?'

'Some whore?' cried Scarpia. 'You have played the whore and dragged me down into Hell.'

A new rush of tears. 'How can you say that, Vitellio? He has never touched me. If I am a whore, then I am your whore. And you know that the count, my husband, gives me very little money and so all the things we enjoy are thanks to Paducci – our stakes at faro, the carriages, our little dinners together, these rooms, this bed? Could you have paid for these things out of your pay as a soldier? Didn't you realise that our happiness came at a price?'

'You have humiliated me,' said Scarpia. 'I am dishonoured. Undone.'

'Oh, come here, you poor provincial,' said Letizia, opening her arms and letting the sheet fall from her breasts. And, filled with self-loathing, Scarpia went to her and, as her limbs closed around him in a now conventional fashion, he resumed what he had begun – his mind working at variance to his body, but taking an oath that he was making love to the Contessa di Comastri for the very last time.

5

The papal treasurer, Fabrizio Ruffo, missed nothing, and, when Scarpia asked to be transferred to some garrison outside Rome, he knew why. At a number of *conversazioni* Ruffo had noticed the mixed looks the contessa had directed at her *cicisbeo bello* – one moment pleading, the next affronted; and, in Scarpia, a disinclination to meet her eyes, a look of gloomy disdain. He had noticed, too, that Prince Paducci did not appear at the Palazzo Comastri: it was said that he had been sick, but when he did return the only symptom of an illness was a livid scar down the side of his cheek, poorly hidden by paste and powder. Scarpia was now rarely to be seen at the Palazzo Comastri: Ruffo had heard the rumours that his protégé had been dismissed from his post as *il bello* in the contessa's triumvirate of *cicisbei*, rumours apparently confirmed when Letizia was seen in her carriage on the Corso with the young Chevalier Malaspina.

The Treasurer Ruffo also knew of the long periods of time that Scarpia spent in the company of Count Palmieri, and he had become anxious that the gaoler was becoming infected by his prisoner's ideas. Ruffo judged Scarpia to be solid in his faith, sound in his instincts and intelligent enough to parry an atheist's argument; but he also knew that Scarpia preferred to act rather than to think; that he was happier on horseback in the open air than in a library reading a book; and that for all his success as a soldier, and the tender rewards he had enjoyed for his courage and good looks, he remained socially ill at ease. Satan might not be able to capture his soul with intellectual arguments, but he might be vulnerable to the force of fashion, which can be as powerful in the realm of ideas as it is in the choice of women's clothes. How many young men, Ruffo asked himself, had become Freemasons not because they accepted the brotherhood's absurd claims of descent from the builders of the Temple of Solomon and the Knights Templar, or the incoherent mumbo-jumbo about the Supreme Being, but because it was fashionable in Paris and Vienna?

Scarpia's request suited Ruffo, who, on taking office and command of the pontifical army, had seen the vulnerability of the Papal States. He had ordered the construction of new coastal fortifications, and though Scarpia might have liked to have been sent further away – to Ancona, perhaps, or to Bologna – Ruffo persuaded him to go to Civitavecchia, where he needed a man he could trust.

*

Ruffo did not know of the shame now felt by Scarpia when he entered the cell of Count Palmieri; that his protégé dared not look his prisoner in the eye, and lived in daily terror that he would be told by his wife that she had been seduced. Worse, the crime he had committed he repeated; he summoned Simona Palmieri to his lodgings and, mutely, she came. Why? Did she hope to buy with her body some advantage for her husband? Scarpia had told her he had done all he could to ameliorate her husband's condition, and had no power to hasten his release. She seemed to accept this, but came all the same. He got little joy from their encounters; the words of St Paul kept ringing through his head: *I find myself doing the very things I hate*. And she seemed to court degradation. Was it to confirm her sense of worthlessness as a wife abandoned in favour of mankind? This was conjecture. They rarely spoke. She came and went like a ghost. It was to escape from Simona as much as from Letizia that Scarpia left Rome.

Looking down over the tiled roofs of Civitavecchia from the Michelangelo Fortress, Scarpia remembered the night he had spent at an inn after landing from Spain. Then he had been disgraced over a woman; now, too, he was disgraced in his own eyes over two others. Here he would lead a chaste and spartan life, devoted to his duties – a military monk, like a Knight of Malta. He confessed his sins to a priest in a small parish church in Civitavecchia who gave Scarpia a harsh penance – daily Mass for a month. 'The wages of sin are death,' he said in a thin but vehement voice. 'Adultery! With two women – one depraved and corrupt, the other helpless and at your mercy. You feel shame? Good. But don't deceive your-self that these are peccadillos. Unrepented, they would send you to Hell. If you cannot contain yourself, you must find a wife, because, as the Apostle Paul teaches, *it is better to marry than to burn*. Find a wife, young man, and sin no more.'

Scarpia suspected that the priest was a Jansenist, banished to this poor parish by the Vicar General; but he was glad all the same, since the priest's severity matched his remorse. As to his advice to find a wife, Scarpia decided it would be no sin to ignore it. Palmieri was right. *Give not thy strength to women.* And what kind of wife could he marry now that he had fallen from favour at the Palazzo Comastri? And at the Palazzo Marcisano, too, he had sensed a new *froideur.* The princess seemed uncomfortable in his presence, and the prince, who had once been so welcoming, looked annoyed whenever he saw Scarpia coming through his door. Only Ludovico welcomed him, but now with a shade of embarrassment in his smile.

Why had he lost favour with the Marcisanos? Was it because of his liaison with the Contessa di Comastri? Had the Chevalier Spinelli let it be known how Prince Paducci had gained the scar on his left cheek? Was Letizia disparaging him now that he was no longer her lover? Easily imagining himself the object of tittering ridicule, Scarpia decided to absent himself from the Roman palazzi altogether and hope for a war in which he could win glory or, if there was no war, demonstrate his abilities as an officer. He might then be asked by a king to reorganise his armed forces like the Englishman, John Acton, in Naples. Gaining a reputation for efficiency was all he could expect from his service in the pontifical army because, for all Ruffo's reforms and extravagant expenditure, there was little chance that the Papal States could confront an invading army or repel the fleet of a major power like Britain or France.

*

Then, at ten one morning, Scarpia was called from the guardroom of the Michelangelo Fortress by Spoletta to say that he had a visitor from Rome, Prince Ludovico di Marcisano. Scarpia was confused. He wanted at first to say that he was too busy to receive him, but the colonel who was in command, hearing that a carriage had drawn up at the gates of the fortress with the coat of arms of the Marcisanos on its door, at once sent an adjutant to tell Scarpia that, should the prince be so inclined, he should invite his illustrious guest to lunch. Scarpia therefore went down to the courtyard, through the gates and over the drawbridge to the coach where he was told by the liveried coachman that his master was stretching his legs. Scarpia turned towards the port, saw Ludovico, and went to join him.

'Ah, Vitellio.' Ludovico turned away from the ships he had been studying and laid his hand on Scarpia's shoulder – a half-embrace. 'Is it inconvenient, this visit? It was such a lovely day and I love the smell of the sea.'

'The stench of the docks?'

'No worse than the stench of the streets of Rome. And to more purpose. Here, things are done. Boats are tarred and refitted. Galleons. Fishing smacks.'

'The fishing smacks are more seaworthy than the galleons,' said Scarpia.

'Yes. We Romans are not great sailors. Our ancestors were, perhaps, but now that inheritance has been dissipated. We are spoilt, irretrievably spoilt.' He started to walk along the quay. 'Thank Providence that you were not born a prince, my dear Vitellio. You might think it is enviable to come into the world invested with titles and properties and great wealth. But they define you before you have had a chance to define yourself. Whereas you – you could be anyone, do anything.'

'My freedom is constrained by my means,' said Scarpia.

'Of course. You are not rich – at least not yet. But you are able and courageous and, I would say, lucky, because older men like Ruffo, who have no children, see in you their younger selves and want to help you. His Holiness has his nephew, Duke Braschi Onesti, and Treasurer Ruffo, it seems to me, sees you as a kinsman who has come from the Kingdom of the Two Sicilies to make his way in Rome – to do what the Romans themselves are too lazy and too cowardly to do.'

'Treasurer Ruffo has certainly been good to me,' said Scarpia. 'And he will do more...'

'If there is more to be done, I would like to do it for myself.'

'Of course, of course. Because you are brave, and audacious and handsome, which no doubt helps because one is always pleased when someone of an agreeable appearance enters the room; that is just human nature. I prefer pretty women to ugly women, though the ugly ones are often more amusing; they have to try harder; but they can be spiteful, too, because they are always aggrieved that nature has treated them unfairly. Not that in our circle a girl's face is her fortune; her fortune is her fortune; but having a pretty face certainly helps. My sister Paola, for instance, has both a fortune and a pretty face and that no doubt accounts for the long line of suitors – a very long line...'

They had come to a café which, because of the warm weather, had an awning over the tables and chairs set out on the pavement. It was inelegant; its patrons were rough; but Ludovico sauntered in as if it was the Veneziano on the Corso, went to one of the tables and, studying the simple wooden chair with an intelligent curiosity, drew it out and sat down. Scarpia sat down next to him. A girl, trembling at the sight of such notable customers – a young man with an elegant coat, breeches, silk stockings and gold buckles on his shoes together with an officer in a uniform with shining buttons and golden epaulettes – melted when Ludovico looked kindly at her and asked for a pot of coffee and perhaps some bread and jam. 'I set off early,' he said not to Scarpia but to the girl, as if to explain his request for such a late *prima colazione*.

'What was I saying?' Ludovico then asked Scarpia.

'The long line of suitors for your sister.'

'Yes. But she has refused them all.'

'*She* has refused them? Surely it is up to her father and mother to decide.'

Ludovico gave a faint smile. 'I am afraid we live in changing times. Or so Paola tells us. She has read novels – *The Sorrows of Young Werther*, *Julie – la nouvelle Héloïse*. She laughs at the Pope's Index of Prohibited Books. And she has read some theology. She tells my poor parents that a marriage is only valid where there is the consent of both parties. And she will not consent. There has been a tempest in our household. My father threatens her with a convent, but she is not intimidated. She says she has spent most of her life up until now in a convent and some are quite comfortable and it is better to live with other women than with a man she dislikes.'

'But surely she can find one among the many?'

'The many suitors? She says not. But there is one whom she says she *would* marry.'

'Then let her marry him.'

'He is not a suitor.'

'But he exists? He is not a chimera?'

'Oh yes, he exists. And she says she loves him.'

'Well, then, let her marry him.'

'We are inclined to do so even though he is not a man my parents would have chosen.'

'But if they don't agree to a marriage, she might run off with him.'

'Or worse.'

'Worse?'

'There was a case recently of a girl who hired two bullies to throw her father out of the window because he would not let her marry the man she loved.'

'Paola would not do that.'

'Perhaps not. But she is very strong-minded.'

'So we see.'

'Even for a husband she loved, she would be a handful.'

Scarpia thought of Paola, then said: 'I cannot believe that any man who was lucky enough to be loved by Paola would regard her as too much. Does he know? Has he been told?'

'Not yet.'

'But he must know Paola.'

'Yes, he knows Paola.'

'And does he love her?'

The girl came with the *prima colazione*. Ludovico stirred sugar into the thick black coffee in his cup. Her presence imposed a lull in their conversation, and gave time for Scarpia to seek an answer a question that had been lurking in his own mind: why had Ludovico come all the way from Rome to tell him about his family's difficulties with his sister? How did this fit in with the coldness and confusion shown to him by the Marcisanos during his recent appearances at their receptions? It was therefore with a low, hoarse voice that, when the girl had gone, he repeated his question. 'And the man? What are his feelings for her?'

Ludovico looked up from his coffee. 'Only you can answer that, Vitellio. You are the man she loves.'

*

Ludovico di Marcisano had risen early to come to Civitavecchia and was tired. With exquisite condescension, he accepted Scarpia's invitation to rest in his quarters and, after feeling the hard mattress on his bed with the same look of bemused curiosity he had directed at the chair in the café, lay down. He awoke an hour later and was taken on a tour of the ramparts by Scarpia and then, gently declining the colonel's invitation to join him and the other officers for lunch, went with Scarpia to an eating house in the town. They did not return at once to the morning's topic of conversation. Instead, they talked about travel. Scarpia told Ludovico about his youth in Naples and then Sicily, and then about his brief stay in Spain.

'Is the story true,' asked Ludovico, 'that you landed in Algiers during the bombardment to rescue a girl you loved?'

'For which I was cashiered,' said Scarpia, 'and learned...' He hesitated.

'Not to put your heart before your head?'

'That women are unpredictable. They change their mind.'

'They do indeed, and that in my view shows the wisdom of the Church in establishing marriage as an institution. Women change their minds. You have perhaps noticed this among Romans as well as Spaniards? And of course men too can change their minds. But fathers and mothers cannot change their minds about their children. They are there and marriage must endure for a lifetime for the sake of the offspring, and all the titles and property that are bequeathed to the offspring, and future generations.'

'Of course.'

'A great mistake is being made by the Americans, I think – I have read about the constitution they are preparing for their republic. They say that each citizen has the right to life, liberty and the pursuit of happiness. Life, of course, but liberty? How can a country be governed without some form of constraint? And, as I understand it, this liberty that is to be enshrined in their constitution will not mean freedom for their slaves or a vote for their wives or indentured servants. We are born into a certain condition. A man might wish he was a woman or a woman a man, but he is what he is. As to the pursuit of happiness – how is happiness to be defined? Are wealth and honours a source of happiness? I have known miserable princes and happiness in the poor. Indeed, it is the view of the French ambassador, Cardinal de Bernis, that Rome is the happiest place in the world precisely because no one strives to be richer than anyone else. All accept the estate into which they are born, and all recognise that they are children of God in whose eyes the prince is no better than his coachman and it is the duty of the rich to serve the poor. And yet love ... I can understand my sister. It would be good for a woman to have a husband whom she loves, and be sincere in the vows she makes in a church. All the infidelity we see – men with their mistresses, women with their lovers – is because they marry for advantage, not for love. Paola says this and she is right. And even my father is coming round to that view. They sense that there is change in the air and anyway are quite terrified of Paola and know that if they thwart her she is quite capable – well, not of throwing them out of a window, perhaps, but eloping with the man she loves, if he is so inclined –' this with a sideways glance at Scarpia – 'or pretending to have a religious vocation, which, of course, the Church would have to respect.'

'How can I marry your sister?' said Scarpia. 'I am no one. I have nothing.'

'All that has been – or rather, I should say, *could* be arranged. My father has spoken to Treasurer Ruffo, who understands these things. He would not want his protégé simply to be bought by a wilful heiress. He has told me to tell you that if the idea of becoming the husband of my sister is something you might consider, then arrangements could be made to put you – if not on an equal footing, then on a footing that would be less obviously *un*equal. He has the ear of the Pope, and one of the advantages of being the Pope is that as the vicar of Christ he can do what he likes. Our aristocracy may be composed of ancient families – though not all are as ancient as they pretend – but popes themselves, and cardinals, often come from the humblest background. This is not France with a *noblesse d'épée* and *noblesse de robe*. If popes can make emperors, kings, princes and dukes like Duke Braschi Onesti, our present pontiff could, should Ruffo ask him, make a Sicilian gentleman a baron and endow him with a property that would provide him with means.

He would do it, I like to think, not just to please Ruffo, but as a favour to a family which of course he knows well.'

*

At four in the afternoon, Ludovico returned to Rome. 'Will you call on us?' he asked through the window of his coach. 'There is a *conversazione* on Thursday evening. Paola will be there. She will know that I have spoken to you. Of course you must feel under no obligation to marry her. You may not be an American but you have the right to pursue happiness as you see fit, and you may feel that by marrying a Marcisano you would be less free. But if you decide to accept our proposal, then know that we would be happy to welcome you into our family.'

6

The next day, Scarpia was summoned to Rome by Treasurer Ruffo. At the Quirinale Palace, he waited in the antechamber with the twenty or thirty others clutching their petitions but, as soon as the secretary saw him, he was taken into Ruffo's presence. The treasurer greeted him warmly and immediately got down to business. 'I have been told by Prince di Marcisano,' he said, 'that he is ready to countenance a marriage between you and his daughter Paola.'

'So I understand.'

'I must ask you on your conscience whether you have done anything to seduce the young woman – not necessarily in body but in mind.'

'Most certainly not. I was … my affections were directed elsewhere.'

'It is possible for one's affections and ambitions to go in different directions.'

'The possibility of marrying Princess di Marcisano never crossed my mind, Monsignor. I am as taken aback as you are.'

'Does that mean that you are inclined to refuse?'

'I would defer to your advice, Monsignor.'

Ruffo looked perplexed. 'I am not a priest, Scarpia. I cannot guide your conscience. But if you are not called by God to a celibate life – and it seems clear that you are not – then you should find a wife. The Church teaches that marriage is a sacrament, but it is not a sacrament that is conferred by a priest. The couple are joined by God when they exchange their vows. But their choice must be freely given. I do not mean by that that they should base their judgements on the heady feelings described as love in romances by irreligious Frenchmen. Quite to the contrary – such feelings are fickle and so are a bad basis for a lifelong union. You should choose a woman you can love with a sensible affection, free from passion, and above all one you can respect. You should not be influenced solely by worldly considerations, though here clearly there are substantial advantages of that kind. However, there are ways to lessen that temptation and these I have taken. The Holy Father, at my request, has agreed to confer on you the title of Baron and the fief of Rubaso that is at his disposal: the last of the d'Angelos has died without issue, leaving his estate to be disposed of as His Holiness sees fit. It will bring you an annual income of five thousand scudi a year.'

'But why –' Scarpia began, astonished at what was proposed.

Ruffo held up his hand. 'The Holy Father understands perfectly the position into which one of the leading families in Rome has been put by a wilful daughter. He does not wish to see the Marcisanos humiliated by the marriage of their daughter to a pauper. Therefore it will be as Baron Scarpia of Rubaso that you will either accept or refuse what Prince di Marcisano proposes. The thought of her fortune should not tempt you because you will be well able to do without it. No one will blame you if you baulk at the thought of marrying such a strong-willed girl. But you may feel, as I do – I who have known her since she was a child – that Paola di Marcisano is an exceptional young woman whom any man would be glad to make his wife.'

*

On the Thursday following this conversation with Ruffo, Scarpia attended the *conversazione* in the Palazzo Marcisano. The prince and princess greeted him with a tentative friendliness; Ludovico took him by the arm and led him to a table to offer him an ice cream with the same exquisite courtesy he had shown when offering him his sister. 'You have spoken to Ruffo?' he asked.

'Yes.'

'Is what he proposes to your satisfaction?'

'I am to be a baron to make me a worthy match.'

'So I understand. You will gain an income, and perhaps a wife, but you will lose your liberty. A baron married to a princess is inevitably constrained.'

'I admire your sister,' said Scarpia. 'I will happily exchange a lonely liberty for her hand.'

'Good. And from that admiration will come love, perhaps.'

'Of course.'

'You must talk to her. I don't know where she is.'

Both young men turned to face the crowded room. 'I suspect that much of the chatter is about you,' said Ludovico. 'Word of the match has leaked out.' They crossed the room. No one yet congratulated Scarpia, but the faces that at previous receptions had been indifferent or even hostile now smiled. Neither the Contessa di Comastri nor the Chevalier Spinelli nor Prince Paducci were present. Ludovico stopped to talk to a cousin; Scarpia walked on and at the end of the gallery saw Paola talking to her friend,

Graziella di Pozzo. She was wearing an embroidered yellow silk dress with a tight waist and modest lace-trimmed décolletage. He went up to her. She blushed. 'Signor Scarpia. How fortunate for us that you were able to take time off your duties to pay us a visit.'

Scarpia bowed. 'Fortunate for me, Principessa.'

'You know the Principessa di Pozzo, I think?'

'I do.'

Graziella di Pozzo gave a slight curtsy, glanced at Paola to see whether she wanted her to remain or to go, and judging that she wanted her to go, said: 'Will you excuse me? I have to see if my mother is still standing.'

Paola took hold of her arm. 'Wait,' she said as if alarmed at being left alone with Scarpia. And then, releasing her grip on the girl's arm: 'No, your poor mother. I will see you later.'

With a quick look at Scarpia, then a furtive smile at Paola, Graziella turned away into the crowd of guests. Paola looked at Scarpia and said in a fast whisper: 'You don't have to talk to me. You needn't say anything. You didn't have to come.'

'Paola…'

'Well, we can't really talk *here*. Come, we'll look at the Raphael, though that won't deceive anyone because they'll know a soldier doesn't care much about art.'

Scarpia followed her into the side gallery where some of the finest paintings of the Marcisano collection were displayed and they stood as if studying the Madonna and Child. They said nothing. Paola's breast was heaving as if she had just run a race. 'Is this how you mean to go on?' said Scarpia.

'To go on?'

'Insulting your husband?'

'Well, *do* you care about art?'

'I recognise beauty, I like to think. And not just in art.'

Paola blushed. 'In the Contessa di Comastri, perhaps?'

Scarpia said nothing.

'If we are to marry, you must promise never to see that bitch again.'

'That won't be difficult,' said Scarpia. 'I will make that promise, and many more.'

'Do you *want* to marry me?'

'Yes.'

'You never said so. After the carnival ... You surely remember *that*. Or perhaps you kissed so many women that I was just one among many.'

'You were the Harlequin?'

'Who else?'

'And the woman with you?'

She laughed. 'Ludovico. He loves to dress up as a woman.'

'I wasn't sure that it was you.'

'Did you not suspect?'

'It crossed my mind.'

'Why did you not ask?'

'Because if I had been wrong, you would have despised me for my conceit, and if I had been right, well, what good would it have served? Whatever I felt or might have felt, I was in no position to ask for your hand, nor ever would be; and for me to engage your affections...'

'No, quite. Far better to engage those of a married woman.'

'Paola...'

'Well, it's the custom, I suppose,' she said, 'so I can't blame you, but it was painful.'

'If I had known –'

'You couldn't have known because, while it is the custom for married women to make eyes at handsome young Sicilians, it is not the custom for an *un*married girl to do the same. We are expected to wait to be bartered by our parents – to make some *good* marriage that will somehow please the families involved and the couple in question have little say in the matter.' She turned to face Scarpia: there were tears in her eyes. 'But you can imagine how feeble and foppish they all are. All they think about is their *figura* – whether their horses and carriages are finer than those of their friends; whether they cut a dash on the Corso. None would ever *fight* or *kill* except in some stupid duel, and then they'd avoid it because the blood might stain their clothes. They wanted me to marry someone like that and have children by someone like that and the thought of it repelled me. They say it's because I've been reading romantic novels, and perhaps that's true. Perhaps the French these days have opened our eyes to a lot of things – to the importance of qualities other than a pedigree and a carriage and what people are wearing at Versailles: and you are the only man I know who is *not* like that and I thought I could respect and even love a man like you, even if he was a provincial, and then I thought that perhaps a man like you wasn't to be found. That in fact it was *you* I could love and respect, and did love and respect, despite your absurd and abject role as the *cicisbeo* of the Contessa di Comastri – but it was just because it was so absurd and abject that proved you were different, and that if you had a companion, a friend, a wife who was Roman, she could ... I don't know...' Paola's tears had now overflowed from her lids and were making wet furrows on her cheeks.

'Listen, Paola,' said Scarpia. 'If I did not think of you as a wife, it was because it never occurred to me that it would be possible that we should marry. Now it is possible and comes as a great blessing. Do you remember when we danced, that first time? How your mother ordered you to take me onto the floor? At once I saw that you were a girl quite unlike any other, but you were quite gauche and scrawny – straight from the convent. Now you remain a girl unlike any other, but you have also become the most beautiful woman in Rome. I would never, *never* have become fond of Letizia if I had imagined that you might be mine. And that, and other things, I now bitterly regret and would ask you to forgive if we are to marry.'

'Other things?' Paola gave him a look of intense scrutiny. 'Well, best not to ask about that. A past is a past and men are allowed one and women are not. And, if I am honest with myself, I would not want to marry a man who had lived like a monk. But now I think we have looked at the Madonna for long enough. We had better rejoin the company.'

'As *fidanzati*?'

She smiled. 'You haven't asked for my hand.'

Scarpia gave a slight bow. 'Will you marry me, Principessa di Marcisano?'

Paola returned his bow with a gentle curtsy. 'I will, Baron Scarpia. It will be a great honour to be your wife.'

PART TWO

Seven

I

On 5 May 1789, the French Estates General convened at Versailles, summoned by King Louis XVI to deal with the bankruptcy of the state. It did not seem at first to Pope Pius VI or his Secretary of State, Cardinal Zelada, that there was any reason to feel concern for the interests of the Church. The First Estate was made up of Catholic clergy – rich bishops and impoverished priests, the Second of the Nobility and the Third of the commons. On 17 June, the Third Estate, which represented 96 per cent of the population of France, proclaimed itself a National Assembly. Two days later, two-thirds of the clergy from the First Estate voted to join it. A Catholic prelate, the Archbishop of Vienne, was chosen to preside over a committee appointed to draw up a new constitution.

Reports of the proceedings of the Estates General, sent to Rome by the papal nuncio in Paris, Archbishop Antonio Dugnani, first caused a measure of alarm when, at the end of July, he described how a mob had stormed the royal fortress in Paris, the Bastille. That alarm turned to dismay as the summer turned into autumn and further dispatches from Archbishop Dugnani reported the abolition of feudal privileges, a Declaration of the Rights of Man, and, in November, the nationalisation of the property of the Church.

It seemed inconceivable to Pope Pius VI that a Catholic king, Louis XVI, could countenance such measures; however, he was advised by the French ambassador to the Holy See, Cardinal de Bernis, that perhaps King Louis had little choice.

In February 1790, all religious orders in France not engaged in education or charitable work were suppressed and their property sequestered by the state. Such suppressions and sequestrations had happened before under the Emperor Joseph in Austria and under Ferdinand in the Kingdom of the Two Sicilies: they did not endanger the practice of the Catholic religion and only frayed at the edges the authority of the Pope. More serious was the drawing up by the new Constituent Assembly in Paris of a Civil Constitution of the Clergy in July of 1790, which stated that all bishops and priests, like deputies, should be elected; and that the Church in France was to sever all links with the Pope. The clergy were obliged to take an oath of loyalty to this Civil Constitution – in other words, to abjure the Pope – with fines and imprisonment for those who refused.

What were the priests to do? Guidance was sought from Rome. Pius temporised, hoping to placate the revolutionaries, but by March of 1791 it had become clear that no compromise was possible. Pius therefore issued an Apostolic Brief condemning the Civil Constitution: any priest who took the oath was to be suspended and, if he had already taken the oath but did not now repent and recant, would be excommunicated from the Catholic Church.

The French Foreign Minister refused to accept the brief when it was delivered by the papal nuncio, Archbishop Dugnani. Diplomatic relations between Paris and Rome were ruptured. The revolutionary government ordered the seizure of the papal city of Avignon and laws were passed condemning priests who refused to take the oath to penal servitude in Guiana. Most of the French bishops remained loyal to the Pope and so too did two-thirds of the lower clergy.

In Paris, priests, monks and nuns were arrested and interned in monasteries and convents now serving as gaols. On 2 September, at three in the afternoon, a crowd broke into the Carmelite convent off the rue de Vaurigard and slaughtered one hundred and fifty priests, among them the Archbishop of Arles. The massacre spread to other prisons throughout Paris and continued for five days. Two hundred and twenty-five priests and five bishops were among the fourteen hundred killed.

This atrocity caused consternation in Rome and increased from a trickle to a flood the flow of fugitives from revolutionary France. In the spring of 1791, the two maiden aunts of King Louis XVI, the Princesses Marie Adelaide and Victoire Marie, had sought asylum in Rome. They were followed by other aristocrats and, after the September massacres, bishops and priests. The city was overwhelmed by refugees: all religious institutions were asked by the Pope to take in their share. Treasurer Ruffo, to finance the relief, was obliged to draw 500,000 thalers from the papal reserves. And for the first time, the term 'Jacobin' was heard on the lips of the refugees to describe members of the political club in Paris based in a former Dominican priory on the rue Saint-Jacques – the via Jacobus. The Jacobins, led by Maximilien de Robespierre, controlled an influential faction in the National Convention and pushed through laws that appealed to the sanguinary passions of the Parisian mob.

By the summer of 1791, it had become clear that the revolution in France could only be defeated by the intervention of outside powers. Already many aristocrats had fled across the River Rhine and in June of 1791 King Louis and his family had fled from Paris to join them. They were stopped at Varennes and brought back to Paris. The Emperor of Austria and King of Prussia warned the revolutionary government of grave consequences if any harm should come to the King and Queen of France. Enraged, the revolutionary government declared war on Austria and invaded the Netherlands, then under Austrian rule. The French army was driven back. A Prussian army invaded France from Koblenz, quickly captured the fortresses of Longwy and Verdun, and threatened Paris. However, it was stopped at Valmy and, with winter approaching, withdrew back across the Rhine.

The revolutionaries were exultant. They had not defeated the Prussians, but checking their advance had shown that the enemy's discipline and professionalism could be matched by fervour and zeal. The National Convention called for a general mobilisation of all male citizens: for the first time in European history a government imposed universal conscription and raised an army of 300,000 men. Led by the Jacobins, the government also turned on the enemy within. The monarchy was abolished, France proclaimed a republic and the king who had conspired against his people was tried, condemned and decapitated by the newly invented killing machine, the guillotine. His wife, Marie Antoinette, died on the same scaffold on the Place de la Revolution nine months later.

*

Giovanni Angelo Braschi, now seventy-five years old, had reigned as Pope Pius VI for seventeen years. In the course of his long term of office, he had had his differences with obstreperous monarchs, but nothing had prepared him for the calamities that had overcome the Church in France. The Pope could but hope and pray that the coalition of powers formed against revolutionary France – Austria, Prussia and Britain – would prevail, restoring both the monarchy and the rights of the Church. He did not join the coalition – there was as yet no threat to the Papal States – but he saw with alarm that French troops, at war with Savoy, had taken the town of Nice on the Mediterranean coast. The road was now open into Italy. What if a revolutionary army should march on Rome? Who would defend the city and the Vicar of Christ? The garrison of the Castel Sant'Angelo? His Swiss Guard?

Hopes were raised in Rome when French royalists seized Toulon and opened the port to a British fleet under Admiral Hood; but then, in December 1793, after a three-month siege by the French republicans, a young Corsican artillery officer, Napoleon Bonaparte, had retaken the city. The British navy withdrew, leaving the French masters of the Mediterranean. The supply of grain to Civitavecchia was now disrupted. Bread became scarce and what was available was adulterated. Discontent was directed against Treasurer Ruffo, who had spent so much money on useless defences. What was the point of making Civitavecchia impregnable if ships carrying supplies upon which Rome depended could be intercepted by the French on the open sea?

In September, a French fleet under Admiral La Touche-Tréville had sailed into the Bay of Naples and, under threat of bombardment, King Ferdinand had been forced to recognise the government that had so recently executed his wife's sister, Marie Antoinette. Would the Pope be obliged to do the same? Pope Pius wrote to the Russian tsarina, Catherine, begging her to send a Russian navy into the Mediterranean: 'We have neither troops nor ships.' Some cardinals urged him to prepare to flee from Rome. He refused. 'My post is by the tomb of St Peter.' Nor would he recognise a republic that had murdered so many bishops and priests.

The pontiff, however, could not avoid the realities of the changed balance of power. When two French artists living in Rome were arrested by the papal police for wearing the tricolour cockade and erecting a statue entitled *Liberty overcoming Fanaticism*, the new French ambassador who had replaced Cardinal de Bernis protested. The artists were released. The ambassador then demanded that French warships should be allowed to put in for provisions at Civitavecchia. The Pope could not but comply, and French sloops flying the tricolour passed beneath the walls of the Michelangelo Fortress so recently strengthened by Ruffo at such great expense.

2

Marriages in Rome at the end of the eighteenth century were private affairs. On occasions, a princely family might give a lavish reception some weeks after the wedding, but the Prince and Princess di Marcisano did not feel that the marriage of their daughter merited a celebration. They bore no grudge against their son-in-law, Baron Scarpia; they knew that he had done nothing to ensnare their daughter; nor could they blame him for acquiescing in her demand that he be her husband: it would have been preposterous for anyone in his position to refuse. However, while the marriage had not caused a scandal, the Marcisanos had been embarrassed, and the Romans entertained, by some mocking pasquinades.

After their wedding, the Scarpias had sailed to Palermo where Vitellio introduced his young wife to his parents, whom he had not seen for seven years. They had spent a month in Sicily – Scarpia showing his bride the Byzantine mosaics in the cathedral of Monreale, the Greek temple at Segesta and the ruined keep at the family's estates at Castelfranco. They had then sailed to Naples, staying with Vitellio's brother Domenico and sister-in-law Sabina. The young couple were received at court by King Ferdinand and Queen Maria Carolina: the gossip about Vitellio's escapades in Spain had been forgotten or, if remembered, had been smothered by the renown he had won in Rome. After their presentation to their Sicilian majesties, General Acton had taken Scarpia aside and questioned him about the fortifications at Civitavecchia and the state of the papal fleet.

During the weeks which followed, Vitellio and Paola got to know their nephews and nieces, the children of Domenico and

146

Sabina, and those of Scarpia's sister Angelina and her husband Leonardo Partinico. They visited the ruins of Pompeii and Herculaneum, spent two nights on the island of Capri, went to the theatre and the San Carlo opera, and contemplated a visit to the family's estates at Barca in Basilicata: Scarpia hoped to show Paola that his mother's family, while not to be compared with the Marcisanos, was nevertheless of some standing in the Kingdom of Naples. However, by now Paola had become pregnant and suffered from morning sickness. After six weeks in Naples, they returned to Rome.

Again, as was customary in a princely family, Vitellio and Paola had been given their own quarters in the Palazzo Marcisano. This suited Scarpia, but not the Prince and Princess di Marcisano. As an unmarried daughter, Paola had been unmanageable; with the new-found liberties of a married woman she became intolerably imperious, and Paola, with her mother fussing because she was pregnant, felt that she was still being treated as a child. They were therefore given a villa belonging to the family beyond the Aventine Hill but within the Aurelian walls – built into the ruins of an ancient temple – a pleasant house with pretty gardens and a small vineyard named after a nymph to whom the temple had been dedicated, Larunda. The young couple moved to the Villa Larunda with a staff to suit their station – a cook, a lady's maid, two housemaids, two footmen, a major-domo, two grooms, three gardeners and Guido Spoletta, the baron's servant.

Paola disliked Spoletta. She found him ugly and coarse and, though he behaved correctly in her presence, he showed a nonchalance that bordered on insolence. She heard from her maid Nunzi that he remained aloof from the other servants, showed contempt for the major-domo, and spent his spare time in Trastevere, where he kept the company of low women and got into drunken brawls. Paola found his presence in her home obnoxious. She liked to see a pleasant image of herself reflected in those around her. When she dressed for a ball, Nunzi took as much pleasure as she did in her fine appearance. The housemaids, the footmen, the coachmen, all looked with unfeigned admiration at the splendour of their young mistress. Only Spoletta eyed her coldly: *You may fool them, but you don't fool me.*

In the early days of her marriage, Paola had intimated to her husband that he might find a better-looking and more congenial manservant. At first gently, then more emphatically, Scarpia made it clear that it was impossible. 'He has been with me for all these years through thick and thin. Without him at my side, in Spain, in Algiers, I would be a corpse.'

Paola did not like to think of her Vitellio as a corpse. He was not just her husband, he was her lover and as such had exceeded all the vague, girlish expectations of sexual love. Imperious with everyone else – with her parents, her brother – she was meek with Scarpia. On those first nights after their wedding, she had offered her soft, draped white body as if on an altar, glimpsing with a delicious terror his dark, lean figure, looking up into his determined eyes, her hands fluttering, not daring to touch or grasp until overwhelmed by ecstatic sensation she clasped his back. He was her stern warrior, her Achilles, her Odysseus returned to the arms of his Penelope.

Paola's pregnancy brought on sickness and lassitude but also a still more powerful cleaving to Scarpia and she had become tormented by doubts. Making love less because of the sickness and lassitude, she began to fear that his affection was waning; that he found her unattractive because of her bulging belly, or perhaps he had never found her attractive and had only married her to further his ambition. Were his endearments sincere? Did he find her dull? Had Letizia di Comastri been more amusing? More passionate? More skilled in the arts of love?

And always there was Spoletta, unavoidable each morning and night, passing her silently with an ironic bow. Did he know better than she did the true feelings of his master, Scarpia? *You bought him. He feels degraded. He longs to escape this pampered life.* Could these be the thoughts that were passing through the head of her beloved Vitellio? Yet when Scarpia himself followed his manservant out of his bedroom, his waistcoat buttoned up, his wig in place, there was only kindness with perhaps a touch of amusement in his eyes.

The birth of a son changed Paola once again. Though still only twenty-two years old, she was now a mother and so decidedly a woman – no longer a girl. When she resumed sexual relations with her husband, it was just as pleasant but less momentous, more routine. Her anxiety was dissipated and her imperiousness returned, but it was that of a matron, not a wilful child. Scarpia, now an equerry to the Treasurer Ruffo, went each day to the Quirinale Palace: Paola reigned alone and unchallenged in the Villa Larunda. But there remained Spoletta – in and out of the villa, she never knew when. Her dislike of him increased. She still dared not press Scarpia to dismiss him, but his presence slowly affected her feelings for her husband. He was a reminder of Scarpia's humble Sicilian origins – a smudge on his escutcheon. Spoletta must go.

One morning, in late autumn, Paola found Spoletta eating a fig in the garden. As was the custom, Paola was easy-going about the behaviour of her servants, but she had not expected to run into Spoletta, found the sight of his blubbery lips sucking out the pink pith of fig disgusting, and was thus provoked to ask him, in a cold manner, to leave the garden and then, as an afterthought, change her mind. 'No, come and sit down. I should like to talk to you.'

She sat down on a stone bench. Spoletta did not sit but stood facing her, licking his sticky fingers and then wiping them on his tunic. He said nothing. He waited.

'Tell me, Spoletta,' she said. 'Has it not occurred to you that you are capable of better things than serving my husband as a valet?'

Spoletta looked at her with no expression, then said: 'I am happy to serve the baron in whatever way he chooses.'

'That is commendable,' said Paola, avoiding his eyes, looking down at her hands, clasped on her knee, 'and of course I understand that when you are on campaigns, you are more than a valet; that you have fought at his side from the beginning and are as good with the sword as you are at dressing a wig – indeed better. But that is precisely my point. You know the international situation as well as I do. It is unlikely that Our Holy Father will ever again put an army in the field. Our destiny will be decided by the great powers. My husband's role is now largely ceremonial. You were companions in your youth; you were inseparable, I understand that. But you … How do you see your future? You are able. You can read. You could aspire to do much more than dress wigs and run errands. If you cared to, and left our household with suitable means, you could surely become more, much more, than you are now.'

Spoletta gave a shallow bow. 'The principessa is kind to think so highly of my abilities.'

'Europe is filled with men and women who have defied their destiny to rise in rank; women, I concede, by exploiting their natural beauty, but men with their native wit. Take a man like the Chevalier de Seignalt, born a Signor Casanova, the son of actors, who has been received by all the monarchs of Europe and received the Order of the Golden Spur from His Holiness the Pope. You, too, if you cut yourself loose from your servile employment here in this household, could achieve great things – and of course, we would not let you go empty-handed into the world.'

Spoletta looked at Paola with his usual insouciant gaze. 'Is this the view of the baron,' he asked, 'or is it just yours?'

'It is mine,' said Paola. 'I have not spoken about this to my husband. He values your services, I know.'

'He could find another valet,' said Spoletta.

'He could.'

'And one, no doubt, who could better dress a wig.'

'No doubt.'

'But there are other things I can do for the baron – things that he would be loath to do himself.'

Paola blushed. Her life had been sheltered. What was Spoletta referring to? Shooting bandits, perhaps, or cutting the throats of Turks? 'Of course,' she said, speaking in a knowing tone to conceal her ignorance, 'you are his right-hand man, and there are times in life when the left hand does not know what the right is doing…'

'And does not want to know.'

'Indeed. And a one-handed man is weak. I understand that. And were my husband to be called upon to fight, then I am sure he would need you at his side. But he should not keep you here as a domestic servant. You should aspire to more. I am told you enjoy visiting the tavernas in Trastevere. Why not become an innkeeper? We could buy you a taverna or an osteria.'

'You are most generous…' An ironic inclination of the head.

'Or you could manage one of our properties. Anything. But I no longer want to see you in my house.'

Again, Spoletta gave a slight bow. 'Should we not consult the baron?'

'No.' She spoke emphatically. 'You are not to come between me and my husband.'

'And if I prefer to remain?'

'Then you can take your chances. But I think you should remember, Spoletta, that Rome is *my* city, not yours, and it would be unwise to antagonise a Marcisano. Someone is killed every night in Trastevere and little would be made of the death of a Sicilian valet.'

*

That night Scarpia was told by Spoletta that he wished to resume his life as a soldier. Scarpia said he understood; Spoletta was not suited to the life of a domestic servant. Scarpia said he would arrange through Ruffo for a return to the garrison of the Castel Sant'Angelo. 'And perhaps,' he added, 'you should look for a wife.'

'A wife?' said Spoletta, with a sniff of derision. 'What would I want with a wife? They trap you, then nag you. I have never met one who is not either a bully or sly.'

'My wife is neither one nor the other,' said Scarpia.

Spoletta said nothing.

Irritated, Scarpia said: 'Well, I dare say women lack refinement in some circles, but no man is complete, I would say, unless he has a wife.'

Lying next to his wife in bed that night, Scarpia told her that Spoletta was returning to the garrison of the Castel Sant'Angelo.

'But what about the taverna?' asked Paola.

'What taverna?' asked Scarpia.

'Oh, I heard from Nunzi that he was thinking of buying a taverna in Trastevere.'

'He said nothing about it to me.'

'Clearly, Nunzi misunderstood.'

This was the first time that Paola had lied to her husband.

3

Three months after the birth of her first child, a son, Pietro, Paola di Marcisano, Baroness Scarpia di Rubaso, began to pay calls in her carriage. Now that she had her own household, she was on easier terms with her parents and her brother Ludovico. The young among Roman society were all her cousins or old friends. She was valued by the older generation: she may have had little formal education, but she had a quick intelligence and had read many books – *The Sorrows of Young Werther*, of course, and forbidden romantic novels that had given her a taste for a warrior husband, but also the works of Voltaire, Jean-Jacques Rousseau, the Scot David Hume (in French translation), and even the atheist Helvetius, whose works were causing so much trouble at the time. 'Your daughter,' Cardinal de Bernis had told her father, Prince di Marcisano, 'has the makings of another Madame de Staël.'

Paola was, of course, a Catholic, and was protected from the virus of scepticism by her *romanità*. All that she was, both within and without, was shaped and coloured by the Roman Catholic and Apostolic faith. Her calendar was punctuated by the feast days of the Church. She revelled in the carnival, but then fasted savagely in Lent. She prayed to the Virgin daily for her intercession on the most trivial matters, and called upon specialist saints to put pressure on God on particular issues. To achieve what at first appeared impossible, securing Scarpia as her husband, she had placed a petition to San Luigi da Gonzaga in the box in the Jesuit church, the Gesù. Later, she had prayed to the Virgin's mother, St Anne, to ensure that she should conceive and bear a healthy child, and had left a petition at the olive-wood figure of the Infant Jesus, the Bambino, at the Aracoeli asking that the child should be a boy. And she had prayed again to the Virgin, leaving a lavish offering at the ancient basilica of Santa Maria Maggiore, to spare her son Pietro when he fell ill. All her prayers had been answered. What reason had she to doubt?

It was not that she did not come across sceptics. The Spanish ambassador, Azara, was a discreet free-thinker of the old school, and the Scarpias met at his receptions Romans with republican sympathies like Cesare Angelotti and his beautiful sister, the Marchesa Domenica Attavanti, as well as Frenchmen and women living in Rome such as the banker Morette, and young painters and sculptors from the French Academy in the Palazzo Mancini. Paola was at first astonished that Azara should admit such people into his embassy, and she would have declined his invitations had not her husband felt a debt of gratitude to Azara, who had been kind to him during his first days in Rome.

In November of 1792, at a reception of Azara's, the Scarpias were introduced by Morette to Hugon de Bassville, the secretary of the French ambassador in Naples, who said he had come to Rome to see the sights. Scarpia reported this to Ruffo. 'The sights!' expostulated the Treasurer. 'He has been sent to organise an uprising. We have seized pamphlets smuggled in from France and a cache of arms has been found in the ghetto. But the Holy Father is terrified of the French. He has said that Bassville must be treated with courtesy and respect.'

In the weeks which followed, Hugon de Bassville openly agitated for the overthrow of the Pope. He gave dinners at the French Embassy at which he toasted the French Republic and called upon his guests to follow the example of Brutus, who had assassinated Julius Caesar. A young French naval officer, La Flotte, was sent from Naples to assist him and, on the afternoon of Sunday 13 January 1793, Bassville and La Flotte took a drive in an open carriage along the Corso. With them were Bassville's wife, his young son, a friend, Amaury Duval, and two servants. All wore large tricolour cockades in their hats and Duval waved a tricolour flag.

The Romans on the crowded Corso were incensed by this display of republican emblems. Angry bystanders told the Frenchmen to remove their cockades. The request was ignored. A stone was thrown at the carriage. Bassville and La Flotte shouted insults at the crowd. A shot was fired. More stones were thrown. The coachman, alarmed, turned down the Vicolo dello Sdrucciolo and into the Palazzo Palombara, the home of the banker Morette. The coach was pursued by an enraged mob, and as the passengers descended there was a scuffle. La Flotte escaped into the palazzo, but Bassville was stabbed in the stomach and, under a fusillade of stones, carried into the police station on the via Frattina.

The riot that had started on the Corso spread throughout Rome. The enraged crowd attacked the French Post Office, the French Academy and houses of known republican sympathisers with cries of 'Long live the Catholic religion' and 'Long live the Pope'. Windows were smashed, and both the French Academy and the house of a Francophile banker, Torlonia, were set on fire. The riots continued into the Monday. A mob from Trastevere crossed the Tiber to attack the ghetto, but found it guarded by papal troops.

Pope Pius VI sent his personal physician, Flajam, to tend to Bassville, but nothing could be done to save his life. After asking for and receiving the last sacrament of the Church, Bassville died. A funeral was held at the church of San Lorenzo in Lucina, after which the Pope provided coaches and an escort of sixty soldiers to take Bassville's wife and son together with La Flotte back to Naples.

4

Like all Catholics in the eighteenth century, Baron Vitellio Scarpia di Rubaso confessed his sins at Easter, and in the last days of Lent of 1793 – soon after the killing of Bassville – he returned to the church of Santa Maria in Vallicella and Father Simone Alberti, who, having given him an introduction to the Treasurer Ruffo, was the source of his good fortune.

Since his marriage to Paola, Scarpia had taken steps to share that good fortune with others. Sponsored by his brother-in-law, Ludovico, he had joined one of the noble confraternities that raised money for charitable institutions such as hospitals, orphanages and schools. He was a conscientious landowner and a just employer. He was devoted to his wife and respectful towards her family, and, if thoughts of other women came into his mind, he quickly expelled them. The sin that most troubled his conscience was a vague discontent. 'I have everything a man could want,' he said to Father Simone through the grille of the confessional. 'I have a title, an estate, a good income, a beautiful and intelligent wife, and the two charming children. And yet I feel frustrated. I am constantly occupied, but yet feel that I have nothing to do.'

'But you serve the Treasurer Ruffo.'

'Indeed I do, and I owe him all. But he himself feels constrained in what he can ask me to do. He could send an obscure Sicilian to hunt down bandits but not the son-in-law of Prince di Marcisano. He deems it beneath me. And so I see to my estates, make polite conversation at receptions and play with my children while all the while Europe is in turmoil and the fiendish Jacobins conspire to conquer the world.'

'Ah, yes,' said Father Simone, his head bowed, 'it is too painful. It is all a terrible trial, and of course we can pray, and for me, a priest, prayer is my métier, but for you, whom God has chosen to fight for the cause of righteousness, I can see that it is hard to be unable to draw your sword...'

'To see others fighting – the Austrians, the Prussians, the Russians, even the English...'

'Indeed. But you are now a Roman. You are under the command of our Holy Father and are part of an army that is, in fact, no army – that, I can see, is hard to bear.'

'Should I enlist in some other army that is actually fighting the French?'

'No, God forbid. You are no longer a young adventurer. You have duties, responsibilities –'

'To twiddle my thumbs.'

'Now, perhaps, yes, to twiddle your thumbs. But the dark clouds have not dissipated. Who knows what trials lie ahead? You can at least stand firm *in spirit*, countering those Romans who are inclined towards republicanism and atheism. Evil actions always start with wrong-headed ideas. The horrors now taking place in France are the progeny of the *conversazioni* of the so-called philosophers in the drawing rooms of Paris. Has not the Church always taught that error leads to evil? Is that not why we have the Holy Inquisition? Was it not thanks to the Holy Inquisition here in Rome, in Venice, in Portugal and in Spain that the iniquitous ideas of Luther and Calvin were smothered and so we were spared the horrors of the wars of religion?

'Satan is subtle,' Father Simone went on. 'The ideals of liberty, equality and fraternity seem to be close to those of the Gospels. Man is free – free, even to sin – that is the difference between a man and a beast – and all men are brothers, equal in the eyes of God. All this is true. But Our Lord also tells us that all authority comes from above, not below. Democracy was all very well in ancient Athens, where the citizens could gather and debate on the Pnyx. But in a nation of millions, most of whom can neither read nor write? How are they to be informed? How are they to choose? How are the impoverished to resist those who would buy their votes? Democracy means factions, and coalitions of factions, with support bought by bankers and Jews. The natural hierarchy is over-turned. The dregs rise to the top and plunder the state. In Paris, grubbing lawyers and pamphleteers – Marat, Danton, Robespierre; and this man who lords it in Naples, Citizen Armand de Mackau! His mother was a governess! And the wretch who was killed – may God have mercy on his soul – Hugon, who added "de Bassville" to his name – the son of a dyer in Abbeville, a defrocked priest, the tutor to some rich Americans, then a journalist! More dregs who have risen to the top. Far better a monarch who is above factions – a good Christian, a father to his people. That is the best form of government and the only one sanctioned by God.'

*

Scarpia agreed with everything said by his confessor. He shared with the Romans their hatred of the republicans, be they Italian or French, and would happily have plunged his sword into Bassville's belly. Who were these vulgar Frenchmen to tell Italians how they should live? How dare they mount this assault on a political system that the Romans had enjoyed for a thousand years? And denigrate their holy faith as superstition, seeking to persuade the people that there is no God! That the Gospels are a fable! The sacraments mumbo-jumbo! To tell the Romans to return to the values and institutions of the worshippers of Zeus!

However, while Scarpia left the confessional reassured that the cause he served was good, he had not brought up with Father Simone the other cause of his concern and frustration – the state of his marriage to Paola. Scarpia loved his wife. He recognised that she was beautiful, amusing, original, intelligent – admirable in every way – and the love he felt for her was based on respect, fondness and, of course, desire. But did it lack passion? There had been times when Scarpia had envisaged a love for a woman that was sublime – the kind of love portrayed in novels, plays, paintings or a piece of music such as Benedetto Marcello's aria, 'Quella Fiamma che m'accende', which he had heard sung by the young soprano from the Veneto before the Pope. The girl's rendering had for a moment made him feel that perhaps he too might one day be consumed by the flames of a transcendent love; but, when the performance was over, he remembered with embarrassment his passion for Celestina and reverted to his conviction that such passion was a weakness – all very well in art and adolescence but an unsound foundation for the concrete affinities of a grown man in real life.

Scarpia did not dwell on the nature of love; however, there was a young French officer then serving in Milan, Henri Beyle, who would one day publish a long book on the subject based on his study of the manners and morals of the Italians at the time. Writing

On Love under the name Stendhal, Beyle would describe a process he called 'crystallisation' whereby all the most commonplace qualities of the beloved became admirable in the eyes of the lover. This had not been the case with Scarpia. The way in which Paola cocked her head in conversation, a little like a parrot, or her habit of raising herself up and down on her toes with her back to the mantel as if stretching the calves of her legs – these and many other mannerisms would have become delightful in the eyes of a lover. Scarpia found them endearing but not delightful; her father, whom she resembled, also cocked his head like a parrot.

However, Scarpia's love for Paola was now far more than an affinity between a man and a woman: it encompassed his powerful feelings for his whole family. When she had become pregnant, he had seen it as a matter for the women of the household; but, when presented with his son Pietro, he had been overwhelmed with novel and powerful emotions – pride, delight, and gratitude to the wife who had endured such protracted agony to bring forth his child.

There had been a second child, a boy, who had died of diphtheria when ten months old and, after the birth of Francesca, another girl who had died of smallpox aged four. The small tragedies were common and to be expected – a quiet sorrow to be shared. They persuaded Scarpia of the efficacy of inoculation and placed small doubts in Paola's mind as to the efficacy of prayer. It also seemed to diminish her enjoyment of making love with her husband. After the birth of Pietro, Paola had happily resumed their conjugal routine, but little by little after the further births and deaths that 'happily' changed to 'willingly' and then to 'why not?'. Was it that she did not want more children – only to see them suffer and die? Or was it, as she had once told him half jokingly, that in Rome it was considered a little ridiculous for a married couple to go on making love for so long.

5

This view had been put to Paola by Graziella di Pozzo. Paola knew, of course, that no one is as likely to feel envy as one's closest friend. Graziella's husband, the Marchese di Ordelaffi, was a dull old stick twelve years her senior and her *cicisbeo*, the *cavaliere* Sodano, had bow legs. Compared to both these men, Scarpia was an Adonis – still slim, dark, handsome. Yet Paola, though apparently confident in her own judgements, was sensitive to her reputation among her peers. She talked as if she lived under the judgement of God, but in reality her behaviour was governed less by her confessor than by a notional committee of slightly older women – the arbiters of what was *comme il faut* and *à la mode*.

Fashions in clothes and morals had hitherto been dictated by the court at Versailles. After the revolution, all had become confused. There was much blushing and tittering when it was learned that fashionable women in Jacobin Paris now wore dresses so décolleté that their nipples were exposed. No one in Rome would go quite so far, but there was an inexorable raising of the waist and lowering of the décolletage. Roman women were accustomed to a certain latitude in the bestowal of their affections and favours after they were married, but again there was blushing and tittering and little gasps of feigned shock at the news of the open liaisons of the Parisian *salonnières* like Josephine de Beauharnais or Madame Récamier. The notional committee was emphatic in its disapproval: adultery must be discreet.

Paola's envoy from this imaginary committee was Graziella. The two young women had grown up together in the convent, and while Paola did not regard her friend as particularly perceptive or imaginative or intelligent, she trusted her as she would a barometer or weathervane to indicate the atmospheric pressure or the direction of the wind. She also relied on Graziella to act as a mirror, enabling her to see herself as others saw her, and just as she had been pleased by Graziella's envy when she had married the handsome Scarpia, so she became perplexed and annoyed when, soon after the birth of her daughter Francesca, she saw the envy give way to a certain smugness as if, when it came to their husbands, the tortoise, Graziella, had outpaced Paola, the hare.

It was apparently the view not just of Graziella but the notional committee of grandes dames that Graziella's husband, the Marchese di Ordelaffi, though old and ugly, had a pedigree second to none, while Baron Scarpia di Rubaso remained a parvenu provincial who, however handsome, looked somehow gauche in the fine coats and tunics and seemed a little out of place at receptions and *conversazioni*. Involuntarily, Paola was affected by this view. The tingling and fluttering she had felt at the thought of being embraced by the wild Sicilian, who was so ready to kill or be killed, had faded as her brooding hero became just another functionary of the papal curia.

Had the time come for Paola to take on a *cicisbeo* like Graziella? When Paola went into society, she took trouble to look attractive, following the fashion for a lower neckline and higher waist so that her bosom and shoulders were all but naked. Young men clustered around at every *conversazione*, but the looks Paola directed at her admirers were not inviting: they were rather mocking, as if to say, 'Do not aspire, you idiots, to possess the body of a Principessa di Marcisano.' The look was softer with older men, the connoisseurs of beautiful women like Cardinal de Bernis who, although no longer the ambassador of France, remained in Rome. In his case her eyes said: 'Well, Your Eminence, how does this compare with a statue by Canova or one of your Dresden figurines? Is there not something to be said for flesh and blood over marble and porcelain?'

There was one man whom Paola could envisage as a lover – a man she had never seen and knew only by repute. He was the same age as she was and, as in a cheap romance, she had initially loathed him when, five years before, she had read in the gazettes of the

23-year-old French brigadier general, Napoleon Bonaparte, who had successfully driven the English out of Toulon. She had loathed him because he served the Jacobin cause, but had nonetheless felt a twinge of admiration for the achievement of one so young. After that, the name of Bonaparte had disappeared until now, five years later, he was named as the outstanding commander of the French armies that had defeated those of Sardinia and Austria in Lombardy and had captured Milan. Here was a new military genius, an Alexander the Great, and Paola, like many other women throughout Europe, forgave him his Jacobinism and dallied with him in her thoughts.

Scarpia was no Bonaparte and, in the eyes of the committee of matrons whose opinion mattered to Paola, he also suffered because of his connection with Treasurer Ruffo – loathed by the nobility for curbing their feudal powers and making them pay taxes. Paducci, Spinelli and Letizia di Comastri started to refer to him as 'Ruffo's *sbirro*': Graziella passed this on to Paola. No open disrespect was shown to Scarpia when he appeared in society; no one wished to fight a duel with a cut-throat Sicilian or incur the displeasure of the Marcisanos. Ludovico remained loyal to his brother-in-law; he even felt some responsibility for his present position; but, after he himself was married to Fulvia di Cardandini, he saw less of him, and Scarpia was not asked to act as godparent to any of his children.

Paola's parents, too, continued to put a brave face on the awkward situation in which their difficult daughter had placed them. Scarpia was always there to remind them of the *mésalliance*; and, however afraid their servants might be of incurring the wrath of the Princess Paola, they were, as servants always are, aware of Scarpia's standing as the bought plaything of their mistress and in waiting on him started to show a subtle disdain.

*

It was much the same at Rubaso, the estate in the Sabine hills that had been settled on Scarpia by the Pope. The estate was not large and the house was not grand, but both were pleasant and productive and Scarpia set out to be on good terms with those who cultivated his land. Rubaso was a two-hour ride from Rome, and at first Paola would accompany him on his visits, but, since the house had been given over with all its furnishings to the Pope, and by the Pope to Scarpia, it always seemed that they were merely guests in another's house.

The last owner, Alberto d'Angelo, had been a devout, benevolent old man, melancholy after the death of both his wife and daughter from smallpox, preserving his house and contents as they had always been, so that the furnishings were now threadbare and out of fashion, but at the same time seemed so much part of the place that it would be sacrilegious to change them. At one time Paola had plans for a refurbishment, but she never put them into effect. After the birth of Pietro, she rarely went to Rubaso. She was preoccupied with running her own household, and, when she wished to leave Rome, there were the several properties of the Marcisanos that were not only more agreeable but were staffed by servants who had been devoted to her since she was a child.

Scarpia did not complain, and went to Rubaso alone. He liked to be there precisely because it was not a property belonging to the Marcisanos; but nor was it in reality a property that belonged to him. The old major-domo, the gardeners, the footmen, the housemaids all treated him correctly; they were polite and went to some trouble to open and air the villa and serve up the best produce of the estate at his table; but the servants seemed to see him not as their master but as an honoured guest of the dead Don Alberto d'Angelo. If Scarpia suggested some improvements to the way the estate was run, the major-domo, or the gardener, or the gamekeeper would say either 'Yes, I think Don Alberto would have done the same had God given him a few more years' or 'Yes, Don Alberto considered that but decided against it'; and it was said in such a gentle but definitive manner that Scarpia could not bring himself to assert his authority and override decisions already made.

6

Treasurer Fabrizio Ruffo, with many urgent matters pressing on his mind, was nonetheless aware that all was not well with his protégé, Baron Scarpia. His friend, the Oratorian Simone Alberti, though scrupulous not to break the seal of the confessional, intimated that all the worldly benefits that the cardinal had bestowed on the young Sicilian had not made him content. Both men agreed that Scarpia's ennui was an unintended consequence of the Treasurer's benevolence: that by asking the Pope to give him a title and a property to make him a less degrading match for a Principessa di Marcisano, he had denied his protégé the sense of achievement that would have come had he won the advantages for himself; and had laid him open to the kind of derision that he knew was being orchestrated by Letizia di Comastri and her circle of friends.

Ruffo was aware that this same circle also put about scurrilous rumours as to the source of his affection for the handsome young Sicilian. Certainly, the dark good looks, the slim figure and the expressive eyes made him a man that another man might love, but Ruffo was confident in his conscience that his feelings for Scarpia were not the sublimated desire of a sodomite but rather those of a father for a son. And a father can quite legitimately look for ways to further the interests of a son.

Treasurer Ruffo's talent was for administration. Day in, day out, his mind applied itself to getting things done. On his desk there was a list of tasks and projects and another with the names of those who could perform the tasks and promote the projects. His responsibilities were vast, and that of matching expenditure with income perhaps the most intractable; but he was also responsible for the defence of the Papal States and he had become aware, like the Pope he served, that the expenditure on fortifications had been largely wasted. Allies rather than ramparts were now the best protection against the French.

Strictly speaking, relations with other governments were a matter for the Secretary of State, Cardinal Zelada, but, inevitably, as the man responsible for the Pope's armed forces, and with the French now occupying Milan, Treasurer Ruffo had an interest in the question of military pacts and alliances. If the papal estates were attacked, which powers could be counted on to join in their defence? To the south was the Kingdom of the Two Sicilies, which had been frightened into recognising the French Republic. To the north, bordering the papal legations, was the Republic of Venice. Venice and Rome had much in common. Both had existed in more or less their present condition for over a thousand years. Neither was the property of a dynasty: both had elected heads of state. Both had an Inquisition. Both passed strict laws on moral conduct that were universally and cheerfully ignored. Both were well past their moment of greatest glory; both were inescapably in decline; yet both still had armies, and was it possible that if the two combined they might be a match for an army sent by the French? What was the state of the Venetian army? What was the morale of its officers and men?

The Venetian army. Scarpia at a loose end. In the mind of Ruffo the administrator, the two things converged on a project. He sent for Scarpia. He explained that, while he had intelligence about the condition of the Venetian army, it came from unreliable sources. The clergy were no judge of military matters; and the patriarch was not wholly to be trusted. He would therefore like Scarpia, posing as a gentleman of leisure, to go to Venice and draw up a report on the preparedness and likely efficacy of any force that the Serene Republic might put in the field.

Eight

I

The Prince General Alberigo di Belgioioso d'Este, the first lover of Tosca, had in his youth fought in the Seven Years War, distinguishing himself in the Battle of Rosbach; but for most of his life his duties had been largely diplomatic and ceremonial and, like many a man later in life, he had grown weary of his main role as viceroy of the Austrian emperor and was more taken with his ancillary activities – the collecting of rare manuscripts, beautiful works of art and pretty women.

Again, like many men later in life, he recognised the limitations placed by nature in the satisfaction of appetites: he ate frugally, mixed water with his wine and, having asserted his *droit de seigneur* over the lovely Floria Tosca, and enjoyed her favours over a number of months, moved her from the Palazzo Belgioioso into comfortable quarters of her own. All this was done with exquisite politeness and, though Tosca made a show of regret at leaving Princess Carlotta and her kind papa, she understood perfectly that having been given a princely start in her career, she must now rely on her own talent to conquer the world.

Tosca had made her debut at La Scala in Cimarosa's *La ballerina amante*. In 1793 she had returned to the same stage in

Zingarelli's *Artaserse*. The opera was repeatedly interrupted by tumultuous applause and by the end of the evening Tosca was famous. In the year which followed, she sang in Parma, Modena, Turin, Ferrara and at La Fenice in Venice. The strength and purity of her voice, the beauty of her face and figure, the poignant expressions she could come up with when playing tragedy, the twinkling wit that showed in comic roles, won her fanatical admirers in every city where she sang. She was importuned by would-be lovers and, of course, impresarios who quickly discovered that Tosca on the billboard would sell every seat in the house.

Tosca did not let her triumphs go to her head. A measure of peasant canniness made her realise that, while her talent might be a gratuitous gift, its development had come from the diligent teaching of her tutors in Golla and the Palazzo Belgioioso. She was willing to flirt with the rich young men who took her to supper after the performance, but she bided her time when it came to choosing a new lover. Her closest friend was the castrato Crescentini, whose fifteen years of experience she could draw on and who was happy to teach her what he knew. He advised her on what engagements she should accept, what roles she should take and what avoid. He also warned her that her success had provoked envy. Supporters of rivals could resort to dirty tricks – eating lemons, making catcalls and, if they outnumbered her admirers, booing her off the stage.

None of this intimidated Tosca. She knew that her fellow countrymen, unwilling to fight foreigners over such unimportant matters as Liberty, Equality and Fraternity or the Divine Right of Kings, were only too ready to do battle over their favourite diva. Italians at the time cared more about music than anything else. In Venice, the year 1792 was known universally as the *anno Todi* because of the triumph of the Portuguese soprano Louisa Todi. One day there would be an *anno Tosca*, and it was for this that she worked so hard.

Tosca was not wholly immune from thoughts about love. A woman who could so convincingly portray Giulietta in Zingarelli's opera *Giulietta e Romeo* could envisage romantic passion. But her practical bent led her to understand, like Stendhal, that there were loves of different kinds. She did not categorise in the systematic manner of the Frenchman, but in her own mind, beyond the elusive *grande passion* that she could imagine, there was *amour d'avantage* – the love for someone like Prince Belgioioso who could further one's career – a kind of tender bartering of influence for pleasure; and what Stendhal called *amour goût* – the enjoyment of a night in the arms of a particularly handsome young man. Such loves, being of a different nature, could be concurrent, though given Tosca's under-standing of the nature of men, it was better that each imagined that she bestowed her favours only on him at the time.

Tosca remained devout, and confessed her sins to priests who on the whole regarded those of the flesh as venial peccadillos. Only Jansenists thought that love outside marriage would jeopardise a young woman's salvation. The ordinary *abate* to whom she confessed was so much part of the culture from which he came that he accepted that it was unreasonable to expect an actress or an opera singer to keep to the same rules as a chaste wife or celibate nun. The buttress of Christian morality had always been the reluctance of the parish to provide for children born out of wedlock: that was why stigma was reserved for the transgressions of unmarried girls rather than their lovers. However, once a woman was married and had a husband who would pay for her offspring, whether he was the father or not, the parish became more tolerant; and it was tolerant too of actresses and divas who, should they have children out of wedlock, could provide for them out of their fees.

Therefore Tosca's laxity was quite compatible with custom and with her faith, and she saw nothing incongruous in rising early after a night of love to go to Mass, or spend lavishly on flowers to be put at a shrine to the Virgin or a favourite saint. She prayed a decade of the rosary before every performance, and never doubted that her success was due to the intervention of her patron saint, one of two girls martyred in Córdoba by the emir Abdur Rahman II. She revered all the virgins and martyrs who had died for the Catholic faith – or simply, like St Philomena, to protect their virtue from some lascivious pagan; but their values were not hers, which was hardly surprising since all the dramas she enacted were about the sexual love of a woman for a man or a man for a woman, not about the love of either for God. Cimarosa, Granacci, Paisiello, Zingarelli – all composed sacred music to be sung in churches; but when they wrote for the opera they wrote about love.

2

Tosca took one false step when, ignoring the advice of Crescentini, she became infatuated with the tenor Panfilo de Lorenzi, who played Romeo to her Giulietta at La Fenice. The expression in her eyes in their duets was so full of feeling that not only was the audience overwhelmed, but Lorenzi too. Lorenzi, small with blond hair and a wispy beard, was the lover of the 22-year-old soprano, Teresa Bertinotti – but she was singing at La Scala in Milan while he was with Tosca in Venice. There started an intense affair. Lorenzi was besotted: their liaison became not just known but notorious. La Bertinotti in Milan was humiliated. Lorenzi begged Tosca to marry him, but Tosca had no intention of marrying anyone, least of all a man who made his living on the boards. Lorenzi became importunate; Tosca became irritated: nothing is more tiresome for a woman than a lover who wants more than she is willing to give. He became possessive, then jealous, and all at once Tosca found that she no longer loved him. She told Lorenzi that their liaison was over, and thereafter put a touch of mockery in her rendering of the arias in which Giulietta assured Romeo of her undying love.

Already the followers of Teresa Bertinotti were furious that their diva should have been thrown over by Lorenzi. Now Lorenzi's admirers were outraged that he had been spurned by Tosca. Tosca's supporters took the line that she was free to love whom she chose. The different factions clashed in La Fenice. There were interruptions and catcalls; lemons were eaten in the front row. At the last performance of the run, the performance hardly progressed. Bertinotti's party booed Lorenzi; Lorenzi's party booed Tosca; Tosca's party booed Lorenzi and shouted abuse at the supporters of the other two. Tosca was elated: she sang and acted as never before and suddenly the mockery in her eyes as she poured out her love for Romeo in the most exquisite sounds became intolerable for Lorenzi. He turned his back on his Giulietta and refused to join her in a duet. Tosca laughed. The conductor persevered, and the orchestra continued playing despite the cries, whistles and catcalls from the audience. The wretched impresario stood in the wings, wringing his hands – cajoling, threatening, begging, his words lost in the din from the auditorium. Fights broke out with fusillades of sweetmeats, crumpled programmes and rotten fruit. Some in the boxes left the theatre in disgust, but others joined in, yelling abuse and throwing anything that came to hand down into the pit – fans, spectacle cases, programmes, even opera glasses, which drew blood when they hit their mark.

The performance hobbled on to the end, but when it came to the curtain call, as each singer stepped forward, the competition between the different factions to drown out the applause of one with the boos of another intensified; and finally Tosca, having curtsied to her admirers, turned to those who were abusing her, extended her graceful arm and with two fingers made the obscene gesture – the *corne* – that she had learned as a child in her village in the Veneto.

The Lorenzistas and Bertinottians, enraged, surged forward, clambering over the pit from which the orchestra had retreated to climb onto the stage. The impresario, stage manager and members of the cast ran forward to protect Tosca. Police entered the back of the auditorium. Stagehands rushed in to wrestle with the vanguard of Tosca's would-be assailants as they clambered onto the proscenium just as Tosca herself withdrew behind the line of her defenders and, picking up her cloak and her maid from her dressing room, slipped out through the stage door of the theatre.

Out in the street she was still not safe, however: partisans of the different factions, who had either been at the performance or simply joined in the hullabaloo, were milling around outside and, seeing two women leave from the stage door, though their hooded cloaks disguised their identity, realised that one might be Tosca and gave chase. The two women hurried away, but Tosca, in her stage costume and high-heeled shoes, could hardly run. They went up a narrow alley but were seen, and turning right and then right again, found themselves at a point on the Grand Canal where those members of the audience who had been disgusted by the fracas were waiting for their own gondolas, or gondolas that were for hire. Glancing over her shoulder, Tosca saw that the crowd was upon her. With an elegant leap, she jumped onto a parting gondola. Her maid made as if to follow, but it was too late – the gondola was too far from the quay. Tosca turned, raised two fingers at her pursuers, waved to her maid, then drew aside the curtains of the enclosed gondola, went in and threw herself down, laughing, onto the banquette, face-to-face with a man who, in alarm at the intrusion, had half drawn his sword.

'Now they will have to swim if they want to catch me,' said Tosca, looking cheerfully into the man's eyes.

'They may follow in a gondola,' he said, returning his sword to its scabbard.

'I can take care of myself,' said Tosca. She reached up with her right hand to a huge pearl at the head of one of the pins holding up her hair and drew out a thin blade around six inches long.

'You won't need to use it,' said Scarpia. 'I shall defend you.'

'But you don't know me,' said Tosca.

'Everyone knows Tosca.'

'You were in the theatre?'

'Yes.'

She laughed again as she pushed the *stiletto* back into her hair. 'What a fracas. Poor Antonelli.'

'Antonelli?'

'The impresario.' Her face suddenly became serious. 'Perhaps he will keep back my money.'

'You were hardly to blame.'

Tosca looked happy again. 'You are right. It was Lorenzi and his terrible friends. I take it you are not one of them?'

'No.'

'And La Bertinotti?'

'I have never heard her sing.'

'No need.'

'I am sure.'

'You are not a Venetian.'

'No. I live in Rome.'

'But you are not a Roman either.'

'I am a Sicilian.' He inclined his head. 'Baron Scarpia di Rubaso at your service.'

'I am Floria Tosca.'

'I know.'

'Of course. You were at the theatre.'

'Where would you like to go?'

'Will you take me home?'

'Wherever you choose.'

Tosca turned and, holding back the curtain, shouted instructions at the gondolier in her strong Veneto accent. 'I shall go home to change,' she said to Scarpia. 'I cannot spend the rest of the evening dressed as Giulietta! And if you like, we will have some supper.'

'It is late…'

'Not for Venetians. They stay up until dawn.'

*

Tosca's lodgings were not far from La Fenice, and when they got there they found that her maid had already returned. The rooms were not large, but they were elegantly appointed and, besides the maid, there was a young footman who seemed to be from the same village as Tosca: she spoke to him casually in their abominable dialect and, when she withdrew with the maid to change, he clumsily served Scarpia with wine from a decanter. Scarpia judged that he could not be more than sixteen or seventeen years old; the maid no older; and Tosca herself little more than twenty. He was, then, among children playing at the adult life.

Yet Scarpia was in awe of Tosca. Such was her natural talent that she emanated a nobility beyond anything a title could bestow. He had gone to the opera because her name was on everyone's lips, and he remembered hearing her ethereal voice when she sang before the Pope. Her role in Zingarelli's opera was not ethereal, but the voice of an impassioned Giulietta had an equal effect. Scarpia had been in the stalls, and when the tumult had started he had left the theatre, not wanting to break the spell cast by Tosca's singing. He had walked to the canal to hire a gondola, and, as it set off towards his *albergo*, he had sat back listening in his memory to the arias he had heard earlier in the evening. And then all at once, there she was – facing him, laughing and behaving as if she had known him all her life.

That familiarity continued throughout the evening. Tosca insisted upon going to the Piazza San Marco, mixing with the crowd, walking under the arcades arm in arm as if he was her *cavaliere servente*, going into a café to drink an aperitif where she was recognised and acclaimed; then leading him to a small restaurant in an alley off the piazzetta where the owners greeted her as if she was the Doge's daughter and seated them at a table placed discreetly behind a screen. She ordered the food in Venetian, which Scarpia barely understood, and, when it came, ate greedily without a trace of ladylike inhibition. 'God, I was starving,' she said. 'I always am after a performance, but tonight, what a performance, what a fight!' Her eyes shone as she relived the battle at La Fenice.

'It was a contrast,' said Scarpia, 'to your recital at the Quirinale.'

She sat back astonished. 'You were there?'

'I was.'

'Did you see me tremble? I was terrified. Think, I had been shut up in a convent and now was singing for the Pope!'

'You sang beautifully.'

'You know, when I sing all my fears disappear. I love to sing. I have always loved to sing. God has given me a voice that is a joy. And it is a joy to use it. Old Monsignor Tochetti used to tell the story in the Gospel about the talents, and how it was one's duty to develop what talents you had been given by God, so to feel one is pleasing God by doing what one likes doing – that is good fortune, is it not?'

'It is indeed.'

'And with it comes admiration and gold and diamonds and beautiful clothes.'

'And love?' asked Scarpia.

'Ah, love.' Tosca's expression changed from elation to a frown. 'That is more complicated, don't you think?'

'Yes. It is more complicated.'

'You can love one man in one way and another man in another way.'

'Perhaps.'

'Lorenzi was nice enough and he was attractive and it was difficult not to enter into the role of his Giulietta. And there was the pleasure of stealing him from La Bertinotti. But then he became importunate and possessive and jealous and wanted me to be his wife! Me, a wife! That was too much. But when I said no, he became angry. He called me the most terrible things. So I returned the insults with interest! Yes, and so from being lovers we became enemies all in a flash!'

'It has happened to others.'

'To you?'

'These things are often easier to start than to finish.'

'Only for fools.'

'Is no love eternal?'

'The love of God and the Madonna, perhaps, but human love ... Well, one has only to look around and you are as likely to find a pearl in the piazzetta as you are to find a couple who have remained in love throughout their life.'

'And Romeo and Giulietta, had they lived?'

Tosca laughed. 'What do you think? It would have been fine for a year or two, but then she would have had babies and, well, that's the course of nature, isn't it? Having babies makes women ugly. It's nature's way of keeping families to a sensible size – unless you are the Queen of Naples, of course.'

'So Giulietta at thirty?'

'*Finita!* But Romeo, at thirty – well, I wouldn't trust him, I can tell you.'

'You cannot imagine meeting a man you would love forever?'

'Yes, I can imagine it, of course. That's what all the operas are about; unless they are about husbands deceiving their wives and wives their husbands. Look at Figaro.'

'Don't you think Figaro would continue to love Susanna? Or Susanna Figaro?'

'Not a chance. Marriage is too dull. Have you ever come across a married couple who do not bicker? And why do they bicker? Because they are bored. So a woman has her *cicisbeo* and a man his mistress and everyone is happy. But lifelong love – it is something one just dreams of, and acts out in operas and plays, but never finds in real life. So why not just have some fun while you can? That's what I told Lorenzi, but he didn't understand.'

'If I were Lorenzi,' said Scarpia, 'I would not want to lose you.'

Tosca smiled. 'How gallant you are, you Sicilians. But I am sure … well, here am I teaching you about love when you have lived longer than I have and must know much more. Tell me about love. Are you in love?'

'I love my wife.'

'*Miracolo!*'

'Not in the way Romeo loved Giulietta, perhaps.'

'You married for advantage?'

It was now Scarpia's turn to frown. 'Yes … in a sense.'

'And she?'

'Not at all. I was a poor match.'

'So she loved you … she was a Giulietta?'

'Yes.'

'And she will love you until death?'

Scarpia hesitated, then said: 'I am not sure.'

*

Tosca asked Scarpia why he was in Venice. He explained. Was he a spy? The idea seemed to amuse her. Scarpia said he was not after secrets but facts that were generally known. Musketry and munitions. Tonnage and cannon. Tosca's eyes wandered. She yawned. Scarpia asked her about the morale of the Venetians.

Would they fight the French? Tosca laughed. Fight the French? They were not mad.

Scarpia's mission in Venice was almost over. He had made an assessment of the armed forces of the Serene Republic and found them wanting. Venice was no longer the formidable naval power that had defeated the Turks at the Battle of Lepanto: its forces were barely sufficient to police and supply their garrisons in Dalmatia. If there was time, new boats could be built or bought and crewed by the tough workers from the Arsenale; and, because of the Venetians' knowledge of the local currents and channels that led into the lagoon, they could defend Venice from a larger force from the sea. But where were the troops that could defend her on land? The best soldiers were scattered in garrisons in Istria and Dalmatia. Those in the Veneto were ill-organised and ill-equipped: their muskets were antique and their artillery obsolete. Their officers were mostly absent in the small gaming rooms, the casinos, dotted around the lagoons. Even when present, they were distracted by thoughts of lawsuits or amorous intrigues. A career in the army was considered the last resort for a penniless younger son.

The state of the army and navy reflected the society from which they came. A century spent in pursuit of pleasure had made Venice the most agreeable city in Europe, and no Venetian could see any reason why his ancient republic should not last for another thousand years. But sybaritism is not a cause for which a man wants to risk his life: soldiering was for uncivilised brutes from the other side of the Alps. And Scarpia acknowledged there was a kind of logic in the pampered cowardice of the Venetians. It is not pleasant living in a belligerent state with so much shouting and bullying and regimentation. And why should men living peaceably together kill others for a cause? Even the poorest Venetians were flummoxed by the slogan Liberty, Equality and Fraternity, because there could be no greater liberty than living in a state where the laws are ignored; no greater equality than when men and women can make of themselves what they will; and no greater fraternity when men are so obliging and women so willing, as if all humanity were guests at the same unending party.

Men fight, Scarpia concluded, who like fighting or strive for the superlative esteem of their fellow citizens that they call glory. Scarpia understood this: he withered in the palazzi and the casinos and flourished on horseback in the hills. He was one of those brutes who felt exhilaration when a musket ball flew past his ear; but he recognised that in Venice, as in Rome, the same exhilaration came not from facing death but from the turn of the cards in a game of faro; and triumph over a rival came not from seeing him bleeding at one's feet but from enticing his wife or mistress into one's bed. Decadent, debilitating, profligate the Venetians might be, but was there not something to be said when men fought over sopranos and contraltos rather than power or money or abstract ideas?

*

They strolled back to the Piazza San Marco: the pale light of the dawn came from the east, gently illuminating the facade of the basilica. The revellers had mostly gone. Would Scarpia fight for the diva now leaning on his arm? He was momentarily bewitched. It was not simply her voice or her beauty that had cast the spell but her gaiety, her simplicity, her ease with a stranger, but there was no suggestion in her manner that she might want him to return with her to her lodgings and make love, nor was there any move by Scarpia to do so. They reached the base of the campanile of San Marco where Tosca's maid was waiting.

Tosca turned to Scarpia. '*Grazie, Signor Barone,*' she said with a curtsy – her face, despite her exhaustion, showing a gentle, ironic smile. 'You saved me from, at the very least, a dunking in the canal.'

'And you saved me from an evening alone.'

'We will meet again?'

'Unless I block my ears with wax, like Odysseus, I shall come whenever I can to hear you sing.'

'And you will let me know? You will come backstage?'

'If I can beat a path through the crowd of your admirers.'

'Simply say your name. I shall come out to greet you, because we are friends, are we not?'

'Yes, we are friends.'

Nine

U pon his return from Venice to the Villa Larunda, Scarpia found Paola entertaining the Marchesa Attavanti. The marchesa was a year or two older than Paola, quite as beautiful though in a different way, with fair hair and blue eyes; and, though related to all the best families and always at the receptions of the Spanish ambassador, was neither within Paola's circle of friends nor a member of that notional committee that decided what was or was not *comme il faut*. The reason for her exclusion from both was her reputation for free-thinking and, more significantly, the active republicanism of her brother, Cesare Angelotti. As a result Scarpia was at first surprised and then a little annoyed to find her drinking tea and toying with a macaroon in his house. Nor did he much like the look she gave him from beneath her long eyelashes – a look which on all previous occasions had been no more than a glance, but now lingered as if to say, 'We may exchange words, but we both know that before all else I am a woman and you are a man.'

'Ah, Vitellio,' said Paola, rising to greet her husband. 'You have made your entry at just the right time, because the marchesa has really come to see you and not me.'

Scarpia gave a slight bow. 'How can I be of service?'

The look lingered a moment longer, but then she gave a little smile before adopting an expression of gentle pleading. 'My dear Baron, my brother has been arrested. He is in the Castel Sant'Angelo. I was wondering if you could use your influence with Treasurer Ruffo to save him.'

Scarpia remained standing and frowned. 'Why has he been arrested?'

'They say he has been conspiring to depose the Pope.'

'And has he? Does such a conspiracy exist?'

The marchesa looked evasive. 'That's such a grand word – *conspiracy*. You know Cesare. Perhaps not well. He is an idealist. He writes down his thoughts. And he shares those thoughts with his friends. And certainly some of those friends are Masons and artists at the Academy. But how could they bring down the government? The idea is absurd.'

'I can certainly talk to the Treasurer,' said Scarpia, 'but he has limited influence with the Inquisition.'

'Of course, I know, but he has the ear of His Holiness. And you were once, I think, at the Castel Sant'Angelo, and Paola tells me that your man Spoletta is part of the garrison, so perhaps you could see Cesare is well treated. I fear they will subject him to the strappado. If only they knew what a sweet man he really is. He would never hurt a fly.'

'I will see what I can do,' said Scarpia.

'I will be eternally grateful,' said the marchesa, once again with a look from beneath her eyelashes to suggest how that gratitude might be expressed.

'What were these writings that led to his arrest?' asked Scarpia.

'Cesare believes there should be new laws to safeguard the value of our currency.'

'Like the worthless assignats issued by the republicans in France?'

The marchesa blushed. 'No, of course not. They are worthless, I know. And I am a woman. I do not really understand these things. But I know my brother. He may be foolish, but he is hardly dangerous. If you could convey that to Treasurer Ruffo, I would be forever in your debt.'

*

Domenica Attavanti departed.

'Is she your new friend?' Scarpia asked Paola.

'Of course not, but she asked to see me, and, since she is a friend of *your* friend Azara, I could hardly refuse.'

'I hear bad things about her.'

'What? Her affair with Pinuchi?'

'And others.'

'Well, that's hardly surprising if you look at her husband, the marchese. And everyone has affairs. It's just that among those republicans people are more open about that sort of thing.'

'All the same, I don't like her.'

'I don't like her either, but she is a friend of Azara and it was apparently Azara who suggested that she approach you.'

'Why doesn't Azara do something?'

'Apparently as Spanish ambassador he cannot interfere in the internal affairs of the Papal States.'

Scarpia nodded.

'Can you do anything?' asked Paola.

'Spoletta will know which palms to grease to make him more comfortable.'

'I cannot help feeling,' said Paola, 'that too much is made of these so-called conspirators.'

'Ideas lead to actions,' said Scarpia, remembering his conversation with Father Simone. 'And the government is vulnerable on the question of the currency. Men like Angelotti take advantage of the discontent.'

*

The next day, Scarpia told Treasurer Ruffo of the visit of the Marchesa Attavanti, and asked about her brother.

'Angelotti is a nasty piece of work,' said Ruffo. 'He's in with the bankers, who have their eyes on the property of the Church. They look to France, where the lands of the religious orders have been sold off at rock-bottom prices to the only people who have money – the bankers, the Jews, the war profiteers. Cluny, Clairvaux, Molesme, all those precious oases of piety and learning, now in the hands of nouveau-riche bourgeois, the ancient abbeys quarried for stone to build their country houses. That's what Angelotti and his friends would like to see happen here.'

Scarpia kept his word to the Marchesa Attavanti: he asked Spoletta to ensure that Angelotti was well treated by his gaolers in the Castel Sant'Angelo. In due course, Angelotti was put on trial. The evidence against him were the seditious pamphlets found in his house, his frequent encounters with known republicans as reported by the spies of the Inquisition, and a large sum of money found in his apartment which he could not explain. As the trial progressed, Angelotti fell ill, or pretended to fall ill. He was allowed to return home under house arrest, and his trial was adjourned with no date set for its resumption.

2

In the summer of 1795, Fabrizio Ruffo was dismissed as Treasurer to the Papal States. He had retained the personal esteem of Pope Pius VI, and was rewarded for his loyal service with a cardinal's hat; but his fiscal reforms had made him so loathed by the Roman nobility that Pope Pius decided that it would be politic to dismiss him. He was offered other minor posts in the curia, but Ruffo saw that he had become redundant and prepared to leave Rome. 'I have done all I can for the Holy Father,' he told Scarpia. 'And now it is better for all that I return to Naples to serve King Ferdinand, who is, after all, my true sovereign. He has asked me to take on the Royal Domains of Caserta. I shall be well employed. But I shall miss Rome, and I shall miss those I have worked with.' He looked at Scarpia – his habitual detachment giving way to an expression of regret. 'It is hard to believe that it is only five years since you came through my door, a dishevelled Sicilian, and now you are a Roman nobleman…'

'All that I am, Your Eminence, I owe to you.'

Ruffo looked pensive. 'I hope you will not come to regret the course your life has taken. Remember the psalm: *Put not your faith in princes.* We rise and we fall. Only Almighty God is to be trusted, and often His will is difficult to discern. We live in terrible times. Satan has been given leave to tempt us in novel ways. It is as bad as the Reformation – perhaps worse, because Luther, for all his obstinacy, still believed that Christ was the Son of God, whereas these new men with their new ideas believe only in man. I fear for the Church, but most of all I fear for the souls of the many who are led astray.'

'I shall remain faithful,' said Scarpia.

'Yes, I know.' The Cardinal's look that had been pensive now became acute. 'But do not underestimate Satan. Beware the glamour of evil. You will remain faithful, I know, but those around you…' Ruffo hesitated. 'I sometimes ask myself whether we did the right thing…'

'The right thing?'

'Ambition is not a sin. You were ambitious. And you have no doubt what you wanted. But the Baron di Rubaso is no match for the Marcisanos and I wonder whether they will be as steadfast as you are. These Roman patricians think only of their own survival and many have survived over the ages by joining the winning side. Until now the interests of the Roman nobility and of the Pope have been the same, but should they diverge...' He again looked intently at Scarpia. 'You may be put to the test, Baron. The pedestal upon which we have placed you may wobble, it may even fall.'

'I shall remain faithful,' said Scarpia again.

The cardinal took his hand. 'You will find me in Naples if you need me. King Ferdinand, after all, is your king too.'

'Indeed, Your Eminence, but I have my wife and family here in Rome.'

'Of course. And you must send my greetings to your wife. You are pleased with *her*, I hope, and she with you?'

'We are very happy, Your Eminence, and both are aware that we owe that happiness to you.'

They had talked enough. Scarpia knelt to kiss the hand of the new cardinal, his patron. The cardinal raised him to his feet. 'God bless you, Baron. Pray for me, and I shall pray for you, for we are all in the hands of God.'

3

In October of 1795, soon after Cardinal Ruffo's departure for Naples, the National Convention in Paris was dissolved and government entrusted to a five-man Directory. It was more than a year since Robespierre had been guillotined and the Jacobin Club closed, but the persecution of the Church in France had not abated. Catholics supporting the royalist cause were fighting an irregular war against the revolution in the Vendée, and the disciples of the *philosophes* saw the Catholic religion as the source of all bigotry, reaction and superstition. One of the five new directors, Louis-Marie de la Révellière-Lépeaux, meant to replace Catholicism with

Theophilanthropism: ceremonies of this new religion had been held in Paris in the cathedral of Notre-Dame.

Another of the directors was Paul-François Barras, whose former mistress, Josephine de Beauharnais, had recently married Napoleon Bonaparte. Barras used his influence to secure Bonaparte's appointment as commander of the French army in Italy. Through a series of brilliant manoeuvres and dramatic victories over the superior forces of the Austrian Empire, Bonaparte conquered Lombardy and established his reputation as a military genius. In pursuit of the Austrians, French troops invaded and then occupied the Veneto; the Serene Republic capitulated; and in Paris the director Révellière-Lépeaux persuaded his colleagues that the time had come to invade the Papal States, take Rome and depose the Pope.

The *casus belli* would be the earlier refusal of Pope Pius VI to accept the humiliating French demands for reparations following the murder of Bassville. Bonaparte was told that he should march on Rome, and at first the historic role of ending the thousand-year rule of the Roman pontiff appealed to him. 'Our intention is to restore the Capitol,' he announced, 'and to set up there in their honour the statues of the men who won renown, and to free the Roman people from their long slavery.' Bonaparte ordered his troops to invade the legations at the north of the Papal States and, meeting little resistance, they took the cities of Ravenna, Ferrara and Bologna.

Pope Pius VI, with no allies to come to his defence, had no choice but to sue for peace. Still refusing to recognise the republican government in France, and so with no legate in Paris, he summoned Azara, the Spanish ambassador, from his country retreat, and asked him to act as a go-between. Azara agreed, and went to Milan, where Bonaparte laid down his terms for a truce. The Pope was to recognise the French Republic and free all political prisoners. He was to send a delegation to Paris to apologise for the murder of Bassville, pay an indemnity of 21 million scudi, and surrender to the French five hundred rare manuscripts and one hundred works of art. All the ports of the Papal States were to be open to French ships, but closed to those of other nations. The French would remain in possession of Bologna and Ferrara and were to be given control of the Adriatic port of Ancona.

Old and unwell, Pius could not but comply. To raise money to pay the indemnity, the Pope sold many of his personal possessions, and pearls and semi-precious stones were stripped from papal vestments and regalia. Pius urged cardinals, prelates and religious communities to do the same, and the citizens of Rome were told to prepare a list of all objects of value in their possession for possible sequestration by commissioners sent by the French.

The Romans were enraged. Posters and pamphlets execrated the French, and French residents in the city were attacked when they appeared on the streets. Afraid that Bonaparte would make this a pretext for an invasion, papal troops were stationed to protect the homes of French citizens and known republicans. Pius urged his subjects to divert their rage into prayers to powers even greater than the all-conquering Bonaparte. Special services were held in the churches to invoke divine protection; barefoot pilgrims climbed the *scala santa* on their knees praying the rosary, and at the service of benediction held in public squares crowds knelt to venerate the white wafer held in a gold monstrance that was to them the body of Christ.

God turned a deaf ear. In the Romagna, French troops plundered and pillaged, ignoring the terms of the truce. Bonaparte was a man, wrote Azara in a dispatch to Madrid, who 'breathed only blood and fire ... I foresee that all the states of the Church and Rome itself will be destroyed'. As a religious sceptic and anti-clerical of the old school, this in itself might not have distressed Azara, but he had lived agreeably in Rome for the past twenty years and had many Roman friends, such as the Marcisanos.

4

Obedient to their sovereign, Pope Pius VI, the Roman nobility now prepared lists of all their significant works of art. The collection of the Marcisanos, assembled over the centuries, was not as magnificent as those of the Colonnas, Orsinis or Doria-Pamphilis, but it nonetheless contained works that might appeal to the French commissaries who were due in Rome towards the end of July. Ludovico was put in charge of drawing up the list, aided by Paola and their old art master, Seventi. The prince and princess wandered around their palace like unhappy ghosts. They had read reports of the massacres of Catholics in the Vendée, and now of the depredations made by Bonaparte's troops in the Romagna. They lived in terror that they would see their possessions plundered, the Pope guillotined and priests drowned in the Tiber as they had been in the Loire.

Ludovico was more sanguine. Things were bad, but they could be worse. With his exact knowledge of his family's history, he remembered the sack of Rome by the brutal German Landsknechts in 1527; the discriminating pillage of the French commissioners would not be as bad as that. The French were high-handed, but they were not barbarians, and could be appeased.

One Sunday in early July, after hearing Mass in their private chapel, and praying for the beatification of Veronica Giuliani, a Capuchin mystic whose cause was dear to the princess, the Marcisano family assembled for lunch. The adults – the prince and princess, Ludovico and his wife Fulvia, and Paola with her husband Vitellio – sat at one end of the table, while the children with their nursemaids and tutors sat at the other. The liveried footmen served the food in the same silver dishes as always, and poured wine from the same cut-glass decanters. The familiar busts remained on their plinths, the fine canvases remained in their gilded frames; but there was all the same a feeling that at any moment the French commissioners might appear at the door.

'Is the list complete?' the prince asked his two children.

'It is, Father.'

'I only hope that they don't take that portrait of our ancestor Prince Alberto.'

'It is a pity it is by Pisanello,' said Paola.

'By Pisanello, is it?' asked the prince. He had an imprecise knowledge of what works there were in his collection in the Palazzo Marcisano, and almost none as to who had created them.

'And the Cellini salt cellar,' said Ludovico. 'That is a charming piece. It might catch their eye.'

'There are far finer pieces by Cellini in the Vatican,' said Paola. 'And I am sure His Holiness can manage without them.'

'Paola, please...'

'You have to admit, Mother,' said Paola, 'that to a large extent our sovereign pontiff has brought all these troubles on himself.'

'Duke Braschi, perhaps...' the princess murmured: it was permissible for the devout to deflect any criticism of the Pope on to his nephew.

'It is not just the duke,' said Paola. 'He may have taken advantage of the crisis to line his own pockets: that's nothing new. But His Holiness, or at any rate Cardinal Zelada, should have seen which way the wind was blowing and trimmed their sails. How can you continue to refuse to recognise a government that is so emphatically established de facto, and why reject as iniquitous all the new ideas?'

'But they are sacrilegious,' said the princess.

'It suits us to say so,' said Paola, 'because we have done well out of the status quo. But privilege has meant that doddering old archdukes are given command of armies because of their pedigree, and so it is hardly surprising that they are defeated by a general with talent.'

'More than talent,' said Ludovico.

'Are we talking about Bonaparte?' asked Scarpia.

'Who else?'

'He is certainly adept at the use of his artillery in support of his infantry, but at Lodi he had twice the number of troops and guns, and two thousand cavalry, when the Austrians had none. It isn't difficult to seem talented with odds like that.'

Paola frowned. 'I seem to recall that there were other battles in which it was Bonaparte who was outnumbered.'

'I dare say,' said Scarpia. 'But there are factors that go beyond strategy. The French army is made up of starving conscripts. They barely have boots on their feet. They may fight for liberty, equality and fraternity but they also fight for booty. So too does Bonaparte. His armies are merely brigands on a grand scale.'

'And what a pity that we have no Baron Scarpia to apprehend them,' said Paola in a tone of icy sarcasm.

Scarpia bowed coldly across the table. 'A Baron Scarpia would do his best if he had the means.'

'I am sure,' said Paola, her tone still sarcastic. 'A Sicilian would be more than a match for a Corsican were he not surrounded by cowardly and indolent Romans.'

'There is no question that we Romans do lack the martial spirit,' said Ludovico, upset at the tone of this exchange between his sister and her husband.

'The Venetians too,' said Scarpia.

'No Roman wants to fight,' said Scarpia's father-in-law.

'We have been told for so long,' said Paola, 'to love our enemies and turn the other cheek.'

'St Augustine taught that war can be just,' said Scarpia.

'Of course, a just war,' said Ludovico, 'but would our war with France be just? Was there justice for all under King Louis? Or did the French have good reason to revolt?'

'They killed priests,' said the princess.

'Which came first, though?' said Ludovico. 'The Church's support for the royalists or the killing of the priests? But all this is beside the point. They are not proposing to kill priests here in Rome, but simply claim the spoils of war. And how can we object when Rome is filled with trophies looted after our conquests.'

'And so our new Caesar can do as he likes,' said the princess miserably.

'I fear so, Mother. There aren't three hundred Romans to hold back the invader as the Spartans did at Thermopylae.'

Scarpia held his tongue. His fondness for Ludovico restrained him from arguing with him in front of the servants and children. And it was not only that defeatism that enraged him, but the slight blush that came onto his wife's cheeks when her mother had said that the new Caesar could do as he likes.

5

Throughout the summer of 1796, and into the early autumn, battles were fought between French and Austrian armies in the valley of the Po. The uncertainty of the final outcome encouraged the Pope's representatives, negotiating a permanent treaty with the French, to reject some of their terms. The Pope and the cardinals were willing to cede cities in the Romagna, to open the ports of the Papal States to French shipping, to pay the indemnities demanded and surrender of works of art, but they refused the demands made of the Pope as head of the Catholic Church. Pope Pius would not disavow all the edicts he had issued condemning the actions of the French since 1789. 'His Holiness,' the French were told, 'would never be a party to such a defamation of the Church, even if his own life were at risk.'

The negotiations collapsed. The truce was now at an end. France and the Pope were at war. The payment of indemnities ceased, and the works of art, some already packed up and loaded on wagons, remained in Rome. There was an enthusiastic response by the Romans to their sovereign's call to arms. A militia was formed to support the pontifical army. The Pope sent to Vienna for an experienced commander and one was dispatched by the Emperor Joseph – an Italian in the service of the Habsburgs, Lieutenant General Michelangelo Alessandro Colli-Marchi. He arrived at Ancona with an entourage of Austrian officers and was met with a rapturous reception when he reached Rome. Ludovico di Marcisano and two of his cousins enrolled in the militia and Baron Scarpia was given command of a company of dragoons.

*

The papal army marched north expecting to join forces with the Austrians in Lombardy, but as it descended from the foothills of the Apennines into the valley of the Po it was met by the news that an Austrian army sent to relieve Mantua had been defeated by Bonaparte at Rivoli and then, on 2 February, that Mantua had surrendered.

Bonaparte, considering the papal army unworthy of his genius, sent a 33-year-old general, Claude Victor-Perrin, to deal with the approaching force. The two armies met near the town of Faenza, twenty-five miles south-east of Bologna. The papal commander, Lieutenant General Colli-Marchi, was old and ill and had to be carried on a stretcher. He commanded seven thousand ill-trained troops as against Victor-Perrin's nine thousand veterans. Colli-Marchi ordered an assault on the French lines. The battle was brief. The Romans were routed with a loss of eight hundred men as against a hundred of the French. The French captured eighteen cannon, eight colours and 1,200 men.

Neither Scarpia nor Ludovico di Marcisano was among the captured or the dead. Ludovico's contingent of militia, bringing up the rearguard of Colli-Marchi's army, did not reach the field of battle. Scarpia, in the vanguard, had led his dragoons in a fruitless charge against the French lines. As he had raised his sabre to strike a French cuirassier, he was hit in the shoulder by a ball from a pistol that threw him from his horse. The cuirassier who had fired the shot rode on. Spoletta, riding behind Scarpia, reined in his horse, dismounted and lifted Scarpia onto his saddle. They rode off the field of battle to the village of Castel Bolognese. Peasants were bribed to take care of Scarpia and a doctor was brought from Bologna to treat his wound. Scarpia was in a fever for ten days. Only five weeks after the battle was he well enough to return to Rome.

*

After the fiasco at Faenza, Pope Pius VI had no choice but to sue for peace. The delegation sent to Bonaparte's headquarters at the small town of Tolentino included the Pope's nephew Duke Braschi Onesti, Cardinal Mattei and Lieutenant General Colli-Marchi. Bonaparte received them with great politeness, but this was a feint. The terms he presented were severe. The Pope's newly raised army was to be disbanded. Lieutenaut General Colli-Marchi and all other Austrian officers were to be dismissed Lieutenaut. The papal territories of Avignon and the Comtat Venaissin were to be ceded to France in perpetuity, and a large part of the Romagna would be incorporated into a new Cisalpine Republic. The existing indemnity of 21 million lire was increased to 36 million. The family of the murdered Hugon de Bassville were to be paid financial compensation by the Pope. All republican prisoners, among them Vicenzo Palmieri and Cesare Angelotti, were to be released, and members of the Roman nobility known to be antagonistic towards the French were to be banished and their property confiscated. The port of Civitavecchia was to be open exclusively to the French navy, and at any future conclave, the French government would have the right to veto the choice made by the cardinals of a new pope.

The papal delegation was given two hours to either accept or reject Bonaparte's demands. Its reply was uncompromising. It could accept his demands of a military, political and fiscal nature, but not those concerning the governance of the Church. Bonaparte dropped his demand for a veto at the next conclave and on 19 February 1797 the treaty was signed. The delegation returned to Rome in triumph: the Holy City had been saved from occupation by the French.

When Scarpia got back to Rome, he received a less rapturous reception. The martial fervour of the Romans had evaporated: valour was out of fashion. A papal decree, ordering the Romans to behave courteously towards the French, was unnecessary: no one wanted to risk banishment or the confiscation of their property. Scarpia was advised by Azara that in the current climate, given his known antipathy towards republicans and the French, he should lie low; he therefore stayed away from the ambassador's *conversazioni* and only left the Villa Larunda with his wife and children to go to Mass on a Sunday. He worked hard at his recuperation, lifting and pushing and pulling to recover the full use of his left arm. Paola treated him kindly. 'How is my hero?' she would ask every morning with the same look of amused affection as when Pietro, shouting 'Look, Mama!', jumped on his pony over a log.

Ten

In the middle of August 1797, the French ambassador to the Holy See, Citizen Cacault, was replaced by Joseph Bonaparte, the older brother of the all-conquering general, Napoleon. He took up residence in the Palazzo Corsini on the via della Lungara with a large retinue, which included an enthusiastic republican, General Maturin-Léonard Duphot. Disregarding all diplomatic conventions, the two men set out to encourage and organise the republican agitators, providing them with funds and tricolour cockades.

Also among the entourage of the new French ambassador was the French painter Armand Ringel, who, together with Girodet, Fabre, Gérard and Gros, had been a student of Jacques-Louis David and was now considered equal to, if not superior to, his master. The Ringel family were originally from Alsace, but had lived in Paris for two generations. Armand's father, a wigmaker like his father before him, had recognised his son's precocious talent and sent him to the Académie Royale in the Louvre. Failing to win the Prix de Rome in 1784, Armand had gone to the Eternal City at his father's expense to study under Winckelmann. He joined the Freemasons at the French Academy, moved in a circle that included the republican Cesare Angelotti, his sister the

Marchesa Attavanti and the young painter Mario Cavaradossi, whose mother was French. Ringel earned his keep by painting exquisite portraits of rich Romans and English families making the grand tour. In 1786, he caused a scandal by seducing both the wife and the daughter of Sir Charles Webster. Sir Charles complained to the Cardinal Secretary of State, and Armand Ringel was expelled from the city.

Back in Paris, Ringel's reputation for depravity was no impediment to a career as a portraitist, and, following the revolution in 1789, actually became an asset – an accoutrement to his Jacobin opinions. He painted superb portraits of some of the republican *salonnières* such as Madame Roland and Josephine de Beauharnais, and one of Josephine's lovers, the young General Bonaparte. He had also painted portraits for the Marseilles silk merchant, François Clary, whose daughter Julie was married to Joseph Bonaparte. Another daughter, Désirée, had been briefly engaged to Napoleon. She was now the fiancée of General Duphot, and had moved into the French Embassy in Rome, the Palazzo Corsini, with her mother.

Ringel had been asked by the Directory in Paris to accompany Joseph Bonaparte to Rome and advise on what works of art should be sequestered and taken to Paris. Now thirty-five years old, he was tall and thin with fleshy lips, narrow eyes and, suffering from rosacea, a strong red knobbly nose. He was proud of his appearance, particularly his long sideburns and thick, curly blond hair which, with the demise of the wig, had come into its own. The demise of the wig had, incidentally, ruined his father, but, despite the kindness his parents had shown him as a child, Ringel was indifferent to the abject conditions in which they now lived. He had married five years before, but left his wife and their two-year-old child to live openly with one of the lesser revolutionary *salonnières*, Giselle d'Annat. He had had a child by Mme d'Annat, and a number of his female models went on, after their portraits were completed, to give birth to babies who grew up to have curly blond hair.

The Directory in Paris had been shrewd in sending Ringel to Rome. Already, many magnificent works of art had arrived in the wake of France's conquering armies in the newly created National Museum of Art in the Louvre – Van Eyck's altarpiece from Ghent, *Adoration of the Lamb*; Rubens's *Descent from the Cross* from Antwerp Cathedral; and Rembrandt's *Night Watch* from Amsterdam's town hall. An altarpiece had been sent from Parma; Titians, Veroneses and Tintorettos from Venice; and Raphaels from Florence. The Directory wanted to make sure that the French commissioners chose equal masterpieces from Rome, and Ringel, having lived in the city, knew where they were to be found.

Many of the Roman nobles, rather than treat their depredators with open loathing or a sullen resentment, gave receptions to welcome them to Rome. Ringel's reputation was such that a number of marchesas and contessas and even two cardinals swallowed their pride and tried to commission portraits either of their families or, more often, of themselves. Though Ringel's fees were now equal to his reputation, he spurned these advances. He had come away from Rome after his earlier stay with a contempt for the lazy, self-indulgent citizens who were content to be ruled by a priest.

However, Ringel did condescend to attend a ball given by Duchess Braschi, the wife of the Pope's nephew, Duke Braschi Onesti, to introduce Joseph Bonaparte and his entourage to Roman society. As a Falconieri, she was rich enough both to contribute towards the indemnity and still provide sumptuous hospitality for the city's French guests. When dancing a *contredanse allemande* with Ringel, the duchess led him to understand that accepting a commission to paint her portrait would not only be financially rewarding but somehow historically significant because of her connection through her husband with the Pope.

Ringel did not care a toss for the duchess's links with the Pope, nor for her position in Roman society, nor particularly for her money, which would be no better or worse than anyone else's. He had grown tired of painting portraits of middle-aged women with their bonnets and wrinkles, and was only interested in those women of an age when the flesh was still firm and the skin still smooth but a measure of maturity gave interest to the face. 'Women until the age of twenty-five are as blank as an untouched canvas; and ten years later, the bloom has gone.' He was on the lookout for a woman around the age of thirty who was beautiful in a distinctive way, and he met just such a woman that evening when introduced by the Duchess Braschi Onesti to Princess Paola di Marcisano.

'So you are Monsieur Ringel?' said Paola, speaking in Italian.

'I am.'

'And you understand Italian. Of course. You lived here in Rome.'

'And you speak French?'

'Soon we shall all be speaking French,' said Paola, 'but you have made it more difficult because those poor royalist refugees who came to the city and were making their living giving lessons in French have now *at your request* been expelled from the city.' The 'at your request' was said with an ironic smile.

Ringel scowled. 'They deserved the guillotine,' he said, 'and ran to save their necks.'

Paola raised her hand to her own neck and held it for a moment over the emerald necklace that lay on the soft flesh of her pale bosom. 'And our necks too, perhaps…'

'Unlikely,' said Ringel.

'Unlikely,' she repeated, as if it meant the sentence had been merely deferred.

They danced a quadrille. 'You dance well, Monsieur Ringel,' said Paola. 'Were you taught as a child?'

'No, Principessa, I was not. My father was a wigmaker.'

'And are not the children of wigmakers taught to dance?'

'Some, perhaps. But this one was not.'

'So how did you learn the quadrille?'

'I was taught by friends after 1789.'

'Lady friends, perhaps?'

'At the time, male dance masters were not to be found.'

'Guillotined, no doubt, for teaching the nobility how to enjoy themselves.'

'Dancing is not a crime.'

'No, of course not, for if it were, you would not be here. But during revolutions some things go out of fashion – like wigs, for example.'

'I see plenty of wigs here.'

'Yes, older men still wear wigs. It has become habitual. Men are not as adaptable to changing fashions as women.'

'Does your husband still wear a wig?'

'My husband?' Paola repeated the word as if it brought something forward from the back of her mind. 'My husband *prefers* not to wear a wig. If he wore one, it would be to make a point.'

'Is he an old man?'

'Not in years. He is three years older than I am.'

'Is he here?'

'He … no, he is not here.'

'He doesn't like dancing?'

'Yes, he likes dancing, but, to be candid, he doesn't like the French.'

'While you?'

'I am obedient to our sovereign pontiff, who has said we must be cordial towards our conquerors.'

'And would that cordiality extend to your sitting for a portrait?'

Paola blushed. The music stopped. He bowed, and she curtsied without making a reply.

'Would you like to take the air on the loggia?' asked Ringel.

Paola clearly heard what he said, but walked ahead of him towards a group that included her brother. 'Ludovico, may I introduce *Citizen* Ringel?'

The two men exchanged bows. 'I have long been an admirer,' said Ludovico. 'When you were here before you did a masterly sketch of our cousin Cosimo di Prata and his family. And a portrait of the Duchess of Palada.'

Ringel frowned, as if he did not like to be reminded of his days in Rome. 'She is now dead, I believe.'

'Yes, she died last year. A good woman. Devout. But –' Ludovico was about to add something, but appeared to think better of it. Instead, he turned to those standing with him and introduced them to Ringel – some showing curiosity at meeting the celebrated portraitist, others a coldness towards the Jacobin come to Rome to plunder its treasures, and one – the *abate* Caltano – an outright repugnance, which he expressed by moving away.

'I have asked your sister,' said Ringel to Ludovico, 'if she would allow me to paint her portrait.'

Ludovico glanced anxiously at Paola, then at Ringel. 'Well, clearly … yes … that does her great honour, since … but her husband … he would, perhaps, permit it.' He glanced again at Paola with a doubtful look.

'I seem to remember,' said Ringel, 'that married women in Rome did more or less as they pleased.'

'It depends on the husband,' said Ludovico.

'And your husband keeps you on a leash?' Ringel asked Paola.

'He is a Sicilian,' said Paola. 'Their customs are different to ours.'

'But even a Sicilian would surely take pride in the beauty of his wife.'

'Of course,' said Ludovico.

'Perhaps,' said Paola.

'And wish to see it immortalised.'

'Immortalised?' said Paola with a smile. 'You mean captured on canvas before it deteriorates with age.'

Ringel returned the smile and gave a slight bow as if to say, 'You read my mind exactly.'

'I am sure Vitellio could be persuaded,' said Ludovico to his sister. 'It is an opportunity not to be missed.'

2

There was consternation, envy and excitement among Paola's circle of friends when it became known that the celebrated Ringel wished to paint her portrait. The general view – the view, that is, of the committee of matrons conveyed to Paola by Graziella di Pozzo – concurred with that of Ludovico: it was an opportunity not to be missed. Graziella made no bones about her envy. 'If he asked me, I would not hesitate.' The two friends stood together looking into a large looking glass with a gilt frame discussing why Ringel should have chosen the one rather than the other. 'My face is too round,' said Graziella. 'And perhaps too plump. You are so lucky to have those high cheekbones. Frenchmen like women with leaner faces. It makes them seem interesting.'

'Seem interesting?' asked Paola with a smile.

'Well, perhaps you are more interesting. Original, anyway – not least in your choice of a husband.'

Paola frowned: she had not yet mentioned the matter to Scarpia.

'And you are taller,' she said. 'More French, in fact.'

'I am not French,' said Paola.

'But you have some French blood in your veins.'

'So do most of us.'

'And are you prepared…?' Graziella looked at her friend with her eyebrows raised.

'Prepared for what?' Paola pretended not to catch the meaning of Graziella's innuendo.

'He is well known to sleep with his models.'

'I shall be the exception,' said Paola.

'You don't find him attractive?' asked Graziella.

'A gangling middle-aged man with those absurd curls, horrible nose and that conceit?'

'Well, he does have something to be conceited about.'

'A good painter is not necessarily an admirable man.'

'And do we only love admirable men?' asked Graziella, whose *cicisbeo*, the *cavaliere* Sodano, not only had bow legs but was generally considered a fool.

'I would not be posing for Monsieur Ringel as Venus,' said Paola firmly. 'I shall be wearing a dress and I shall remain wearing a dress. And one does not fall in love with a man of that kind.'

*

Paola had decided in her own mind to accept the invitation of Armand Ringel, but knew she had to think carefully about how she would persuade her husband to give his consent. Already, Scarpia had been annoyed that she had gone to the Duchess Braschi's ball, and had noticed the trouble she had taken with her appearance. 'If you are fortunate,' he said with a sour smile, 'you may dance with the man who tried to kill your husband at Faenza.'

'I don't imagine that there will be cuirassiers among the guests,' said Paola.

'Just the officers who issued the orders,' said Scarpia.

'As you gave such orders to your men.'

The problem Paola faced with Scarpia was that he was not a Roman. A Roman nobleman had in his blood millennia of placating their conquerors, whether they be Goths or Germans or French. They had been conquered before. They would be conquered again.

They had survived by bending with the wind and, remaining true to the precepts of the religion of which they were the custodians, forgiving their enemies even as they loaded carts with their finest works of art.

Scarpia was a Sicilian. He was possessed by the spirit of vendetta. In this he had much in common with the Roman people who were baffled by their pontiff's courtesy towards the atheist Jacobins, and seethed with fury at the sight of bumptious Frenchmen touring the palaces and galleries choosing which artistic treasures to plunder. Scarpia, had he not been an officer in the pontifical army, would have joined the demonstrations that every now and then erupted in the city. His frustration was palpable, made all the more acute by the passivity and acquiescence of the Marcisanos. Paola could see this, and realised that the question of the portrait might ignite an explosion. Not that there was much he could do if she chose to defy him. As Paola had told Spoletta, Rome was her city, and she would do as she pleased.

However, her pride too came into play. Having defied her parents to marry Scarpia, she did not want her marriage to fail. Scarpia's impetuousness had been clear from the start; it had once been part of his attraction. He therefore had to be brought round to the idea of the portrait – but how? Paola was used to having her way without resorting to subterfuge; not for moral reasons, but from pride, deceit went against the grain; but since it was the view of the committee of matrons that she should accept Ringel's offer, and since she could not but feel a certain exhilaration at being chosen, Scarpia must be persuaded one way or another to give his consent.

*

Two days after the ball in the Palazzo Braschi, she was sitting with Scarpia in their garden in the late afternoon, watching their children play with a ball. She saw the look of pride in their father's eyes. 'Aren't they beautiful?' she said to Scarpia. 'They are both at such a delightful age.'

'Of course they are beautiful,' said Scarpia. 'They have a beautiful mother.'

'And a handsome father.'

'Perhaps.'

'Would it be an idea to find someone to paint them – or perhaps just a pencil sketch – so that we could always be reminded of how lovely they were at this age?'

'Yes,' said Scarpia. 'But who?'

'Did you ever see the family group of those cousins of mine, the di Pratas?'

'I don't think so.'

'It is exquisite – so delicate and true to life.'

'Who was the artist?'

'That Frenchman, Ringel. He has since become famous.'

Scarpia frowned. 'And a Jacobin.'

'Oh, you have to be a Jacobin in France if you want to get on. Look at David.'

'And isn't Ringel in Rome?'

'Yes, he's here at the Villa Corsini. I met him at the ball. He is not unpleasant.'

Scarpia was silent. Paola could see him looking at his children and considering the idea of a great artist capturing their innocence and beauty in a work of art.

'I would not sit for a Jacobin,' said Scarpia.

'It would just be of the children,' said Paola. 'Perhaps with their mother.'

'Isn't he a notorious seducer?' asked Scarpia.

Paola smiled. 'So they say. But I think I would be safe with the children.'

'And without the children?'

'Even then. If you saw him…'

'Not another Bonaparte?'

'Not at all. Terrible teeth, an ugly nose, absurd curly hair. His father was a wigmaker.'

'Do you think he would accept the commission?'

'It's worth a try. Graziella says he has already been approached by Prince Paducci to do a sketch of Letizia.'

Scarpia scowled. 'Paducci can afford his fees.'

'Oh, I don't think it's a matter of money.'

They went on to talk of other things. Paola let the idea germinate in her husband's mind. Two days later, over breakfast, Scarpia said: 'How would one approach this Frenchman, Ringel?'

'I don't know. I could ask Graziella.'

'I would not want to have anything to do with it.'

'No, of course not. Don't worry. Leave it to me.'

3

Negotiations between Paola and Ringel were conducted by the Marchesa Attavanti. It was agreed that Ringel should undertake a pencil sketch of Paola with her children, and at the same time an unofficial painting of Paola alone. To save the baron, her husband, from the humiliation of having a French Jacobin under his roof, Paola and her children would go to the French Academy, where Ringel had been allotted the best and largest studio. After the session with the children, Paola's maid Nunzi would take them to eat ice creams on the Corso, or for a walk in the Borghese Gardens, while their mother sat for her portrait. Domenica Attavanti and Graziella di Pozzo had advised Paola on what to wear. But rejecting their choice of something low-cut and revealing, Paola chose a simple blue dress, with bunched sleeves, a raised waist and a diaphanous gauze covering her bust. Little Francesca wore a long dress that, like her mother's, went down to the ankles, and Pietro a beautiful red tunic with breeches, stockings and shoes with silver buckles.

The three, with Nunzi in attendance, were accompanied by Domenica Attavanti on their first visit to the Palazzo Mancini. They rode not in the coach with the family's coat of arms but in a modest barouche, and little attention was paid to them when they arrived. Ringel was sent for and came down with a preoccupied look on his face as if his mind was on other things, but he welcomed them in a friendly way, nodding towards Paola, then the maid Nunzi, bending down to greet the children, then turning away to say something to the Marchesa Attavanti as, with a wave to the three Scarpias, she took her leave.

Ringel led his models up the shallow stairs to the first floor of the Palazzo Mancini, then to the end of a long corridor and into a cavernous studio with a large window that faced north over the garden. The room was filled with plaster casts of statues from antiquity, huge frames without pictures, easels of different sizes stacked against the walls, faux-marble pedestals, Grecian urns, even two spears and an old shield – props for paintings of classical heroes. In the centre of the room there was a platform with a dark brown backcloth suspended between two poles, and on the platform a sofa with carved walnut borders and hard red-striped upholstery.

Ringel now directed the party towards a room that led off the studio where, he said, they could leave what would not be required for the sitting and arrange their clothes. The room seemed small because of its low ceiling and the kind of clutter one might expect to find in the green room of a theatre – more props stacked against the wall and, in a painted armoire, racks of togas and tunics to go with the wooden shields and spears. There was a large gilt-framed mirror and also a sofa – deeper, wider and more softly upholstered than that on the platform. Involuntarily, at the sight of this sofa, Nunzi directed a quick look at her mistress. Paola ignored the look but nonetheless blushed. She took off her cape and threw it on the sofa, as if it could serve no other purpose than this. Nunzi took the rag doll that Francesca had brought with her and propped it against the arm of the sofa, as if this too would somehow ensure its innocent purpose. Then the three models, starting with Francesca and ending with Paola, passed in front of the mirror and adjusted their clothes and hair before returning to the studio.

Ringel had a large sheet of thick paper pinned to an easel, and on the ledge four or five sticks of graphite. He looked at his subjects, but said nothing about the clothes they had chosen to wear. He helped first Paola and then her children onto the platform and seated them on the sofa. He asked Paola to lean back in an informal pose, and the children, one on each side, to lean against her while looking straight ahead. 'Can you stay still like this?' he asked, adding a promise of biscuits and lemonade at the end of their ordeal.

Both Pietro and Francesca had gathered from the conversations they had overheard, if not understood, and the excitement shown by Nunzi, their mother and her two friends, that sitting for the strange-looking Frenchman to sketch their portraits was something very grand and important, and so they did not need the bribe of biscuits and lemonade to behave well. As he was sketching, Ringel spoke pleasantly about this and that – his deep voice was more attractive than his appearance – and every now and then, when he had said something amusing – or simply said something that sounded amusing to the children because of his French accent – he said, 'No, you must not smile. Simply think pleasant thoughts, about how lovely the weather is today and how lucky you are to have such a beautiful mama.' Then to Paola: 'Please don't frown, Principessa. It makes it look as if you are annoyed with your children.'

Paola smoothed her brow. She kept her eyes not on Ringel but on the back of his easel, glancing only occasionally towards Nunzi, who was sitting on a papier mâché sarcophagus set against the wall. After a while, Ringel stopped talking, absorbed in his work, and his models became imbued with the same concentration, remaining silent and still. Then, after around fifty minutes, he said: 'There, that is enough for today. Now for the biscuits and lemonade.'

The two children clambered off the sofa, stretched the limbs that had remained still for so long, jumped off the platform and, at Ringel's instructions, pulled a long thick rope with a tassel that rang a bell. A few moments later, a servant came in with a tray on which were the promised refreshments. It was placed on a plinth. The glasses were filled. Paola and Nunzi declined the glasses offered by the servant. They waited while, behind them, Ringel set aside the paper on which he had been sketching and adjusted the easel to take a larger canvas. The glasses emptied, the biscuits eaten, the servant withdrew with the tray. Nunzi took Francesca to the side room to recover her cape and rag doll.

'Now,' said Paola to her children, 'Nunzi will take you for a walk and if you are *very* good she will buy you an ice cream, but better make it a secret from Papa because you know he doesn't like you to eat so many sweet things.' The children exchanged delighted, conspiratorial looks and then departed with Nunzi.

*

Paola and Ringel were now alone. The painter, again like a doctor directing a patient, asked his subject to return to the platform and resume her place on the sofa. He followed her onto the platform, stood back to study her pose, took hold of her right arm, placed it along the back of the sofa, then placed the left on her lap. He smelt of sweat and paint.

'May I?' he asked, and, without waiting for her to answer, adjusted a lock of her hair. 'Are you happy with that?'

'With what?'

'With what you are wearing, the way you are placed.'

'You are the painter,' she said. 'I am merely the model.'

Ringel returned to his easel and, as he started to sketch on the canvas with a piece of charcoal, spoke of the charm of her children.

'You have a daughter, I am told,' said Paola.

'Yes.'

'How old?'

'Ten. Perhaps eleven years old.'

'Do you see her?'

'No.'

'Why not?'

'Her mother is insufferable, and has another husband.'

'How is she insufferable?'

'She is dull.'

'Did she become dull?'

'No, she was always dull. But I did not notice it.'

'Because she was pretty?'

'She was pretty and I was young.'

'Many of us make mistakes when we are young,' said Paola, 'but we live with the consequences.'

'For me the consequence would have meant abandoning my art.'

'May artists take liberties that are forbidden to others?'

'All should be free, but, for an artist, freedom of spirit is life itself, a life that is suffocated by a whingeing, petit bourgeois wife.'

'And with the Bastille there fell some of those conventions that bound men to their wives?'

'In a republic liberty is not merely political.'

They continued to converse, but warily. Paola asked him about his earlier time in Rome; about how he had come to know the

Marchesa Attavanti, Cesare Angelotti and Mario Cavaradossi. 'Cavaradossi,' said Ringel, 'is a charming fellow, and a handsome young man, but his talent does not match his looks. Angelotti, on the other hand, has the potential to be a great statesman – a Roman Danton, perhaps – but he is inept.'

'He wanted to assassinate the Pope,' said Paola.

'That is what I mean by his ineptitude. What difference would it make if he were to kill the octogenarian Braschi? They would simply elect someone else. You can depose a pope without killing him …'

'We have lived happily under the popes for a thousand years,' said Paola.

'The nobility, perhaps,' said Ringel, 'but not the people.'

'Bankers and doctors and lawyers are not the people.'

'We must not argue,' said Ringel. 'It will distract me and distort your features.'

'As you please.'

*

Later in the week, Paola returned to the Palazzo Mancini with her maid and her children for a second sitting. All went as before. Ringel, who now had a brush in his hand, answered her questions about Joseph Bonaparte and his wife Julie. 'And tell me about General Bonaparte,' asked Paola. 'You painted his portrait, I believe?'

'We had only a few sittings. He was very busy.'

'Was he polite, amusing, or what?'

'He was businesslike. But I knew him already. I had met him with the Clarys. He is a soldier, but holds artists in great esteem.'

'Women find him attractive?'

'Of course.'

'Though they say he is small.'

'He is small, but his face is intriguing. An acute intelligence, an inflexible will.'

'And his wife, Mme de Beauharnais?'

'An exceptional woman.'

'I am told that she is older than he is?'

'Yes, six years older.'

'And was married before?'

'Yes. Her husband was guillotined in '94. She has two children.'

'And they say…' Paola blushed. 'They say that she had a number of lovers before her marriage to Bonaparte.'

'Barras was one of them, and there were others. Apparently a night with Josephine is like no other.'

'But does not the general mind?'

'About the lovers? No, he is no prude. But he would mind if he knew about Lieutenant Charles.'

Paola's face went an even deeper pink – blushing not so much because of the indelicacy of the subject as at the thrill of finding herself with someone privy to the secrets of the Bonaparte family. 'Who is Lieutenant Charles?' she asked.

'An officer in the hussars. Ten years younger than Josephine. A buffoon, but handsome and amusing. He makes her laugh.'

Both were silent as Ringel worked on the portrait. Paola looked at the back of the easel, but could not avoid the face of the painter in her field of vision. Little by little the man whose eyes flitted between her and the canvas seemed to change shape, his features darkening, the eyes receding under his brows yet glowing, his nose growing longer and pointing at her whenever he looked up – pointing at her and hovering as if it were the brush in his hand.

The session ended. Ringel did not escort Paola down the wide staircase to the entrance of the Palazzo Mancini, which she at first thought was somewhat discourteous, but then accepted as an aspect of his disdain for convention. Nunzi and the coachman were waiting; the children were called from where they had been playing in the garden. They returned home.

At the third sitting, the following week, the children needed no prompting to find their positions on the podium, but after only half an hour Ringel let them go. He removed the parchment from the easel and replaced it with the canvas, put away his pencils and took up his brush. All seemed to be going as before, though there was less conversation. Paola's odd questions about this and that received abrupt answers: she sensed that Ringel was in a poor mood. She remained motionless looking at the easel and slipped once again into a trance – the brush, the angry eyes, the bulbous nose.

Then, suddenly, the spell was broken. '*Merde*,' said Ringel, throwing down his brush.

Paola was startled, not just by the gesture but by the use of such a crude word.

'What is the matter?'

'This is all hopeless.' He pointed at his easel.

Paola abandoned her pose and leaned forward with a look of concern. 'Hopeless? Why hopeless?'

'Because here I am painting the frills and bows on your dress as if you were just another bourgeois wife whose husband has paid me a fat commission.'

'But my husband has not paid you a fat commission, though of course –'

'That is not the point. I chose as my model not the Baroness Scarpia di Rubaso but a beautiful woman, and here I am painting a blue dress.'

'But there is my face and, well, my arms,' said Paola.

'Let me show you something,' said Ringel. He went to a table by the wall, shuffled through some papers and came back with what appeared to be several pencil sketches. He mounted the platform, brusquely told Paola to make room for him on the sofa, and sat down next to her. 'When I was in Paris,' he said, 'I went to visit David. He is working on a most extraordinary painting – a subject from antiquity – the legend of the Sabine women. As you know, they were abducted by the Romans, who were short of women; their fathers came to avenge their rape, and the women placed themselves between the two armies.'

'I know the legend,' said Paola. 'My brother would say we are descended from those Sabine women.'

'David's painting will be a masterpiece. I cannot begin to describe its splendour. And at the centre are three figures – two helmeted warriors, one with a raised spear, another a raised sword, both with shields, and between them a young woman, her arms outstretched to keep the antagonists apart. Now these –' he showed Paola the papers he held in his hand – 'are two discarded sketches of that woman which David gave to me and said I could keep. See the way, even in these sketches, the look of gentleness on her face, and the way that gentleness is expressed in her whole body, which we see lightly shrouded, falling over her thigh, clinging to her breasts.'

Paola looked at the drawings. 'He is a skilled draughtsman.'

'Of course. But he is much more, because you see in this painting that the essence of a woman is as much in her body as in her face. And it is that essence that I want to capture in you, not in a portrait in which you might be the wife of a banker, but like a woman from antiquity – a vestal virgin perhaps, or even one of your ancestors, a Sabine woman.'

Paola said nothing.

'The great glory of art in our age,' Ringel went on, 'is to depict humanity in all its beauty and grandeur – including the beauty of women. Think not just of David but the marble statues of Venus by Canova –'

'I will not pose naked as Venus,' said Paola.

Ringel smiled. 'I am not asking you to pose naked,' he said, 'but to exchange this dull dress for a costume from antiquity – there are a number in the armoire.'

'And what?' asked Paola. 'Sit in the same pose here on the sofa?'

'If you have the strength and patience,' said Ringel, 'I would like you to stand by a column or a plinth.'

Paola turned to look at Ringel, as if to assess the sincerity behind his words. He was looking not at her but at David's sketches: he seemed genuinely enthralled by his master's art.

'Very well,' she said. 'Let's see if I can find something to wear.'

They climbed down off the platform and went together into the room with the armoire and sofa.

'Perhaps I could be the nymph Larunda,' said Paola.

'Who was Larunda?'

'She is our household goddess. Our villa is built in the ruins of her temple.'

Ringel opened the armoire and sifted through the costumes. 'Was she beautiful?'

'According to Ovid, she was beautiful, but talked too much. She told Juno that Jupiter was having an affair with Juturna, the wife of Janus. Jupiter cut out her tongue and ordered Mercury to take her to the gates of the underworld. But Mercury fell in love with her. They made love on the way and she gave birth to twins.'

'Would this suit Larunda?' Ringel took from the rack by the armoire a white muslin dress that, to judge from its pristine condition, had not been worn before.

Paola took the hanger and held the diaphanous dress at arm's length. 'Yes. That will do.'

Ringel left the room. Paola, with some difficulty, removed her blue dress, wondering how she would put it on again without Nunzi to help her. She then removed her underclothes, stockings and shoes and put on the muslin dress. There was a tape which she tied beneath her bosom; the skirts fell to below the knee. She looked at herself in the gilt-framed mirror. The shadow of her pubic hair could be seen through the muslin and her nipples made pinnacles in the white cloth. She could pass for a nymph.

Paola walked barefoot into the studio. Ringel had pushed the sofa to the side of the platform, and replaced it with a column on which he had placed an urn. He looked at her with a professional eye. 'That's fine, don't you think?'

'It is revealing,' said Paola.

'Which is as it should be,' said Ringel. 'Beauty should not be concealed.'

She mounted the platform, and stood by the plinth.

'Could you try looking at the urn? Imagine that it contains the ashes of your father?'

'Do you want me to look sad?'

'No. That was a bad idea.' He followed her onto the platform. 'Perhaps there should be a garland in your hair. But we can find that later.' He took her arm and placed her elbow against the column. 'And if you could just turn your head a little this way.' His face was close to hers: again, the smell of sweat and paint. 'Could you remain standing like that?'

'I think so.'

'And the fall of the cloth. That is all-important.' He pulled the muslin down over her left breast, his knuckle brushing against her nipple; then the same with the right. 'If you could turn your leg a little…' He went behind her and crouched to first raise and then drop the muslin so that it fell over her flank. He rearranged the creases and she felt his fingers trace their lines on her buttocks.

'Surely,' she said, embarrassed that she was breathless as she spoke, 'you won't portray me from behind.'

'No, but the whole thing must look right. Of course the angle from the front matters more.' He came round, not looking her in the eye, apparently intent on arranging the robe covering her body.

He knelt once again to adjust the hem, his nose an inch from her thigh. She stood motionless, looking down at his curly locks. Her breathing quickened.

'There,' said Ringel. 'I think that's about right.' He stood up, climbed down off the platform and returned to his easel. 'You cannot imagine,' he said, starting to sketch with charcoal on the blank canvas, 'what a fine work this will be – equal, I hope, to anything by David or Canova.'

Paola barely heard what he was saying. Words did not penetrate the trance. She stood without moving, her breathing now subsided, but her body still taut. Her mouth was set in a smile, her eyes looked at the back of the easel, at his three fingers clutching the charcoal, and at his nose – always the nose.

After half an hour, Ringel stopped sketching. 'That will do for now. We have made a fine start.'

Her body relaxed. She stepped down from the platform in her bare feet.

'Will you need help putting on your dress?' asked Ringel in a matter-of-fact tone of voice.

'That would be kind,' said Paola.

They went into the side room. She stood facing the mirror. He came up behind her, reached round to untie the band beneath her breast, and lifted the dress up over her head. Naked, she turned and embraced him. He led her to the sofa. She lay back, looking not into his glowering eyes but at the point of his knobbly nose.

*

'Did the principessa change her dress this afternoon?' asked Nunzi as she helped Paola change for dinner that evening.

'No. Why?' asked Paola.

'Because someone very clumsy has buttoned up the back.'

'Oh, that...' said Paola. 'Monsieur Ringel wanted to see how I would look in one of those costumes.'

Nunzi understood that there was no need to say more.

4

The graphite drawing of Baroness Scarpia di Rubosa and her two children by Armand Ringel was completed by the beginning of October 1797, and delivered, handsomely framed, to the Palazzo Marcisano. The parchment on which it had been drawn measured 30 x 40 centimetres. At the centre was Paola with her arms crossed, one to hold the hand of Francesca, the other to hold that of Pietro. The girl leaned against her mother, the boy sat erect. All faced the artist. Paola's expression was gentle, Pietro's impish, Francesca's amused. The hair, the eyes, the features were all sketched in intricate detail. The children's necks were lost in the ruffles of their clothes, while Paola's neck and shoulders rose gracefully from the modest neckline of her dress. The lace and embroidery on the clothes were detailed only to the waist, after which they were subsumed into a cursory depiction of the folds of the mother's dress.

The prince and princess gave a small reception to show the drawing to their friends. Ringel was invited, but did not attend. All who saw it acknowledged the Frenchman's genius. There were comparisons with Raphael, with Leonardo and, of course, with Ringel's master, Jacques-Louis David. Paola moved among her guests with her husband and two children, at times taking Vitellio by the arm. Fulvia, Ludovico's wife, came up to them. 'Prince Spalato wants to commission Ringel,' she said, 'and asks how much you had to pay.'

'It was not a commission,' said Paola. 'He wanted to draw Roman children with their mother and we were fortunate in that

217

he chose these.' She looked down at Pietro and Francesca at her side.

Fulvia returned to the Prince Spalato and repeated what Paola had said.

'Your sister-in-law is being modest,' said Domenica Attavanti, who was standing next to the prince. 'Monsieur Ringel said he wanted to draw the most beautiful woman in Rome.'

'In the eyes of a Frenchman,' said Prince Spalato, who thought his wife had a right to that claim.

'In the eyes of a man, at any rate,' said the marchesa with a smirk.

Scarpia, who had imagined that the drawing would hang on a wall in his home, the Villa Larunda, was persuaded by Paola that it should remain at the Palazzo Marcisano to fill a gap left by one of the works taken by the French. '*The Lord gives, the Lord takes away*,' said Scarpia acidly as he acquiesced.

'The truth is,' said Paola, 'that we have been treated leniently by the commissioners. The Dorias, the Colonnas, the Orsinis and, of course, the Holy Father, have had to part with much more.'

Was that leniency thanks to the influence of Armand Ringel? Scarpia did not ask. He remembered how Paola had wrinkled her nose in disgust when describing the physical appearance of the French painter, and felt confident that if Paola entertained thoughts of a lover, it was still of the inaccessible Bonaparte. A more observant man might have noticed that when on occasions he proposed joining her at night, though she never refused him, the look she gave him had subtly changed from 'why not?' to 'if I must'.

Paola continued to go out in the barouche on odd afternoons accompanied by Nunzi, supposedly to pay calls on her friends. The coachman, Arturo, came from her father's stables and could be trusted not to let it be known that his mistress alighted at a house close to the Palazzo Mancini. This had been taken by Ringel to continue his study of Paola – a study with the eye but also with the fingers, the lips and the tongue – a study that transposed the beauty of the goddess Larunda onto canvas, but also the body of the beautiful Roman into an instrument of mutual pleasure.

The sittings continued throughout October and November, and only became less frequent when Paola found, among the few costumes that were draped over the arm of a sofa, a waistband she had admired beneath the bust of her friend Graziella di Pozzo. There could be no doubt but that it was the same waistband: it was embroidered with beads of coloured Venetian glass, three or four of which Paola had once noticed were missing from one of the strands. 'You are painting a portrait of the Marchesa di Pozzo?' she asked at one sitting in a nonchalant tone of voice.

'She told you?' asked Ringel. 'She said that she would rather you did not know.'

'You find her beautiful?'

'No. Not, at any rate, in comparison to you. But she has a voluptuous figure and is prepared to pose as Venus.'

'Who is a greater goddess than Larunda.'

'A greater goddess, but not a greater beauty,' said Ringel.

'And ... in other ways, how does she compare?'

Ringel frowned. 'Does one compare a peach with an orange? They are simply different fruits, and one appreciates the variety.'

'Of course.' Her tone was ironic.

'You are surely not jealous?' said Ringel.

Paola did not reply.

'You presumably continue to perform your conjugal duties with your husband.'

'I have no choice.'

'You could feign illness.'

'He would smell a rat.'

'There is always a way,' said Ringel, 'but I don't either demand or expect it. One does not own a lover. We are free. Possessiveness is an odious remnant of feudalism, when women were bought and sold.'

Paola did not argue, and when they made love after the sitting the thought of her rival somehow enhanced her enjoyment, so the session ended with them both sated and exhausted.

On leaving the studio, Paola took the waistband, and when she was next alone with Graziella, she handed it to her, saying: 'You left this at Monsieur Ringel's studio.'

Graziella's face went a deep red. 'What? No. That isn't mine.'

'Yes, look, where the beads are missing,' said Paola.

'He must … I must …'

'You are posing as Venus, so I understand.'

'I never thought … I never meant …'

'To offend me? But I have no rights over Monsieur Ringel,' said Paola. 'He explained the position. I am a peach. You are an orange. Or perhaps it is the other way around. He likes variety. *Il est comme ça.*'

These last words seemed to satisfy both women: a genius like Ringel was not to be judged as other men. Both continued to visit him and, if anything, became closer friends.

5

Armand Ringel had never worried much about the reputations of the women he seduced. Even under the old feudal order, kings had their mistresses, cardinals their catamites and, where a lover was powerful or distinguished and a mistress a well-known beauty, affairs were something to boast about, not hide from the world. Reputations might have been important among the bourgeoisie, but since 1789 the revolutionaries had appropriated not just the property but the sexual freedom of the nobility. Ringel did not boast about his conquests, but it was taken for granted that the women who sat for him would also sleep with him if he so chose. It was therefore clear to those who visited Ringel's studio, and were shown his work in progress, that the model for his painting of the nymph Larunda was unlikely to be an exception to the rule; and while many of those visitors were French, and so did not identify the model, some were Romans who did. As a result, however inconspicuous the visits paid by Paola to Ringel's studio, and however much was spent on paying servants for their discretion, it soon became common knowledge that Paola was not just sitting for another painting by Ringel but also, as the Chevalier Spinelli put it, 'lying recumbent for him as well'.

Scarpia no longer moved in the same circles as the Chevalier Spinelli but, so porous was the skin of Roman society – so eager were masters and mistresses to share gossip with their servants and their servants with the servants of different households – that small rumours quickly became large certainties, confirmed by the pursed lips of Nunzi and the coachman. The fall of the Princess di Marcisano delighted the servants, because it showed that their masters and mistresses were no better than they were, and it thrilled their masters and mistresses because it had been so long awaited and watched for. No woman of such beauty and distinction had hitherto gone for so long without a *cavaliere servente*.

The frisson was spiced, of course, by the fact that the cuckolded husband, Baron Scarpia, was a Sicilian with the unsophisticated, perhaps even barbaric passions that the Romans associated with the mongrel inhabitants of that island. Wagers were taken on whether he would be able to sustain the stoical sangfroid expected of the Roman husband when deceived by his wife. Letizia di Comastri said she knew from experience that Scarpia was quite capable of using his sword. Prince Paducci, fingering the scar on his cheek, concurred. Perhaps, the Chevalier Spinelli suggested, Ambassador Bonaparte should station a grenadier outside Ringel's studio and escort him when he went out and about.

Impatient as all were for the inevitable next act of the drama, no one dared to inform Scarpia of his new status, either with an anonymous letter or even a pasquinade. The Marchesa Attavanti, who had heard Letizia di Comastri's remark about Scarpia and his sword, took it upon herself obliquely to warn Paola. 'People seem to think,' she said, 'that you are still paying visits to Monsieur Ringel, and that if the baron, your husband, should find out –'

'That's nonsense,' said Paola sharply. 'It is the *cavaliere* Sodano who should look to his laurels.' The *cavaliere* Sodano was the *cicisbeo* of Graziella di Pozzo.

The marchesa sighed. 'As you please.'

If Paola deceived herself about what others knew, so, too, Scarpia deceived himself about what was going on. He noticed, vaguely, his wife's reluctance to sleep with him and her growing passivity in the conjugal bed. He noticed, too, her flushed complexion and the furtive glances when she returned from those afternoon calls on her friends. He no longer went to receptions or *conversazioni*, and when he occasionally noticed a smirk on the face of a servant or an embarrassed look on the face of a friend, he ascribed it to the derision directed since Faenza at all the officers of the pontifical army.

More difficult to interpret were the anxious looks that Paola's parents directed at him and their daughter when the family gathered at the Palazzo Marcisano, and the gentle but uneasy manner in which his brother-in-law, Ludovico, talked to him about life's vicissitudes – quoting Horace and the Stoics to the effect that they must be borne with patience and equanimity; that human feelings are as ephemeral as mist; that a marriage is built on common interests, not fickle emotions; that honour lies in courage and endurance.

In the end, it was Spoletta who told him in a matter-of-fact tone of voice that his wife was 'being fucked by the French painter when he takes time off from fucking her whore friend di Pozzo'. They were in the guardroom at the Quirinale Palace. Scarpia's face went pale. His mouth felt dry. 'That's impossible,' he said. 'The picture was finished a month ago.'

'Apparently there's another of your wife as a half-naked nymph.'

'How do you know?'

'Everyone knows. And I've followed her coach. She goes to his studio two or three times a week.'

'It's impossible,' said Scarpia, the words spoken from his lips contradicting the feeling in the pit of his stomach.

'All women are whores,' said Spoletta. 'The princess is no exception.'

Scarpia sat down on the bench that ran along the wall of the guardroom. He hid his face in his hands. He did not listen to Spoletta's coarse philosophising on the nature of women, but tried to sort out his own thoughts. All at once he understood the smirks, the odd looks, Paola's radiance on some afternoons, her lifelessness when they made love. He felt anger rise within him as if he had taken a deep breath of rancour to fill his lungs; but almost at once the anger subsided and left only sadness in its wake. He felt at once an impulse to return to Sicily – never to see his faithless wife again; but then he remembered his children and his duties as an officer in the pontifical army. Should the man who had faced a phalanx of French dragoons flee from a domestic skirmish? *Così fan tutte*. If he were now to show that he minded, the smirks would become outright laughter. The jealous Sicilian would become a figure of fun.

Scarpia could play the role of a Stoic if that was what the circumstances required. On his return to the Villa Larunda that evening, he greeted his wife courteously and, meaning to avoid looking into her eyes for fear of what his expression would reveal, glanced at her and realised what he had noticed but never acknowledged to himself – that for many months Paola had in fact avoided looking at him.

They dined, more or less in silence, and after the servants had withdrawn, and they were sitting alone, Scarpia said to Paola: 'I understand that you are sitting for a second portrait by Monsieur Ringel.'

Paola blushed. 'Most certainly not.'

'It is common knowledge.'

'Well, certainly, he started something when I was there with the children and now I occasionally look in so that he can finish it off.'

'Why didn't you tell me?'

'You would have made a fuss.'

'Is it a portrait?'

'More … you know … something from antiquity.'

'You pose as what?'

'Larunda.'

'Clothed?'

'Of course.'

'And does he sleep with you as he does with his other models?'

Paola blushed more deeply and stood up. 'Really, Vitellio, these are not questions a husband puts to his wife.'

'They might be questions that a man puts to a woman he loves.'

She frowned. 'We are not children, Vitellio. We have been married for ten years and the reasons for marrying, well, I was then a child and you quite reasonably saw an advantage in taking me as a wife.'

'That is unfair. I was ready to love you, and did.'

'And I loved you, Vitellio, but one grows up and one changes, and as one changes so do one's feelings.'

'My feelings for you have not changed.'

'You still see the advantage –'

'I did not marry you just for the advantage.'

'Not *just*, perhaps, but it surely played a role.'

'You were very beautiful ... you are still beautiful.'

'But not for much longer ... And when a man, another man, a man who...' Her voice faltered, and then suddenly became indignant rather than rueful. 'You surely know how feelings change. Weren't you in love with Letizia di Comastri?'

'I was not in love with her, no. It was ... she was ... she, too, was very beautiful and –'

'And she took to you, and who can blame either her or you? Life is short, Vitellio, and God has not called us to the religious life. We are human and weak and surely we must be tolerant of one another's weaknesses as Jesus was with Mary Magdalene and the adulterous woman?'

'He told her to sin no more.'

'Of course, and when I can muster the strength, I will sin no more; but think what it is like to be a woman, Vitellio, a beautiful woman, who since the age of fourteen has seen the faces of men light up when she enters the room, but knows that soon those looks will be directed elsewhere. She is in her last years in bloom. Soon she will be shrivelled and ignored. And then a man comes along – a man who promises to capture her beauty, to immortalise it – a man who could have his pick of any woman, but desires *her* –'

'Have I not always desired you?'

'Oh, of course, Vitellio. But you're my husband, and a husband, night after night, year after year...' Paola, who had been facing away from Scarpia, now turned and looked at him with an expression that was at once sad and mildly mocking. 'You should not have married a Roman, Vitellio. We are too fickle, too pleasure-loving, too frivolous, too cynical, too insincere. We feel we have God in our pockets – a God who is so all-forgiving that we can surely forgive ourselves.'

They retired to their rooms. Nunzi reappeared to help her mistress undress; so, too, Scarpia's valet. When they were once again alone, they remained in their separate bedrooms.

6

The Pope's injunctions to his subjects that the French were to be treated courteously had been accepted by the aristocracy, but had confused the people of the street, who, having been told by their priests that the Jacobins were devils intent on the destruction of the Church, could not understand why the agent of Satan, Joseph Bonaparte, had been received cordially by the Pope at the Quirinale Palace; nor why they must stand by and watch as the city's finest works of art, of which even those who did not own them were proud, were being loaded onto carts to be taken to Paris. Despite the papal edicts, strutting Frenchmen were threatened and insulted in the street. So, too, the zealous republicans who had come to Rome from other parts of Italy to partake in the glory of overthrowing the Pope.

On 27 December 1797, there was a large demonstration by these foreign agitators, shouting 'Long live liberty!' and 'Long live the Republic!' Stones were thrown at the papal troops. A company of dragoons dispersed the crowd, but the republican agitators regrouped on the Pincio. Once again, the dragoons were attacked, this time with knives as well as stones. Two troopers were dragged off their horses and killed. Enraged, their companions drove the crowd back down the Lungara towards the French Embassy, the Palazzo Corsini. There General Duphot came out with drawn sword to defend the republicans. 'Long live liberty!' he shouted. 'Courage! I am your general!' He advanced on a corporal and four soldiers from the papal army by the Porta Settimanas. The troopers, on the order of their corporal, raised their muskets and fired. Duphot was shot in the head. His body was carried into the Palazzo Corsini, where he was found to be dead.

In the Quirinale Palace the news was received with dismay: it was the case of Bassville all over again, but far more serious because of the general's links to the Bonaparte family. Cardinal Doria Pamphili, who had replaced the exhausted Cardinal Zelada as Secretary of State, went at once in person to the Palazzo Corsini to apologise for what had occurred. Joseph Bonaparte was not to be appeased. Whatever his personal feelings might have been at the loss of a friend and future kinsman, Duphot's death provided the *casus belli* that the Directory had been demanding for some time. He immediately demanded from Cardinal Doria post horses to enable the French mission to leave the city.

The cardinal pleaded with him to stay, but the ambassador was inflexible, and the next day left Rome for Paris with his wife, his children and the entire diplomatic staff. Among the party was Armand Ringel, who took with him rolled-up canvases of unfinished paintings, including those of the beauties of antiquity, the goddess Venus and the nymph Larunda.

*

When the news of Duphot's death reached Paris, the Directory ordered the commander of the French army in Italy, Napoleon Bonaparte, to march on Rome. Bonaparte delegated the task to his chief adjutant, General Berthier. As the French army advanced down the peninsula, the cardinals urged Pope Pius to flee to Naples. He refused, awaiting his fate with pious resignation: he was ready, if it was the will of God, to die for the Catholic faith.

Of course, all knew that it was unlikely that even the fanatical enemies of the Catholic religion in the Directory would dare execute a pope; and it was clear that even if such an order should be sent from Paris, no general would want to make the occupation of Rome more difficult by antagonising the population. However, there were lesser figures in the papal government who could be punished for opposing liberty without causing a stir.

When Scarpia returned home from duty at the Quirinale Palace on 14 February, he found Paola sitting by the fire. He sat down on a chair at a distance from his wife. 'Cardinal Doria, Duke Braschi and Azara have surrendered the city,' he said. 'The French will be here tomorrow.'

'You must leave,' she said.

'I am not a coward,' said Scarpia.

'Of course you are not a coward,' said Paola, 'but nor are you a Don Quixote. Your name is on a list, and, when the French enter Rome, you will be arrested. You and your man Spoletta.'

'I have committed no crime.'

Paola laughed – a dry, dead laugh. 'A crime is in the eyes of the beholder. To them you are an enemy of liberty…'

'To them?'

'The French.'

'Have you heard from your lover? Did he tell you about the list?'

'He is no longer my lover and he has returned to Paris.'

'Who, then?'

'Angelotti is with Berthier.'

'And so the warning comes from the marchesa?'

'Yes.'

Scarpia was silent. Then: 'I don't like to run from the field of battle.'

'There is no battle. We have surrendered.'

Scarpia paused again, then asked: 'And will you come with me?'

Paola looked down at her knees. 'I am not on the list. Nor are the children. My father, Ludovico … They are not thought to be enemies of the republicans.'

'And you, of course,' said Scarpia, 'are known to have been friendly towards the French.'

Paola said nothing.

'So I am to lose my wife and children as well as my home?'

'We will join you later.' She spoke without conviction.

'I am their father,' said Scarpia.

'Of course. But you will not be much use to them either dead or in a dungeon.'

*

Scarpia and Spoletta left Rome that evening by the Appian Gate. The next day, 15 February, the anniversary of the election of Pope Pius VI to the papacy, French troops marched into Rome. General Berthier proceeded to the Capitol, where he proclaimed, in the name of the French Republic, a new political order. After a thousand-year rule, the Pope was deposed. The donation of the Emperor Constantine was abrogated by the will of the people. The tyranny of priests was over. Wreathed with laurel, and standing in front of the statue of Marcus Aurelius festooned with tricolour flags, the French general proclaimed a republic. 'Descendants of Cato, Brutus and Cicero, accept the homage of free Frenchmen on the Capitol, where you so often defended the rights of the people to celebrate the Roman Republic! These sons of the Gauls, with the olive branch of peace in their hands, will re-erect on this hallowed spot the altars of freedom that were set up of old by the first Brutus. And you, citizens of Rome, who are recovering your lawful rights, remember the blood that flows in your veins! Turn your eyes to the monuments of glory that surround you! Regain your ancient greatness and the virtues of your fathers!'

Giovanni Braschi, Pope Pius VI, was now a prisoner in the Quirinale Palace. When told that he had been deposed, he simply bowed his head and said that he accepted the inscrutable designs of divine providence. On 17 February, he was ordered to prepare to leave the city. Pius said he wished to die by the tomb of St Peter. 'You can die anywhere,' the French officer replied. It was made clear that, if he refused to leave, he would be forcibly expelled. Early in the morning on 20 February 1797, after hearing Mass, the ailing eighty-year-old pontiff climbed into a coach at the Cortile de San Damso with two priests and his doctor, Tassi. It was still dark. Escorted by a small contingent of French soldiers, the coach passed through the streets unnoticed. With no ceremony and no farewells, the supreme pontiff of the Roman Catholic Church left the Eternal City.

PART THREE

Eleven

I

With the eviction of the Pope and the occupation of Rome by General Berthier's army, the only principality in Italy that remained free of the French was the Kingdom of the Two Sicilies. Its king, Ferdinand, was, of all Europe's enlightened despots, the least enlightened and the most despotic. He was a Bourbon – brother of the King of Spain and cousin of the King of France. His wife, Queen Maria Carolina, was a Habsburg – sister of the Emperor of Austria and Marie Antoinette, the decapitated Queen of France. Ferdinand ruled, in his own view, by divine right – his subjects children who never grew up.

Ferdinand was coarse, sensual and unaffected. His brother-in-law, the Emperor Francis, described him as 'ugly, though not absolutely repulsive: his skin is fairly smooth and firm, with a yellowish pallor; he is clean except for his hands; and at least he does not stink'. The Italian historian, Bernadetto Croce, saw him as the prototype of the plebeian nobleman, 'with plebeian speech, habits and gestures' – closer to his coachman than his ministers, 'being a fine driver himself, good-natured with all and beloved as a *bon signore* for his improvidence, admired for his pomp and luxury, easy to compete with in jokes and jibes'. He ate with his fingers, spoke with a vulgar accent, used crude language and, as a result, was close to the common people. 'The truth is,' wrote Goethe, 'the Neapolitans lead a coarse life, but one that is free.'

Ferdinand loved hunting and it was rare that he allowed matters of state to interfere with the chase. In the royal palace in Naples there were chickens, pigeons, ducks, geese, partridges, quails, canaries, cats, dogs – and caged rats and mice which Ferdinand would release and hunt over the marble floors of the state apartments. He loathed reading, and while never abdicating his right to rule, left the routine administration of his kingdom to others. His contempt for learning, like his coarse sensuality and vulgar language, enhanced his popularity with the mass of his subjects. They, too, thought reading a waste of time. 'In Naples,' wrote the French Abbé Galiani, 'there are at most only twelve people who can read.'

Ferdinand's wife, Queen Maria Carolina, when she had arrived as a young princess from Vienna, had been fond of reading and encouraged it among her entourage. It became smart for young Neapolitans from the aristocracy and bourgeoisie to hold advanced views and meet to discuss them in Masonic lodges. Maria Carolina herself favoured Freemasonry until it became apparent that if one did away with God, or reduced Him to a vague 'supreme being' with no particular link to the Catholic Church, then the divine right of kings became problematic – indeed was rejected altogether by just the kind of people the Queen had encouraged to read books.

Maria Carolina, who from the age of twenty-four had taken it upon herself to fill the vacuum left by her husband's disinclination to rule, had grown into a formidable woman. Her model was her mother, the Austrian Empress Maria Theresa, and she had inherited her mother's strong will, considerable intelligence and sense of duty. She was extravagant and lavished gifts on her favourites, both men and women. There were rumours of liaisons with her male favourites, but nothing was ever proved. She had eighteen children of whom nine died in infancy, mostly from smallpox, and one was stillborn.

The events in Paris in 1789 divided irrevocably the enlightened despots from their enlightened subjects. Ferdinand and Maria Carolina heard with dismay of the humiliations endured by King Louis XVI and Marie Antoinette following the fall of the Bastille. All at once advanced views were proscribed. Anyone who talked about liberty, who read foreign newspapers, who wore trousers rather than breeches, who had a moustache, a beard or even side-burns, or eschewed the powdered wig in favour of a Brutus haircut, was considered a Jacobin, plotting the downfall of the king. And such suspicions were not unfounded. A Patriotic Society was formed in Naples by a group of young noblemen and middle-class intellectuals – patriotism being now the preferred term for republicanism since Robespierre had given Jacobinism a bad name. A conspiracy to overthrow the king led by a lawyer named Blasi was uncovered: Blasi was tortured and executed and his co-conspirators sent to the galleys.

When, in 1793, the news reached Naples that first King Louis of France and then Queen Marie Antoinette had been guillotined by the Jacobins in Paris, the Sicilian monarchs' political antipathy towards republicans became a visceral and implacable loathing. The spirit of vendetta, common among Calabrians and Sicilians, now entered the blood of their Spanish and Austrian sovereigns. Under a portrait of her sister that Queen Maria Carolina kept in her study was written: *Je poursuiverai ma vengeance jusqu'au tombeau.* But how was that vengeance to be pursued? The Kingdom of the Two Sicilies was large in territory and prosperous in times of peace; but its people, subject for so many centuries to pugnacious invaders – the Normans, the Germans, the French, the Spaniards – had lost any martial spirit themselves. Few engaged in events outside their parish: most lived happily from day to day.

Soon after the dismissal of the Marchese Tanucci at the instigation of Queen Maria Carolina – a fall that had precipitated the exile of Vitellio Scarpia's father to his estates in Sicily – the queen had been advised by her brother, the Austrian emperor, that her kingdom, with a short land frontier but long coastline, should concentrate its resources on building a powerful navy. Who could they recruit to undertake such an ambitious programme? A minister, the Prince of Caramanico, recommended an Englishman, John Acton, who had built up the naval forces of Tuscany, and had done well in a recent attack by the Tuscan fleet on Algiers. Queen Maria Carolina's kinsman, the Grand Duke of Tuscany, agreed to release him, and in 1779 John Acton was appointed Admiral of the Neapolitan Fleet.

Acton was then forty-three years old and unmarried. He was the cousin of an English baronet, Sir Richard Acton, of Aldenham Hall in Shropshire. Several members of the Acton family, among them the fifth baronet, had converted to Catholicism and, because it was hard for a Catholic to rise in the professions in Protestant England, had sought employment abroad. Edward Acton, John Acton's father, had studied medicine in Paris, worked as a doctor in Besançon, and in 1735 married the daughter of the president of the Parlement of the Franche-Comté, Anne Cathérine Loys. In 1750, at the age of fourteen, their son John had been sent to serve with his uncle and namesake, Commodore John Acton, commander of the fleet of the Grand Duke of Tuscany. On the death of this uncle, the nephew took over his command until he was poached by the King and Queen of Naples.

Acton was described by his descendant, the historian Harold Acton, as a man with 'a fine presence, magnetic, penetrating eyes and a slim, agile figure'. He was not handsome, but was 'dignified and self-assured'. He immediately impressed the king and the queen with his decisiveness, sound judgement and ability to see things through. Queen Maria Carolina gave him her wholehearted support. Both the king and the queen came to trust Acton and rely upon him rather than their home-grown advisers. His duties were extended from the navy to the exchequer and eventually to the entire governance of the kingdom.

Acton was also liked and admired by the British ambassador in Naples, Sir William Hamilton: the two Englishmen felt an affinity and favoured an alliance between Naples and Great Britain. They encouraged King Ferdinand and Queen Maria Carolina to see the British Mediterranean fleet as a useful instrument in the pursuit of their vendetta against the Jacobins.

Sir William Hamilton was a connoisseur of precious and beautiful antiquities, and had in 1783 been given for safekeeping a living embodiment of classical beauty in the form of a young Englishwoman, Emma Lyon, the daughter of a blacksmith in Ness in Cheshire. Emma Lyon, also known as Emma Hart, had worked as a housemaid for a doctor, then for an actress in London who had taught her to act and dance. At the age of fifteen Emma became the mistress of an English rake, Sir Harry Featherstonhaugh, who passed her on to a friend, Charles Greville, the second son of the Earl of Warwick. When Greville ran out of money and sought to marry an heiress, Emma became an embarrassment, and so he sent her to stay with his widowed uncle, Sir William Hamilton, in Naples. There she became first Sir William's mistress and, in 1791, his wife – enchanting the visitors to the ambassador's residence by enacting *tableaux vivants* of figures from antiquity – poses she had learned in London.

There was one man, however, who exercised a greater influence over the Neapolitans than Hamilton, Acton or even King Ferdinand and Queen Carolina: this was the Roman martyr, St Gennaro (Januarius), executed during the persecution of Christians by the Emperor Diocletian fifteen hundred years before. He had been bishop of Naples and was now its patron saint – the reality of his martyrdom visible in an ampoule containing his blood. Three times a year, the ampoule at the centre of a gold monstrance was displayed to the crowd assembled in the city's cathedral where, on occasions, the dry russet powder liquefied before the eyes of the devout. This miracle was for the Neapolitans a portent of the utmost importance; and when it failed – when the powder remained powder – it was taken as an omen of disasters to come – wars, storms, the plague or the eruption of Vesuvius, the volcano that loomed over the city.

No monarch had ever questioned the power of St Gennaro to intervene in favour of the people of Naples. Quite to the contrary: the rich and mighty sought to ingratiate themselves with the saint by donating stupendous treasures to his shrine. His skull was contained in a silver reliquary, and around its neck hung a necklace with emeralds, sapphires and diamonds. The golden mitre worn by the archbishops of Naples when displaying the blood of St Gennaro was studded with over three thousand diamonds, 164 rubies, two hundred emeralds and fifty garnets. No conqueror had ever dared seize these precious relics from the shrine of St Gennaro, but rather had added to its treasures to secure his favour and, more practically for the sceptics, the support of the superstitious *lazzaroni* whose first loyalty was to their patron saint.

2

When Vitellio Scarpia fled from Rome to Naples in February of 1798, he stayed with his brother Domenico and visited almost daily his sister Angelina and her husband Leonardo Partinico. The family were in mourning because their father, the *cavaliere* Luigi Scarpia, had died the month before; Domenico and Angelina had recently returned from his funeral in Sicily with their mother, Marcella, who was now living on Domenico's estate at Barca, her childhood home.

All were now older; Vitellio's nephews and nieces were on the verge of maturity; but none had changed so much as Vitellio himself. Ten years had passed since he had visited the city as the newly ennobled Baron di Rubaso with his bride, Paola di Marcisano – elated with his good fortune and a little disdainful of his provincial siblings. Now, he was all but destitute, his salary as a soldier stopped, his estates at Rubaso expropriated by the French – a refugee without a home, a wife, a family or even a servant, because he had sent Spoletta on to Palermo.

Scarpia's appearance reflected his change in fortune: he retained his slim figure and still had a good head of hair, but there were lines in his face, shadows under his eyes – eyes that would sometimes as before light up with amusement, but more often expressed bitterness and dejection. His brother and sister had heard the gossip about Paola and the painter Ringel, but pretended to accept Vitellio's assurance that in due course his family would join him.

Scarpia presented himself at court, and put his sword at the service of his sovereigns, King Ferdinand and Queen Maria Carolina; but Naples was at peace. Despite their loathing of the French, Bonaparte was thought invincible; Austria was reluctant to take him on, and the Kingdom of the Two Sicilies was in no position to do so on its own. Their Majesties might hope and pray for the defeat of their enemies, but even Acton advised caution. To commission Scarpia, an officer who had been proscribed by the French, would be noted by the French ambassador, Citizen Trouvé, and be taken as a sign of the government's unfriendly intentions.

Moreover, Scarpia was a Sicilian, and King Ferdinand and Queen Carolina held the martial skills of their own subjects in low regard. Only foreigners from north of the Alps were considered capable of command. A Swiss, Baron Rudoph de Salis, employed as inspector general of the Neapolitan army in 1787, had been replaced by a Hungarian, Joseph von Zehenter, in 1790. Certainly, Scarpia had established a reputation, but it was more for personal courage than military skills. A minor command in the papal army at the disastrous battle of Faenza was not enough to secure a commission in the Neapolitan army without influence at court. Scarpia had no powerful patron to back him. His brother was a loyal but docile member of the minor nobility; his brother-in-law was suspected of republican sympathies and was fortunate not to have been implicated in Blasi's plot to kill the king.

There remained Cardinal Ruffo, now enjoying a sinecure as comptroller of the royal palace at Caserta and superintendent of King Ferdinand's colony at Leucio. Scarpia called upon him at Caserta and was received with unfeigned affection. 'My dear Baron,' said the cardinal. 'I feared for you when I heard that the French had taken Rome. You came here. Quite right. Discretion is the better part of valour and the Lord helps those who help themselves. The princess remained in Rome? That is understandable. Even the French would not dare touch a Marcisano. And your father. I am sorry to hear of his death. Punished for the sins of Tanucci, I fear, but from everything I hear, he was an admirable man.'

The cardinal was now fifty-five years old, but to Scarpia he seemed little changed. Resignation to the will of God, and the sense that he had served Him as best he could, clearly removed many of the sources of anxiety that would have taken their toll on a layman. His concern now was for his protégé, Scarpia, for whom he still felt the same paternal affection that the young Sicilian had aroused in him when he had first appeared as a destitute young adventurer in the Quirinale Palace thirteen years before. However, it is always easier to do something for a youth than for a middle-aged man. Ruffo had posts within his gifts, both in the running of the immense palace at Caserta or the king's colony of silk weavers at Leucio, but none were suitable for a man of Scarpia's rank and standing.

'Alas, I have no influence at court when it comes to commissions in the army,' he said to Scarpia. 'The only man that matters there is Acton. He is a Catholic, of course, and his mother was French, but in essence he is an Englishman – cold, calculating, and concerned first with the interests of his sovereigns, then those of Great Britain, which he regards as synonymous as those of his sovereigns, and only lastly, if at all, the interests of the Catholic Church. And if he was to listen to anyone, it would not be to me but our Archbishop, Cardinal Zurlo, who regards me as an interloper and an embarrassment, and would as soon thwart my wishes as seek to fulfil them.'

'Would you advise, then,' asked Scarpia, 'that I seek service with the Russians, perhaps, or the Turks?'

'The Turks? God forbid. I know they are now our allies, but they remain infidels. No, you should wait. Are you in need of money? I could appoint you as an honorary gentleman in my household, which would bring a modest stipend.'

'Thank you, Your Eminence, but following my father's death I now have the income from our estates in Sicily.'

'Then go to Sicily and bide your time. The present peace cannot last indefinitely. The French are infected with a malign virus – there is no inoculation against Jacobinism as there is now against smallpox: it is in its nature to spread. And now added to the virulence of the Jacobins' satanic ideas is the ambition of Bonaparte, who will not rest until he is master of the world. There will be war and when there is war you must be here, not in St Petersburg or the Porte.'

3

S carpia travelled south to his brother's estate at Barca to visit his
mother. He found her well cared for by the family's retainers,
many of them the sons and daughters of those she had known as a
child. Domenico was a benign landlord and the family was regarded
with affection, while Vitellio was a hero who had won glory in the
service of the Pope.

His mother's mind was half gone. She knew that there were
sources of unhappiness and disappointment in her own life and that
of her son, but could not remember what they were. At times she
mistook him for her husband, Scarpia's father, and adopted the old
tone of irritation. And yet senility had to some extent softened her,
and now that she was helpless she became almost affectionate, as if
understanding that one must curry benevolence when one lost the
power to command. Her decrepitude enhanced the melancholy felt
by Scarpia since he had left Rome. *O quam cito transit Gloria mundi!*

*

Scarpia travelled on along the dusty roads of Calabria. He stayed
for three days with Cardinal Ruffo's brother, the Duke of Baranello –
telling him of what had passed in Rome as they sat on the terrace
of the duke's *castello* at Bagnara with its view of Sicily over the
narrow strait of Messina. The duke provided a boat to take him to
Messina, where he was met by Spoletta and taken to the villa in
Bagheria. The dust sheets had been removed from the furniture;
servants had been employed; and on that evening, after a good
dinner, sitting alone on the terrace in the late-summer sun, looking
out to sea and smoking a cigar, Vitellio Scarpia, despite his melancholy, felt almost content.

In the weeks which followed, Scarpia paid a courtesy visit to the
viceroy in Palermo, and went to Castelfranco, to pray at the tomb of

his father, and take possession of the estate that was now his. He looked over Ottavio Spoletta's accounts, joking with Guido, the son, about the discrepancies, saying that they were too obvious – that the old factor was losing his touch. But Scarpia had now no wish to grow rich at the expense of tenants. In the villa at Bagheria, he needed little: his establishment was modest and his descents into Palermo rare. He received invitations from cousins, neighbours and friends from his youth, but in those first weeks he declined them, giving as an excuse that he was unwell.

Scarpia's indisposition was not wholly feigned. Physically he was well enough to hunt boar with Spoletta at Castelfranco, and ride out every day from the villa at Bagheria, but when this was reported to the disappointed *salonnières* of Palermo, the old Principessa Calamatina, who had known Scarpia as a child, would say, 'He is licking his wounds,' tapping her head to indicate where the wounds were to be found. Scarpia was suffering from an odd mixture of contentment and dejection – contentment because he was out of the fray, his ambition in abeyance, secure in his childhood home; dejection because as he sat in his father's study he remembered the day when the *cavaliere* had given him his sword, his blessing and those ducats and sequins and florins as seed corn for his future good fortune.

Now, fifteen years later, he was back in the same room, sitting on the same chair, surrounded by the same books, with no position, no fortune, a wife who had been happy to be rid of him and children she had infected with her disdain. Scarpia felt the presence of his father and wished that he was present to answer his son's questions. He was overwhelmed with regret that he had seen almost nothing of his parents in recent years. He looked around at the spines of books on the shelves as if his eye might alight on the work of a sage who would bring him peace of mind. There were the Greek philosophers, Plato and Aristotle; the Roman authors,

Cicero and Pliny the Elder; the great historians, Suetonius and Herodotus; the great theologians, Augustine and Aquinas; the free-thinkers who had removed the certainties – Montaigne, Voltaire, Rousseau; and the Catholic apologists who had tried to sustain them – Bossuet, Pascal. Which should he read? Philosophy was said to be a consolation for life's vicissitudes, but none, so far as he could remember, gave a consistent explanation of the purpose of a man's life. To do the will of God? To pursue fame and fortune? Could one do both? Soldiering was a noble profession, but only if the cause was right. Scarpia had killed others in the service of the Pope, and what can better define righteousness than the cause of Christ's vicar on earth? But what of the Bourbons? Were righteousness and legitimacy one and the same? Or was legitimacy merely a tag, like liberty, to promote the interests of one set of men and women over others? 'Since justice cannot be enforced,' Pascal had written, 'we justify force so that justice and force go together and we have peace, which is the sovereign good.' What was the source of their legitimacy other than descent from conquerors who had imposed their rule by force?

And what if a new conqueror appears? Scarpia thought back to the moment when all Europe was astonished by the military triumphs of Bonaparte and Paola's affections had strayed. He looked again at the spines of the books that surrounded him, rebuking their authors for failing to warn him about women as the arbiters of men's reputations. Of course the authors were mostly celibate; or they lived in less refined epochs when women were chattels rather than the custodians of men's self-esteem. Beyond the humiliation of being cuckolded by the libertine Ringel, Scarpia felt a retrospective resentment against all the women he had thought he had loved. It is men's fatuous vanity, he now realised, that persuades them that they are the predators, when it is in fact the woman who seduces the man.

Yet even as Scarpia inveighed against women, he longed for one to be there with him – not simply to satisfy his desires, but as a companion in mind as well as the flesh. When he thought back to the first years of his marriage to Paola, what he now realised he had most valued was not the pleasure of making love to a beautiful woman but the exchange of smiles, the shared laughter, small physical intimacies – a caress, or the holding of hands. He thought of them both standing arm in arm looking down at Pietro lying in his cradle; the gentle halo of love that seemed to hover over this new family. Could he have done anything to preserve that precious affinity? Or had he always been no more than a means to an end – Paola's smiles and embraces the ties to secure a man from outside her circle whose seed would invigorate the etiolated genes of the inbred Marcisanos?

What had been his mistake? What had lost him her affection? Was it simply that by fathering two children he had served his purpose? Or was it that historical events had changed her feminine perception of his strength? The dashing young officer in the papal army with a record of heroic escapades had seemed superior to the foppish young Romans who were put forward by their parents for her to marry. But then the French had appeared in Lombardy; the extraordinary young Corsican had routed the armies of the Austrian emperor; and at Faenza the papal army was shown to be not just feeble but absurd.

Looking out through the window of the study in the villa in Bagheria, Scarpia thought back to those early years of his marriage, blushing to remember his conceit at being the husband of the Principessa di Marcisano, achieving at one stroke fame and fortune, not realising that it rested on the whim of a woman. And how foolish he had been to treat her so well – to be courteous, affectionate, tolerant, forgiving – when the affection had been taken for weakness, his love his Achilles heel. Ringel was callous with women; she had surrendered to Ringel. Perhaps Spoletta was right. Women purport to admire courtliness; in reality, they succumb to brutes.

4

Every morning Guido Spoletta would go down to Palermo and return with the gazettes that carried news from Naples, but also from Rome. From these reports, Scarpia learned that the holy city and former Papal States now had a republican government, and a constitution based on the model of antiquity with a Senate, a Tribunal and five Consuls – one of them Cesare Angelotti. The bronze angel on top of the Castel Sant'Angelo had been renamed 'The Liberating Genius of France', painted the red, white and blue of the French tricolour flag, and a Liberty bonnet put on its head. Crucifixes had been replaced by Liberty trees, statues of the saints by busts of Cato and Brutus. Patriots rather than penitents now processed through the streets of the holy city, acclaiming the Nation rather than God. A grandiose memorial service was held for the republican martyr, General Duphot, in St Peter's Square – men in togas extolling his heroic virtue while young women in diaphanous costumes danced around a papier mâché altar. At the Piazza di Spagna there had been a ritual burning of the archives of the Roman Inquisition, where half-naked youths with wings attached to their shoulder blades lit the bonfire and, at the summation of the ceremony, a naked woman symbolising Truth was seen rising from the Ashes of Superstition. The Roman hoi polloi, watching from the Spanish Steps, had booed and jeered, and pelted the performers with rotten vegetables.

General Berthier did not want to antagonise the Romans by holding republican ceremonies inside any of the city's great Catholic basilicas; however, while the clergy remained in possession of their churches, anything of value in the sacristies was seized by the French – reliquaries, monstrances, even cruets and chalices used in the Mass. The city was plundered. Gold and silver bars to the value of 15 million scudi had been taken from the vaults of the Castel Sant'Angelo, and anything of value from the Vatican, the Quirinale and the palaces of the cardinals and patricians. Pearls and precious stones from the papal tiaras and regalia were removed from their settings and sent to Paris. So too Rome's finest works of art – the *Laocoön Group*, the *Apollo Belvedere*, the *Dying Gaul*, *Cupid and Psyche*, *Ariadne on Naxos*, the *Medici Venus*, Raphael's *Madonna di Foligno*, *Madonna della Sedia* and the *Transfiguration*, and Titian's *Sacra Conversazione* – all were loaded on to carts and sent to Paris. Treasures and artworks not deemed of sufficient quality for the new Musée du Louvre were sold off at auction and went for knock-down prices to the merchants and bankers who had ready cash. So, too, the properties of the papal loyalists such as Scarpia's estate at Rubaso. Cesare Angelotti bought for a pittance the palace of the Grand Master of the Knights of Malta on the Aventine Hill.

The republican government was a fiction: in reality, Rome was ruled by the French commander-in-chief, first General Berthier and later General Massena, who pillaged the city as effectively as any Goth or Vandal. French troops were billeted in monasteries, convents and even private homes; their generals in requisitioned palaces, their wives bickering over the allocation of quarters. They gave lavish parties to celebrate their triumph that frequently degenerated into drunken orgies which earned them the contempt of their unpaid troops. A group of two hundred junior officers protested at the greed and depravity of their superiors – at one point Massena, fearing mutiny, fled the city.

With no munificent princes or cardinals to distribute their largesse, the economy of the city collapsed. The paper currency issued by the

French became worthless. The people went hungry. The only group that seemed to have profited from the occupation were Rome's Jews, liberated from the ghetto and now full citizens of the republic. A group of Jews was attacked by a mob in Trastevere. French troops were called in to restore order. There was a riot. Some soldiers were killed. Twenty-two protesters were arrested and later shot on the Piazza del Popolo. More demonstrations and isolated assassinations let to further reprisals. The cells of the Castel Sant'Angelo, which had once held republicans like Count Palmieri, were now filled with papal loyalists, or those thought to have hidden their property from the French. Two priests who had replaced a Tree of Liberty with a crucifix were shot.

Some Romans, it was reported, were collaborating with the French. The Vicar General of Rome, Cardinal Somaglia, had let it be known that he no longer wished to be addressed as 'Your Eminence' but 'Citizen Somaglia'. Young men from noble families were to be seen on the Corso with their hair cut short and wearing tricolour scarves. One news sheet published a list of princely families who had declared themselves in favour of the republic: the Sforzas, the Santa Croces and the Marcisanos. The name of Ludovico di Marcisano cropped up in the columns, and at one republican ceremony 'the prince's sister, the Princess Paola, was dressed becomingly as the nymph Larunda'. 'Young married women,' the correspondent went on, 'and some not so young, are now to be seen wearing light, clinging Grecian tunics, and some have dropped their Roman *cicisbei* in favour of handsome French officers.'

Was Paola among these women with French lovers? Scarpia remembered how his first rival in her imagination had been Bonaparte; and, while he did not imagine Paola in the arms of the Corsican, whose name was now mysteriously absent from the gazettes, he could envisage her taking up with some proxy; and sure enough there came a report in one of the Neapolitan news sheets that the Princess Paola di Marcisano had been seen riding in an open carriage on the Corso with the French Major General Gaston de Jouve. Scarpia might have missed the item, had Spoletta not pointed it out.

*

The knowledge that his wife had a French lover made plain to Scarpia that he had lost her forever. Her loyalties had changed. She was not just the mistress of an enemy, but, to judge from the reports of her participation at republican ceremonies, had become a Jacobin herself. It pained Scarpia to think of Paola making love with a Frenchman, but it pained him more to imagine the Frenchman playing with Pietro and Francesca and infecting them with Jacobin ideas. These thoughts became so painful that Scarpia tried to put them out of his mind, and form a crust of indifference over his depression. He told himself that he was still only thirty-six years old, and should not spend the rest of his life brooding over his misfortunes. He descended from Bagheria into Palermo – first visiting a tailor, and then, with new clothes to match his new mood, paying calls on the Sicilian *salonnières* such as the Princess Calamatina, going to the theatre and the opera, not so much to listen to the wailing of the minor divas as to pay court to some of the dark Sicilian beauties whose smiles and lingering glances encouraged him to whisper insincere endearments in their ears.

5

The spring was warm; the heat of the summer approached, and the end of the season in Palermo was at hand; but before the leading families left their town houses for their country estates, two pieces of news reached the city that excited the dozy guests at the *conversazioni* of the Princess Calamatina.

The first came from Messina, where a boat had arrived from the island of Malta to say that the island, only sixty miles off the south coast of Sicily, had been taken by the French. At first the news was disregarded as an absurd rumour: Malta had been garrisoned by the Knights of Malta since the sixteenth century and the fortress at Valetta was impregnable. But further dispatches confirmed the rumours. Bonaparte had decided to conquer Egypt. A French fleet of seventeen warships and four hundred transports, secretly assembled at Toulon, had set sail for Alexandria. Permission had been sought for ships to put into Valetta for fresh food and water. The Grand Master of the Knights of Malta, Ferdinand von Hompesch, had said he would allow only two ships to enter the harbour at a time. This restriction would have delayed the expeditionary force for several weeks, during which time it might have been discovered and engaged by the British fleet. Bonaparte ordered soldiers and cannon to be landed on the western part of the island and, after a twenty-four-hour bombardment of Valetta, von Hompesch surrendered.

It was disturbing to think that Malta, so close to Sicily, was in the hands of the murderous Jacobins, and there was relief when the French armada sailed on to Egypt. Bonaparte's absence from Europe promised a period of peace, and the Bourbon loyalists could hope that the expedition might turn out badly. Only Scarpia was disappointed: his recall to arms would be indefinitely postponed. However, he was distracted by the other piece of news that excited the citizens of Palermo: Prince Luigi Alturo had persuaded the diva Tosca to come to Sicily and sing in Giuseppe Curcio's new opera, *La disfatta dei Macedoni*.

It was well known that the prince was besotted with Tosca, a diva now so celebrated that she had sung before the King of Prussia in Potsdam and the Tsarina Catherine in St Petersburg. She could command any fee she chose, and Prince Alturo had mortified his wife and enraged his children by mortgaging some of his estates and selling works of art to English collectors to pay for gifts for Tosca, and now to guarantee a princely fee and all the costs of bringing her to Sicily.

The season was over; the opera house was closed; but the prince's project did not require an auditorium. The opera would be staged in the open air in the ancient Greek theatre at Taormina. Scarpia decided to attend the performance. He arranged to stay with his cousins, the Petofrescinis, in their villa near Messina, and, when the day came, it was simply as one member of their large party that he took his place on the stone benches of the theatre sculpted into the side of a hill. In the light of the setting sun, there was a view of the sea and the volcano, Mount Etna, wisps of smoke arising from its craters. The dry air was scented by pine. His cousins were dull; their friends more so; and though he was seated next to a sallow young woman who was pretty enough, she was too fresh from the convent to be of interest, and blushed at everything he said.

Curcio's opera was poor, but the audience had not gathered from the four corners of the island to be engaged by a drama or even listen to fine music. It was the voice of Tosca that they had come to hear, and a roar greeted her appearance, dressed simply in a Grecian tunic, her hair raised in plaited strands. She was no more lovely to look at than any other woman, but when she opened her mouth and her voice rose to the highest rows of the amphitheatre, all fell silent and were overwhelmed. Her acting, too, enchanted the audience – her elastic features, her shifting expressions – all the feelings of love and grief indicated by the libretto conveyed by the movement of her limbs and the look in her eyes. The fluttering fans were closed and lay limp on the laps of the ladies, their hands now gripping scented handkerchiefs to wipe away their tears. There were even men to be seen weeping as Tosca sang.

Scarpia did not weep, but he was affected. Here was a woman whose art was sublime and embodied all that was beautiful in a living person. The dumpiness was lost not in a skilfully tailored costume but by the way in which the sound transformed the form of Tosca into the quintessence of feminine beauty. To the women, she became everything they would like to be; to the men, everything they would like to possess.

The opera ended. A great roar rose into the night air and echoed off the mountains as the audience stood and applauded. They would not let Tosca go; there were twelve calls for her to reappear; she was bombarded with *bravas* and the ground before her strewn with roses. Tosca curtsied. She smiled. She pointed to the other singers, the orchestra, the conductor, the artistic director, and finally to Prince Alturo himself, who came forward to acknowledge the gratitude of his fellow Sicilians.

A select few, among them the Petofrescinis, had been invited by the prince to a reception given in the ruins of the city. Hundreds of torches lit the ancient forum. Silver dishes piled with sumptuous food were laid out on the white tablecloths covering trestle tables, while liveried footmen attended to the guests. Scarpia followed in the wake of his hosts. He ate. He drank. He shared with friends and acquaintances the same enthusiastic judgements of Tosca's performance, and saw, over the shoulders of the guests, the huddle that had formed around the prince and his diva like bees around their queen. Should he push through this wall of admirers to pay his respects? Would she remember him from Venice? It seemed unlikely. How many male admirers had she entertained since then? Dozens. Perhaps hundreds. Certainly, too many for her to recall a single encounter with a Sicilian soldier.

Scarpia watched her receive the extravagant obeisance of her admirers, and felt a mix of emotions – admiration that she treated them all so gracefully, and astonishment that this daughter of peasants from the Veneto should now manifest the gentle imperiousness of a princess, handing her empty glass to Prince Alturo as if he were a flunkey. He felt a quiet contentment, even pride, that she had once sat in his gondola, had admitted him to her chamber while she changed her clothes and then had supped with him alone in a Venetian cantina.

Then, just as these thoughts were going through his head, Tosca's gaze, sweeping over her admirers with a gracious indifference, suddenly alighted on Scarpia. Their eyes met. Scarpia smiled and gently inclined his head. For a moment her brow contracted as if she could not place him. Then it relaxed and her eyes moved on.

*

Scarpia, too, moved on. The night remained warm. The guests, already intoxicated by the opera, were kept at a pitch of delight by the savoury delicacies, sorbets and sweetmeats, and glass after glass of ice-cold white or warm red wine. The women gathered in clutches, sitting on gilded chairs, while groups of men leaned against the warm stones of toppled temples, the smoke of their cigars rising into the pine-scented air. There was a moon which lit the ruins beyond the line of flaming torches, and Scarpia, unable to think of anything more to say to his cousins and their friends, left the forum and walked away, intending to find a better view of the moonlit sea.

He stopped and sat on the base of a fallen pillar. He was looking at the light of a boat sailing close to the shore when he heard a movement behind him and then a hand on his shoulder. He turned and looked up into the face of Tosca.

'So, Baron,' she said archly, 'you could not be bothered to pay your respects?'

Scarpia stood. 'I never imagined –'

'That I would remember you?'

'You have so many admirers.'

'I have many admirers, but not many friends.'

'Am I your friend?'

'More than a friend, surely? You saved me in your gondola. Don't you remember? Were it not for you, I might have been torn to pieces by the angry crowd.'

Scarpia laughed. 'If only that were the case, I would have something to be proud of.'

Tosca sat down on the slab of marble and, by a glance over her shoulder, invited him to join her. Scarpia sat down beside her, feeling her warmth as well as that of the sun retained in the stone. She had changed from her Grecian tunic into a longer dress, tied by ribbons at her shoulders and drawn in by a belt beneath her breasts. She took hold of his hand. 'I thought of you, after our adventure. Do you remember? We talked about love.'

'Yes.'

'And you told me that you had a wife who loved you and whom you loved.'

'Yes.'

'And I said it was a miracle.'

'Yes.'

The low tone with which Scarpia answered her led Tosca to turn and look into his face. 'Is she here, your wife? I would like to meet her.'

'No. She is in Rome.'

'And the miracle?'

'It turned out to be false. She now loves someone else.'

'Ah!' There was a touch of satisfaction in Tosca's exclamation.

'And our views differ,' Scarpia went on. 'She is now a patriot, a friend of the Jacobins, while I...'

'You are loyal to your king.'

'Yes.'

'And if you had stayed in Rome, you would have been imprisoned?'

'Almost certainly.'

'So you fled. Bravo.'

Scarpia blushed. 'A tactical retreat. In due course I shall return.'

'Of course.'

'I have estates here in Sicily,' said Scarpia.

'So you pick olives and make wine…'

'Our people do that, yes.'

'While you amuse yourself.'

'As best I can.'

'But without a wife.'

'Without a wife.'

'But an inamorata?' She looked quizzically into his eyes.

'No. No inamorata.'

'No wonder. Sicilian women are all Africans.'

Scarpia smiled. 'And the women of the Veneto?'

Tosca looked down at her bosom as if to make an appraisal. 'Well, what do you think? Could you love a woman from the Veneto?'

'Only too easily.'

Tosca looked steadily into his eyes, then said: 'Let's walk further away. Sooner or later the prince will come looking for me.' She rose and put her arm through Scarpia's. 'He thinks I am obeying a call of nature.' She glanced at him – an impudent look in her eyes.

'No doubt he hoped that he would be the one walking with you in the moonlight.'

'I am sure. But he paid me to sing, for nothing else. He doesn't own me. No one owns me. I am Tosca.'

'And doesn't Tosca have a lover?'

She did not reply, but tightened her hold of his arm. They walked on for a while in silence. Then she said: 'You cannot imagine how one feels after singing here, under the moon and the stars. I felt the gods were watching, the pagan gods, coming out of their temples, and Venus was there filling me with a longing; and then I saw you, over the heads of Prince Alturo and all those absurd old men. I saw you looking at me with such a sad and serious look on your face, and I remembered you and Venice and how chivalrous you had been and how you had asked for nothing...'

They reached a cluster of pine trees. Tosca stopped, then drew him into the shade from the light of the moon. 'And I felt that terrible longing and thought – now he shall have his reward.' She placed her arms on his shoulders and looked up into his eyes. Then she closed her eyes and tilted her head. Scarpia kissed her. She drew him further into the darkness. Scarpia took off his tunic, spread it on the yellowed grass strewn with pine needles, and laid her down on the hard ground. '*Dio, dio, Santa Maria,*' she said as he caressed her. Then, deftly, she freed one hand to reach under her skirts to remove the garment beneath. Scarpia untied the ribbons on her shoulders. '*Dio, dio...*' He kissed her neck, her eyes, her ears, her breasts. Her embrace became stronger; her kiss enduring; and, as they made love, she first whispered and then cried again '*Dio, dio...*' and further words in a dialect that Scarpia did not understand.

*

They walked arm in arm back towards the forum. As they saw the light of torches and heard voices, they stopped. Tosca tightened the belt beneath her bodice; Scarpia retied the ribbons at her shoulders and brushed pine needles off the back of her dress.

'Will that do?' he asked her.

'Of course. And anyway, who cares? Let people think what they like.'

'Tosca is invulnerable?'

'Yes.' She looked up at him again, her face suddenly severe. 'And you must be invulnerable too. Do not fall in love with me, Scarpia. I have my life and you have yours. Tonight … this … has been a joy. But I belong to no one and the future is uncertain. We may never meet again. Farewell may be adieu.'

Twelve

On 3 September 1798, a sloop flying the white ensign of the British navy sailed into the Bay of Naples. Two British officers, Captain Hoste and Captain Capel, were rowed ashore. They reported to the British ambassador, Sir William Hamilton, that a month before the British fleet had found and annihilated the French fleet off the coast of Egypt in Aboukir Bay. Bonaparte, whose army had defeated the Mameluks and taken Cairo, was cut off from France. The British were now masters of the Mediterranean.

Sir William immediately took Captain Capel to the royal palace, where the king and queen were at dinner with their children. On hearing the news, King Ferdinand embraced his family. 'Oh, my dears, you are now safe.' Queen Maria Carolina laughed, wept, kissed her children, her husband, ran from the room, then returned, again burst into tears, and embraced all those around her. 'Oh, brave Nelson! Oh God, bless and protect our brave deliverer! Oh, Nelson! Nelson! What do we not owe you! Oh, conqueror. Saviour of Italy.'

Three days of celebration were proclaimed by the king. Emma Hamilton ordered a new dress embroidered with gold anchors. Sir William Hamilton wrote to Nelson: 'Come here, for God's sake, my dear friend, as soon as the service will permit you. A pleasant retreat is ready for you in my house, and Emma is looking out for the softest pillows to repose the few wearied limbs you have left.' When Nelson reached Naples on the *Vanguard* on 22 September, he was greeted by a flotilla of five hundred boats and barges carrying musicians and choirs singing 'Rule Britannia' and 'See the Conquering Hero'. The barge of the British ambassador, as it drew alongside the *Vanguard*, was saluted by a salvo of thirteen guns. Emma Hamilton, after greeting Nelson, fell in a swoon into his arms. The short, half-blind, one-armed rear admiral was enchanted. An hour later, a 21-gun salute proclaimed the arrival of the royal barge. King Ferdinand himself came aboard the *Vanguard* to congratulate the saviour of his family and throne.

The British Embassy where Nelson stayed when he came ashore was illuminated by three thousand lamps spelling out his name. General Acton gave an official dinner in his honour, and Sir William a party at the British Embassy for eighteen hundred guests. Emma Hamilton arranged every detail of this reception and, after the arrival of their guest of honour, remained at his side throughout the evening, indispensable as an interpreter for her compatriot, who could speak no foreign language.

After many months at sea, Nelson appreciated the attentions of such a beautiful woman. He had been touched when she had fainted into his arms on the deck of the *Vanguard* and, if he recalled from his earlier visit that Lady Hamilton was an accomplished actress, and that perhaps the swoon had been well rehearsed, it hardly detracted from the charm of her attentions. In the days which followed the reception, she continued to keep his company, and it quickly became evident that the services provided by Emma went beyond interpreting and entertaining the conquering hero. Her husband, Sir William Hamilton, raised no objection: if the battered admiral had lost an arm and an eye in the service of his country, he could hardly begrudge him the ministrations of his much younger wife.

Nelson had a wife in England, but he was not in England, and in Naples the moral climate was more tolerant, and the hot sun heated the blood. Queen Maria Carolina, whose mother, the Empress Maria Theresa, had policed the chastity of her courtiers, was so besotted with the pretty adventuress from Cheshire that in her eyes she could do no wrong. Historians have wondered why a queen so proud of her lineage should befriend an English strumpet. The republican historian, Pietro Coletta, thought it simply a means to manipulate Nelson, but in fact there was no need: the Austrian queen and English admiral were of a like mind when it came to affairs of state. Queen Maria Carolina had been ill when Nelson first arrived on the *Vanguard*, but when she was well enough to receive him, they agreed that they should now stop the celebrations and pursue the war. Time was being lost. 'The boldest measures are the safest,' Nelson told the queen. The Kingdom of the Two Sicilies should abandon its policy of procrastination and wage war against the French.

'The queen thinks as we do,' wrote Nelson after this encounter, but what can be done with 'a country of fiddlers and poets, whores and scoundrels'? However, it was not simply the easy-going nature of his subjects that caused King Ferdinand to hesitate before going to war. The British might now rule the waves, but on land it was a different matter. Lord Grenville in London advised Hamilton and Nelson against attacking the French without Austrian support. He was ignored. General Acton, Admiral Nelson and Queen Maria Caroline overcame the king's doubts. A levy was imposed on the communes of the kingdom to raise 40,000 fresh troops.

The regiments required officers. Baron Scarpia, in his villa in Bagheria, received a note from Cardinal Ruffo: 'My dear son in Christ. The time has come. The king will have use for your sword.' He sailed at once to Naples, where he was welcomed at court and given a commission, but not a command: it was still held that only soldiers from north of the Alps made competent generals. Scarpia was placed in a regiment led by a French émigré, Roger de Damas. To take overall command, a Bavarian general, Karl Mack, Baron von Leiberich, was dispatched from Vienna.

Mack reached Naples on 16 October. 'General,' said Queen Maria Carolina, 'you must be to us by land what my hero Nelson has been by sea.' The army Mack was to command was assembled at the military base near the northern border of the Kingdom of Naples at San Germano. The whole court accompanied him to review the troops. Queen Maria Carolina, wearing a blue riding habit adorned with gold fleurs-de-lis, rode along the lines in a coach-and-four, followed by members of the nobility and the ambassadors of allied nations, among them Sir William Hamilton and his wife Emma sitting next to the victor of Aboukir Bay. Mack was impressed. 'If only we had an enemy worthy of such a superb army,' he told the queen.

General Roger de Damas, Scarpia's commander, was sceptical. The regiments might look formidable when drawn up on parade, but the soldiers were no more than peasants in uniform with no experience of manoeuvres and little of fighting beyond the pursuit of personal vendettas. Their commanders were foreign generals whose language they did not understand.

At a council of war it was agreed that four thousand troops under General Naselli should be transported to Livorno by the British fleet to attack the French from the north, while Mack's legions would invade the Roman Republic from the south. At the last moment, King Ferdinand heard from his son-in-law, the Emperor Francis, that Austria would not support him unless first attacked by the French. Again, he hesitated. Exasperated, Nelson told Ferdinand that it was too late to turn back. His choice was either to go to war, ready to die and trusting to God to aid his just cause, or to wait in Naples to be deposed and no doubt guillotined by the French. Ferdinand was persuaded. He issued a proclamation that was read from every pulpit of the kingdom appealing both to his people's patriotism and their religious faith. He, Ferdinand, King of the Two Sicilies, was leading his army to Rome to oust the foreign tyrants, restore the Pope to the throne of St Peter, and secure for his people security and peace.

2

The invasion of the Roman Republic began at dawn on 22 November 1798, in heavy rain. No bridge had been built over the River Melfa, so the soldiers had to wade up to their necks in the cold water. The Liberty trees were felled as they came upon them and the tricolours torn down, but there was no fighting: the French forces withdrew towards Rome. The carriages of King Ferdinand and General Acton, accompanying the army, became stuck in the mud; so too the cannon and baggage wagons. After three days of a slow advance, the vanguard of the army made contact with a French contingent, but the orders were only to fire if fired upon, and it was allowed to retreat unharmed. On the sixth day, the army reached the gates of Rome and found them open: the French had withdrawn from the city, leaving only a garrison of four hundred men in the Castel Sant'Angelo.

On 29 November, King Ferdinand, accompanied by Mack and Acton, made a triumphal entry into the city. A throng of ecstatic Romans greeted their deliverer with cries of '*Evviva il Re di Napoli*': bells were rung from all the churches. The king proceeded on horseback to the Palazzo Farnese, the splendid palace he had inherited from his grandmother, Elisabeth Farnese. From here he sent a letter to Pope Pius VI, exiled in a Cistercian monastery in Tuscany, urging him to return to Rome and reclaim his throne. He invited the cardinals and members of the Roman nobility to a reception to celebrate the liberation of their city: those who had shown republican sympathies had fled with the French.

To prevent the Roman populace taking any revenge, the king sent troops to guard the ghetto – too late to save two Jews who were thrown into the Tiber and drowned. A young officer, Gennaro Valentino, who had dazzled his commanders in the first days of the campaign with his courage and solicitude for his men, was put in command of a hastily formed Roman militia to protect the ghetto and houses of known republicans from the mob. Scarpia, with the permission of General de Damas, sent a contingent under Spoletta to the Villa Larunda and himself took a troop to the Palazzo Marcisano. At both they found the owners absent: they were told by the servants that the Prince and Princess di Marcisano had gone to the country, while Prince Ludovico and Princess Paola had left with the French.

So distracted were they by this lightning triumph that King Ferdinand, John Acton and General Mack forgot about General Naselli's army in Tuscany which, for want of orders, remained encamped outside Livorno. Mack, taking the French withdrawal to mean that their forces were in disarray, determined to pursue and destroy them. Orders were given to be ready to march in two days. Damas with Scarpia as his interpreter inspected his troops and judged that they were unfit for battle. The baggage wagons had yet to reach Rome: the men remained soaked to the skin and many were barefoot, having lost their boots in the mud. Their muskets had rusted from the constant rain and the mules which pulled the cannon were as weak and exhausted as their human masters. 'I tell you,' Damas said to Scarpia, 'the six days' march from Naples has damaged this army more than a month of fighting in any war.'

Mack was not to be deterred. Leaving Rome in the hands of a new governor, the Swiss General Burckhardt, a Council of Nobles and Gennaro Valentino's Roman militia, he led his army out of Rome to the north on 3 December. It was split into four columns – that in the centre, which included the regiment of Roger de Damas, was commanded by Mack himself. The French general facing Mack was Jacques Macdonald, a descendant of Irish Jacobites, who had made his headquarters in Civita Castellan on the road to Loretto. An assault on Civita Castellan, a fortress surrounded by deep ravines, was the first of many reverses. Far from being in disarray, the French had simply regrouped, and now counter-attacked across a swathe of the peninsula. In numbers, the armies were evenly matched, but the French troops were both more experienced and better trained.

There was another factor that worked in their favour. A number of the middle-ranking officers in the Neapolitan army were republican sympathisers who would later fight for the republican cause. They encouraged their men's natural inclination to cut and run, and by 6 December the Neapolitan front had collapsed. The retreat quickly became a rout. King Ferdinand, afraid that he would be captured and guillotined, slipped out of Rome in disguise and fled back to Naples. The next day, the French reoccupied the city – entering from the north as the last contingents of the Neapolitan army were departing from the south.

At a *pourparler* arranged under a flag of truce, the Neapolitan General Burckhardt offered to leave Gennaro Valentino in command of the Roman militia to preserve order during the interregnum. His offer was accepted. However, once the French had regained control of the city, Valentino was arrested and sent to the Castel Sant'Angelo. The French commander-in-chief, General Championnet, disowned the agreement made by his junior officers. He ruled that Valentino's militia had not been a unit of Mack's army, but a band of Roman partisans, and therefore its commander had none of the rights of a prisoner of war.

Valentino was known to be a zealous Bourbonist and a favourite of Queen Maria Carolina. This made him all the more attractive to Championnet as a candidate for exemplary justice. After a peremptory trial, he was condemned to death. Championnet determined that the execution should be a public demonstration of the republicans' implacable resolve. At midday on the last day of 1798, the young Neapolitan officer was led from the Castel Sant'Angelo to the Piazza Montecitorio, escorted by contingents of French soldiers and a military band. 'When he arrived at the Piazza Montecitorio,' wrote the diarist Antonio Galimberti, who witnessed the scene, patriots howled at him, shouting, 'Death to the tyrant!' He was quite fearless, and without a blindfold he knelt and took off his own hat and prepared for death holding a crucifix in his hand. At the first volley of shots he fell, struck in the forehead; a second volley was fired into him as he lay on the ground.

The republican *Monitore*, in an account of the execution published the next day, acknowledged 'the insane courage' with which Don Gennaro Valentino had faced death.

3

General Championnet was not in Rome to witness Valentino's execution. In early December he had been ordered by the Directory in Paris to pursue the retreating Neapolitans to their capital city. He met little resistance from the professional soldiers in the service of King Ferdinand. The Spanish commander of the well-stocked fortress at Civitella surrendered to the French without a fight. The fortress at Pescara, well provisioned and armed with sixty brass cannon and four mortars, was yielded by its royalist French commander, Colonel Picard, to his revolutionary fellow countryman, General Duhesme. The fortress at Gaeta, garrisoned by four thousand soldiers, seventy cannon, 20,000 muskets and provisions for a year, was surrendered by the Swiss Marshal Tschiudy to a feeble French force under General Rey.

More resolute in resisting the French were the peasant irregulars and the destitute *lazzaroni* who rallied to defend their *patria*, the city of Naples. They called upon their patron saint, Gennaro, for assistance, but on 16 December the phial containing the dried blood of the saint was held aloft and failed to liquefy. Was Providence angry that so many blasphemous republicans remained in the city's dungeons waiting for the French to set them free? A crowd gathered outside the royal palace, calling upon the king to give them arms to kill the Jacobins. One of the king's envoys, mistaken for a Jacobin, was stabbed in front of the palace – his bleeding body shown to King Ferdinand when he appeared on the balcony as proof of the loyalty of his subjects.

The sight of the mutilated corpse of his servant persuaded King Ferdinand that his people were quite as dangerous as the French, and that the time had come to withdraw to the other half of his kingdom, the island of Sicily. Nelson, returning from Livorno, and seeing at once that the war he had instigated was lost, ordered the evacuation of all British subjects and the royal family. Queen Maria Carolina sent chests filled with her clothes, jewels, plate and the royal treasure to Emma Hamilton at the British Embassy, which were duly shipped out to the British men-of-war. Sir William Hamilton chartered two Greek ships to carry his unique collection of antiquities, and the possessions of French émigrés. These joined the twenty merchant vessels and two Neapolitan men-of-war, the *Archimede* and the *Sannita*, commanded by the dashing Neapolitan naval commander, Admiral Caracciolo.

Caracciolo assumed that the honour of conveying the royal family to safety would fall to him, but at nine o'clock on the night of 21 December, King Ferdinand and Queen Maria Carolina, with their children and grandchildren, left the royal palace by a secret passage, and were rowed not to the *Sannita* but to Nelson's flagship, the *Vanguard*. The reason given was that *Sannita* was undermanned: as many as three hundred sailors had deserted. However, Caracciolo was mortified, and blamed his humiliation on Nelson.

The fleet sailed on the night of the 23rd. King Ferdinand remained on deck, chatting with Sir William Hamilton and any British officers who could speak Italian or French about the prospects for shooting woodcock in Sicily. The wind grew stronger; the gale turned into a hurricane. Sails were shredded: the foreyard was lost. The crew of the *Vanguard* were told to prepare to fell the mainmast. The royal passengers, prostrate with seasickness, were cared for by Emma Hamilton. Her husband, the old ambassador, when the storm was at its worst, primed two pistols, saying he would rather blow out his brains than drown. The king's loud voice was heard promising lavish gifts to St Gennaro and St Francis of Assisi if they would intercede to save him and his family. The Austrian ambassador, Count Esterhazy, threw a bejewelled snuff-box into the sea, not to placate Neptune but because inside the lid was a miniature of his naked mistress and he did not want it to be found on his sodden corpse.

The storm continued throughout Christmas Day, and that evening the six-year-old Prince Carlo Alberto died in the arms of the ever-solicitous Emma Hamilton. When the queen was told, she said simply: 'We will all soon join him.' Nelson's temper was not improved when the *Sannita*, captained by Admiral Caracciolo, drew close to the *Vanguard* and signalled an offer of help. Its sails trimmed, its masts intact, it was noted with some pride by King Ferdinand that the Neapolitan Caracciolo had mastered the seas better than Nelson.

The fleet that had left Naples had been widely dispersed by the storms – some ships being blown back to Calabria, others north to Sardinia. However, late on Christmas night the *Vanguard* finally reached Palermo. The Queen disembarked at once: King Ferdinand waited until morning and at nine o'clock, after a good breakfast, landed with his hunting dogs in that part of his kingdom still under his command.

4

The only general in Mack's army who had shown both courage and competence was Roger de Damas. Mack's dispatch to Damas ordering him to retreat had been intercepted by treacherous officers. As a result, he had found himself surrounded by superior French forces. Imposing complete silence on his men, and leaving the campfires burning to deceive the enemy, he evacuated his entire regiment in the dark, and after a long march north, reached the town of Monterosi. 'He slipped out of my hands,' wrote the French General Kellerman, 'like a piece of soap.'

Damas continued the march north, pursued by the armies of Kellerman and Macdonald. Kellerman's forces caught up with him at the town of Montalto, but were beaten back. In this engagement, Damas was wounded – his jaw shattered by grapeshot. He withdrew into the fortress of Orbetello on the Tuscan coast. Disabled by his wound, he had no choice but to resign his command. He decided to join the court in Sicily, and asked Scarpia to go with him.

Scarpia, during the few weeks of action against the French, had formed a close bond with his commander: Damas was the man he would like to have been, and might have been had he not married Paola di Marcisano. As they bivouacked at night, Damas would tell of his exploits – joining the Russians under Prince Potemkin to fight the Turks on the Black Sea, then serving in the Prince de

Condé's army of émigrés fighting the Jacobins on the Rhine. His amorous adventures, about which he talked freely, were as intriguing as his exploits on the field. Damas was cultured and witty, and if a little conceited, the conceit was justified. The calm with which he marshalled his men, the strict discipline he enforced which enabled them to escape encirclement by the French, his insouciance as the heads or limbs of men standing next to him were blown off by a cannonball or their bodies lacerated by grapeshot, and the stoicism he showed now that half his jaw was shot away, had greatly impressed Scarpia, who hitherto had had little experience of major campaigns.

It was clear that Damas had become equally attached to Scarpia, their camaraderie one of the few happy bi-products of the cruel war. Moreover, both Scarpia and Spoletta had proved indispensable to Damas, because they spoke the language of the Neapolitan conscripts who, despite their inexperience and lack of training, had shown great courage and endurance. The soldiers would now be shipped back to Naples by Nelson. Scarpia therefore agreed to go with Damas to Sicily.

The two men, accompanied by Spoletta, landed at Messina. From here Damas was carried on a litter to Palermo, where he received a hero's welcome. King Ferdinand and Queen Maria Carolina, General Acton and Admiral Nelson all congratulated him on his extraordinary achievement in escaping encirclement by the French. Damas disliked the two Englishmen, blaming them for the disastrous war. But King Ferdinand was in no position to dispense with either: it was a British fleet at Palermo, and a British garrison at Messina, that protected him from the French.

Moreover, Nelson's position in the affections of Queen Maria Carolina was stronger than ever. Soon after Damas's arrival in Sicily, she gave an extravagant reception in Nelson's honour with effigies in a Temple of Victory of Nelson, his mistress Emma

Hamilton, and her *mari complaisant*, Sir William Hamilton. The eight-year-old Prince Leopold, Ferdinand and Maria Carolina's second son, escorted the British admiral into the temple and placed a crown of laurels upon his head. The king then announced that he had made Nelson the Duke of Brontë, with estates that brought in eight thousand ducats a year.

While Nelson was being lionised in Palermo, a French frigate left the port of Alexandria in Egypt with an all-important passenger bound for Toulon. Bonaparte had had enough of his adventure in the Levant: political confusion in Paris demanded his return to France. Had Nelson been alert at his post, the future French emperor might have been captured and the course of history changed. 'Bonaparte should build a shrine to Lady Hamilton,' Damas later wrote in his memoirs. 'She should head the list of all the happy chances that led him to the throne.'

Thirteen

On the mainland of Italy, the abandoned subjects of King Ferdinand and Queen Maria Carolina continued to fight the French. For a moment they seemed to have the advantage over the invaders, but the Austrian commander, General Mack, and the viceroy appointed by King Ferdinand, General Pignatelli, decided that the war was lost. They asked for an armistice. General Championnet was astonished: he had been on the point of ordering a tactical retreat. His terms for a cessation of hostilities were harsh, and, though accepted by the king's representatives, were, when announced in Naples, rejected by the common people. The impoverished *lazzaroni* seized arms from the regular troops and stormed the fortresses overlooking the city – the Castel Nuovo, the St Elmo, Carmine and Ovo castles. Their arsenals were expropriated and all their prisoners set free – political prisoners and common criminals alike. An armed band set off to arrest General Mack, who, forewarned, surrendered to Championnet. General Pignatelli fled to Sicily dressed as a woman.

In the city of Naples, the mob now chose its own leaders: Paggio, a flour merchant, and Michele il Pazzo – Michael the Mad. It plundered the houses of republicans and attacked anyone who looked like a Jacobin. The middle classes were dismayed. Feeling that a republic would be preferable to anarchy, a number changed sides. The Patriotic Society asked Championnet to send his soldiers into the city and through subterfuge took from the *lazzaroni* the fortresses that overlooked the city. The *lazzaroni* continued to resist, fighting the French from street to street, facing grapeshot, mounted dragoons, cannonades from the 'patriots' in the St Elmo fortress and fire from republicans in the upper storeys of their homes. There was slaughter on both sides – a thousand French, three thousand *lazzaroni*.

After three days of fighting, it became clear to the surviving *lazzaroni* that they could not win. The time had come to quit. The king was gone: why leave his possessions to be plundered by the French? The mob broke into the royal palace and stripped it bare. Michele il Pazzo was taken prisoner, but instead of being shot by the French, he was reassured by Championnet: they had come as liberators, not conquerors. A guard of honour was placed before the shrine of St Gennaro.

*

In the midst of the fighting, on 22 January, the republicans in St Elmo had planted a Liberty tree in the courtyard of the castle, raised a tricolour over the ramparts and proclaimed a republic. A poetess, Eleonara Pimentel, who had joined her brothers in the fortress, composed a Hymn to Liberty. To establish a pedigree in classical antiquity, the republic was named after the pagan Greek settlement that had preceded the city of Naples, Parthenope. Names of those who it was thought should now govern this Parthenopean Republic were sent to General Championnet – the first being Carlo Lauberg, a defrocked priest, who had returned with the French wearing a French uniform and with a wife.

A *Te Deum* was sung in the cathedral to celebrate the founding of the republic and a Tree of Liberty planted in front of the royal palace, now renamed the National Palace. All the royal emblems – the crowns and fleurs-de-lis – were hacked off the building. The city was lit up for three nights of celebrations. There were impassioned speeches, wild dancing and impromptu civic weddings which, wrote the republican historian Pietro Coletta, 'had rather the character of bacchanalian orgies than civil ceremonies'. The *lazzaroni* were quiescent, while the bourgeois republicans, released from the dungeons of the Bourbons, or free to leave the homes where they had been hiding for so long, put on their finest clothes and took their places in the loggias in the San Carlo Opera, now the National Theatre, to listen to an opera by Tritto composed for the king's birthday, *Nicaboro in Jucatan*.

2

News that half their kingdom was now a republic reached King Ferdinand and Queen Maria Carolina in Palermo at the end of January 1798; so too the report of the execution of Gennaro Valentino. Unable to formally mourn the death of her young favourite, the queen's grief festered and sharpened her desire for revenge. Scarpia and Damas, though used to the death of friends on the field, were incensed that Championnet had broken the promise of a safe conduct and executed a fellow soldier in cold blood. Scarpia was particularly affected – the young Valentino had seemed a younger and better self – and his heart hardened towards the Jacobins and the French.

In Palermo, further reports that senior officers hitherto loyal to the king such as the Prince of Moliterno and the Duke of Rocaromana had gone over to the republic dispersed the euphoria that had come with the feting of Nelson. A thin layer of snow had settled on the city, and the royal family shivered in their draughty, ill-furnished palace. Only the king remained in good health and good spirits. Queen Maria Carolina, depressed and herself unwell, had to tend sick children and a daughter-in-law dying of consumption. She also knew that, for the first time in their marriage, her husband had lost faith in her judgement. It was she who had advised him to attack the French; she who had sent for Mack; and it was therefore she who was responsible for their present plight.

The position of the royal family in Palermo was not only uncomfortable but precarious: the Sicilians might be loyal to their monarch but they disliked his Neapolitan entourage and so Ferdinand felt obliged to replace some of his Neapolitan ministers with Sicilians. Acton was still responsible for foreign affairs: alliances were formed with Russia and Turkey, and Britain remained the guarantor of the safety of the royal family, but Nelson's fleet was required in other parts of the Mediterranean, leaving only one warship in the harbour at Palermo. Charred hulks were all that was left of the once fine Neapolitan navy, and its dashing admiral, Francesco Caracciolo, with no role to play, was given permission to return to Naples to secure his property from the republicans and the French. Once there, he deserted the king and offered his services to the Parthenopean Republic.

The hopes of the Bourbons were for the spring, when military campaigns against the French would resume. The Russians had promised to send a fleet into the Mediterranean and land troops in Italy. The Turks were now allies, and the British remained implacable in their war against those whom Nelson called 'the enemies of the human race'. Austria, too, was stirring from its pusillanimous inertia. It was possible that an Austrian army with Russian support might defeat the French forces in northern Italy. In the meantime, there was little to do but wait.

*

There was one man, however, who was not prepared to wait, seeing more at stake than the ousting of foreign invaders and the restoration of legitimate monarchs to their thrones. Cardinal Fabrizio Ruffo, Comptroller of the Palace of Caserta and the Royal Colony of Leucio, had fled with the court from Naples to Palermo. However, Ruffo was more than the holder of a minor office in the court of the King and Queen of the Two Sicilies; he was also a prince of the Roman Catholic Church and saw with dismay in the establishment of the Parthenopean Republic a far greater catastrophe than the transfer of power from the Bourbon monarchs and their favourites to republican lawyers, doctors, disaffected aristocrats and defrocked priests. What alarmed Ruffo was not the sequestration of estates or the removal of royal emblems from public buildings, but the supplanting with the Tree of Liberty of the Cross of Christ.

The Catholic Church had been the religion of the state throughout Italy since the reign of the Roman Emperor Constantine in the fourth century. With the collapse of the imperial administration in the Dark Ages, it was the Church that had filled the void – its literate priests replacing the imperial magistrates, its bishops the prefects, and at the apex of the administration of the Western Empire not a new Caesar but the Pope. At a time when the forefathers of the Bourbons and Habsburgs were mere chieftains of barbarian clans, popes such as Leo and Gregory had defended the integrity of Christendom. When the followers of Muhammad who had swept over North Africa, Syria, Palestine, the Iberian peninsula, the Balkans and all that now constituted the Kingdom of the Two Sicilies, it was the popes who had called upon Christians to resist them, and reconquer the lost nations for the Holy Catholic Faith.

What was the French Revolution but another assault on Christendom under a new guise? Satan, who had seduced the faithful with the zeal of a Muhammad, the unworldliness of a Cathar *parfait*, the evangelical fervour of a Luther, now misled with promises of liberty, equality and fraternity. Where deceit failed, apostasy was enforced by terror – the Saracen's scimitar, the Protestant's pike or the Jacobin's guillotine. And there was always concupiscence, a favoured tool of Satan to achieve his ends.

Ruffo was no fanatic. He could understand that in this life it was hard to distinguish the wheat from the chaff; that there were some who sincerely believed that liberty, equality and fraternity could contribute to human happiness and lead to a better life. He recognised the great disparities in the distribution of God's gifts in this world; but the way to redress the imbalance was through the giving of alms, not social revolution.

Ruffo also had an attribute beyond his zeal that distinguished him from most of those in the court of King Ferdinand and Queen Maria Carolina: he was a Calabrian. The estates of his brother, the Duke of Baranello, lay just on the other side of the Strait of Messina at Bagnara; Ruffo had been born at San Lucido, another of his family's domains. He knew and loved his people and had been kept well informed by dispatches from the clergy on the mainland and knew that there was no popular support for the Parthenopean Republic. 'It is clear, Your Eminence,' wrote the Bishop of Ottavini, 'that with good leadership the invaders would have been repulsed. But the army was led by foreigners with no love of our *patria*.' Another described how, in his diocese which abutted that of Naples, a number of the leading citizens, hitherto loyal to the king, were declaring themselves republicans and replacing crucifixes with Liberty trees. 'Human nature is weak, Your Eminence. They see whose hand now fills the trough. The Jacobin poison is spreading and will spread further in the wake of the French.'

*

Early in February, Ruffo sent for Scarpia. They had met frequently following Scarpia's arrival in Palermo with Roger de Damas – either at court, or at the receptions of the Princess Calamatina, and once at Scarpia's villa in Bagheria, when Scarpia had given a reception in honour of the man who had raised him from obscurity in Rome. Now Scarpia was summoned to the episcopal palace in Palermo where Ruffo was residing, and was shown by his secretary into the cardinal's private apartments.

Ruffo was standing by his desk, and when he looked up, Scarpia noticed that his usually placid features were flushed and his eyes, normally expressing no more than curiosity, benevolence and a measure of affection, were enlivened by some sort of excitement. 'Ah, Baron,' he said. 'I am glad you are here.' Ruffo did not offer Scarpia a chair, or sit down himself. 'I have just come from the king and will leave tomorrow.'

'Leave?'

'For Italy. I have persuaded the king, the queen and General Acton that we must act now, not await the spring. I intend to cross the Strait of Messina and raise the standard of revolt in the name of our Holy Faith. I have alerted our people at Bagnara.'

'But with what forces?'

'With no forces but that force that is invincible – trust in the providence of Almighty God.'

'Let me go with you.'

The cardinal smiled. 'Of course. I knew I could count on you. Your mother is from Basilicata. Your brother has estates at Barca. Would his people respond to an appeal?'

'Without a doubt.'

'I thought as much. The peasants are loyal,' said Ruffo. 'They are loyal to the king, but above all to God and His Church. The Jacobin poison has infected Naples and some towns, but it has not yet spread to Calabria or the Abruzzi. There is every chance that we can check it before it does. Enough of these Austrian, Swiss and German generals. If we, their natural leaders, call upon the people, they will follow us to victory or death.'

'Your Eminence can count on me.'

'I leave tomorrow, but you must send first to Barca to prepare the ground. Then sail to Sapri and go from there to Barca. Once you have raised a force, send word to me at Bagnara so that we can coordinate our tactics. The king has made me his viceroy. I have full powers to act in his name.'

*

On 7 February 1799, Cardinal Ruffo landed on the coast of Calabria with two clerics and four retainers. He was met by members of his family and escorted to Bagnara, where he was met by an enthusiastic crowd. The next morning, during Mass in the packed parish church, he preached his crusade. Cries of *Una guerra santa* and *Viva il re* came from the congregation. In the days which followed, volunteers came from all over Calabria; priests and friars, eager to serve this prince of the Church – their congregations, incited by sermons to take up arms against the atheistic republicans; soldiers from the disbanded baronial armies; landowners and peasants loyal to the Bourbons; and a fair number of thieves and bandits who saw the possibility of plunder in this holy war.

Ruffo named his ragbag force *il Armate della Santa Fide in Gesu Cristo* – the Army of the Holy Faith in Jesus Christ. These *sanfedisti* had white crosses sewn onto their sleeves, and wore the red cockades of the Bourbons on their hats. Ruffo led his army out of Bagnara towards the towns of Gioia Tauro and Rosarno, which opened their gates. Horses, arms and provisions were provided at Monteleone. At Mileto, the cardinal told the magistrates, officials and prominent citizens of the holy purpose of his crusade; of the powers that had been conferred upon him by the king; of the terrible consequences of resistance, and the advantages of acquiescence – among them six years of exemption from taxes and a share in the property expropriated from the rebellious republicans. The city opened its gates and the cardinal led a solemn procession through the streets to the church, where a *Te Deum* was sung to thank God for this early triumph.

The *sanfedisti* now marched across the instep of the foot of Italy towards the Adriatic. Maida and Cutro surrendered, but at Cotrone on the coast they met resistance from the republican citizens and thirty-two French soldiers whose boat had been blown off course on its voyage back from Egypt. The walls were weak; the defenders had few arms and little ammunition. After the first assault, they sued for peace. Ruffo would accept only unconditional surrender. This was refused, the siege continued, and finally the defences collapsed and the city was sacked.

Catanzaro was the next obstacle in the path of the Holy Army – a city with substantial fortifications and 16,000 citizens well armed and supplied. A delegation came to negotiate with Ruffo, saying they were quite willing to resume their loyalty to the king. Ruffo agreed that, if the civil guard was replaced with Bourbon loyalists, and 12,000 ducats paid towards the costs of his crusade, no vendetta would be pursued against the republicans and the city would be left in peace. His terms were accepted: the Bourbon standard was raised over the city. With his hinterland secured, Ruffo now led his *sanfedisti* north towards Naples.

*

The news of Ruffo's success encouraged those already fighting a guerrilla war against the French, among them the notorious Fra Diavolo. These drew on a pool of the disaffected – soldiers from the disbanded private armies, retainers of expropriated

Bourbonists who had lost their livelihoods, servants thrown out of work and some disillusioned by the Parthenopean Republic.

In Naples, General Championnet had been replaced by General Macdonald. To stop the advance of the *sanfedisti*, Macdonald first issued ferocious proclamations: any town that rose against the republic was to be razed to the ground. All rebels and accomplices of the rebels were to be shot, whether they be laymen, cardinals, archbishops, abbots or priests. He then dispatched General Duhesme to stop Ruffo with an army of six thousand men. Accompanying this French force were a thousand republican volunteers under Ettore Caraffa, Count of Ruvo and heir to the Duke of Andria. A republican from his youth, Caraffa had been imprisoned in the fortress of Saint Elmo in 1796, had escaped, fled the kingdom, and returned with the army of General Championnet. Now, with Duhesme, he besieged the city of Andria north of Bari, a fief of his family in the hands of the Bourbonists. Andria was taken. Ettore Caraffa, to prove his zeal, insisted on punishing its citizens. The population was slaughtered and the buildings burned to the ground – 'a marvellous instance of self-denial', wrote the historian Pietro Coletta, 'or thirst for vengeance'.

Another zealous republican, Giuseppe Schipani, led an army of twelve hundred patriots due south from Naples, hoping to add to that number of those fleeing before the advancing *sanfedisti*. Schipani was a trained soldier; a junior officer in King Ferdinand's army, he had been dismissed for his liberal views but reinstated as a general when the republicans came to power. He now passed through Salerno, Eboli, Albanella, Controne and Capaccia, all in republican hands, and first saw a Bourbon flag flying from the bell tower of the church of a small village, Castellucia. His mission was to engage the forces of Cardinal Ruffo, but he was provoked by this gesture of defiance and decided to take this little Bourbon outpost en route.

The citizens of Castellucia, seeing the approach of an army equipped with artillery, assembled in the church and decided to surrender. 'But it happened,' wrote Pietro Coletta, 'that a Captain Scarpia was present who accused them of cowardice.' If they were prepared to fight, he would take command, but if they were not, he would withdraw with his men and fight on better terrain, leaving them and their womenfolk at the mercy of the republicans. 'They answered with one voice, demanding war,' and, after being blessed by their parish priest, were deployed by Scarpia to meet the imminent assault.

When the republican troops reached the outskirts of the town, they were met by 'a brisk fire of musketry from invisible enemies'. General Schipani, with drawn sword, led them on, but when they reached the gates of the town, they encountered a further fusillade. The spirit of the republicans faltered; Schipani ordered a retreat; and as his men fell back, the Bourbonists leapt out from behind the walls and pursued the fugitives down the slope, killing some and capturing others. Schipani fell back with his remaining troops into the city of Salerno.

3

Scarpia, accompanied by Spoletta, had landed as planned on the mainland of Italy at the port of Sapri in the Gulf of Policastro. He had been met by three of his family's retainers – the majordomo and two grooms – and the news that their mistress, Marcella di Torre della Barca, had died three days before. They rode to Barca and the next day Scarpia buried his mother. He was the only child to throw a handful of earth on her coffin: his brother Domenico was under house arrest in Naples.

Scarpia had no time to grieve, and anyway felt that he might soon join her. He had sent word in advance of his arrival, and there gathered at Barca over the next few days not just feudatories and tenants of his mother's family but the bishop of the diocese, a number of the local clergy and a dozen neighbouring landowners – excited by Cardinal Ruffo's landing and impatient for further news from Palermo. Scarpia had letters from King Ferdinand and Cardinal Ruffo which he showed to the bishop who in turn blessed his mission and promised eternal rewards to those who should choose to join the Army of the Holy Faith.

Scarpia now organised his men according to their ability – trained soldiers to form the vanguard, the untrained to follow on behind. The number of volunteers doubled day by day. Five men led by a Tommaso Crivelli arrived with dispatches from Cardinal Ruffo. 'I send you these witnesses to the cruelty of the enemies of the faith. Their wives and children were all killed in Andria.' Why had Ruffo sent them? To stiffen his resolve? Yet in the same letter Ruffo urged Scarpia to be merciful. 'Remember, we are emissaries of Christ. Those who submit must be treated well and even the defeated merit clemency. Vengeance is to be left to the Lord.' The cardinal's sentiments did not seem to be shared by Crivelli and his friends. They sat apart from the other volunteers, priming their pistols and sharpening their swords.

After only a week of rudimentary training, Scarpia felt ready to lead his force north from Barca. Most of the neighbouring communes had already proclaimed their loyalty to the king. Others further afield sent out civic leaders as he approached to negotiate their surrender; and, following the guidance given to Scarpia by Ruffo, cities were spared if they replaced their republican magistrates with Bourbon loyalists and contributed towards the costs of the campaign. It was only by chance that Scarpia was present in Castellucia to rally its inhabitants against the assault by the republicans under Schipani.

Scarpia first met outright defiance when he and his men reached the commune of Certosino di San Marco that they met defiance – the gates closed and the republican tricolour flying from its ramparts. It was the largest of the towns they had yet encountered. Scarpia was told by the peasants who lived nearby that the chemists, notaries and merchants were all republicans; they had raised a militia and, forewarned of Scarpia's approach, had called in a small contingent of republican troops from Salerno. This was led by a *signor nobile* and had two cannon.

The town was invested and bombarded with Scarpia's few cannon. A breach was made in the wall. Scarpia led his soldiers through the opening, a pistol in his left hand, his German sword in the right, clambering over the rubble of the breach and the soft corpses of the defenders. As they advanced up the street, a cannon fired shrapnel, which lacerated a number of his men. Scarpia took cover under arches and in doorways, and, as he moved forward, felt both horror and a strange elation as he saw faces blown off by grapeshot, ducked the bayonets of his adversaries and, reaching the cannon, fired at one soldier with his pistol and plunged his sword into the belly of another. The sound of shrieks and shots stunned his ears; the smell of blood and dust clogged his nostrils; expressions of fury, fear, shock and pain passed before his eyes, as instinct drove him to kill before being killed.

The defenders of Certosino di San Marco retreated into narrow streets. The *sanfedisti* followed, Crivelli and his men, like eager staghounds sniffing prey, bounding ahead of their commander and dodging the bullets fired from snipers on the roofs of the houses as if they were gnats – any instinct of fear overwhelmed by their thirst for revenge. In their wake was a trail of decapitated bodies, and when the city was finally taken, there came first the shrieks of women, and then the file of the triumphant victors returning to camp with heavy portmanteaus, bulging pockets and wearing absurdly handsome clothes.

Thirty prisoners were taken. Crivelli demanded that they be shot. Scarpia hesitated. With Crivelli were not just the men who had come with him but a number of others whose families had suffered from the republican atrocities at Andria. A cry went up. 'Death to the Jacobins. Up against the wall.' Scarpia silenced them. 'We are ordered by the cardinal to offer every prisoner the chance to repent.' A priest with a Bible was summoned and, with Scarpia sitting in judgement at a trestle table in the central square, the prisoners were brought forward. One by one they fell on their knees and begged to be forgiven. One by one they laid their hand on the Bible, swore to repudiate the republic and remain loyal to God and the king. The line shifted forward. Scarpia glanced at the besmirched and bloodstained faces of the frightened men; and then, at the end of the queue, a figure in the uniform of an officer, the *signor nobile*, his head tilted upward in disdain and a face that showed no fear – a figure, a head, a face which Scarpia recognised: that of his former prisoner, Count Vicenzo Palmieri.

Spoletta too recognised the prisoner from the Castel Sant'Angelo and muttered to Scarpia: 'You see who we have here?'

Scarpia nodded.

'Better not be too friendly. It might be misunderstood.'

The queue advanced. Clearly, Palmieri had recognised Scarpia long before he himself had been recognised, lowering his head every now and then to glance at his captors with scorn and then darting a look almost of amusement at Scarpia. He had aged – the smooth, youthful features that Scarpia remembered were broken by lines and wrinkles – and the eyes that had so often looked idealistically into the middle distance, as if the future could be discerned in the ether, now focused on the priest with a look of complete contempt.

'And do you repent?' The priest put the question as Palmieri came before Scarpia.

Scarpia leaned forward. Involuntarily, his thoughts had turned to Simona Palmieri, and for a moment, forgetting Spoletta's warning not to treat his captive as a friend, he was about to greet him as if the two men had met at a reception, but he was wrenched out of this absurd reverie when Palmieri, in answer to the priest's question, spat on the Bible and then, half turning, spat in Scarpia's face.

The *abate* shrank back with horror and, after a momentary hesitation, wiped the spittle off the holy book with the sleeve of his cassock. A roar of rage went up among those surrounding Palmieri and the *sanfedista* on his left slapped his face. Scarpia was not angry. He wiped his face with a handkerchief, already stained with dirt and blood, and then raised it to command those pushing forward to belabour Palmieri to desist. 'Wait, wait,' he said. 'Let the man speak…' He said this though Palmieri had shown no inclination to add words to his actions. He darted a questioning look at Scarpia, rather as if he had departed from the script, and was perhaps encouraged to say something by Scarpia's look of confusion. The pulsing blood had ebbed in his veins with the image of Simona Palmieri: he felt that the spittle on his face was deserved.

Palmieri now turned away from Scarpia and faced the angry men surrounding him. 'Soldiers! Peasants! My brothers! My friends! Don't you see you have been deceived? You have been fighting for a cowardly king who cringes in Palermo, leaving it to his lackeys to fight his wars. Don't be duped by superstition! Do you think God is on the side of greedy despots? Or does He want you to share the goods of this earth and be free?'

'But you do not believe in God,' said Spoletta suddenly – his voice not raised but rasping and clear.

Palmieri hesitated. 'God, if He exists –'

'If He exists!' the priest repeated. And then, holding the holy book aloft: 'He spat on the Bible!'

'Sacrilege! Blasphemy!' The cries went up from the crowd.

'Citizens,' shouted Palmieri, 'we are approaching a new century. We are living in the age of philosophy and science. We can feed the hungry and cure the sick. We can inoculate your children against smallpox and teach you to read.'

'And San' Gennaro?' cried a voice.

'San' Gennaro?' Palmieri repeated in a tone of bewilderment.

'He is the enemy of San' Gennaro,' cried another Neapolitan.

'And of Christ,' said the priest.

'I am your friend,' said Palmieri. 'I am your brother. I fight so that you may be equal and free.'

'We don't want your liberty and equality,' said a voice in coarse Calabrian from the crowd. 'We want our king and our Holy Faith!'

The crowd shouted their approval. 'The king! Our Holy Faith!' And, as if judging that the time had come to settle the matter, Crivelli now stepped forward to the trestle table and, looking first at Scarpia, and then turning to face the crowd, cried: 'Enough! This man and his friends say they want to free us, but how do they free us? With rape and pillage and slaughter. My wife, my daughter, both violated and then killed in Andria. Are we to let this man go free?' He turned once again to face Scarpia and repeated his question: 'Are we to let this man go free?'

Scarpia raised his hand. The crowd was silent. He turned to Palmieri. 'Do you refuse to accept the pardon offered by His Eminence Cardinal Ruffo in the name of King Ferdinand to those who repent?'

'I refuse.'

'Then I hereby pronounce sentence. You will be shot at dawn.'

There was a growl from the crowd.

'Why wait?' asked Crivelli. 'Let us shoot him now.'

Again, the growl from the crowd.

'I am your commander,' said Scarpia. 'We will do as I say. The prisoner will be shot at dawn.'

*

It was not long until dawn. The crowd of soldiers dispersed, some to sleep in the camp outside the walls to guard their booty, others in rooms in the deserted houses. Palmieri was led away to the dungeon of the *castello* and Scarpia with Spoletta withdrew to the rooms above. They did not sleep. 'I cannot let him be killed,' Scarpia said to Spoletta. Spoletta's lack of a rejoinder suggested that he knew why.

Some food had been found for them: they sat together eating cold chicken, cheese and bread.

'There will be trouble if you let him go,' said Spoletta.

'I know.'

'You can't count on the priest to show any mercy. He would happily burn him at the stake.'

'Can we count on anyone?'

'Perhaps a dozen of the men from Barca.'

'Get hold of them. They shall be the firing squad. Tell them to put powder into their muskets but not shot. And tell Palmieri that when the shots are fired, he should fall as if dead.'

'And then?'

'Take away his body. Throw it on a dungheap.'

'Shouldn't you be the one to tell him?'

'No. If it is me, he might refuse.'

'He might refuse anyway and laugh in our faces or wriggle once he is down.'

'Then the men can finish him off with bayonets. We will have done what we can.'

*

Palmieri was led out to be shot in dim light shortly before the sun had risen. He was escorted out of the eastern gates of the town by a contingent commanded by Spoletta. The priest accompanied the condemned man, ready to absolve him should he choose to repent before meeting his Maker. Many of the *sanfedisti* were still drunk and so asleep, but Crivelli and his contingent from Andria, together with thirty or so others, stood by the gates to see that justice was done. Outside the eastern gates there were terraces with olive trees and vines. Palmieri was placed against the wall of the town close to the gates, his eyes covered by a scarf. The soldiers stood in a line facing him, raised their muskets and fired at Spoletta's command. The quiet of the early morning was shattered by the sharp sound. Palmieri fell to the ground. There was a moment of silence and apparent paralysis. The priest crossed himself. Spoletta walked forward to the wall and, looking down, fired his pistol into the corpse – the *coup de grâce*. Then he gestured to four of his soldiers, who lifted the body of Palmieri onto a bier improvised with their muskets. They carried it away from the wall and tipped it over the edge of a terrace.

'Food for the dogs,' said Spoletta to Crivelli.

'We must return to bury it,' said the priest.

'Later,' said Spoletta. 'Now it is time for Mass.'

All now followed the priest back into the town and to the church. A *Te Deum* was sung to give thanks for this victory of God's army. The priest assured his congregation that their comrades who had died in the battle were now in Paradise and, making the sign of the cross over the congregation, absolved them of any sins that might have been committed in the heat of battle. At ten in the morning, the army broke camp and marched north. The surviving citizens set about burying the many dead. When sent by the priest to find the body of Palmieri, they returned to say that it had already been carried off by the dogs.

4

By the middle of April 1799, throughout the Abruzzi, Calabria and Puglia, only Pescara and a few towns garrisoned by the French remained in republican hands. The contingents led by

Scarpia and the other Bourbonist irregulars, Pronio, Mammone and Fra Diavolo, had been as successful as Cardinal Ruffo. A force of five hundred English marines landed at Castelmare and, joining with the *sanfedisti*, took the city of Salerno. The Parthenopean Republic was reduced to a few square miles around the city of Naples and events in the north of Italy now led the French to waver in their support. On 5 April 1799, in the valley of the Po, a French army under General Scherer had been defeated by an Austrian army under the Hungarian Pal Kray; and three weeks later, at Cassano d'Adda north of Milan, the Russian General Alexander Suvorov routed a second French army led by General Moreau. It was clear to General Macdonald in Naples that he could expect no reinforcements, and that his lines of supply were now at risk. It was time to withdraw from Naples, but how should he present this desertion to his republican allies? As common sense. In an address to the Legislative Council of the Parthenopean Republic on 1 May, he told its members that the cost of supporting the French army of occupation was crippling the Neapolitan economy and, since the presence of a foreign army had provoked the insurgency, its absence would bring an end. If the friends of Liberty showed the courage of their convictions, they could easily deal with the *sanfedisti* themselves. 'A state that depends upon foreign arms cannot consider itself to be wholly free.'

Macdonald's speech was met with enthusiastic applause. So intoxicated were the senators with their own ideals that they failed to see that they were being left in the lurch. On 7 May, leaving French garrisons in the St Elmo and the Castel Nuovo fortresses, General Macdonald departed from Naples and led his army north towards the frontier of the Roman Republic. The republicans in Naples reorganised their forces and prepared for the city's defence. Stringent measures were taken to pre-empt a rising by the Bourbon enemy within.

A conspiracy by two brothers called Bacher was uncovered. The Bachers and their friends planned to seize the fortress of St Elmo and massacre prominent republicans. They would mark the doors of those to be killed and issue safe conducts to supporters of the king. Gerardo Bacher, the younger of the two brothers, gave one such safe conduct to a young woman he was courting, Luisa Sanfelice. She passed it on to her lover, a zealous republican, Ferdinando Ferri. Ferri went to the police and the conspirators were arrested. Luisa, who had only thought to save her lover from the pogrom, was declared the Saviour of the Republic and Mother of the Nation. These were titles she would later come to regret.

The successful suppression of the enemy within could not save the republic. A general, the Duke of Rocaromana, an early hero of resistance to the French who had gone over to the republic, now saw the error of his ways, threw himself at the mercy of Cardinal Ruffo and offered to serve as a private in the Army of the Holy Faith. The cardinal welcomed back this prodigal son and gave him command of all the forces in the Terra del Lavoro. The encirclement of the city was now complete. Pronio controlled the land around Capua; Fra Diavolo and Mammone had united their forces around Sessa and Teano, and Scarpia had secured the surrender of Cava and Salerno. All placed themselves under the authority of Cardinal Ruffo, whose coalition now included Neapolitans, Sicilians, Romans, Tuscans, English, Portuguese, Dalmatians, Russians and Turks – the Muslim soldiers an anomaly in the Army of the Holy Faith.

As the Bourbonists closed in on the city, the members of the Legislative Council attended a performance of Alfieri's *Timoleone* at the Patriotic Theatre. Rumours circulated of French victories in northern Italy and the imminent arrival in the Bay of Naples of a French fleet carrying 30,000 men. Using the last of the depleted stocks of oil, the city was illuminated to celebrate these phantom French victories. There was a ball at the Fondo Theatre and on 2 June, after Cardinal Zurlo had excommunicated his rival, Cardinal Ruffo, a *Te Deum* was sung in the church of San Lorenzo even as a priest was shot for shouting 'Long live the king'.

Cardinal Ruffo awaited an auspicious day to launch his assault. St Gennaro was out of favour for having appeared to favour the French, so Ruffo chose the feast of St Anthony of Padua, 13 June. After kneeling before the Blessed Sacrament, the cardinal mounted his horse and, dressed in his purple robes and carrying a drawn sword, led his troops towards the Maddalena Bridge. Seeing his advance, the members of the republican government retreated with their families into the Castel Nuovo and ordered the execution of the Bacher brothers: they were shot in the courtyard of the castle, together with three of their companions and eleven other Bourbonist prisoners.

As Ruffo's troops advanced into the city, they were met with fusillades from the fortresses and, more effectively, from gunboats in the harbour commanded by Admiral Caracciolo. Unlike the Duke of Rocaromana, he had remained loyal to the republic. Only when the sea fort of Vigliena was captured by a contingent of Calabrian *sanfedisti* was Caracciolo forced to withdraw. The Carmine castle was also taken, which gave the cardinal control of the port.

With the republicans holed up in the fortresses, and the *sanfedisti* still on the outskirts of Naples, anarchy took hold of the city. The half-starved *lazzaroni* emerged from their cellars and turned on anyone who was or might be a Jacobin. Men and women were stripped, slaughtered, dismembered – their heads kicked around as footballs or held aloft on pikes, their flesh roasted to fill empty bellies. Women who were deemed republican sympathisers were stripped to see if a Tree of Liberty had been tattooed on their bodies, made to pose naked as Liberty, jeered at, pelted with filth, and raped.

There was now a momentary stalemate and, despite the extraordinary success of his venture, and being so close to victory, Cardinal Ruffo felt overwhelmed. He was dismayed by his failure to control the *lazzaroni* or even the Calabrians in his army, and his inability to move further into the city while the fortresses were in the hands of the enemy. In a dispatch to Acton, he wrote:

I am at the Maddalena bridge, and from all appearances the Ovo and Nuovo castles are about to surrender to the Russians and *cavaliere* Micheroux. I am so exhausted and worn out that I do not see how I shall be able to bear up if this goes on for another three days. Having to govern, or more precisely to curb, a vast population accustomed to the most resolute anarchy, and having to control a score of uneducated and insubordinate leaders of light troops, all intent on pillage, slaughter and violence, is so terrible and complicated a business that it is utterly beyond my strength. By now they have brought me 1,300 Jacobins; not knowing where to shelter them I have sent them to the granaries near the bridge. They must have massacred or shot at least fifty in my presence without my being able to prevent it, and wounded at least two hundred whom they dragged here naked. Seeing me horrified at this spectacle, they consoled me by saying that the dead men were truly arch-villains, and that the wounded were out-and-out enemies of the human race, well known to the population. I hope it is true, and thus I set my mind at ease a little. By dint of precautions, edicts, patrols and preachings, the violence of the people has considerably abated, thank God. If we obtain the surrender of the two castles, I hope to restore calm there entirely, because I shall be able to employ my troops with this object.

Cavaliere Antonio Micheroux, a Neapolitan officer who had been acting as liaison between the court in Palermo and the Russians and Turks, was sent by Cardinal Ruffo to parley with the republican General Massa in command of the Castel Nuovo and Colonel Méjean in command of the French garrison in the St Elmo. Their terms for surrender included immunity from arrest or prosecution for the republicans and passage for the French troops and any who chose to go with them from Naples to the port of Toulon. And a large sum of money for Méjean.

Cardinal Ruffo knew quite well that these terms would be rejected by his vengeful monarchs. 'No pity must be shown,' Queen Maria Carolina had written to him, 'and the weeds that poison the rest must be hunted down, destroyed, annihilated and deported.' But if clemency was anathema to the Bourbon monarchs, revenge affronted the Christian conscience of the cardinal. 'What is the use of punishing?' he had written to Acton. 'Indeed, how is it possible to punish so many persons without an indelible imputation of cruelty?'

On 19 June, Ruffo accepted the proposed terms. The French would surrender to the Russian, Turkish and English troops and march out with full military honours. The Neapolitan republicans could choose between sailing to Toulon with the French or remaining unmolested in Naples. All their Bourbonist prisoners were to be released, but an archbishop, a bishop and two generals would remain as hostages to ensure that the provisions of the treaty were kept. The treaty was signed by Russian and Turkish representatives and, on the 23rd, by the senior British officer, Captain Foote.

Foote was aware, as was Cardinal Ruffo, that these lenient terms would not have been approved by Acton, Nelson or the Bourbon monarchs; but it made military sense to take control of the two fortresses overlooking the city in case a French fleet should arrive to relieve them. In the event, on the 24th, the day after the treaty had been ratified by Captain Foote, it was not a French fleet but eighteen British men-of-war that sailed into the Bay of Naples. On the quarterdeck of the flagship *Foudroyant* stood Admiral Nelson and Sir William and Lady Hamilton. Captain Foote, who had put his signature to the treaty with the republicans, went aboard and told his three compatriots what had been agreed. All three were incensed. Nelson told Foote that he had been misled by 'that worthless fellow Cardinal Ruffo who was endeavouring to form a party hostile to the interests of his sovereign'.

There now followed a struggle between Nelson and Ruffo as to whether or not the terms of the treaty should be respected. Ruffo was rowed out to the *Foudroyant* to explain to Nelson in French – the 'Frog language' that had to be interpreted by the Hamiltons – what factors had led him to enter into his commitments in the name of the king. At first, Nelson seemed to accept the treaty, but then on 28 June letters arrived from the king and queen in Naples telling him to abjure it. British warships turned their batteries on the boats that were to take the republicans to France. Those who had already boarded were surrendered and transferred in chains onto British men-of-war. The republicans protested to Cardinal Ruffo at this breach of the treaty. Ruffo sent Micheroux to protest to Nelson. Nelson ignored him. He had a note from King Ferdinand that authorised him, if necessary, to arrest Ruffo. Ruffo was now powerless, and nothing demonstrated that impotence more than the treatment of Admiral Caracciolo.

*

Unlike the Duke of Rocaromana, who had deftly changed sides, Caracciolo had remained loyal to the republic to the end. Ever conciliatory, Ruffo had sent him a message advising him to flee, and offering him a safe conduct through the encircling army. Instead of accepting this offer, Caracciolo had hidden on his mother's estate close to Naples, but had been betrayed by one of the servants. At nine in the morning of 30 June, he was brought aboard the *Foudroyant*. At ten, Nelson convened a court martial under an Austrian, Count Thurn, and five Neapolitan officers. Caracciolo was found guilty of treason and sentenced to be hanged. Nelson ordered that the sentence should be carried out that afternoon on Caracciolo's own flagship, the *Minerva*. Caracciolo asked that, as an officer, he be shot rather than ignominiously hanged. The request was relayed to Nelson, who refused. At five, Caracciolo was hanged from the yardarm of the *Minerva*. He was forty-seven years old.

It was said later that Lady Hamilton was rowed around the *Minerva* to see the body dangling before it was cut down and, weighted with shot, dropped into the sea. Charles Locke, the British consul, dining on the *Foudroyant* that night, described how Emma Hamilton fainted when the roast pig was decapitated before her because, she said, it reminded her of Caracciolo; but, upon recovering, she 'ate heartily of it – aye, and even of the brains'.

*

On 10 July, King Ferdinand sailed into the Bay of Naples on a Neapolitan warship with General Acton. The king refused to set foot on dry land, but over the next five weeks re-imposed his rule from the deck of the *Foudroyant*. Ruffo made one last appeal for the treaty he had signed in the name of the king to be respected. His request was ignored. He offered his resignation, but rather than accept it the king made him Captain General of the Realm and President of the Supreme Council. These were empty roles that left Ruffo powerless to prevent Ferdinand taking revenge on the defeated republicans. A high court was set up, the Giunta di Stato, to try the political prisoners – most of them intellectuals, professionals, academics and cultured members of the nobility. Pietro Coletta claimed that 30,000 were held in Naples alone and 'about three hundred of the first men in the kingdom perished'. Harold Acton wrote that, of the arrested eight thousand, 105 were condemned to death, 222 to life imprisonment, 322 to shorter terms in gaol, 288 to deportation and 67 to exile. The rest were set free.

The effect of the exemplary sentences was greater than the numbers suggested. General Orenzo Massa was hanged: so too Eleonara Pimentel, the feminist firebrand who had edited the republican news sheet, the *Monitore*. Luisa Sanfelice, whose rash warning to her lover of the Bachers' conspiracy had led to the brothers being shot in the last days of the republic, was sentenced to death. Her execution was postponed because she was pregnant, but after the birth of her baby, despite many appeals for clemency, she too was hanged. No exceptions were made for gender, age, rank or distinction. Noblemen, scholars, even bishops were hanged, their executions delighting delirious crowds of *lazzaroni*. Ruffo's fear that punishing the republicans would lead to the imputation of cruelty was well founded. Roger de Damas later described the Giunta di Stato as 'a tribunal of blood', while later histories such as that of Pietro Coletta canonised the victims of the Bourbons' vendetta as martyrs of the republican cause.

If there were punishments, so, too, were there rewards. Cardinal Ruffo, according to Coletta, was given properties that brought in a revenue of 50,000 ducats, a salary of 24,000 ducats as Captain General of the Realm, and a stipend of 9,000 ducats to be held in perpetuity by his family. The Russian Tsar Paul sent him the Order of Saints Andrew and Alexander with a letter praising him for restoring a kingdom to its legitimate monarch. The *cavaliere* Micheroux, who had arranged the surrender of the fortresses, was enriched and made a marshal. The leaders of the royalist insurgents such as Fra Diavolo, Mammone and Pronio were rewarded and given the rank of colonel in the Neapolitan army. Scarpia too was made a colonel, awarded the Order of Constantine, made a baron of the Kingdom of the Two Sicilies, and given estates close to those of his brother at Barca.

5

In the few moments of repose in the course of the campaign that had now ended, Vitellio Scarpia had thought of little besides tactics, logistics and how to hold together his fractious force of family retainers, arrogant noblemen, priests, peasants, bandits, turncoat soldiers, legitimist zealots and anarchic adventurers. The heightening of the senses and the pulsing of the blood that could be so exhilarating in battle was tempered by the knowledge that he was leading many men to their death. The youth who fought with such bravado in the morning was a corpse by sunset. The next day another took his place.

Scarpia led his soldiers, in the vanguard of any assault on a city, a pistol in one hand, a drawn sword in another and Spoletta a pace or two behind him. He led not simply to set an example and inspire those behind him but because he felt his life had little value. Who would mourn him if he was killed? His parents were now both dead. His brother and sister hardly knew him and his wife and children were estranged. Scarpia would never take his own life, but he minded less than most the thought that he might lose it. At each encounter he expected to be killed or badly wounded like Damas, and every evening felt almost bemused to find that he was both alive and unhurt.

Now the task was done. The God-given order had been restored. The foreign Jacobins had left the kingdom and the domestic Jacobins were in chains. The *sanfedisti* could now enjoy both their spiritual and material rewards, but, perversely, Scarpia was in no mood to do so. Once again rich, further ennobled and bedecked with medals and decorations, Scarpia felt neither triumphant nor even content. Like Cardinal Ruffo, he felt dishonoured by the king's rejection of an agreement made in his name. The thought of so many of the country's intelligentsia, who had been promised their liberty, being abused, tortured and some hanged, disturbed Scarpia and, awakened by nightmares, he relived the terrors of the war that had just come to an end.

Scarpia was familiar with irregular actions; he had fought the brigands in the Papal States, but these actions had been mere skirmishes, the shots fired as at game, while in many of the assaults on the recalcitrant cities he had found himself in an abattoir. In the papal army, his motives and those of his men had been to do their duty and earn their pay. With the *sanfedisti*, motives had been less uniform and frequently confused. Cardinal Ruffo's reasoning was clear. All men and women were destined to die and after death faced an eternity either in Heaven or in Hell. Outside the Church there was no salvation: thus all who would discredit and abolish religion were doing the work of Satan. They must be defeated by fair means or foul.

Did the end justify the means, however? Some of Scarpia's men were inspired not by devotion to God or to their Bourbon king, but by greed, loathing and lust – a terrible joy in killing and plunder, in the hacking off of limbs and heads and seeing blood spurt from bodies, of trampling on corpses, of breaking into homes, scooping up coins, jewels, fine clothes, anything silver or gold, feeling a particular hatred for the republicans in the towns they had taken because they were literate – doctors, chemists, writers, bankers, scholars – and taking revenge for their disdain by raping their wives and daughters.

Time and again, Scarpia gave orders that women were to be well treated, and sent to convents for their safety. Spoletta, whose task was to relay these orders to the men, received them with a smile. He did not dispute them, but, Scarpia suspected, was the first to ignore them. Threatened punishments were no deterrent, because the urge to rape came with the bloodlust of battle. And knowing that Scarpia was not immune to these feelings, Spoletta would bring before him some lovely, trembling woman on the pretext that she merited interrogation, leaving her for Scarpia to enjoy what Spoletta regarded as the legitimate spoils of war.

And at times Scarpia had been tempted, not only because he too had felt the same bloodlust, but because he saw in the eyes of these women a pleading to be taken under his protection, preferring to submit to a handsome and well-bred officer if it saved them from the brutish soldiers below. But when the bloodlust ebbed, so too did the temptation. Conscience, honour and self-respect regained their control over his thoughts and actions. Had he raped a woman, Scarpia would have been unable to face his own reflection in a mirror or look Cardinal Ruffo in the eye.

*

Scarpia had never lost his respect for his friend and patron, Cardinal Ruffo. There had been times during the campaign when he had been called to Ruffo's headquarters to discuss strategy, and there he was struck by the modesty and wisdom of this generalissimo and prince of the Church. Ruffo slept under canvas like his men, and every evening he did the rounds of their bivouacs, talking to his Calabrians in their native dialect, comforting the wounded, reassuring the fearful, listening to their complaints, settling their quarrels, calming their anxieties – not just as their commander but also as their pastor. And later, around the campfire, he would encourage his officers to give their views, and never humiliate those whose opinions were crass and ill-informed.

However, Scarpia never felt he knew what thoughts were to be found in the deepest recesses of the cardinal's mind. He made a great display of the Catholic religion from the altars he had erected before the gates of a recalcitrant city, preached the duty of each and every man to fight for the Holy Faith, promised eternal happiness for those who should die and absolution for any sins committed in the heat of battle. But was God on their side? Was it prayer and the intercession of the saints that had led to their victory? Or was the success of the *sanfedisti* due more to the victories of Kray and Suvorov in Lombardy, which had forced Macdonald to withdraw?

One evening, when dining with the cardinal in his tent, Scarpia had asked Ruffo quite what he expected from the intercession of the saints.

Ruffo had looked up, as if surprised by the question. 'I never expect too much.'

'It is said by Cardinal Zurlo that San' Gennaro's blood liquefied to indicate his support for the republic and the French.'

The cardinal smiled. 'Poor Gennaro. He must be confused. I ask for one thing and my brother in Christ, Cardinal Zurlo, for another.'

'Can we count on his help, all the same?'

'I think so, don't you? After all, he will surely see that Cardinal Zurlo prayed with a bayonet held to his throat.'

'Yet the blood liquefied. Can a saint perform a miracle under duress?'

Ruffo smiled again. 'It is best, I think, not to speculate as to what a saint can or cannot do. We know that they are with Almighty God in Heaven and can intercede on our behalf. We know that miracles occur for *nothing is impossible for God*. The illiterate *lazzaroni* know this too, and in their faith there is more wisdom than in the whole of Diderot's *Encyclopédie*.'

'But sometimes, Your Eminence, the most devout men can make bad soldiers.'

'Certainly.'

'And scoundrels like Bonaparte make good ones.'

'The Devil is given his due. Remember the Book of Job. Satan wanders through the world for the ruin of souls, and the Lord leaves him free to test us. But remember, too, the vision of Constantine at the Milvian Bridge. He saw the cross in the sky and heard a voice saying *In hoc signo vinces*. With this sign you will conquer. We too raise the cross and will conquer.'

'Yet the crusaders at Hattin went into battle with a relic of the True Cross and they were defeated.'

The cardinal sighed and wiped his mouth with his napkin. '*We see through a glass darkly*, my dear Baron. We cannot presume to know the will of God. God is beyond our understanding. We can only defer to the holy wisdom of the Church, listen to our conscience and do as our conscience commands.'

'But surely many of the Jacobins believe in their cause, while some of our soldiers are only after booty.'

The cardinal's expression did not change. 'Of course. There are Jacobins who believe that they are fighting for the good of mankind, but they reject the guidance of the Church and that is the sin of pride. Man is a delicate mechanism, Vitellio. He can easily be set off course. We know from God through revelation the truths about our condition, and distortions of these truths can have grave consequences through many generations to come. It is from God that we know that man is more than an animal; that each one of us is of equal worth; that marriage is sacred, ordained by God, one man to one woman, and then think back to the polygamous pagans or of the Saracens who take four wives or the licentious Anabaptists of Münster. Yes, there may be Jacobins who act in good conscience, but their ideas are like a plague, and those who bring in foreign armies to infect the innocent must be resisted. They must be driven out of Italy just as the Saracens were driven out of Spain.'

301

'And we may recruit brigands to do the work of God?'

'Two thieves were crucified with Jesus. One good, one bad. The Lord will know which is which.'

'Does the end justify the means?'

'*Cum finis est licitus, etiam media sunt licita?* No, not at all. St Augustine taught quite clearly that nothing wrong can be done for the sake of a good end and St Thomas confirmed it. *Ea, quae secundum se mala, nullo fine bene fieri possunt.* But St Augustine also taught that war can be just and, if the aim of the war is just, and no evil means are *deliberate* or *intended*, then there is no sin. St Bernard reached the same conclusion when he approved the crusades. We are not fighting the Jacobins for their property or for revenge. We are fighting to defend our Church and our king. Evil may be done, but it is incidental. It is not the intended means, let alone the end.'

*

We are not fighting the Jacobins for their property or for revenge. These words of the cardinal had sounded in Scarpia's ears when, staying with his brother in Naples, he had received the deeds to estates confiscated from republicans in Basilicata. Were these not just as much booty as the jewels and plate pillaged by his troops? And as he heard of the sentences of death handed down on some of Naples's most distinguished men of letters – Cirillo and Pagnano, de Filippis and Fiorentino – and then women like the foolish Eleonora Pimentel and the impetuous Luisa Sanfelice, and the sixteen-year-old son of the Marchese Genzano, he asked himself was this not revenge?

Scarpia could calm his conscience with the thought that it was not he nor even Ruffo who was taking revenge, but King Ferdinand and Queen Maria Carolina who dismissed all appeals for mercy. Scarpia's own family was not unaffected by the purge of republicans because, while his brother Domenico had remained loyal to the king, and had been held as a hostage by the republicans in the Castel Nuovo, his brother-in-law Leonardo Partinico and his sister Angelina, who had supported the republic, were arrested and imprisoned, and only released as a favour to Scarpia.

Scarpia was made welcome in the homes of both his brother and sister: he was a hero in Domenico's household, and the Partinicos realised that they owed him their liberty, perhaps even their lives. However, being with these two happy families made Scarpia miss his own; talking to his nephews and nieces made him yearn to embrace and fondle his own children, whom he had not seen for well over a year. He was now a rich and respected figure in the Kingdom of the Two Sicilies – approved of by Acton, favoured by the king and queen – but he was conscious he took little joy in the fruits of his triumph with no woman to share them.

There were a number on offer – Bourbonist *salonnières* eager to reward their hero, or frightened former republicans ready to barter their bodies for his patronage and protection. If he wanted a mistress, he could take his pick from among some of the most beautiful women in Naples; and if he wanted a new wife, an annulment of his marriage to Paola could surely be arranged, leaving him free to marry the daughter of a leading Neapolitan family – his sister had a number of candidates in mind. But Scarpia did not want a new wife nor a mistress. Bored, despondent, feeling old, though not yet forty, Scarpia remembered the relative contentment he had felt alone in his father's library and returned to Palermo.

Fourteen

General Jacques Macdonald, after leaving the Parthenopean Republic to its fate, led his army north – first to Rome where he picked up what reinforcements could be spared, then on over the Apennines to Florence and through Tuscany towards Milan. He was stopped at the River Trebia just short of Piacenza by a combined force of Russians and Austrians under the Russian General Suvorov. The French outnumbered the allies, but were defeated. Macdonald fled with the rump of his army to Genoa. Around five thousand of the allies were killed and nine thousand French – among them Major General Gaston de Jouve, the lover of Paola di Marcisano.

When the news of Jouve's death reached Rome, Paola consulted her friends Graziella di Pozzo and Domenica Attavanti as to whether or not she should go into mourning. If Jouve had been her husband, the etiquette was clear: withdrawal from society for six weeks and, when the widow reappeared, a year dressed in black. But Jouve had not been her husband. The marchesa argued that certainly Paola should not seem unaffected by the death of a patriotic hero, but that the whole ritual of mourning smacked of popish superstition. Graziella agreed and suggested a compromise – a day or two of retirement – perhaps even a week – during which time her seamstress could make some dresses in subdued colours: she had seen some bales of fine grey silk that would match the mien of a bereaved lover.

After the marchesa had left, but with Graziella still with her, Paola practised that mien in front of the mirror and rigidly retained it even as Graziella shook with laughter. The marchesa would have strongly disapproved of such levity around the death of a patriot, but Graziella had known for some time that Paola had grown bored of her brigadier and had been delighted to see him depart with Macdonald. She had not wished him dead, and as she sat alone in the Villa Larunda in semi-mourning, she thought back fondly of her farouche Frenchman with his hairy torso and scratchy whiskers; of his jolly good nature and the loud laugh that always accompanied his own jokes. After the mercurial Scarpia, who at one moment had played the debonair adventurer and then had become maudlin and philosophical – a Werther overcome by Weltschmerz – Jouve had been easy to live with: Paola could under-stand Josephine taking a hussar as a lover while Bonaparte was campaigning in Italy.

Jouve had also been right for the time – the time being the new era of Liberty, Equality and Fraternity, the overthrow of a medie-val theocracy and the rebirth of the civitas of antiquity in which the ancestors of the Marcisanos (if that thousand-year-old rumour was to be believed) had played a prominent role. Jouve had been a warrior; in one of the *tableaux vivants* in which Paola had appeared, lightly draped, as the nymph Larunda, the major general had also taken part attired as Mars with a thick leather breastplate moulded to his hirsute torso, metal slats over his woollen tunic and a helmet with a horsehair mane – all borrowed from the costumier at the Argentina theatre. Ludovico had appeared in a toga, and so too the young artists from the Villa Medici and their Italian friends such as Mario Cavaradossi, and, of course, presiding over them all, the Consul of the Roman Republic, Cesare Angelotti.

There had been something exhilarating about the republican festivities. Perhaps some of the symbolic changes had verged on the ridiculous: the bronze statue of St Michael the Archangel on top of the Castel Sant'Angelo, renamed 'The Genius of Liberty', dressed in a tricolour cape and a republican bonnet. But Paola had seen with what joy young Roman girls danced around the Liberty trees in flimsy costumes and, as the warm air caressed their bodies, had chosen handsome young men with whom to celebrate their liberation. At a reception given by the Principessa di Santa Croce, a sour *abate* had said that throughout history sexual licence had been a driving force of political revolution. Was her affair part of that phenomenon? Why, then, had she gone off Jouve? Was it because he laughed so loudly at his own jokes, or had she turned against the French because they were plundering her city?

All the festivities and celebrations could not hide the comprehensive looting of Rome by the army of occupation. Ludovico excused it by the right of conquest. 'After all, Rome is filled with statues taken from Greece and obelisks from Egypt.' And when she had complained to Jouve, he had said: 'You must understand, my little cabbage, that, as our great General Bonaparte once said, an army marches on its stomach, and France has a large army with a prodigious appetite and it is many months since our soldiers have been paid.'

Though the French soldiers might not have been paid, their senior officers, among them Jouve, seemed to have plentiful resources; so too the leading republicans such as Cesare Angelotti, who suddenly found the money to buy the confiscated palace of the Grand Master of the Knights of Malta on the via Dondotti for the knock-down price of 5,200 scudi. It became quite clear to Paola that Angelotti's concept of fraternity extended no further than members of his immediate family whom he enriched through the buying and selling of confiscated properties; and that his idea of liberty was also relative because he exercised his powers as consul in an arbitrary fashion. 'Be careful,' said a pamphlet lodged with Pasquino. 'Don't let Angelotti hear you, because when he's in a rage, he's a real beast.'

The Marchesa Attavanti, Angelotti's sister, defended her brother, saying that he deserved some reward for what he had suffered for the republican cause. And: 'It's all very well for those who have property already to criticise those who have had to acquire it.' Paola made no response, but felt this was an unsatisfactory excuse for Angelotti's venality. Others took the same view. Angelotti was pilloried in the republican broadsheets and attacked when he rode out in his luxurious carriage. He was finally forced to resign as consul and was only spared prosecution for corruption by claiming immunity as a member of the Senate.

Paola was also dismayed by the regular executions by firing squad of both common criminals and political offenders. As the material conditions of the Roman poor deteriorated and the people went hungry, there were more protests and more executions – of those who stole bread or hoarded it, of thieves, bandits, deserters but also dissenters: two clerics were shot in November 1798 for replacing a Liberty tree in their village with a cross. However, the execution that tested Paola's new loyalties the most was that of Gennaro Valentino, the young commander of the Roman militia during the Neapolitan occupation who, after receiving a safe conduct, had been shot by the French. Why had Championnet reneged upon his officers' promise? Jouve had been evasive. The general himself had never given his word. Junior officers had exceeded their authority. Valentino might have worn the uniform of a Neapolitan officer, but he was a Bourbonist fanatic at the head of a force of *sbirri*, arresting and imprisoning patriots whom he would have executed had he had the chance.

Paola asked the Marchesa Attavanti at a reception if this was true. Cesare Angelotti, standing with his back to Paola, overheard her question and turned to answer her. 'We had to make an example.'

'Because he kept order?'

'Precisely. Because he was young and able and handsome and admired by too many people.'

'And honourable,' said Paola.

'And honourable,' said Angelotti with an ironic bow and condescending smile. 'It is precisely the lackeys of the despots who are appealing who must be crushed.'

Paola had seen the force of Angelotti's reasoning perhaps more clearly than he did himself. The limpid idealism of a Valentino showed up the hypocrisy of the corrupt patriots and rapacious French. The execution had been dishonourable and cruel. It had cast doubts in her mind on the benevolence of the republic, and tarnished in retrospect all those ceremonies and celebrations in which she had taken part. She now began to regret her appearance as the nymph Larunda at republican pageants and blushed to think of Ludovico in a toga. At the time, it had seemed like a dressing-up party but now, decidedly, the party was over, and it was time for the costumes to be put away.

2

After the week agreed upon with her friends, Paola came out of her mourning and reappeared in society wearing a pale grey silk dress. Many commiserated with her loss of Jouve, and she displayed to perfection the well-practised manner of a bereaved lover. She was surprised to find that the defeat at Trebia seemed to have had little effect on her republican friends, who surely had as much to mourn as she did. How could the republic survive without its

French protectors? Yet Angelotti, Cavaradossi and the Attavantis all behaved as if nothing had changed: the march of history could not be reversed.

Both the frenzied celebrations and vindictive executions continued even as the allies marched on Rome. In August 1799, two Florentines – a father and his son – were shot for carrying arms, together with a priest who had urged his congregation to rise against the French. In September, on the anniversary of the founding of the French Republic, with the allied armies coming ever closer to Rome, there were horse races, fireworks, a military parade and a grand ball at the Apollo theatre. At a gala dinner at the French Embassy, the French commander, General Garnier, promised the Roman republicans to defend their city to the last drop of his blood; a week later, he reached agreement with the allies for its surrender.

The terms were lenient: neither side wished to see the orgy of vengeance that had followed the fall of the Parthenopean Republic. There was to be no triumphal entry into the city. The Neapolitan army entered silently from the south, the British from the west, the Austrians and Russians from the north. A contingent was sent at once to protect the Jewish ghetto. Those Roman republicans who chose to do so could leave with the French and those who remained would be protected. The French troops retained their arms, and were escorted by British marines down the dusty road to the port of Civitavecchia from where ships of the British navy would take them to France.

Who should now govern the liberated city? The legitimate ruler was the Pope, but there was no Pope. At the end of August 1799, the aged and ailing Pius VI, having been taken as a prisoner to France, had died upon reaching the city of Valence. Before being bundled out of the holy city, Pope Pius VI had ruled that the next conclave should be held where a majority of cardinals were to be found at the time of his death. This had been Venice, then controlled by the Austrians, and in November the cardinals of the Roman Catholic Church assembled in the Benedictine monastery of San Giorgio in Venice to elect a new Pope. The conclave dragged on for months and, while awaiting the outcome of the election, the allies appointed as interim governor of Rome the Neapolitan General Naselli. The fleur-de-lis banner of the Bourbon King of Naples was raised over the Castel Sant'Angelo.

Baron Scarpia did not return to Rome with Naselli. Paola was disappointed. She had, on his behalf, and thinking of the interests of their son Pietro, successfully reclaimed the estate at Rubaso. She had hoped that he might be grateful to her for that, and even return to live with her under the same roof at the Villa Larunda. She was now over thirty years old. Her children were growing up; soon Pietro's voice would break and they would be looking for a husband for Francesca. Although it was only two years or so since Paola had 'succumbed' to Ringel, and an even shorter period since she had been the mistress of Jouve, she looked back on both with some embarrassment, which, in Paola, was akin to remorse.

Many different factors go to create a frame of mind. With legitimacy now in the ascendant, it seemed sensible for Citizeness Marcisano to become Princess di Marcisano once again – Princess di Marcisano, but also Baroness Scarpia di Rubaso; and with middle age on the horizon, it seemed appropriate that she should enter it on the arm of a husband. Of course, a marriage can be annulled, but Paola looked at other men and realised that there was none she preferred to Scarpia. She told herself that she had never, in fact, disliked him; that her liaisons with Ringel and Jouve could be ascribed to a kind of fever which women sometimes catch at a certain stage in life; and once it had run its course leaves them wiser – aware of the advantages of remaining with the father of their children and the love of their youth.

There was a further factor which she toyed with in her reflections: Scarpia's success as a general in Cardinal Ruffo's campaign against the French. She looked back beyond the Don Quixote of the Battle of Faenza, back beyond 'Ruffo's *sbirro*', to the dashing young officer who had captured the bandit Ponzio Adena and whom she had chosen to marry, and thought that perhaps she had been right to recognise something heroic in the Sicilian and insist upon his new blood to revitalise the stock of the Marcisanos. No one now, seeing him decorated, enriched and ennobled for his feats of valour on the field, could dismiss him as a *sbirro*.

Paola knew that Scarpia might not return. The lands he had been given in the Kingdom of the Two Sicilies were greater than those at Rubaso; and clearly there was more glory to be enjoyed in Naples and Palermo than there would be in Rome. No doubt there were beautiful women – and younger women – who would be more than willing to share his bed, and she did not deceive herself into imagining that he might be yearning for her; but she knew that Scarpia, too, was approaching middle age and that, while young men might want to make love to a woman as an end in itself, older men warm towards the by-product of that youthful desire – namely their children.

Pietro was now twelve years old – slender and handsome like his father but with the softer manner of his uncle Ludovico. He had picked up the Marcisanos' sense of election from his grandfather and uncle, but Paola could see his father in the occasional glint in his eye and in the way in which, when riding or fencing, his body became taut like the string of a bow. She could see what Pietro could not see – that his languid uncle and crotchety grandfather were unsatisfactory models of manhood. Pietro never spoke about his father; he understood that he had had to flee from the French and had accepted that they could not follow; but when the subject of Scarpia's triumphs came up at table, she could see a discreet blush of pride suffuse his cheeks.

Francesca, now ten years old, was quite unlike her mother or father and was thought to resemble the old prince's aunt Matilda. She was small, cheerful and utterly confident in her right to dominate the entire Marcisano household. She was far cannier than Paola had been at that age, managing to glean from the cooks and maidservants all the gossip about her mother and her friends. When Jouve first came to the Villa Larunda, and was introduced by Paola to her children, Pietro was mute and looked embarrassed, but Francesca had asked in a by-the-way tone of voice: 'Are you descended from a walrus?'

Jouve had taken the question in good heart. 'No, not a walrus,' he had said, stroking his whiskers, 'a lion!' And he gave a roar and the loud laugh with which the Marcisanos were to become familiar. Francesca had not laughed or even smiled. 'You don't sound like a lion,' she said, 'you sound like a donkey.' From then on, the children always referred to Jouve as 'the donkey'.

When it became clear to Paola, in the course of the autumn of 1799, that Scarpia might be staying in Sicily not for the attractions of that place but because Rome held painful memories, and that he might believe both his wife and children to be irretrievably estranged, she thought of writing to him, but could not think of how to put what she wanted to say. She decided instead to order two miniature portraits of the children, which somehow or other she would arrange to fall into his hands. She commissioned a talented miniaturist, a friend of Cavaradossi's, and by the end of November she had the two enchanting likenesses set in little gold-and-enamel lockets.

In Paola's mind, recovering her husband and the father of her children was a necessary part of the reordering of her life. However, the cornerstone of that reordering was not a reconciliation with Scarpia but a reconciliation with God. Paola was a Catholic, and no amount of cavorting around Liberty trees or posing as a pagan goddess or venerating Eros in the arms of French lovers would alter the impress made on her soul by a convent education. Moreover, Catholicism was a religion perfectly attuned to her present mood of regret. The forgiveness of sins was an article of the Apostles' Creed.

The Marcisanos had a tame chaplain to whom the members of the family routinely confessed, but Paola did not respect him – it was more than his job was worth to give harsh penances or refuse absolution. For the profound confession she had in mind – a baring of her soul – she wanted a priest who would not be intimidated by her rank or afraid to chastise her. She remembered that Scarpia had told her how his own life had taken the turn that eventually led to their marriage after confessing to the Oratorian, Father Simone Alberti. Paola had known Father Simone – they were related many times over – but she had been too afraid of his severity to confess to him before. Now, she wanted severity; she felt she had sinned and wanted not to be excused but punished and then forgiven. There was a further consideration at the back of her mind. Father Simone might be used to persuade Scarpia to return under the conjugal roof.

*

Father Simone Alberti was an experienced confessor and that experience had taught him that repentance is sometimes adulterated by worldly concerns: the Prodigal Son, after all, had only returned to his father because he was hungry. Therefore, when he received a note saying that Princess Paola di Marcisano would like to make her confession to him, he realised that he would need God's help to discern the sincerity or otherwise of her repentance. He knew, as did all in Rome, of her embrace of Jacobinism and her liaison with a French brigadier. He knew too that to be fully accepted back into society under the new Bourbon regime she must be seen to be reconciled with the Church. But cynicism in a confessor was itself a sin and so Father Simone, when Paola entered the confessional, was ready to give her the benefit of the doubt.

'Bless me, Father, for I have sinned.'

The man who sits in obscurity behind the grille of a confessional, listening to the penitent's list of transgressions, acts *in persona Christi* and while as a man he is ready to comfort and counsel a soul in distress, he is trained to beware of letting human sympathy affect his moral judgement – a failing all too common with a repentant woman. It was not that the rustle of silk, the waft of rich scent, the dim outline of a gentle face and large, lowered eyes could provoke in Father Simone improper desires – even as a young man, mortification of the flesh had first tamed and then killed his sexual instinct – but he loved women and was always ready to make allowances for a nature that he saw as distinct to that of man. Eve had been created by God after He had offered Adam other creatures as a companion, and so was herself in a sense a creature from the animal kingdom – a creature with a soul, but less governed by reason than by instinct, and so less responsible for those sins which stem from the exigencies of the species.

To an educated woman at the time – a Madame de Staël, a Mary Wollstonecraft or an Eleonara Pimentel – such an attitude would have seemed demeaning, but Father Simone's formation had taken place when the views of Aristotle and Aquinas on the irrationality of women had been widely accepted. Dom Simone had not known sexual love, but he had vicariously experienced it through the tearful revelations from the other side of the grille. He understood that God intended it to bind a husband and a wife, but he knew that few of the married women who confessed to him had loved or desired the husbands chosen for them by their parents. He knew that just because, in the words of St Paul, *woman was made for man and not man for woman*, a sexual passion could grow so strong that it appeared to be the whole point of her existence, and so to abandon it a form of death. Of course, it was not the point of her existence; that was salvation, and disordered love jeopardised that salvation; but death and the world to come were dim and unconvincing prospects to a woman whose body yearned for her lover and tingled at the thought of his touch.

Father Simone therefore listened to Paola's account of her affairs with Ringel and Jouve with a sympathetic ear. He accepted with little further interrogation her assurance that she repented of both liaisons and would, with the help of God, never commit such sins again. The Oratorian was more severe – far more severe – when it came to her collaboration with the atheist Jacobins, failing to perform her Easter duties and appearing as a pagan goddess at their blasphemous ceremonials. What an example to set to the people! She, a Marcisano! It was one thing to endanger her own salvation through her sins against chastity, but quite another to cause scandal and lead others astray. How many young women may have abandoned the sacraments, perhaps even their faith, after seeing Paola dancing around a Liberty tree? 'Certainly, as our first pontiff, St Peter, wrote in his Epistle, *love covers many a sin*,' said Father Simone, 'and the Church has always been understanding of human weaknesses. But when such weaknesses are harnessed to unbelief! When we turn from the worship of Jehovah to that of Baal, the god of fertility; for what is the Jacobin's Liberty tree but the phallus – the maypoles of the German barbarians or the high ground spoken of by the prophet Ezekiel? *You have piled whoring on whoring, and built yourself a mound at the beginning of every road and a high place at every crossroads*, says the prophet, and again, *You have laid down for those big-membered neighbours, the Egyptians –*'

'He was French,' said Paola.

'My dear child, I was merely quoting from Scripture to illustrate the Lord's anger at the adulterous Jerusalem. *The Lord your God is a consuming fire, a jealous God.* But remember also the prophet Isaiah:

315

Do not be afraid, you will not be put to shame, do not be dismayed, you will not be disgraced … Does a man cast off the wife of his youth? says your God. In excess of anger, for a moment, I hid my face from you, but with everlasting love I have taken pity on you, says the Lord, your redeemer.'

'Do you think,' asked Paola softly, 'that a man might be persuaded to take back the wife of his youth?'

'A man? You mean…' The priest hesitated as if he had forgotten for a moment to whom Paola was married. 'Yes, Baron Scarpia.' A further hesitation. Then: 'He must take you back. You will be cleansed of your sins. If God forgives you, then he must forgive you. But, is he in Rome?'

'No. He remains in Palermo.'

'Of course, he is a Sicilian. They have strong passions. But there is goodness in Scarpia, I know, and after all *nothing is impossible for God.'*

'I pray every day,' said Paola, 'or at least most days, that he will find it in his heart to forgive me.'

'In his heart. Yes, he must, for Our Lord says we must forgive those who have injured us *not seven times but seventy-seven times,* and we must forgive them *from our heart.'*

'I thought, perhaps,' said Paola, 'that if you were to write to him and say that you knew that I longed for him to return…'

'Of course.'

'It is not just for me, but for our children. They have gone too long without their father.'

'The children, yes.'

'I have two miniature portraits and thought if he was to see how fine they now were, it might tempt him to return.'

'Not simply tempt him,' said Father Simone, 'but remind him that he has responsibilities under God, and that there are things more important than wounded pride. The forgiveness of sins is an article of our faith: *Confiteor in remissionem peccatorum.* For those who are truly repentant, as I know you are, my dear child, there is the warmest welcome back into the arms of the Father.'

Paola made her act of contrition. The words were those she had been taught at the convent and she wondered if they were a sufficient expression of repentance for adult sins; but they seemed to satisfy Father Simone. The penance he gave her, however, was adult and severe – not because of her adultery, but because of her political apostasy, which was so much worse. She was to make a month's retreat in the convent of the discalced Carmelites, wearing a scratchy horsehair habit, drinking only water, eating only bread and vegetables, and joining in their Office, starting with matins at four in the morning. Paola bowed her head to denote her meek acceptance of such a well-deserved punishment. Then Father Simone made the sign of the cross with his raised hand saying: '*Ego te absolvo a peccatis tuis, in nomine Patris et Filii et Spiritus Sancti. Amen,*' and Paola left the confessional shriven and pure.

3

Towards the end of October 1799, at ten in the morning, Vitellio Scarpia was sitting in the library of the villa in Bagheria reading the gazette fetched by Spoletta from Palermo when a servant brought him a packet that bore the seal of the Oratory in Rome. When the servant had left the room, Scarpia broke the seal and opened the packet. Inside was a letter and, wrapped in silk, two closed lockets of enamel and gold. Scarpia opened the lockets and saw in one the portrait of an enchanting young man and in the other an equally delightful likeness of a girl. He then turned to the letter.

My dear son in Christ,

I am sending you at the request of your wife these depictions of your dear children, Pietro and Francesca. It is now almost two years since they have seen their father and she deems that they suffer as a result. She would have you either summon them to join you in Palermo or return to take your rightful place in Rome. She hesitates to write to you herself; she feels she is not worthy of your thoughts and feelings; however, I would be failing in my pastoral duties were I not to inform you that she greatly regrets her offences over the past two years – offences against God and against you, her husband. She begs forgiveness and again it is incumbent upon me as a priest to remind you that mercy is at the heart of our Catholic religion. Time and again in the Holy Gospel Our Lord asks us to forgive those who sin against us as he forgives our sins against Him: *dimitte nobis debita nostra sicut et nos dimittimus debitoribus nostris.* Do not let Satan harden your heart. Forgive as Christ forgave the woman taken in adultery and think of the rich reward you will receive in the love and respect of your children.

Pax Domini, Simone Alberti

Scarpia sat in the autumn sun, light filtering through the windows, with Father Simone's letter on the desk and the two open lockets in his left hand. He gazed at the portraits of his children and longed to be with them – to hold them, to embrace them, to look into their eyes. He imagined himself back in the Villa Larunda and wondered whether it would be possible to return. Or should he summon them to Palermo? The children, perhaps, but not Paola. King Ferdinand and Queen Maria Carolina would never receive a former Jacobin, whether or not she was repentant and at peace with the Church.

A month before, General Acton had asked Scarpia to go to Rome with General Naselli. Scarpia had declined. He had assumed that Paola and his two children had left the city with her French lover. When he had later learned that the lover was dead and that

Paola and his children had remained in Rome, he still hesitated. Did she want him back? Did he want live with her once again under the same roof? Scarpia had been held in Sicily by indecision. He had abandoned the idea of finding another wife. Paola had been faithless, but that was nothing unusual in her circle and, if Father Simone was to be believed, she now regretted what she had done. God demanded that he forgive her; not to do so would in itself be a sin. And there were their two children, who yearned for him as he yearned for them.

Later that day, Scarpia told Spoletta that he had decided to return to Rome.

'To Rubosa?'

'No. To the Villa Larunda.'

'To live with the princess?'

'And my children.'

Spoletta glanced at the letter from Father Simone open on Scarpia's desk, and then at the lockets in Scarpia's hands. Scarpia held them up for him to see. 'Pietro and Francesca. Aren't they enchanting?'

Spoletta studied them silently, then said: 'One never knows what comes from the skill of the artist.'

Scarpia laughed. 'All the more reason to see them in the flesh.'

'And the Princess Paola?'

'She is their mother.'

Spoletta said nothing.

'And my wife.'

'Of course.' He looked back at the letter. Scarpia saw his glance but did not offer to let him read it.

'Prince Naselli will give me a post.'

Spoletta nodded.

'I am kicking my heels here,' said Scarpia.

'It is your home.'

'I put down roots in Rome,' said Scarpia.

'I would not trust the princess,' said Spoletta. 'She wants to get back into the good graces of the king and queen.'

'Quite possibly,' said Scarpia. 'I am under no illusions. But I cannot bring her here. Nor can I separate her from the children. If I wish to be with them, I must go to Rome.'

4

On 19 January 1800, the start of Rome's first carnival season of the new century was marked by a ball at the Alibert theatre. A decorated pavilion had been built on the stage to serve as a ballroom and the boxes were festooned with the Bourbon colours – white silk trimmed with gold. Two boxes had been knocked into one to accommodate the governor of the city, Prince Naselli, and his entourage. There were 1,200 guests, among them the ambassadors of the friendly powers, officers from the Neapolitan, Austrian, Russian and Turkish armies, and Roman patricians – legitimists mingling with former republicans, some cutting their erstwhile enemies, others affecting a particularly Roman disdain for political differences: '*Sub specie aeternitatis,*' said the Prince Paducci to the Chevalier Spinelli, 'what do these little squabbles matter? And Rome is, after all, the Eternal City.'

'And we mustn't be outdone by the Scarpias,' said Letizia di Comastri. 'Look at them, arm in arm, the cut-throat Sicilian with the grenadier's whore.'

'If I am not mistaken,' said Spinelli, 'the late Major General Jouve was a hussar, not a grenadier.'

'But you do not dispute the rank of the lady in question?'

'The rank? No. Promoted by the great Ringel to the first whore of Rome.'

'And now she plays the Magdalene,' said Paducci.

'And she plays it well,' said Letizia. 'That blue dress clinging to her body. She must have lost at least twenty *libbra grossa* during her month with the nuns.'

'And him,' said the Prince Paducci, fingering the scar on his cheek. 'Ruffo's *sbirro*. Didn't we always say he was a murderer?'

'But he has done well out of it,' said Count Malaspina, still the *cavaliere servente* of Letizia di Comastri. 'Look at the orders and ribbons on his chest. And they say King Ferdinand has given him estates in Calabria twice the size of Rubosa.'

The Alibert theatre was lit by a thousand lamps and candles, but the light and the warmth they gave out could not smother a sense of unease. As the revellers gossiped, danced, drank the wine and ate the delicacies served by bewigged footmen, they could not forget that outside in the streets the people were hungry. Bread was expensive and the flour adulterated with barley, fava beans and even hay. There had been riots; bakeries had to be protected by armed guards; and republican agitators were back at work. On the same night as the ball at the Alibert theatre, a young lawyer, Gregorio Silvestri, convicted of a Jacobin conspiracy, was executed on the Piazza del Popolo.

The timing of the execution – one of only two for sedition – was to impress the guest of honour in the governor's double box at the Alibert, the first minister of the Kingdom of the Two Sicilies, the Englishman General Acton. He had come to Rome on a tour of inspection because although the dispatches from Naselli to Palermo had reassured King Ferdinand and Queen Maria Carolina that all was well, Acton had heard from a number of other sources that Naselli's administration was ineffective; that hunger had led to desperation; that murder and theft were commonplace and went unpunished; that while the French had kept order under the republic through fear, the allied forces were ridiculed and despised.

The Scarpias had taken a box with the Marcisanos and the Marchese di Ordelaffi, the husband of Graziella di Pozzo. They could see across the theatre the box of the Comastris with Paducci, Spinelli and Malaspina in attendance; and also that of Marchese and Marchesa Attavanti, with the painter Mario Cavaradossi seated next to the beautiful marchesa. Under the terms of the treaty, republican sympathisers like the Attavantis were to be unmolested, but there remained a *froideur* between legitimists and patriots: few paid calls on the boxes of those of a different political persuasion. Ludovico had been a patriot, but the presence of Scarpia in his box frightened off his former friends; and, for Paola, cutting republicans such as Domenica Attavanti was a necessary proof of her firm purpose of amendment.

Halfway through the evening, a young officer in the uniform of the Neapolitan army came to the Marcisanos' box and, after saluting Scarpia – blushing with pride to be addressing this celebrated leader of the *sanfedisti* – presented the compliments of General Acton and his request that Baron Scarpia spare a moment to visit him in his box. Scarpia rose, gave an apologetic nod to his wife and his sister-in-law Fulvia, and followed the young Neapolitan out of the box. He was led along the semicircular gallery past the entrance to Prince Naselli's double box to one next to it, which, when he entered, was empty except for Acton, adorned with bejewelled orders, and a secretary wearing a drab suit. The curtain was half drawn and the two men sat at the back of the box, out of sight of the throng and less exposed to the hubbub that came from the music and chatter.

Acton rose and greeted Scarpia as he entered. 'I am sorry to interrupt your festivities,' he said.

'I am at your service.'

The young officer withdrew. The secretary moved to a seat next to the door while Acton drew up a gilt chair for Scarpia, before returning to his place on the upholstered banquette at the back of the box. 'This may seem a strange place to attend to business,' said

Acton, 'but it is convenient to have all those one might want to see under one roof.'

'I am at your service.'

Scarpia knew Acton already: he had seen him a dozen times in Palermo and, while he did not warm to the bloodless Englishman, he did not share the loathing felt by his friend Damas. There had been times when Scarpia was ready to feel affronted that no Neapolitan or Sicilian was thought competent to act as first minister to the king, but he recognised Acton's abilities – his pragmatism and efficiency – and when he ran through in his mind the likely candidates he concluded that the kingdom was better ruled by a man with no clan or family to fatten from the trough.

'I have been asked by His Majesty, King Ferdinand,' said Acton, 'to report on what is going on here in Rome. Prince Naselli has assured us that all is well, but it appears that this is not so.'

'He has faced particular difficulties,' said Scarpia.

'Of course,' said Acton. 'But it seems to me that his administration is ineffective. The people go hungry while grain rots on the quays at Civitavecchia and there is crime in the streets.'

'Prince Naselli is constrained by the terms of the treaty.'

'But the treaty does not prevent him imposing order.'

'The Romans only acknowledge the authority of their Pope,' said Scarpia. 'The state of *sede vacante* has always meant a measure of anarchy – even at the best of times.'

'But we cannot simply await a new pope,' said Acton. 'And there is no knowing who it will be. Consalvi seems the obvious choice, but the emperor won't have him. And it is not just what is going on in Venice that concerns me, but events in Paris.'

'Bonaparte...'

'Precisely. He calls himself First Consul but to all intents and purposes he is a dictator. He now commands not just the army but the whole French nation, and it is only a matter of time before he returns to Italy. There will be war in the spring, and for that reason it is vital that Rome should be secured.'

'Do you mean to strengthen the garrison?'

'A garrison can hold the Castel Sant'Angelo but it cannot contain the enemy within. We must eradicate the Jacobins...'

'But the treaty ...'

'The treaty. Of course. We cannot have a purge as in Naples. But the amnesty covers sedition only until the signing of the treaty. Any subsequent conspiracies – any plots *now* to revive the republic – can be punished with the full rigour of the law. Silvestri, who was hanged tonight, planned to raise a force of six thousand Jacobins to attack our troops from the rear. Perhaps six thousand is an exaggeration, but there are without doubt a number of so-called patriots who are only biding their time. Many of those who were to leave with the French remain in Civitavecchia. I have been told that Angelotti is planning to return. We cannot incarcerate all of the Jacobins, but we can deal with their leaders. A snake without a head may slither, but it cannot sting.'

'The prince surely understands this.'

'We cannot count on Naselli,' said Acton. 'He dithers. He is soft. Nor do I have much faith in the people he has appointed to enforce the law. In Naples perhaps we have gone too far, but here we have not gone far enough. His Giunta di Stato is useless.'

'This is Rome,' said Scarpia. 'The public prosecutor is a priest – Monsignor Barberi. Agostino Valle, who defends the accused, is a former Jesuit who once worked for the Rota and runs rings around the judges, knows how to exploit the different jurisdictions, adjourn cases *sine die*, and even after a conviction, count on a pardon from the Pope.'

'That is the point,' said Acton. 'Sooner or later, there will be a new pope, and once he returns to govern Rome then all hope of

eradicating our enemies will be gone.' He paused. 'Do you remember Gennaro Valentino?'

'I will never forget him.'

'Shot by the French with the gleeful Jacobins like Angelotti
rubbing their hands. Is he not to be avenged?'

'If Angelotti ever returns to Rome –'

'It is not just Angelotti. There are others, here in Rome and in
Civitavecchia, strutting around as if no one can touch them. We
must act now, and I have been asked by the king to offer you a
commission to hunt down his enemies. You are the only man we
can trust.'

Scarpia hesitated. 'Am I to serve under Prince Naselli?'

'You are to serve apart from Prince Naselli. You will have a
warrant direct from the king. You will work from the Palazzo
Farnese and the Castel Sant'Angelo. Naselli will not interfere. You
must be implacable, Scarpia. Do not let sentiment cloud your
judgement. You must ensure that, when a new pope returns to the
holy city, the Jacobin monster has no head.'

*

The interview was at an end. At a gesture from Acton, his secretary –
the pale young man who had remained silent throughout the two
men's conversation in the corner of the box, hidden from the revellers by the curtain – now rose and summoned the officer to escort
the baron back to his box. When Scarpia had left, the secretary
returned to his chair.

Acton was weary. He leaned forward, resting his elbows on his
knees and looking down as if studying the buckles of his shoes.
After a minute or so, he sat up, looked out of the box at the glittering spectacle of boisterous Romans, then turned to his young
secretary.

'What did you think?'

'It was an honour to meet such a hero.'

'A hero, yes. Scarpia is courageous and also able. We saw that in Basilicata. He is loyal to the king and he loathes Jacobins. All that is clear enough. My only misgiving is that he has picked up from Ruffo a propensity to show mercy. He is unwilling to go for a kill when his man is down.'

'You are thinking of Palmieri?'

'Apparently he ordered the balls removed from the muskets for a fake execution.'

'Certainly Palmieri remains alive. He is with the French.'

Acton brooded, then said: 'Doesn't Scarpia have a man, Spoletta?'

'Yes. He is his servant, his adjutant, his *bravo*.'

'Talk to this man Spoletta. Find out the truth of the matter and, if the story is true, make it clear to him that the position of his master and his own prospects would be jeopardised if such a thing were to happen again.'

5

It was now more than a month since Scarpia had returned to Rome. He had not upon arrival gone to the Villa Larunda but had stayed at the Oratory as a guest of Father Simone Alberti. He had confessed his sins to the priest, among them his surrender to passion in the pagan surroundings of Taormina; and later had a number of long conversations with the Oratorian on many subjects – the unease he felt about the terrible cruelty of some of the *sanfedisti*; the sin, if it was a sin, of letting Palmieri go free to rejoin the Jacobin armies; the sin, if it was a sin, of *accidia* – the dejection that had come over him after the war was won.

Father Simone reassured him. 'You are a soldier, my dear Baron, and in performing our duty as a soldier you have had to take the lives of your enemies and perhaps of necessity do cruel things. But even in the heat of battle, a man may be pure in spirit; he may love his enemy, yet he takes his life. Remember the centurion who begs Jesus to cure his daughter but feels unworthy that he should come to his house. Our good Lord tells him to return home where he will find his daughter cured, but he does not tell him to give up his profession. And another centurion, Cornelius, whom St Peter visits and welcomes into the community of Christians – a soldier of the Ithaca cohort stationed at Caesarea but *a devout and God-fearing man* – he has no doubt killed the enemies of Rome in performing his duties, but Peter does not ask him to lay down his sword. No, a soldier may also be a saint.'

Scarpia confided to Father Simone the conflicting feelings which tormented him – a longing to live with his children and reluctance to return to his faithless wife. The priest had repeated what he had said in his letter: that to forgive was a clear commandment of Christ; that Paola was repentant and it would be sinful to spurn her contrition. He must now go back to his wife and children.

*

Four days after his return to Rome, Scarpia had left the Oratory for the Villa Larunda. The household had been forewarned of his arrival. Paola was awaiting him in the atrium with Pietro and Francesca. She was dressed demurely in a simple but elegant dress with a modest décolletage. Her hair was raised in a bun exposing her graceful neck. Her face was pale but, as Letizia di Comastri had observed, she had lost the plumpness that had come over her during the feasting and roistering with Jouve. As Scarpia approached, she gave a deep curtsy. 'Welcome home,' she said softly.

'Yes, welcome home, Signor Padre,' chimed in the children, as if this was a line that they had rehearsed. Each took hold of a hand to kiss it; he gathered them up in an embrace.

As Paola rose from her curtsy, Scarpia might have stepped forward to embrace her too, but he felt no inclination to do so. The curtsy and lowered eyes, their expression hidden by the lids, denoted a readiness to surrender, an acquiescence to his will – but even as this became apparent a voice whispered in his ear: 'Is she play-acting?' 'Is she posing for a painting by Ringel – *Penelope at the Return of Odysseus?*'

That night, Scarpia returned to his bedroom, Paola to hers. Nothing seemed to have changed except for a prie-dieu installed in Paola's bedroom facing an ebony crucifix with an ivory figure of Christ. The base of the prie-dieu showed the impress of two knees, and looped over the side was a rosary with silver links and ebony beads. When both Nunzi and Scarpia's valet had retired, Scarpia glanced through the open door to Paola's bedroom and saw her on her knees telling the beads. Sensing his presence, she rose, rehung her rosary on the prie-dieu, and turned towards him. She looked exquisite in a soft silk gown; a delightful scent lingered in the air. 'We are so pleased that you have returned,' she said to Scarpia, looking directly into his eyes. What were they expressing? He could not tell. Was she inviting him into her bed? Or conveying a penitential acquiescence should he choose to reclaim his rights as her husband? Did she want him to make love to her, *faute de mieux*? Scarpia could not tell. Did he want to make love to her? Back in the setting of their early passion, the sight of the bed on which they had known so much joy might have kindled a mature desire had it not been blocked by the thought that on that same bed Paola had made love to her French brigadier. The mind might forgive, but the body has a will of its own, and Scarpia could not bring himself to embrace a woman who, for all the scent dabbed on her body, still held the odour of another man.

*

In the weeks that followed, Baron Scarpia and his wife, Princess Paola di Marcisano, lived as might a brother and sister under the same roof. If Paola felt spurned, she did not show it, apparently willing to be a good wife in any way her husband might choose. It seemed as if Scarpia's imaginary rival that had once been Bonaparte was now Christ. To all outward appearances, the month's mortification of the flesh in the Carmelite convent had not just led Paola to lose weight but had brought about an inner conversion. The French novels were gone; instead, open on the escritoire, was St Teresa of Avila's *Way of Perfection*. Nor did Paola see any of her old friends such as Graziella di Pozzo or Domenica Attavanti: he even heard Paola mention the latter to Pietro as 'a very wicked woman who has led many astray'.

Paola was often out of the house. She went to Mass at six every morning at the nearby church of Santa Maria della Pace, returned for breakfast with Scarpia and the children, then often went out again, either to visit her now decrepit parents or, three times a week, to the women's hospital, San Salvatore, where, with other noble ladies, she donned an apron and bathed the sick. She also visited the Sisters of Our Lady of Loretto, whose particular apostolate was to reconcile separated husbands and wives. She made little of her charitable works, and only told Scarpia about them when asked, saying, 'There is so much suffering,' and, 'Providence has been so good to me, and I have done so little in return.'

Among the few visitors to the Villa Larunda was her brother Ludovico, who seemed to have had a similar change of heart. At first Ludovico was awkward in Scarpia's presence – apologetic, almost obsequious. 'You saw things so clearly,' he said. 'You were immune to all the folly.' He said this as if intending a compliment, but he could not purge from his way of saying it a trace of his old condescension, as if Scarpia's immunity from radical thinking, although to be welcomed, was somehow the product of his less than princely Sicilian origins. Like Paola, he too had become ostensibly more devout, resuming his work at the charitable confraternities.

The repudiation of their republican sympathies, and the renewed religiosity of Paola and Ludovico, should have been welcomed by Scarpia, but incomprehensibly they were not. He was exasperated by Ludovico's condescension – his implicit assumption that religions and ideologies, like fads and fashions, come and go but the standing of Rome's patricians was timeless – and by his inability to understand what was going on in Paola's mind. Had she really undergone a conversion? Were her prayers sincere? Were her good works the product of God's grace? Or had she simply read the signs of the times, seen that Jacobinism had had its day and, like an actress, taken on a new role?

*

On 14 March 1800, the conclave of cardinals in Venice elected a new pope, the Benedictine Father Gregory Chiaramonti, Bishop of Imola. The choice was a compromise and surprised many because, after the establishment of the Cisalpine Republic by the French, he had preached acquiescence in the new order. 'Christian virtue,' he had said, 'makes men good democrats ... Equality is not an idea of philosophers but of Christ ... and do not believe that the Catholic religion is against democracy.'

The new Pope's liberal outlook did not change the determination of the Roman republicans to seize power in the city before his return. To thwart them, Scarpia formed a small team – Spoletta as his adjutant, three clerks to collate intelligence and four *sbirri* recruited by Spoletta to undertake the less savoury aspects of their work. It was Spoletta who set up the network of informers – paying out petty bribes to domestic servants in the homes of those known to have Jacobin sympathies.

With the carrot also went the stick. The strappado was close to the Villa Farnese on the via della Corda – the machine gave the street its name. It consisted of a crossbar with ropes and pulleys that would lift a man by his arms tied behind his back and then drop him suddenly to within an inch or two of the floor – *tre tratti di corda* being the usual punishment for breaches of public order.

All depended now on events in northern Italy. The Russians had withdrawn from the coalition, but the Austrians retained an army of 100,000 men in the valley of the Po. The French remained besieged in Genoa, but the new First Consul, Napoleon Bonaparte, was assembling an army to relieve them. Could the military genius turn the tables once again? For the republicans, there was everything to hope for, and for the Bourbons everything to fear.

Then, just as Bonaparte was leading his newly formed army over the Alps by St Gotthard Pass, Spoletta brought information that he had gleaned from a housemaid at the Palazzo Attavanti. There was a mysterious guest who never appeared at meals but was treated with unusual consideration. She had been told to use the best linen sheets for his bed and saw that the best food on the finest china was taken to his room, not by a lackey but by the marchesa herself. The housemaid was told to clean his room between specified hours in the morning – between nine and ten – when the guest would be elsewhere – it was thought, in the marchesa's bedroom. At first the servants thought he might be her lover; but once he had returned to his own room while the maid was still dusting and, though she lowered her eyes and hurried from the room, she recognised the guest: it was Cesare Angelotti, the marchesa's brother.

The Attavantis had a number of retainers; Scarpia therefore did not want to risk an imbroglio by arresting Angelotti in their palazzo. However, he felt that sooner or later he would go out to meet with other conspirators. It was a matter of keeping watch, day and night. Angelotti was cunning. He lay low. It was the marchesa who busied herself going to and fro, no doubt leaving notes or verbal messages with her patriot friends. Moreover, she was posing as St Mary Magdalene for Mario Cavaradossi, who as a gesture of reconciliation had been commissioned to paint a mural depicting the repentant sinner in the church of Sant'Andrea della Valle. The painter was undoubtedly a conduit for messages from Angelotti to his republican friends.

Then, on 19 May, as the marchesa left the palazzo in her coach, Spoletta, affecting to be a passer-by, noticed an unusual disarray in the livery of one of the coachmen and saw, beneath his tricorn hat, the face of Angelotti. He followed the coach with his *sbirri*. It went as so often before to Sant'Andrea della Valle. The coachmen climbed down and, while one opened the door for his mistress, and then took hold of the bridles of the horses, the other went with the marchesa towards the church. Before he could go in, Spoletta's *sbirri* had seized him and, fending off an assault by the marchesa with her parasol, dragged Angelotti off to the Castel Sant'Angelo.

Fifteen

I

Shortly after the opening of the carnival of 1800 in the Alibert theatre, the first opera of the new century was staged at the Apollo. It was Cimarosa's *L'italiana in Londra*, and was judged mediocre. For the second half of the evening's entertainment, the company performed a ballet, *Gli sogni di Telemaco*, which provoked jeers and catcalls from the audience. A month later, *I matrimonio in cantina* closed after only one performance.

Under Governor Naselli, many of the statutes of pontifical Rome had been reinstated – Jews were once again required to live in the ghetto – but one of the changes made under the republic had remained: women were permitted to appear onstage. At the Valle theatre, to open the carnival, the diva La Bussoni appeared in an opera composed and staged by Luigi Caruso. La Bussoni loathed Caruso – she had wanted to sing in an opera by his rival, Guglielmi – and so sabotaged the first performance by singing in an inaudible whisper. '*Cavi la voce,*' shouted Caruso from the pit. La Bussoni pretended not to hear. The audience took up the cry, '*Cavi la voce!*' and when she paid no attention, whistled and jeered her off the stage.

The management of the Valle capitulated and put on an opera by Guglielmi but, though La Bussoni sang with full voice, the show was a flop. Ash Wednesday, the first day of Lent when the theatres were closed, came as a relief – giving time for the Roman impresarios to plan for what would follow Easter. On 27 April, the Valle opened the spring season with Paisiello's *La spaz-zacamino*, but they sold few tickets and those who did attend booed the performance. In May, Paer's *l'intrigo amoroso* did better; and *Roma liberata* at the Alibert by the Neapolitan composer Giuseppe Curcio, which depicted the Christian Emperor Constantine liberating Rome from the pagan Maxentius, just as King Ferdinand had freed it from the atheist Jacobins, was approved by Prince Naselli and his entourage; but neither opera was enough to save what looked to be a disastrous season.

There was only one hope of salvation – Floria Tosca. The desperate impresarios wrote to their agents in Venice, Vienna, Berlin and St Petersburg – no one quite knew where Tosca was singing at the time – offering her any inducement if she would come at once to sing in Rome, perhaps in the title role in Guglielmi's *La morte di Cleopatra*, or better still, Rosina in Paisiello's ever-popular *Il barbiere di Siviglia*. Their appeal reached Tosca in Vienna, where she had triumphed as Susanna in Mozart's *Le nozze di Figaro*. She was toying with an invitation to sing in Berlin. In pecuniary terms, it far outdid the one she now received from Rome; but for reasons that were neither pecuniary nor professional, she was inclined to accept it. She was in love.

Tosca was now aged twenty-six and at the height of her powers. She exulted in those powers; she lived to feel her voice fill a thea-tre, to entrance an audience and hear their frantic applause. For all the genius of the composers, the arias of a Cimarosa, a Granacci, a Paisiello or a Mozart were only black dots and lines on a page until given substance by Tosca; and then the mix of melody and pure sound created a quintessence of beauty that for her audience was a glimpse of Heaven. Tosca's talent gave her a unique and extraordinary power that was acknowledged by every crowned head of Europe, and their homage, and that of other highly placed admirers, she had come to accept as her due.

And Tosca had become accustomed to behave like a monarch, treating with impresarios as Queen Maria Carolina might with the ambassadors of foreign powers, and choosing lovers with the insouciance of Catherine the Great. She was not a wanton; there had been perhaps no more than a dozen – or a dozen she liked to think about – since she had lost her virginity to the great Prince Alberigo di Belgioioso d'Este – one or two of them fellow performers, like the odious Lorenzi; the odd nobleman in the mould of Prince Alberigo whose power was in itself an aphrodisiac and whose influence could further her career; and three or four attractive men she had felt drawn to at a particular time and in a particular place like Baron Scarpia in Taormina.

Tosca had performed twice in Rome during the republic – one of the first women to appear on the Roman stage. She had been vexed by the law that had banned them under the popes, but she had also remembered that it was thanks to Pope Pius VI that she had been able to pursue her career. Tosca remained a Catholic – an unquestioning believer – with a particular devotion to the Virgin Mary – a woman who understood the feelings of women and so was willing to intercede with her son on their behalf. She had no political sympathies, one way or the other, but was irritated to see crosses supplanted by Liberty trees and the festivities on saints' days replaced by absurd republican ceremonials; play-acting, in her view, should be confined to the theatres and liturgies left to the Church.

On the other hand, novelty had its attractions; Tosca rather liked the young men with their Brutus haircuts who talked so loftily about liberty, equality and fraternity even though all three might be tosh. One young man in particular who took her fancy was the painter Mario Cavaradossi, whom she met at a reception given in her honour after her first gala performance in Rome. In fact, he was not so young – he was well over thirty – of medium height with a fine figure, strong features, dark brown eyes and a conceited manner that she found somehow endearing. She sensed that his conceit was fragile, recognising him as the kind of man who set goals to prove that he was as fine as he thought himself to be. His goal that evening, at the Palazzo Colonna, had been to ask Tosca, in an almost offhand way, if she might like to sit for a sketch, and, when she agreed to his suggestion and went next day to his studio, to attempt to seduce her – an attempt which succeeded all too easily because she saw something poignant in his bravado, found him handsome and had not made love with anyone for quite a while.

Tosca was a year or two younger than Cavaradossi, but there was something in him that brought out a motherly tenderness as they lay together half dressed on the sofa in his studio. She had enjoyed the encounter despite his slightly inept impatience – odd, she thought, since he must surely have experience of other women, some of whom might have taught him that on the whole women preferred their lovers to take their time; or had he thought she would take impetuosity for passion? She was touched when she caught his quick sidelong glance to see how she now felt after their bout of love. He was a dear, posturing and perhaps not particularly intelligent man and, to judge from the canvases in his studio, a mediocre painter; but with a little bit of tactful coaching he could be a delightful lover and, for reasons she did not bother to analyse, he was what she felt like at the time.

Their affair should have lasted no more than a week, because Tosca was due to move on to Milan; but, to the dismay of her entourage, she cancelled the engagement, claiming to be ill. She remained in Rome, giving out that she was tired, but she had enough energy to receive Cavaradossi in her lodgings, visit his studio and spend three days in a delightful love nest – a small farmhouse, the Casa di Ferruto, half an hour's ride from the Argentina theatre on the Appian Way belonging to a republican friend of Cavaradossi's. There, away from the impresarios, musicians and admirers, without even a maid or valet, she tactfully taught him that passion did not mean making love at a gallop; and the staying power he showed at a canter brought Tosca's senses to a high pitch of delight.

Where Tosca's senses led, her emotions followed. She found she grew increasingly fond of the absurd young painter, listening as if enraptured to his monologues about liberty, the rights of man and the metric system. He was a proud conspirator, showing her the rungs in the side of the well in the garden that led down to an empty cistern which had been used as a refuge for republicans on the run from the papal police during the reign of Pope Pius VI. 'Patriots would hide out there for as long as a week.' And he was eloquent on the evil of his adversaries, citing the terrible atrocities committed by Bourbonists in Naples – the monstrous Fra Diavolo who played football with severed heads, Mammone who fed his followers with human flesh, Pronio who raped young girls and then impaled them on sharpened stakes, and the notorious Scarpia who drank his victims' blood from their skulls. 'And to think Scarpia once lived here in Rome. If only then I had known what was to come, I would have thrust a dagger into his heart!'

Tosca had thought it prudent not to mention that, if this was the same Scarpia she had known in Sicily, the story of his cruelties seemed unlikely. She showed a polite interest in Cavaradossi's political intrigues and his views on philosophy and art but, having never read Rousseau or Helvetius, and being unfamiliar with the paintings of David or Ingres, she could not turn his monologues into a conversation. At first she thought that listening to him would be enough, but by the third day of their stay at the Casa di Ferruto, she saw that her lover was growing restless – that his monologues were not enough to entertain him. She sensed that he was bored, and his enthusiasm when she suggested a return to Rome proved that her apprehensions had been correct. They went back to the city and accepted some of the invitations to the grand palazzi that had been piling up for Tosca, or went to the more intimate *conversazioni* given by Cavaradossi's republican friends. At both she arrived on his arm and remained with him throughout the evening. Cavaradossi was no longer bored, and he took some pride at being on public display as Tosca's lover, but he was clearly embarrassed by her occasional attempts to contribute to a discussion – the inanity of what she said and her coarse accent revealing that, for all the beauty of her voice, Tosca's mind was that of a peasant from the Veneto.

Tosca could not remain in Rome indefinitely: the lavish fees from past engagements were always quickly spent on sumptuous lodgings, the finest cooks, a large and pilfering body of servants, and gifts for her lovers – in Rome, diamond-studded snuffboxes, watches, ebony canes with ivory handles, soft leather boots, fine tailored tunics – gifts which she forced upon Cavaradossi, who affected a republican indifference to material things. If she remained off the stage for long, the impresarios might find they could manage without her – replacing her with Angelica Catalini or Teresa Bertinotti – and then Tosca might be deprived of what she valued more, even, than the love of Cavaradossi – appearing onstage before an audience and enrapturing them with her voice.

Tosca suggested timidly to Cavaradossi that he might accompany her to Milan. Cavaradossi was, as she had feared, indignant: much as he loved Tosca, he had imperative reasons, both professional and political, for remaining in Rome. They therefore parted, but, rather than leave Cavaradossi with the severe warning she had delivered to Scarpia – that he was not to fall in love with her – she made anguished protestations of lasting affection which he accepted as if they were another pair of gold cufflinks or white kid gloves, and returned with a nonchalance that was not in itself insincere but suggested that such protestations in Rome were a currency as debased as the paper money.

Tosca was no fool: she sensed his indifference and thought that she too should try and cultivate a certain detachment; but in Milan, in Venice and then in Vienna, she could not eject Cavaradossi from her thoughts. She had mused ceaselessly on the time she had spent in his company; she wrote to him frequently and received one or two replies; and to her dismay she found that, together with her fond memories, came not just schemes for a future reunion but daydreams of their sharing a home – of her cooking macaroni and washing his clothes as her mother had done for her father. The idea was absurd – it was a decade since Tosca had cooked anything or washed any clothes – but some instinct inherited from the Veneto told her that the kind of love she felt for the handsome young painter could only be fulfilled in cooking, washing, and even bearing a child.

2

This, then, was Tosca's frame of mind when the plea came for her to return to Rome and save the opera season from disaster. Tosca accepted at once. She reneged on her commitment to go to Berlin, wrote to Cavaradossi to say she was returning, and hired a coach to take her south over the Alps. Upon reaching Rome she was installed in her old lodgings and sent a note to Cavaradossi to announce her arrival. There was only a week to rehearse before she appeared onstage as the eponymous heroine in Paisello's *Nina, o sia la pazza per amore*. The role of a crazed maiden singing gentle arias with flowers entwined in her hair suited Tosca's mood because she did indeed become almost demented when her note to Cavaradossi was not answered. Worse, her lackey said he could not be sure whether Cavaradossi had even received it. Perhaps he was not in Rome. Perhaps he was on the run. Even the apolitical Tosca could understand that Cavaradossi's position under the allied occupation was not the same as it had been under the republic. He was no longer a member of the governing elite, the darling of the patriots, the insouciant hero of the Roman revolution. Perhaps the letters she had sent from Vienna and then Venice telling of her planned arrival had not reached him either? Or was he lying low in his friend's farmhouse, the Casa di Ferruto, maybe with another woman?

Tosca's anguish at Cavaradossi's absence from the first night of *Nina* so enhanced her performance that the audience went delirious: the season was saved. But Tosca could not rest on her laurels: she had also agreed to play the role of Rosina in *Il barbiere de Siviglia*. Even as she was rehearsing, enquiries were made on Tosca's behalf as to the whereabouts of Cavaradossi. All sources agreed that he was in Rome but were shifty as to what he was doing. This confirmed Tosca's suspicions that he had another woman. No one came up with the name of a rival, but she was told that he spent much of his time in the Palazzo Attavanti, and that he was working on a mural of St Mary Magdalene in the church of Sant'Andrea della Valle for which the Marchesa Attavanti was posing as a model.

So agitated was Tosca – so taut were her nerves, so vivid her imagination – that the suspicion became a certainty and she determined to confront her fickle lover and his new mistress where she was sure to find them – in the church. With the help of her maid – the same young girl from the Veneto whom Scarpia had met in Venice – she prepared herself for the encounter, choosing a simple dress of beautiful blue velour, full at the hips and tight at the bust. Deft dabs of powder and a touch of French rouge concealed the lines and shadows that agitation had brought onto her face; and she inserted a tortoiseshell comb and three hairpins to hold up her thick-plaited hair – the last being the long pearl-topped silver *stiletto* with which she could defend herself or, in this context, take revenge on a rival and faithless lover.

Tosca walked with her maid the short distance to the Theatine church of Sant'Andrea della Valle and at the entrance told the girl to wait outside. She pushed back the heavy leather curtains behind the open door and went alone from the bright summer sunlight into the sumptuous baroque gloom. There was no congregation, but she could hear singing from behind the altar.

Tibi omnes Angeli;
tibi caeli et universae Potestates;
Tibi Cherubim et Seraphim
incessabili voce proclamant...

An old man in a black cassock stood at the back of the church.
'Is this a Mass?' Tosca asked him.
'No, the *Te Deum*.'
'Why a *Te Deum*?'
'Haven't you heard? Bonaparte has been defeated at Marengo.'

Tosca had heard; her maid had woken her with the news, but such were her other preoccupations that it meant nothing to her.

'And where is the chapel of the Magdalene?' she asked the sextant.

He nodded towards the right side of the church. 'But it is under scaffolding. It is being restored.'

Tosca made a deep genuflection towards the high altar, then walked down the aisle towards the chapel. It was hidden from view by a wall of sackcloth attached to scaffolding. She went to the pillar to the right and silently pulled back the sackcloth. A shaft of sunlight from the stained-glass window illuminated the fresco of St Mary Magdalene. Beneath it, Tosca could see two figures – a

341

man and a woman – the woman as tall as the man. The man was Cavaradossi; he was whispering in the woman's ear.

'Traitor!' she cried, advancing on Cavaradossi.

Cavaradossi turned. 'Floria! You! Here!'

'You betray me with this whore!' – the exclamation sounded all the more vehement for being in the dialect of the Veneto. Tosca pointed scornfully at the woman but saw first that she was ugly and then that she was not a woman but a man.

'Floria. This is my friend, the *cavaliere* Angelotti.'

'Angelotti? Mario, I thought…'

Cavaradossi stepped forward and took her in his arms. 'You silly girl. You thought I no longer loved you?'

'Yes.'

'Of course I love you, but I had to save my friend. The vile Scarpia seized him. He was held in Castel Sant'Angelo, condemned to death. His sister begged me to save him.'

'His sister?'

'My model, the marchesa. Only that could keep me from answering your note.'

'Ah, Mario,' she said again, tears coming into her eyes.

Over the sound of the voices singing the *Te Deum*, there came the boom of cannon.

'Do you hear that?' said Angelotti. 'It means my escape has been discovered. And one of the first places they will look for me is here.'

'Yes,' said Cavaradossi, 'we must leave.' He looked at Tosca. 'I am taking Cesare to the farm. He can hide there until we can smuggle him out of Rome. When he is gone, my life will be yours. I promise you, Floria. My life will be yours.'

After a last ardent kiss, Cavaradossi pulled himself away from Tosca and led Angelotti, a shawl over his head, through the opening in the hessian out of the chapel and into the church. Tosca, overwhelmed with joy and relief, fell to her knees in front of the altar to give thanks to Mary Magdalene, the patron saint of fallen women. She raised her eyes and met the demure gaze of the half-naked woman, her long blonde hair draping her breasts, kneeling in a way that revealed long, luscious flanks. It was in the realist style of David – Cavaradossi was one of his pupils – and, though greatly inferior to the work of the master, managed to suggest that, while the saint might be repentant, she could still provoke a man's desire.

As she gazed at the mural, Tosca remembered that his model was the Marchesa Attavanti, and she remembered, too, the rumours picked up by her servants that she was not just his model but his mistress as well. She tried to dismiss her suspicions; had not Cavaradossi just kissed her and assured her of his love? But she knew quite well that men are fickle, and the more she looked at the expression on the face above the altar, the more she became convinced that the look was of promise, anticipation, acquiescence. She glared at the blonde hair, blue eyes, long legs and curved breasts and, in a moment of self-doubt, compared them unfavourably to her own black hair, short legs and heavy bosom. A terrible rage rose within her. What she had at first simply suspected now became certain.

There were sounds behind her. She turned. Four men had entered the chapel – two in uniform, two wearing frock coats and breeches. The first came towards her. He stopped as he recognised her. 'Tosca!'

She stood and curtsied. 'Baron Scarpia.' She was taken aback by how much older he seemed, and the look of weariness on his face.

The second man wearing a frock coat – shabbier and uglier than Scarpia – came up behind him. 'Is this the marchesa?' he asked Scarpia.

'No, this is Floria Tosca.'

'La Tosca!' He looked at her scornfully. 'A funny place to rehearse.'

343

'I was praying.'

'Of course.' The scornful tone remained in his voice.

Scarpia said to the man, 'Look behind the altar and in the confessionals.'

Spoletta gestured to the two *sbirri* to follow him.

'Did you come here to see Cavaradossi?' Scarpia asked Tosca.

Tosca blushed. 'I came to see the mural...'

Scarpia smiled – a sad smile. 'Of course. But also the artist, perhaps...'

'He isn't here.'

'No, he isn't here,' Scarpia repeated.

'What do you want of him?' asked Tosca.

'He must answer some questions.'

'About what? His opinions? I can answer them for you.'

'About the escape of Angelotti.'

'Who is Angelotti?'

'A Jacobin. An enemy of the state.'

Tosca turned away. 'I know nothing about politics.'

Scarpia looked up at the mural. 'So you came here to see this. You have not seen Mario Cavaradossi or Cesare Angelotti.' He said this as if summarising her answers to questions he had not in fact put to her, and with no apparent expectation that she should make a reply. Tosca remained silent.

Spoletta returned from his search behind the altar holding a fan and a woman's chemise. 'The artist's model seems to have left these behind,' he said. Then, with a leer at Tosca, he added: 'And there is a straw paillasse behind the altar which suggests that our Jacobin's model did more than pose.'

Tosca blushed.

'Perhaps it was for the painter's siesta,' said Scarpia. He nodded towards orange peel and an apple core on the step of the altar. 'It would appear that he ate here at midday.'

'Perhaps they took a siesta together,' said Spoletta, holding up the chemise with another smirk at Tosca.

'Anyway,' said Scarpia, 'if our bird was here, he has flown.'

'And the painter too,' said Spoletta.

Scarpia signalled to Spoletta and the two *sbirri* to leave the chapel. He then turned to Tosca and asked in a low voice: 'Are we still friends?'

'Of course.'

'You are not performing tonight, I think. Would you care to dine with me at the Palazzo Farnese?'

Tosca hesitated. Would she not be with Cavaradossi? Or would he remain at the farm with Angelotti? There was no way of knowing, but nothing was lost by keeping on good terms with Scarpia. She curtsied. 'I should be delighted.'

Scarpia turned as if to go, then looked back at Cavaradossi's unfinished mural. 'What do you think?'

'It is a fine painting.'

Scarpia smiled. 'It is perhaps better than it might have been. He is not a talented artist.'

'Then why was he chosen?'

'It was commissioned as a gesture of reconciliation.'

'I am sure they will be pleased with the result.'

'I am told the fathers find the portrait of the Magdalene too ... realistic.'

Tosca laughed. 'Yes, for priests.'

'Clearly,' said Scarpia, with the detached manner of a critic, 'the artist wishes to convey that the penitent Magdalene remains a desirable woman. There is even a touch of irony in the depiction, perhaps, as if the painter is saying through the very sensuality of his model that chastity is absurd. His own desire is projected into his painting.'

Tosca frowned and said nothing.

'And clearly from the expression in her eyes, one can deduce that the model feels the same desire…'

'In the painting, perhaps,' said Tosca.

'And, knowing Domenica Attavanti as I do, we may assume in life.'

'You want to torment me.'

'Torment you? No, Floria. You can love whom you like. But do not deceive yourself. Do you imagine a man could paint a woman in such a pose and not wish to possess her? I tell you, artists always sleep with their models.'

Scarpia left the chapel. Tosca waited, then went out into the nave of the church. She went to the statue of the Virgin Mary, took a gold ducat out of her purse, put it into the metal strongbox by the altar, took a candle from the bucket beneath it and, after lighting it from another candle, placed it on the stand. She then fell on her knees. *Remember, O most gracious Virgin Mary, that never was it known that anyone who fled to thy protection, implored thy help or sought thine intercession was left unaided* … But her thoughts were not with her prayer. Her mind seethed with the terrible certainty that what Scarpia had said was true. The model was his mistress. But yet she loved him. She must find him. Warn him. Confront him. Reclaim him. She would go at once to the Casa di Ferruto, not in her finery in her own carriage but incognito in a humble two-wheeled, two-seated cart – a *sediola*.

3

King Ferdinand's viceroy, Prince Naselli, governed Rome from the Palazzo Farnese, the embassy of the Kingdom of the Two Sicilies. The prince might have resided at the Quirinale Palace like the French commander, General Garnier, or even at the Vatican, because both remained unoccupied during the period of *sede vacante*; but had he done so, it might have seemed to the Romans and to the allies – the Russians, the English and the Austrians – that King Ferdinand had plans to make his rule permanent and annex the Papal States to his kingdom. If there ever had been such plans, they had been abandoned. The cardinals had already arrived in the city and the newly elected Pope, Pius VII, was expected in two weeks' time.

The prospect of this imminent transfer of power had put great pressure on Prince Naselli. The new Pope, when Bishop of Imola, had shown himself sympathetic to the cause of democracy; he was likely to pardon those who had been conspiring against him and would certainly not permit further executions. Time, then, was short, and the wretched Prince Naselli, who himself lacked his monarchs' vindictive streak, was pelted by letters from King Ferdinand and Acton in Palermo, and Queen Maria Carolina in Livorno en route to Vienna, insisting that active Jacobins, and particularly those responsible for the judicial assassination of Valentino, should be dealt with before the transfer of power. Naselli had passed on these instructions to Baron Scarpia, relieved that, if things did not turn out as his king expected, there would be some-one else to blame. He was delighted when Angelotti was arrested, but then dismayed when he escaped. He had impressed upon Scarpia the overriding importance of finding the fugitive and executing the sentence already passed of death.

The Palazzo Farnese was large and had many magnificent rooms on the *piano nobile*, but there were equally spacious if less ornate rooms above and it was in a suite of these rooms that Baron Scarpia worked to hunt down Jacobins. So pressing was the work that he often stayed there overnight, only returning to the Villa Larunda when time allowed. The Palazzo Farnese was therefore both a temporary home as well as his office, and he was well tended by servants, among them a major-domo to whom, on his return from the church of Sant'Andrea della Valle, he gave instructions to prepare dinner for a single guest.

Scarpia sat down at his gilded desk and, with a bemused smile on his face, thought about his unexpected encounter with Tosca. When they had parted at Taormina, she had said *addio* – intimating that they were unlikely to meet again. She had told him not to fall in love with her – a command that had been unnecessary because his desire, too, had been a matter of the moment, an intoxication brought on by the sound of her voice. Certainly, the memory of the moment lingered, but with the passing of time it had grown feebler, and finally had faded altogether, driven out of his mind by the horrors of the *sanfedista* crusade.

Coming across Tosca in the church of Sant' Andrea della Valle, Scarpia had noticed only that she seemed to have grown stouter and had not lost her coarse Venetian accent. He had been told of her passion for Cavaradossi, and had seen at once how he could take advantage of it to find Angelotti. He suspected she was lying; that she knew where her lover had gone and, with him, Angelotti. He had stimulated her jealousy by pointing to the lascivious pose of the Marchesa Attavanti, anticipating that she would then rush to confront him. He had given orders that she was to be followed when she left the church.

4

When Floria Tosca reached the Casa di Ferruto in her hired *sediola*, she asked the driver to wait under an umbrella pine, then rang the bell at the gate. Cavaradossi himself came to open it and, when he saw Tosca, a look of displeasure came onto his face.

'What are you doing here? This is madness. You will have been followed.'

Tosca frowned. This was not the welcome she had anticipated. 'I have come to warn you and I am disguised. Look…' She pointed at the simple dress she had borrowed from her maid.

'Even so.' Cavaradossi looked up and down the road, and seeing no one other than the driver of the *sediola*, opened the gate and let her in. He embraced her cursorily, making clear that now was not the time for love, and so, despite the jealousy of the Marchesa Attavanti that seethed within her, Tosca decided it was not the moment either to take her lover to task about his relations with his model. As he led her into the living room which held such sweet memories for Tosca, she managed to drop the role of a jealous mistress and adopt that of a courageous patriot. She was thus able to meet the look of annoyance that came onto the face of Angelotti when he rose from a chair by the fire. He made no attempt to greet her politely but looked angrily at Cavaradossi. 'What is she doing here?'

'I have come to warn you,' said Tosca. 'The *sbirri* came to the church. With them was Baron Scarpia.'

'You know Scarpia?' asked Angelotti.

Tosca blushed. 'Know him? No. How should I know him? A man who drinks blood out of skulls! But he told me who he was and he questioned me. He knows that Mario arranged your escape. They searched the chapel. They found the fan, the women's clothes, the remains of your lunch. The baron asked me if I had seen you, and if I knew where you had gone. I said that I did not. That I too was looking for Mario. Why else would I be there? To look at the painting?' Involuntarily, Tosca darted an angry look at Cavaradossi.

Cavaradossi did not notice her glance: he was preoccupied. 'If he knows that I helped you escape,' he said to Angelotti, 'then he may search my house and my studio, but no one knows about this farmhouse. It belongs to a friend.'

'But if la signorina Tosca was followed?' asked Angelotti.

'I was not followed,' said Tosca angrily. 'No one would recognise me, Tosca, dressed like a servant and riding in a *sediola*.'

'There is a hiding place,' said Cavaradossi to Angelotti, 'where even if they come here they would never find you.' He turned to Tosca. 'You, Floria, must go back to Rome. I will hide Cesare in the well and then set up my easel. They can arrest me, but what can they prove? And when Angelotti is gone, my dearest Floria, I will send for you and all will be as it was before.'

5

Tosca arrived at the Palazzo Farnese in a flustered state. After another uncomfortable half-hour in the *sediola* listening to the tedious talk of the driver, she had had only a short time to take a bath, rest, change and eat a handful of nuts and raisins before setting off again, this time in her own coach, to dine with Baron Scarpia.

Had Scarpia had time to take a bath and rest? Certainly, Tosca noticed, he had taken some trouble over his appearance, but then so had she. He wore an embroidered blue coat and waistcoat, black breeches, white stockings and silver-buckled shoes; she, a long dark red silk dress with bows beneath the low-cut bodice. Her hair had been dressed by her maid; Scarpia's was tied back in a pigtail. He was sitting at a leather-topped desk when she entered, but rose and ushered her to a chair. Pointing to the papers piled on his desk, he apologised for the disarray. 'I am afraid this room must also serve as my office.'

The footman who had shown her in returned with two glasses of chilled white wine on a silver tray. Scarpia sat down opposite her and turned his glass in his fingers as if looking for words to compose a toast.

'To happier times,' he said.

'Yes,' she said. 'To happier times.'

They both drank from their glasses.

'And they will come soon, the happier times,' said Scarpia. 'Bonaparte has been defeated. The new Pope is on his way from Venice. We expect him to reach Rome in around ten days' time. Then my work –' he gestured towards the table piled with papers – 'my work will be done.'

'Couldn't you be the *sbirro* of a pope as well as a king?' asked Tosca with an impertinent smile.

Scarpia did not react to the insult. 'You must be hungry,' he said, 'if you have had no lunch.'

Tosca was hungry, but how did Scarpia know that she had had no lunch?

He led her into a dining room next to his study. It was dimly lit, with candles in a silver candelabrum. They sat opposite one another at a polished table with an inlaid veneer. While one footman filled their glasses, another served first Tosca and then Scarpia with fresh langoustines and mayonnaise. They talked easily together, as former lovers often do. Tosca told Scarpia malicious stories about her rival divas and Scarpia gave her the gossip about the court in Palermo. The langoustines were eaten and followed by freshly made ravioli and then guinea fowl in a chanterelle sauce. Tosca ate with gusto. 'And is it true,' she asked, 'that you drank the blood of your enemies out of a skull?'

Scarpia smiled. 'No. But I saw things I do not like to remember. All war is terrible and civil war worst of all. Men descend into savagery and behave worse than beasts.' He looked up from his food. 'And that is the point, Floria. There are always many things wrong with a settled order – inequality, injustice, a chasm between the rich and the poor – but disorder is worse, and to force change leads to chaos, destroying all the certainties upon which people base their lives. Their brute instincts are unleashed. Cain turns against Abel. That is why I pursue men like Angelotti. They use liberty, equality or fraternity as slogans to stir up the people in pursuit of their own ends.'

Tosca laughed. 'But, Vitellio, you are so handsome when you talk like that. Just like Mario.'

Scarpia gave a brief snort of exasperation. 'Cavaradossi is unworthy of you,' he said. 'He is a third-rate painter, a posturing Jacobin, a would-be demagogue, a gigolo…'

Tosca felt her face flush at the word 'gigolo'; if only he knew how reluctant dear Mario had been to accept the gifts she had pressed upon him; but instinct told her that if Bonaparte had indeed been defeated and the return of a Roman republic postponed, then Scarpia would retain great influence and might be persuaded to protect Mario.

'Mario is an idealist,' she said firmly. 'He risks his life for liberty.'

'He risks his life for Angelotti,' said Scarpia irritably, 'because he knows there will be rich pickings with the return of a republic.'

'Oh, politics bore me,' she said with a wave of her hand. 'Can't we talk about something else?'

A footman came into the room to take away their plates, refill their glasses and serve them with sorbets.

'You are to sing in *Il barbiere di Siviglia*?' Scarpia asked Tosca.

'Yes,' said Tosca. 'I hope you will attend.'

'Of course.'

'With your wife, perhaps?' She gave a mischievous smile.

'Perhaps with my wife,' said Scarpia, 'although she now regards the theatre as frivolous. She has become very devout.'

'Devout? Why devout?'

'She did penance in a convent. It seems to have changed her.'

'Penance for what?'

'Sleeping with Jacobins.'

'Huh. You will not find *me* in a convent for that.'

'No. I don't see you in a convent.'

'And where *do* you see me, Baron Scarpia? Beneath an olive tree in Taormina?'

Scarpia smiled sadly. 'No longer.'

Tosca leaned across the table and looked intently into Scarpia's eyes. 'And that is quite right, Vitellio, because I love Mario and I can only be happy with him.'

'And will he be happy with you?'

'Of course.'

'I am glad you are so sure.'

'He loves me.'

'The priests would say –'

'The priests!'

'They would say,' Scarpia went on, 'that the love of a man and a woman is meant by God only for marriage and the procreation of children.'

'Then God means me to love Mario because I would like to be his wife and bear his children.'

'Truly?'

'Truly!'

'And would he like to be a husband and a father?'

'I am sure.'

'We can ask him.'

'When?'

'In a moment.'

'How?'

'I have invited him to join us with his friend Angelotti.'

Tosca was confused. 'But…'

Scarpia turned his head towards sounds of movement that came from the other room. 'This must be them.'

'But how did you find them?'

'One of my men followed a maidservant in a *sediola*.'

'*Dio mio!*'

The door opened. Cavaradossi, dishevelled, his hands tied behind his back, was pushed into the room by Spoletta. He looked first at Scarpia, then at Tosca, both with equal contempt.

'Mario!' She ran forward to embrace him.

Cavaradossi spat in her face. '*Puttana!*'

Scarpia, who had also risen from the table, looked at Spoletta. 'And our other guest, Angelotti?'

Spoletta shook his head. 'Nowhere to be found.'

'But he must have been there. There was no time to send him somewhere else.'

'He had certainly been there – there were the women's clothes. And he could not have escaped – the house was surrounded – but we looked everywhere. We pulled up the floorboards. We searched the barn and the stables.'

Scarpia frowned and turned towards Cavaradossi. 'Well, we shall have to ask our guest to tell us where we can find his friend.'

'Never,' said Cavaradossi.

'Then you will have to be persuaded.'

'Never,' said Cavaradossi again.

'If you tell us,' said Scarpia, 'then we will cut loose your hands, set another place at table, and I have no doubt that His Sicilian Majesty will show his appreciation –'

'Never,' said Cavaradossi for a third time. Then, with a look of loathing directed at Tosca, 'It is only weak women who betray their friends.'

'Ah, no, Mario,' said Tosca, now weeping, 'I did not betray you. I was followed. I swear on the Madonna, I did not know.'

'Weakness is not unique to women,' said Scarpia. 'The strappado has revealed weakness in men.'

'No,' cried Tosca.

'You would not dare,' said Cavaradossi.

'I have no choice,' said Scarpia. 'There it is, waiting in the street below. I am commanded to recover the prisoner Angelotti. It is my duty.'

'Have mercy,' cried Tosca.

'Did they show mercy to Gennaro Valentino?'

'Valentino was a lackey of the Bourbons,' said Cavaradossi.

'And I too am a lackey of the Bourbons,' Scarpia replied with a mock bow, 'and it is my king's command that I use any means necessary to apprehend Cesare Angelotti.'

'Do your worst,' said Cavaradossi.

'As you wish,' said Scarpia.

He turned to Spoletta. 'Take him down.'

'*Tre tratti di corda?*'

'Yes.'

Cavaradossi gave a last look of disdain at Tosca as Spoletta pulled him to the door and out of the room.

Tosca, weeping, turned to Scarpia and fell to her knees. 'I beg you, no, do not torture him, do not be so cruel.'

Scarpia looked into the face now smudged with mascara. 'I have no choice.'

'You once loved me, Scarpia, and for that moment I loved you. Is that not enough?'

Scarpia looked at her sadly. 'I wish you well, Floria, but I must do my duty.'

Tosca looked away towards the window then, with a flushed face and a desperate expression, back at Scarpia. 'And if I were to tell you where to find Angelotti?'

Scarpia looked sharply at Tosca. 'You know?'

'Would you then spare Mario the *corda*?'

'Of course. There would be no need.'

'And release him?'

'Yes.'

'I trust to your honour, Scarpia.'

'I will keep my word.'

'In the garden of the house, there is a well. In the well, there are rungs set into the side. Halfway down, there is an opening to a cistern. That is where you will find Angelotti.'

Scarpia went to the door and gave orders to a *sbirro*. He returned and gestured to Tosca to sit back at the table. Her appetite had gone, but she dared not refuse. Both cut into their sorbets with their silver-gilt spoons, but only Scarpia raised his to his mouth: on Tosca's plate the cold crystals melted into a pool of coloured liquid. There was a commotion in the salon. They both rose from the table and went through to find Cavaradossi, still with his hands tied behind his back, held not by Spoletta but two *sbirri*. He looked furiously at Tosca. 'You told them.'

'I told them nothing.'

'I heard them. You told them about the well.'

'For you, Mario.'

'For me. There is no me. I am shamed, dishonoured, brought down by a whore.'

'I could not bear for you to suffer,' said Tosca. Her tone was that of a nursemaid who has been cruel to be kind.

'And now? Do I not suffer?'

'Mario, you are alive!'

A lackey entered and handed Scarpia a letter. He opened it with his silver knife, read it rapidly, frowned, then turned to Cavaradossi. 'It may alleviate your suffering, *cavaliere*, to know that we were misinformed about the Battle of Marengo. Bonaparte counter-attacked. Melas is defeated. The French have won.'

'*Vittoria!*' cried Cavaradossi.

Scarpia looked again at the letter, his brow puckered, then said: 'Marengo is a long way from Rome.'

'Release me, you viper,' said Cavaradossi, 'and I will put in a good word.'

Scarpia smiled. 'The Pope will reach Rome before Bonaparte and my orders are to wrap up our business here before he comes.' He nodded to the *sbirri*. 'Take him to the Castel Sant'Angelo. Lock him up while we wait for Angelotti.'

'You are done for, Scarpia,' shouted Cavaradossi as he was dragged from the room. 'You cannot stop history!'

*

Scarpia and Tosca were once again alone together, but neither spoke. Scarpia returned to his desk to prepare the passports and safe conducts that he had promised Tosca. He was tired. He wished it all to be over. He glanced at the letter telling him of Bonaparte's triumph at Marengo. Would the French now march on Rome? Would the new Pope be deposed? A second republic installed with Angelotti revered as a martyr and Cavaradossi acclaimed as a hero? Scarpia would have to flee once again, but this time Paola and the children would come with him, and how much happier he would be than he was now, playing with Francesca in the garden of the villa in Bagheria, or riding with Pietro among the pine trees in the hills above Castelfranco. Cavaradossi was welcome to fame and fortune – and to Tosca.

Tosca was also tired, and she too was thinking, struggling against the befuddlement caused by the wine to think through what had happened and what should be done. She had betrayed Angelotti. So what? She owed nothing to that pig, who had treated her with contempt, and if his death was the price for saving Mario, it was a bargain. But Mario did not see it that way. Clearly, he believed that she was the accomplice, if not the mistress, of Scarpia. Why else would she be dining so intimately with a man she did not know? How could she persuade him that Scarpia was not her lover? That he was merely her friend? A friend! The man who drank his enemies' blood out of a skull! Would friendship be any more excusable than love? What if Mario continued to spurn her? What if he despised her for saving his life? What could she do to win back his love? How could she convince him that she had not sold herself to Scarpia? *What could prove beyond doubt that he was her only love?*

An hour passed. Both Tosca and Scarpia were preoccupied with their own thoughts. The low light seemed to change the man whom Tosca glanced at every now and then, from the handsome Sicilian, so gallant in Venice, so attractive in Taormina, into a hooded falcon waiting to pounce on two innocent lovers, tear them to pieces and eat their flesh. But his days were numbered. Bonaparte had won the Battle of Marengo. The French would return to Rome. The republic would be restored, with Cavaradossi a hero and perhaps Tosca a heroine should she, like Luisa Sanfelice in Naples, do something heroic for the cause.

*

A footman came in, renewed the candles and offered both Tosca and Scarpia glasses of Marsala which Tosca accepted but Scarpia refused. When the footman had left the room, Scarpia got up from his desk and crossed to Tosca.

'Listen, Floria,' he said. 'This is what I propose. When Spoletta returns with Angelotti, he will be taken to join Cavaradossi in the Castel Sant'Angelo where both men will be shot at dawn.'

'So you will break your promise?'

'No, I shall keep my promise. Cavaradossi will not die. There will be no shot in the soldiers' muskets. You will be allowed to see him before his execution, and you must tell him that when he hears the shots he must pretend to be dead. Then when the firing squad withdraws, you can both leave. I have prepared passports and safe conducts for you both.'

Tosca took the papers from Scarpia, but felt no gratitude: she was merely receiving, after all, no more than the fee for her betrayal of Angelotti. And while she might have saved the life of her lover, Mario, she had by no means secured his love. Would he accept clemency he believed she had bought with her body? She knew Mario. He would rather die than be dishonoured. He might well refuse to play dead.

Sounds came from the outer chamber. The door opened and Spoletta entered accompanied by a *sbirro* but no one else.

'Angelotti?' asked Scarpia.

'He cheated us,' said Spoletta. 'He slipped from our grasp and threw himself down the well.'

'He is dead?'

'Yes. Drowned. We climbed down and fished him out.'

'You have his corpse to prove it?'

'We do.'

'Good. Send it to Naselli.'

'And the other?' said Spoletta.

'He must be shot. A firing squad at dawn but, Guido, *it is to be an execution like that of Count Palmieri.*'

'The same as Count Palmieri?'

'The same as Count Palmieri.'

'Are you sure?'

'I am sure.' Scarpia glanced at Tosca. 'La signorina Tosca is to be allowed to see him before his execution.'

Spoletta bowed. 'Very well.'

*

Spoletta left with the *sbirro*. Scarpia turned to Tosca. 'Go to the Castel Sant'Angelo,' he said. 'Tell Cavaradossi what he has to do. Spoletta knows what has been arranged. And when the pantomime is over, leave Rome. Go north to the French. Later, when they retake Rome, you can return and fulfil your engagements.'

'But you will not be there to hear me sing,' said Tosca, going towards the door, and standing before a gilt-framed mirror to straighten her dress and adjust her hair.

Scarpia came up behind her, holding open her cloak. 'No, this time it really is *addio*.'

'Yes, Scarpia, *addio*.' Tosca drew out the pearl-handled *stiletto*, turned, and thrust it through the white silk of his shirt into his chest. The blade met no resistance. She pushed it to the hilt, straight at his heart. Scarpia gave a choking cry and looked down as blood spurted from the wound onto the bodice of her dress. Then he looked up into her eyes. 'But, Floria...' A look of astonishment was followed by one of sadness and then, as he staggered and fell, again that melancholy smile. He fell to the floor and, after some further convulsions, lay still.

*

Tosca's coach was waiting outside the Palazzo Farnese. She had left a shawl on the seat and now wrapped it around her shoulders to keep out the damp of the dawn, and cover the blotch of blood on the bodice of her dress. She did not have long. She had dragged Scarpia's body behind the curtains, and no doubt the footmen would not disturb their master alone with a woman until well after dawn. In her hands she held the papers which would take her through gates and past guards, and when they were alone she would pull back the shawl and show him the bloodstains to prove that her love for him knew no bounds. She had killed the viper. And she had saved his life.

At the outer gates of the Castel Sant'Angelo, Tosca showed the laissez-passer signed by Scarpia. The gates were opened. Her coachman whipped the horses to take the coach up the steep road through the cavernous interior of Hadrian's Mausoleum, over the draw-bridge and onto the concourse at the top. There, after a further scrutiny of her papers, she was shown into the governor's quarters. The officer of the guard rubbed his eyes, looked with puzzlement at Tosca, then at the papers, then asked her why she was there.

'I am permitted to see the prisoner Cavaradossi before his execution.'

The officer looked at the order signed by Scarpia, then told a soldier to fetch Spoletta. Tosca sat, waiting for Spoletta to appear. When he did so, he showed no surprise at her presence. 'You wish to see the prisoner? Of course. I will take you to his cell.'

Tosca followed him out of the guardroom and along the ramparts to the room where Cavaradossi was held. His hands were no longer tied, but when he saw Tosca he made no attempt to embrace her. He looked away from her, his head tilted in a heroic pose.

Tosca turned to Spoletta. 'I wish to talk to him privately.'

'Of course.' Spoletta smiled, a smile that was somehow terrible, but Tosca did not pause to wonder what it might mean. He went to the door. 'You must be quick. The sun is about to rise.'

Tosca crossed the room to Cavaradossi. 'Mario, you are saved. There will be no balls in the muskets. You are to fall and play dead and then, when the soldiers withdraw, we may leave the *castello*. I have passports – we can fly from Rome.'

Cavaradossi turned, as she knew he would, with a look of contempt. 'And what price have you paid for this clemency?'

'Not the price you think, Mario. I will confess, yes, I was once Scarpia's lover – once, on one night. But now and forever there will be only you, and to prove it – see!' She drew back her shawl to uncover the darkening stain on her bodice.

Cavaradossi looked down at the blotch of congealed blood, then up again at Tosca.

'What is that?'

'His blood.'

'Scarpia's?'

'Yes. He is dead.'

'You killed him?'

'For you.'

A flush came onto Cavaradossi's face. 'So the monster is dead. *Brava*, Floria! You are now truly a patriot.'

Tosca looked into his eyes, hoping for an expression of love rather than republican esteem. And she was rewarded. '*Brava*, Floria,' he said again, and embraced her.

'Ah, my love,' she said.

'Yes, yes.' He let go of her. 'And I am to play dead? Play dead and then come alive and leave Rome?'

'Yes.'

'What if Scarpia's body is found?'

'I hid it behind the curtains.'

'But the curtains will be drawn at dawn.'

'Yes.'

'We must move quickly.' Cavaradossi went to the door of his cell and hammered on it with his fist. 'Soldier, I am ready.'

The door was opened by Spoletta. 'If you will follow me. And you, signorina, might like to watch the rise of the sun from the battlements or, if you prefer, and turn the other way, see the act of justice.'

Tosca smiled. Yes, she would watch the charade. With a last smile at her reconciled lover as he was led off by a squad of soldiers, she climbed onto the ramparts overlooking the basilica of St Peter's – pink in the light of the rising sun. She heard the roll of drums. She saw Cavaradossi reappear, blindfolded and his hands once again tied behind his back, escorted by ten soldiers. She watched as he was stood against the wall of the tower that crowned the *castello* and the squad of soldiers was lined up to face him. Their muskets were raised. She heard Spoletta shout the order to take aim and then fire. She heard the shots. She saw

Mario fall. Joy filled her heart. He lay there motionless. How well he feigned death. Spoletta handed over the command of the soldiers to a corporal who marched them away. Tosca waited. How long would it be before he rose? She saw that Spoletta had remained. Would he give the signal? Nothing happened. Mario did not move. She stepped down from the ramparts onto the stones of the small square and went to Spoletta. 'Can we now go?'

'Of course. You have your passport.'

'And Mario?'

'He has already left. He is on his way to Hell.'

Tosca turned towards the inert body of her lover. 'But he is alive,' she said. 'Scarpia promised.'

'I had my orders too,' said Spoletta. He turned away.

Tosca ran towards Cavaradossi. He lay face down with no marks on his back but a trickle of blood ran from under his body. She turned him over. The blood came from six holes in his breast. His face was pale, his eyes unfocused. Cavaradossi was dead.

'*Dio mio*,' cried Tosca, 'Mario. He promised me ... he swore on his honour.' There was no one to hear what she said, except perhaps a voice within Tosca: 'This is Scarpia's revenge.' And another voice, that of the peasant from the Veneto, which said that she still had the passports and safe conducts, and that lingering by the body of her dead lover would accomplish nothing. She stood and walked back towards her coach. Spoletta was talking with the officer of the guard. What the officer said seemed to agitate him; he turned and crossed the courtyard to Tosca.

'The baron is dead,' he said. 'He has been murdered.'

Tosca stepped back. She saw a twisted look on Spoletta's face – a blend of anger and anguish.

'He is dead?' she asked lamely.

Spoletta looked straight into her eyes, and what he read in those eyes led him to lower his glance and see, in the light of the risen

363

sun, the blotch of blood on Tosca's dress. 'It was you. Of course. Who else?'

Tosca looked down at her bodice and pointed towards the corpse of Cavaradossi. 'It is his blood.'

'That is not fresh blood,' said Spoletta. 'It is caked and dry.'

Tosca turned to climb into her coach, but Spoletta seized her by the arm. 'You vile whore,' he shouted. 'What did you hope for? To escape? To claim a crime of passion? An appeal to the Rota? A pardon from the Pope? Is that what you imagined?' Spoletta laughed and with his two huge hands took hold of Tosca by the waist and lifted her over his shoulder. She shrieked and struggled but could not escape his grip. Spoletta took seven strides to the castellated ramparts, lifted her high above his head, and threw Floria Tosca over the wall.

Postscript

Barnaba Chiaramonti, elected Pope in Venice on 14 March, took the same name as his predecessor and was crowned with a papier mâché tiara as Pius VII. He then sailed on an Austrian ship, the *Bellona*, to the port of Pesaro from whence he travelled by coach over the Apennines to Rome. He reached the Eternal City on 3 July 1800, returning to the seat of St Peter two years and four months after the exile of his predecessor, Luigi Braschi Onesti, Pope Pius VI.

Eight days before his return, a large crowd had followed the coffin containing the body of Floria Tosca from the church of Sant'Andrea della Valle to her grave. The way she had died as reported by the governor of the Castel Sant'Angelo – throwing herself from the ramparts after the execution of her lover – was an operatic drama suddenly transposed to real life. Canon law forbade the burying of a suicide on consecrated ground, but there was no cardinal or bishop in Rome who dared hold Tosca responsible for what she had done. To the grieving crowd, she was indistinguishable from the heroine she had played so well in *Nina, o sia la pazza per amore*. Tosca had been driven mad by love.

In contrast to the grandiose interment of Tosca, the funeral of Baron Scarpia at Rubosa was simple, conducted by the Oratorian priest, Father Simone Alberti, and attended only by his widow, his two children, his brother-in-law, Prince Ludovico di Marcisano with his wife and children, and Guido Spoletta. It was officially announced that he had been killed by a Jacobin assassin as he was sitting at his desk – an assassin who then escaped – although soon all Rome believed the alternative version put about by the servants at the Palazzo Farnese – that he had been stabbed by Tosca. But why? Some said it was in revenge for ordering the death of her lover; others that he had tried to ravish her and she had killed him rather than submit. The circle around Prince Paducci, the Chevalier Spinelli and the Contessa di Comastri preferred this version. So too did the Romans.

The death of a man who had served the legitimist cause with such distinction would normally have led to public obsequies organised by the state, but in the interregnum there was no one to give such a command. Prince Naselli had left Rome, Cardinal Ruffo was in Naples, and those cardinals who were in Rome awaiting the arrival of Pius VII had no wish to tarnish the new pontificate with an unseemly scandal. Sir John Acton, in Palermo, having inherited the baronetcy and estates in England from his cousin, was preoccupied with arrangements for his marriage to his thirteen-year-old niece. Queen Maria Carolina was in Vienna. King Ferdinand, who had remained in Sicily, was busy hunting.

With the consent of his wife, Paola di Marcisano, Guido Spoletta took the body of Baron Scarpia back to Sicily in a lead-lined coffin where it was placed in the family sepulchre at Castelfranco alongside ancestors. The title of Baron of both the Papal States and the Kingdom of Two Sicilies passed to Pietro Scarpia together with the properties that had belonged to his father. Paola continued to wear black long after the prescribed period of mourning for her husband had ended and never went into society, devoting her life to charitable works and religious devotions. Her only extravagance was the commissioning from the sculptor Canova of a fine monument to her husband in Carrara marble. It was erected in the chapel at Rubaso and every year on the anniversary of his death Paola, Pietro and Francesca came from Rome to Rubaso to attend a Mass said for the repose of his soul.

Acknowledgements

The idea of writing the story of Baron Vitellio Scarpia came to me after reading Susan Vandiver Nicassio's book *Tosca's Rome: The Play and the Opera in Historical Perspective.* In this superb study of Puccini's opera, *Tosca*, Professor Nicassio establishes just how inaccurate and partisan is its portrayal of the political realities of the time. The libretto was based on a play, *La Tosca*, written in the late nineteenth century by an anti-clerical Frenchman, Victorien Sardou: thus the chief of police of the Papal States, Baron Scarpia, is the sadistic agent of reaction while the republicans, Cesare Angelotti and Mario Cavaradossi, are heroes. Angelotti and Cavaradossi, she tells us, were based on real historical characters with similar names while Baron Scarpia, a Sicilian, appears fleetingly in histories of the time as the leader of a guerrilla army fighting for the Bourbon cause.

Can one perpetuate an injustice on a historical character? Could an English novelist do something to redress the calumny of a French playwright, filling in the gaps left by history with invention? This is what I have tried to do, and I wish to thank Susan Vandiver Nicassio not just for giving me the idea for this novel, but for the richly detailed portrait of the period to be found in her book.

My gratitude also goes to those historians on whose works I have drawn in writing this novel: Maurice Andrieux's *Daily Life in*

Papal Rome in the Eighteenth Century and *Daily Life in Venice in the Time of Casanova*, both translated by Mary Fitton; *The Bourbons of Naples (1734–1825)* by Harold Acton; *The History of the Popes from the Close of the Middle Ages*, Volume XL, by Ludwig, Freiherr von Pastor, translated by E. F. Peeler; *History of Naples from the Accession of Charles of Bourbon to the Death of Ferdinand I* by Pietro Coletta, translated by S. Horner; *Memorie Storiche Sulla Vita del Cardinale Fabrizio Ruffo. La contestazioni dell'abate sanfedista alle opere di Vincenzo Cuoco, Carlo Botta e Pietro Coletta* by Domenico Sacchinelli; *Goethe's Travels in Italy*, translated from the German by the Rev. A. J. W. Morrison and Charles Nesbit; *Memoirs of Comte Roger de Damas 1787–1806*; *The Memoirs of Jacques Casanova de Seingalt*; *Nelson and Ruffo* by F. P. Badham; *Imperial City: Rome, Romans and Napoleon, 1796–1815* by Susan Vandiver Nicassio; and *Jacques-Louis David* by Anita Brookner.

I would also like to express my gratitude to my agent, Gillon Aitken, for his faith in the novel; to all at Bloomsbury, in particular my editor, Michael Fishwick, for his inspired insight into how early drafts might be improved; to John Warrack, who corrected my errors about eighteenth-century opera; to Lucy Beckett for her sound advice.

A NOTE ON THE AUTHOR

Piers Paul Read is best known for his number one *New York Times* bestseller *Alive: The Story of the Andes Survivors*, which documented the 1972 crash of Uruguayan Air Force Flight 571 and was later adapted into a film. He has written sixteen novels which have won a number of awards, among them a Hawthornden Prize, a Somerset Maugham Award and a James Tait Black Memorial Prize. Most recently he published *The Dreyfus Affair*, a compelling non-fiction account of the infamous case of a miscarriage of justice in France in the nineteenth century. He lives in London.

A NOTE ON THE TYPE

The text of this book is set in Adobe Caslon, named after the English punch-cutter and type-founder William Caslon I (1692–1766). Caslon's rather old-fashioned types were modelled on seventeenth-century Dutch designs, but found wide acceptance throughout the English-speaking world for much of the eighteenth century until replaced by newer types towards the end of the century. Used in 1776 to print the Declaration of Independence, they were revived in the nineteenth century and have been popular ever since, particularly amongst fine printers. There are several digital versions, of which Carol Twombly's Adobe Caslon is one.